THE DOVECOTE

Also by Sue Sully

The Bluebell Pool
The Scent of May
The Barleyfield
The Shingle Beach

THE DOVECOTE

Sue Sully

St. Martin's Press
New York

Library of Congress Cataloging-in-Publication Data

Sully, Sue.
The dovecote / Sue Sully.
p.   cm.
ISBN 0-312-13471-1 (hardcover)
1. World War, 1914–1918—England—Dorset—Influence—Fiction.
2. Artist colonies—England—Dorset—Fiction.   3. Women
potters—England—Dorset—Fiction.   4. War widows—England—
Dorset—Fiction.   5. Dorset (England)—Fiction.   I. Title.
PR6069.U326D68   1995
823'.914—dc20   95-23934   CIP

First published in Great Britain by Headline Book Publishing

First U.S. Edition: September 1995
10 9 8 7 6 5 4 3 2 1

THE DOVECOTE

PART ONE

Chapter One

The wrought-iron entrance gates stood slightly ajar as if to invite her into the courtyard. A dovecote stood at its centre, large and square, raised on stone pillars and clad with wooden boards silvered with age; the roof-tiles had a soft coating of moss, like those of the low, wistaria-covered barns and garages enclosing the courtyard on three sides.

Esther watched the doves perch, their feathers white against the roofs. More doves strutted on the ledges in front of the small arched entrance holes, making a soft-throated crooning sound; they spread their tail feathers in the sunlight. Others fussed with their beaks into their back neck feathers, or tucked their heads into the fold under their wings. When they flew it was with a whistle of wings, like the singing of a lasso.

The courtyard was so tranquil that it seemed detached from the world she had left behind; a world of doctors and experts, of artificially hushed voices and attempts to jolly her out of herself, and everyone's baffled, ill-concealed impatience. Her mother had said, 'But it's 1920. Christopher's been dead more than two years,' as if a new decade should have made all the difference. They couldn't understand why, after all that time of bearing up, of getting over things and getting on with her life, she should suddenly collapse at the Fieldings' New Year's party and cry for three whole days without stopping.

Weeds grew among the cracks in the paving of the courtyard; the place had an air of neglect, but without a full-blown sense of decay that might have rendered it oppressive rather than beautiful. It seemed deserted. The house beyond the courtyard was invisible, hidden by the barns. A high red-brick wall ran close to the edge of the road and a tree in full white blossom hung over its edge.

Esther listened to the seductive murmur of the doves and drew closer to the entrance gates. Her figure, framed by the bars, gave the impression that it was not the courtyard but she – by her exclusion from it – who was being confined. Her look of despair reinforced this idea of exclusion. A beautiful face and striking, with its square jaw and full yet resolute mouth. Her hair, worn in a chignon without a hat, was fair and thick. It was a strong face; the unhappiness clouding it would not be of a trivial kind, decided the watcher in the shadows of the barn, as Esther grasped the leading edge of the gate and pressed her cheek against the metal.

Esther remembered her mother's words again, 'All we want is to help you find peace,' and her grip tightened on the gate. How could they talk of peace and say that it was all over, when the dead still haunted every living moment, when her parents too had been touched by grief? Her own brother, killed in the early months of the war, friends of her father, sons of friends. So many lives reduced to memories, so many hopes turned sour.

The watcher from the barn moved out of the shadows and crossed the courtyard. Doves flew up into the air with a flurry and clatter of wings. 'Why not come in and have a look around?'

Esther stepped back from the gate, startled to see the woman standing there. 'I'm sorry . . . I was attracted by the doves and I thought the house was empty.'

'Far from it. The Dovecote's always full of activity. And my doves come in many different forms.'

Esther, puzzled by this last remark, glanced again at the birds on the roof. She wondered if the stranger was a little mad. She looked mad. She had very intense, dark brown eyes in a sallow skin, a hawk nose and a high forehead. Her clothes were eccentric: a long, shapeless skirt, a paint-spattered blouse, a woollen cardigan with holes in the pockets, and her buttoned boots were caked with mud. 'Do you mean that you breed several varieties?'

The stranger spoke with an energy that carried her words along in a rush. 'I don't breed them, they look after themselves, though I toss them a little grain from time to time. Are you renting the cottage up the road? We wondered what you'd be like. I'm Julia – Julia Brassington.' The woman held out her hand. 'I should explain. The house is called The Dovecote. The doves who live in it are all uncommon. While I can't say I breed them, I would lay claim to some nurturing.'

Esther still did not understand.

'I mean my protégés. My friends. My artists. I call them my doves. You must think I'm completely mad.' The woman laughed as if pleased by the idea, and tossed back her short black hair. 'They all think we're mad in the village, but we don't care. We've found peace in our Dovecote. And how many people can say that – after the disastrous last few years? I paint,' she added with a flash of intensity from her dark eyes. 'Some of the others paint too, some of us work with wood, some with clay.'

'How strange,' Esther said involuntarily. 'I'm a potter. That is – my husband was a craft potter before the war. I used to paint the pots he made.'

The woman clapped her hands together; her fingers were long and nicotine-stained. 'I knew it. I knew as soon as I saw you that you belonged.'

Esther was immediately resistant to the idea. 'Oh, no. I'm only here for a holiday. I have a home, my work, a little girl – my parents are looking after her.' She found herself talking quickly, saying too much, as if the woman's way of letting her words run away with her were

4

catching. Or perhaps it was the illness, she told herself; perhaps her mother had been right and she was still not fully recovered. 'We can look after Cassie for another week or two. It's too soon to go back to The Folly. You need to get right away from everything, darling.' Like a child, like Cassie when she had been told by her grandmother to put away her clothes, to be a good girl, to eat up her dinner, Esther had packed a suitcase and let her father drive her to the railway station. She had kissed her daughter and her parents goodbye and taken the train for Dorset.

'Are you going for a swim?'

Esther looked down at the string bag containing her bathing suit. Had she really contemplated swimming when she set out that morning? It seemed she had, for the bathing suit was neatly wrapped in a striped towel. 'I suppose I might. If it's not too cold.'

'Be careful. The tides here can be strong.' The woman smiled and the expression at once transformed her face, lighting her deep-set eyes with gentleness, making her seem mysterious, even beautiful. 'Why don't you come and visit us while you're here? I'm sure you'll find our little community interesting.'

Esther's reply was noncommittal. She knew that the last thing she wanted was to spend the next few weeks being sociable with strangers. She said goodbye and moved on. She would avoid the woman in future, she told herself. She couldn't face the company of The Dovecote, nor any sort of company yet. She remembered the Fieldings' house, the New Year's party, her mother's observation that she and Giles ... 'You've been on your own a long time. Christopher would expect you to live a normal life again and Giles is such an old friend. You get on so well. Besides – you'll soon be thirty. Cassie needs a father.'

The road was hot from the glare of the sun, white and dusty and reminiscent of village roads on the French coast. She and Christopher had been drunk with the sun that very first summer together. But this was Dorset, England, and to think of France with nostalgia seemed a kind of sacrilege now, after the Somme.

Everyone had been drunk in one way or another during those golden years long before the war; if not with love and sunshine, then with a kind of desperation that the old ways of life shouldn't change. She and Christopher had been full of plans. He would throw pots and she would raise their children. They had married on the strength of his first large commission, defying her parents' protest that she, at nineteen, was too young and Christopher too irresponsible for marriage. All their reservations had been proved wrong, thought Esther. The marriage had been perfect. *Nothing* – she emphasised the word with a swing of the string bag – nothing could have been more perfect.

The road departed from the high brick wall encircling the gardens of The Dovecote and sloped more steeply downwards. A few houses clung to the bottom of the hill where the road veered towards the village. A man, leading a horse and cart loaded with milk churns, walked steadily

5

some hundred yards in front of her. A woman, hanging washing in her garden, ignored her, and Esther walked on, reassured by the absence of many people and by the air of stolid calm – for, after months of seclusion, it had taken all her courage to set out that morning.

A butcher leaned in the doorway of his shop, smoking a cigarette; he nodded to her as she passed and Esther said good morning.

'Reconnoitring', Christopher had called this early exploration of their surroundings. He had used the word with a boy-scout enthusiasm for a military turn of phrase. Do you remember? Esther asked him silently as she turned a corner into the village square. Oh, how naïve we were in those days.

She saw the war memorial, too late to avoid it. How could anyone have expected that her walk would bring her face to face with a list of local dead? A high Maltese cross, mounted on a flight of gleaming Purbeck marble steps, stood in a corner of the churchyard wall: the villagers must have been proud of their achievement in raising the money for such a monument. The dais beneath the cross had a bronze plaque inscribed with names set into each vertical face, and the dates – '1914', cast in bronze on one side, and '1918', on the other – were qualified with a central plaque bearing the words 'Our Glorious Dead'.

Esther read a few of the names and shivered involuntarily. It was as if she held again in her hand the letter from one of Christopher's fellow officers, explaining that they had been unable to retrieve the body for burial. The man was honest and she had been grateful for it, but there had been no talk of glory.

She did not finish reading the memorial plaques but walked angrily away, swinging her string bag over her shoulder. *Our Glorious Dead.* The words seemed a personal mockery. Christopher, duped into uniform, crushed into the mud of Flanders had not been glorious. But alive, she thought fiercely – laughing with his head thrown back as he said that he was going to make pots that would be the envy of all potters, diving from a rock, beads of water on his golden body glistening in the sun, the look in his eyes when he held his daughter for the first time; Christopher, laughing down at her in the shade of the apple trees, lying on the grass beside her, or on the pillow in the bedroom of The Folly, his face drowsy with love – yes, he had been glorious when he was alive.

Esther reached the isolated track to the beach. The sun glittered on the sea as it dragged at the pebbles with long drawn-out sighs. She walked along the shore and found a place under the cliff where the expanse of pebbles was broken by patches of brown sand and a large rock made both a seat and a table for the rudimentary picnic of bread and cheese she had brought with her. She had discovered the inconsequence of food when there was nothing and nobody to enhance the routines of breakfast, lunch and dinner. If it had not been for her child's need for a pattern to their existence, she might have let go of time altogether. Instead the petty details of her life had merged into the dreary business of bearing up under the burden of widowhood.

Everyone had thought she was being stoical, but it was as if, on the surface, her emotions had been frozen, while inside, undetectable until the Fieldings' party, she had all the time been going crazy with grief. Esther stood for a long time staring at the empty glitter of the sunlight on the sea. She remembered with a vivid intensity the open horizon, the brilliance of the sun and of their love for one another – and she knew now why she had come or, perhaps unconsciously, been directed to the sea. She began to strip off her clothes. The beach and cliff were deserted. It was May, still too early in the year for the place to attract holiday-makers. She undressed slowly, half reluctant to acknowledge the growing certainty of her intention, then stood in her underwear, feeling the weight of the string bag, the striped towel wrapped round her heavy bathing suit, the same black wool bathing suit she had worn – or rather, not worn on their honeymoon in France. She glanced up to the cliff path as if to make sure it was empty and, unfastening her hair-comb with one hand, shook her hair free then pulled off her vest and cami-knickers.

The chill of the air raised goosepimples on her flesh. She folded her underclothes and laid them on top of the rest of her clothes on the rock, then, hugging her arms across her breasts, crossed the pebbles to a patch of dark, level sand where the shifting ripples of foam linked the land and the sea.

The cold water made her gasp as it lapped her thighs and stomach. She struck out with long strokes, her hair streaming behind her, warm against her back. There was nothing ahead but the horizon, nothing below but the water and, in the near distance, the cliffs, the beach and the rock with her belongings.

Esther's mood became one of detachment, as if whatever might happen in the next moments were predetermined. The sun dazzled on the water and she saw again the flash of sunlight on Christopher's body. She saw him dive, to disappear for long, terrifying seconds, and then rise, laughing behind her to swim with her in his arms, the sea warm as it lapped their chins, his mouth close against her ear. She closed her eyes and the sea supported her and moved in currents between her legs. She heard his voice in her head. Do you remember the Côte Sauvage?

'Of course I remember. How could I ever forget?'

His voice was as clear and as warm with love as it had always been, his arms encircled her, his body buoyed her up in the water. If she opened her eyes would she see him? She didn't know. He never came to her except like this, in the darkness of her own mind, in the middle of the night, or in dreams. When she turned and lit the lamp beside the bed the room was always empty, though she could have sworn he breathed beside her on the pillow. Do you remember? he insisted.

'We swam.' The water salted her lips and the sun was warm against her back. 'I was so frightened when you dived.'

And afterwards – because I swam out so far.

'I was so frightened of losing you.'

7

Are you frightened now?

'No, because you're here with me.'

The water lapped Esther's chin and ears. The gentle slap of sound was soothing. Far away the cries of sea-birds carried on the wind. She did not open her eyes, but swam towards the light of the horizon beyond the red and gold world behind her closed eyelids. His voice was close beside her, familiar, persuasive as always. You see? There was nothing to be afraid of. You'd only lost me for a short while. If you swim out as far as the horizon I'll be with you for ever. We'll be together for always and never ever be parted.

Esther's hair was heavy against her back, the weight of it dragged her low in the water and the waves touched her gently, inviting her to sink deeper. The taste of salt on her lips was the taste of his flesh, the weight of the water was his love enveloping her, drawing her to him . . .

A wave hit her face and Esther swallowed a mouthful of sea water. It caught the back of her throat and filled her nose and the sensation of being suffocated was not the warm, embracing darkness she had expected but was violent and unpleasant. She struggled and coughed and flailed with her arms to stay afloat, treading water, fighting for gulps of air that cut and seared, until her terror had subsided and she could breathe again.

She had swum out about fifty yards from the shore. The beach and cliff lay in brilliant sunshine, but the sea was green and cold beneath her. Esther turned round and round to survey the empty horizon and the empty beach and she felt the weight of her grief return with a self-mocking resignation. So, she couldn't even go to him and end it all with any vigour. She thought of Cassie and began to swim slowly towards the shore. Her child might manage without a father, but she still needed a mother. How could she have contemplated leaving her like that? Was the insanity of grieving so much stronger than the ties of motherhood?

Esther stopped swimming and trod water again. She could see the cliff path, snaking up from the shore and winding among gorse bushes on the top of the cliff. A house stood above the shoreline, its gardens running right down almost to meet the path. A flash of light had caught her attention, the sun glinting on the house windows, but also a pinpoint of reflected sunlight among the trees of the garden. She saw a movement. Someone with binoculars? The idea that someone had been watching from the cliff was disturbing. Esther was conscious of her nakedness as she raised her hand to shade her eyes and stared hard at the flicker of the reflection, letting the owner of the binoculars know they had been seen.

At once there was a movement among the trees, a brief impression of a figure that swiftly disappeared. Esther imagined the watcher sneaking away through the garden; only then, as she considered its position on the cliff, did it occur to her that she had passed the house earlier on the road: whoever had been watching her must have been someone from The Dovecote.

Despair and her indifference to living all at once took second place to a very worldly feeling of indignation, and Esther struck out more strongly for the shore. The cliff loomed closer and the house and garden left her field of vision. She had a vague idea of confronting Julia Brassington, demanding she be allowed to interrogate the woman's 'doves' and give the owner of the binoculars a piece of her mind. There was a heavy pull to the sea. Esther remembered the woman's warning about the strength of the tide. She realised too that she was beginning to tire, for with each forward stroke towards the shore the current seemed to be pulling her back. She had once been a moderately strong swimmer, yet, though she thrust with all her strength against the current, her arms and legs felt increasingly heavy.

A cry of frustration broke from her. She rested briefly, a large wave swamped her and she swallowed water again. Esther choked, a pain burned her throat and chest. With the next wave a feeling of panic engulfed her, sucking the energy from her, and it occurred to her that, whether she wanted it or not, she was going to be swept out to sea.

Esther heard his voice before she saw him. 'Don't give in! I'm coming!'

She struggled to keep her head above the slap of the waves and saw him swim towards her, his fair hair dark with the water, his streamlined body, the flash of golden limbs. 'Christopher?' She closed her eyes and seconds later his arms enfolded her, he was beneath her and his hands were locked firmly under her chin.

He didn't speak and she let herself sink, unresisting, trusting his hands and his superior strength as his body bore her up. Then they reached shallow water and he let her go; he helped her to her feet as the pebbles dragged against her shins. They staggered up the beach and, coughing, Esther fell to her knees on the sand.

'Has no one told you about the tide?'

Esther, conscious again of her nakedness, sat and hugged her arms around her. Her flesh felt like cold orange peel and she began to shiver violently. 'Where did you come from? How did you know I was there?'

'I was on the cliff path – didn't anyone tell you about the tide?'

'Yes. I was told, but I've always been a good swimmer.'

'You obviously over-estimate yourself.' He sounded angry.

'I haven't swum for a long time.'

He did not answer. He turned suddenly and walked away from her and Esther thought he was so annoyed by her stupidity that he was leaving. Then she saw that he was making for the pile of her belongings further along the beach. He returned, carrying them and his own clothes bundled in his arms.

As she watched him walk towards her she was struck again by the similarity to Christopher. He was much younger – early twenties perhaps – and the hair was a little darker, but the fit, tanned body, the sudden rueful smile after his anger . . .

'Are you going to be all right?'

9

Esther nodded. His drawers were soaked and clung to his thighs. She found herself staring and looked away. 'I'm sorry,' she said. 'I've put you to a lot of trouble – your clothes.' She was seized by another fit of shivering.

He crouched beside her with her towel and wrapped it round her shoulders with a sudden tenderness. 'Here. Try to get warm.' The gesture was extraordinarily intimate, and, as if he too were suddenly aware of it, he moved away and, still soaked through, pulled on his trousers and a pullover.

Esther, wrapped in the towel, felt foolishly weak. After a while she said, 'I know this is going to sound silly, but I thought you were my husband.'

He glanced up and down the beach. 'I don't understand. I imagined you were alone.'

'Oh, he's not here. I pretend he is sometimes, but –' she began to dry her hair with the corner of the towel – 'I know really that he's not here.' She looked at him. 'He's dead. For a moment I almost believed he had come back.'

He showed no surprise. He didn't shift his glance from hers in embarrassment, nor put on an air of sympathy, and Esther was encouraged to go on, to talk to him as she had talked to the doctors, except that the stranger didn't adopt the professional pose of detachment that always made her feel as if she were talking to herself.

'We were married for eight years. We have a child – a daughter. He joined up during the war – like everyone else – like all the other sheep.' Esther dug her hands into the pebbles. 'What one needs, and what we don't get, is a sense of conviction that it was all worthwhile, that they didn't die in vain – that *he* didn't die for nothing.' She looked at him. The stranger's expression was unfathomable. 'I keep asking myself, what was the point to his life? What's the point of mine?'

At last he spoke. 'You have your little girl.'

'Yes. I have Cassie.'

'There's your answer.' He shifted his feet and, glancing out to the horizon added, 'It's a lot more than some can say.'

She looked at him again. The resemblance to Christopher was strong, but the stranger's features, though youthful, were harder than those of her husband. His jaw-line was lean, where Christopher's had been softened by a sheltered and comfortable upbringing.

'I'm sorry,' she said suddenly. 'I expect you were there as well.'

'Yes.'

'I'm sorry,' she said again.

'It's best forgotten. It's time we put it behind us and got on with what's left of our lives.'

'We can't pretend it didn't happen. So many memories are bound up with the war.'

He turned, avoiding her eyes, and he seemed angry again. 'I shouldn't swim out so far again, if I were you.'

10

'I won't.'

'Are you sure you'll be all right?'

Esther smiled. 'I'm sure. I even feel hungry now.' She reached for her string bag. 'It's only bread and cheese, but you're welcome to share it.'

He shook his head, suddenly awkward. 'I'll leave you to it.'

It was only when Esther watched him leave the beach and make for the cliff path that she realised she hadn't thanked him for saving her life. She hadn't even asked him his name.

'So, we meet again. And you've been swimming after all.' Julia Brassington walked towards her as she neared the courtyard gates. 'I hoped you would pass by again on your way back. I so much wanted to ask you some more about your work as a potter.'

Esther, annoyed at being waylaid by the woman for a second time, said, 'I thought you had a potter in the community.'

Julia pulled a face. 'Rowena's an amateur. When I invited her to join us I was hoping she would do more than dabble. She has artistic flair but she wastes it on cooking. We take it in turns to cook. It's part of the philosophy of The Dovecote – to dispense with servants and wait on one another. Our aim is for mutual development and support, domestically, artistically and spiritually.'

'It sounds very pleasant,' Esther said. A weariness had come over her since leaving the beach, and it had taken all her stamina to climb the hill. She wanted nothing more than to get back to her cottage and lie out in a deckchair all afternoon; 'to rest', as the doctors had instructed, and let the sun soak away all thought.

'It *is*,' Julia said with sudden enthusiasm. 'It is so very pleasant. We live for art and for one another. We try to be as "wise as serpents and harmless as doves". It all works really splendidly. I don't know your name, do I? Should I? I mean, are you a *famous* potter?'

Esther shook her head, disconcerted by the woman's energy and her rapid way of talking: it was as if the words would burst from her if she didn't release them quickly enough. 'I'm Esther Norbrook. My husband was the potter.' She emphasised from habit that Christopher's had been the superior skill. Esther was struck by a sudden vivid picture of him, seeing the way he used to sit at the wheel, all his concentration on the ball of clay, his forearms and hands spattered with clay and water. She saw him pressing his thumbs to open up the pot as it took swift shape, like a living thing under his hands. 'My husband was killed in the war.'

'Poor you.' The words were spoken with gentle sympathy.

Esther glanced up to the dovecote as one of the doves flew from the roof with a whir of wings, the sun lighting its broad tail feathers. She swallowed the sudden threat of tears. She cried so easily these days.

Julia followed her gaze. 'Beautiful – don't you think?'

It was the only word to describe the scene. Esther absorbed the

11

soothing murmur of the doves and the ache of holding back tears faded. 'Quite beautiful,' she said.

'There have always been doves here. It's one of my earliest memories – seeing and hearing them go in and out of the dovecote.'

'You've lived here since you were a child?'

'The Brassingtons have lived here longer than some of the so-called locals can remember. My parents, when they were alive, always kept doves. I miss them. One never appreciates one's family until it's too late, don't you think? But what is death? Nothing at all.' She smiled. 'Have you got half an hour?'

Esther opened her mouth to say a firm no and found herself instead begin to waver, feeling an unexpected curiosity about the house beyond the courtyard.

'It would be interesting for the rest of the community to meet you.' Julia opened the gates wider and stepped to one side, nodding, smiling. 'You never know. We may have something to offer.'

Esther went with her across the courtyard towards an arched gateway in one corner. She drew in her breath in an exclamation of pleasure as she saw a two-storey, red-brick mansion, covered in wistaria, lying beyond a broad expanse of lawn: a shallow flight of steps led to the open front door under a cracked and weathered portico; on either side, gigantic urns spilled torrents of pale flowers against the house walls. Some distance from the house a tortoiseshell cat crossed a corner of the garden and rolled over on the grass, where a man in a white shirt and flannels was hoeing flower borders.

The barns around the courtyard were backed on this side by a broad pavement, raised above terraces of flowers; the path ran the full length of the outbuildings, dissolving eventually into a jumble of sheds and barns and a court stacked with timber. Esther's eye was drawn back to the garden, with its impression of control and glorious chaos, of sunlight and colour and deep, mysterious shadows. Statues, a fountain pool and formal lawns gave way to beaten pathways among wild grasses and the black shade of ancient cedars. A belt of wind-swept trees screened the cliff, but the blue glint of the sea shone through them, and the sound of the sea, surging, ebbing, breathed faintly on the wind.

'Do you like it?' Julia laughed, tossing back her hair. She hugged her arms about her, delighted with Esther's reaction.

'It's perfect.'

'You're right. You're so *right*. And that's why I love it and why, when people come here, they don't ever want to leave. You'll see. But come along–' she seized Esther's arm. 'You must come inside and meet everyone.'

They crossed the soft springing turf of the lawn, and Esther, half curious, half wishing she hadn't accepted the invitation, remembering that she didn't want to meet people, followed Julia into the entrance hall.

The stone floor was covered in a woven matting; a battered and ancient high-backed settle, cluttered with hats and walking sticks, boots and coats and piles of books, stood beneath a broad oak staircase leading out of the immediate cool darkness to a sunlit galleried landing. Handmade artefacts were everywhere: heavy, stoneware pots, a shell-encrusted bowl of pot-pourri, set off-centre on a grotesque, shell-encrusted stone table, a beautifully turned wooden chair standing beside a brightly coloured wall-hanging. Despite the sense of clutter, the arrangement of objects seemed precise. Contemporary portraits of disturbing intensity filled the walls, alongside water-colour landscapes and impressionistic paintings of the sea.

The sound of voices came from a room at the end of the corridor ahead of them. Esther listened to the musical rise and fall of conversation and breathed the musty smell of the house. She let her eyes adjust to the light and the mix of paintings and furniture. Her glance fell on a framed print near the stairs: it was of a Rossetti painting of Dante's Beatrice in an attitude of sublime ecstasy, the eyes closed, the body slumped, the hands resting, palms upwards in the figure's lap.

'She is in a state of trance.' Julia came to stand beside Esther. She sighed. 'It's very beautiful, don't you think?'

'She is beautiful. But I can't say I like the painting.' Esther found the picture unsettling in the heavy gloom of the hall.

'That's because you don't understand it,' Julia said; and she turned away abruptly.

Esther followed her into a low-ceilinged sitting room, as full of sunlight, space and colour as the hall had been cluttered and dark. The room was furnished with chintz-covered sofas and modern oak furniture, so unusual and striking in its straight, uncompromising lines, that Esther turned to her companion with a look of wonder.

'Joseph Kilburn is the designer. He's young. You won't have heard of him yet, but you will. Remember the name. I commissioned the furniture from him. He has the use of one of our workshops and his work is selling very well.' She smiled and again a gentle light softened her eyes and face. 'I believe it is my purpose to help people reach their full potential, Esther. Both as artists and human beings. It's wonderful what we achieve here, helping people to find themselves. We aim at mutual development through love. I have a lot of love to give. It's my nature to love. You might say that love is the ruling energy here. The others will tell you.' She sprang to the door. 'Stay there. Don't move. I'll fetch some of them in to meet you.'

Esther walked across the room, bemused by Julia, beginning to be seduced by The Dovecote. There was a sense of energy in the house, transmitted not only through its owner but in its atmosphere. Esther's glance fell on the simple lines of a sideboard with ebony legs and ebony inlaid drawers; it was the work of a designer with vision as well as of a gifted craftsman. She hesitated and, unable to resist, stroked the polished surface. She turned as she heard footsteps and Julia again breezed into the room.

A woman accompanied her, dark and pretty with a slightly desperate air of youthfulness. She wore a flowered overall, on which she wiped her hands. The apron and the gesture seemed out of harmony with her red lips, the permanently waved hair and the fingers clustered with rings.

'This is Rowena, our culinary enthusiast,' Julia said with a faint air of dismissal as Esther shook the limply offered hand.

'Julia's told us about meeting you this morning.' Rowena eyed Esther shrewdly. She smiled suddenly. 'We've all been wondering about you.'

The man and woman who followed were not easy to place. A married couple, or lovers? Esther could not tell, but it was clear that they belonged together.

'Meg acts as our secretary,' Julia said, introducing the woman – in her sixties, small and neat and giving an impression of emotions kept under tight control; her smooth white hair was worn in a bob. 'Meg does the bookings and the accounts. Peter is our lamp-man and the handyman indoors. He trims the lamps, fills them and polishes them. We all keep our own rooms clean and have a rota for the rest of the house. A baker calls every day. We get our milk and eggs from a local farm and have our own produce from the garden. Freddie – you saw him outside – does the garden. Joseph cuts firewood and fetches and delivers. Oh, and then there is Violet – she comes from the village to wash up and do the dirtier jobs. There! That's all there is to know about us.'

'Not quite all,' prompted Meg quietly.

The others looked at her and it seemed to Esther that, almost imperceptibly, Julia shook her head. She smiled, turning away from Meg. 'I haven't told you about our artistic lives. Peter, Meg and I paint. Rowena joined us initially to develop her skills as a potter. Meg does water-colours, though I'm constantly trying to persuade her to try oils. With oils one has so much more freedom. I tell her, "Look at what I've achieved with Peter."'

Peter was large and stoop-shouldered, with an impression of power in his back and arms, giving him a top-heavy appearance. He had a mane of untamed white hair and expressive hands, and he regarded Esther with a far-away expression in his pale blue eyes. 'I have not always been a painter. I played a violin in my youth. On street corners in Budapest for a few pennies. But that was a long time ago. A sad memory of times when one starved – long before I met darling Julia.' His eyes, still regarding her, became troubled. 'But I think you have sad memories too.'

Esther was startled. He continued to regard her calmly, without challenge, and, surprised at how easily the words came, she said, 'No. Not really. I only have happy memories of the past.'

'Julia tells us you work as a potter,' Rowena said, removing her overall and revealing a dress, fashionably draped across her shoulders. She threw down the apron and sat on the sofa, crossing her legs as she reached for a box of cigarettes beside her. She handed the box round and Julia and Peter each took one.

'There's not much to say, really,' Esther said. 'I studied design when I was younger. I rent a cottage near Bath with a small pottery studio and a wood-fired kiln. My husband and I made craft-ware mostly – vases, bowls, that sort of thing. Christopher was very skilled . . .' She tailed off. Why was it still so difficult in front of strangers to say that he was dead?

'Esther's husband was killed in the war,' Julia told them quietly. The others regarded Esther with a mixture of compassion and interest. Peter said, 'Ah' softly.

'We could do with a decent pottery teacher at The Dovecote.' Rowena looked for affirmation to Julia.

'As I told Julia – I'm only here on holiday.'

'Would you give some informal lessons?' Julia said. 'Just while you're here? People would be so interested. I would pay you, of course, since you're not a resident member of our community.'

Esther hesitated.

'We don't expect anyone to share their skills for nothing. You do believe in selling your skills?'

'I've sold hardly any of Christopher's pottery since the war,' Esther said. 'There was no market, of course, except for utility ware . . .'

'But not for much longer.' Julia regarded her steadily. 'The world is moving on. People want colour and beauty again. They want to see and own beautiful things – don't you think?'

The question invited confidence, but Esther did not want to think. Nor did she want to hear that the world was moving on, with its implications of forgetting. Her gaze fell again on the oak and ebony sideboard. Joseph Kilburn's furniture at least fulfilled all the criteria of beauty. It looked expensive too: the community was clearly not impoverished.

The door opened, rescuing her from an immediate reply about the pottery classes. Esther recognised the man in the white shirt and flannels who had been working in the garden. He had raffish good looks and a slick of dark hair that fell carelessly over his forehead. Esther noticed Rowena stiffen watchfully as he came forward.

'So, you're the young lady from the holiday cottage. We've all been dying to meet you since Julia told us about you. I'm Freddie. I'm the jobbing gardener round here.'

'I thought everyone was an artist?' said Esther, conscious of the slightly too ardent pressure of his hand.

'Freddie is a wood-turner,' said Julia. 'He's too modest to say how good he is.'

'I'm rather new to it,' Freddie admitted with a grin. 'An amateur really, with a lot to learn, but I make tolerable wooden bowls. Julia has let me set up a lathe in one of the sheds.'

'He's the jobbing gardener,' said Rowena with a touch of resentment.

15

'And he's not a bit modest. What Freddie has failed to add, Esther, is that he is also my husband.'

'Yes, my darling. And you're the cook.' Freddie's response echoed his wife's tone of malice.

Rowena laughed suddenly. 'Isn't it jolly? He used to work in the City before we met Julia. You'd never think it, to see him chiselling wood and hacking up potatoes.'

Julia puffed at her cigarette, holding it between nicotine-stained fingers. 'Stop bitching at one another, you two. Where is Joseph? I told him I wanted him to meet you.' Suddenly she seemed annoyed.

'Trust Joseph,' said Meg. 'He'll shut himself in his workshed just to be awkward.' She turned to Esther. 'He has what people generally call an artistic temperament.' She glanced at Julia with a strange expression and added, 'In Joseph's case, artistic temperament is sometimes a euphemism for being darned obstinate.'

'You only say that because you don't understand him properly,' snapped Julia.

'No one understands Joseph.'

'Oh, Meg, do be quiet. You know Julia understands us all.' Rowena too glanced at Julia, and it occurred to Esther that everyone's attitude to their patron was moderated by a vague unease, a suggestion of wariness.

'Come and see the pottery studio.' Julia leaped up with a sudden change of mood, and stubbed out her cigarette. 'Rowena, you don't mind?'

'It's your studio, Julia darling. I only borrow it from time to time. My province is the kitchen.'

Esther followed Julia out of the drawing room and across the hall once more.

'Well! Somebody new to stir us up a bit,' said Freddie when they had gone. He took a cigarette from the box on the table and lit it, narrowing his eyes against the smoke.

'Stir who up? You or Julia?' Rowena went to the window to watch Esther and Julia cross the lawn. She drew on her cigarette and folded her arms. 'Anyway, I don't think this one will stay long. She looks too self-sufficient.'

'I'm not so sure,' said Peter quietly. 'Julia seems very determined, and you know what that means. Come hell or high water...'

'If Julia does get her way, we shall have to get used to it,' said Meg. 'You're forgetting – Esther has been bereaved. She needs our help.' It was not clear from her expression whether Meg spoke with deep sincerity or an even deeper cynicism. 'Actually, I rather like her. Anyone with half a mind can see she's vulnerable.' She glanced at Peter, who raised his eyebrows and smiled at her gently.

'We are all vulnerable. It's why we depend so heavily on darling Julia,' he said.

Freddie laughed ruefully. 'Isn't that how she likes us?'

'It's how she liked Joseph,' remarked Rowena, turning away from the window.

'Ah, Joseph,' murmured Meg enigmatically.

Rowena laughed. 'Perhaps that's what all this is about. Perhaps Julia is growing tired of him at last.'

'Rowena is so – uncommitted,' Julia complained as they crossed the lawn.

'Rowena seems committed to her cooking.'

'But I didn't invite her to live with me and be my chef!'

'Food can be a form of art as well.' Esther thought of the lingering, sensuous meals that she and Christopher had once shared. She fell silent. Why did the strongest memories strike so unexpectedly and with a force that was physical in its intensity?

'You're remembering something,' Julia said gently.

'I spend much of my time remembering.'

'That's not a bad thing. But you shouldn't draw in on yourself with your memories the way you do.'

Esther said nothing, annoyed that Julia should presume to know her at all.

They entered a long, low barn that had been turned into a workshop, with windows overlooking the garden. In front of the windows stood a row of kick wheels. Unfinished pots were ranged on shelves along the wall, and work-tables filled the centre of the room. The end wall was taken up by an open flight of stairs. Esther glanced involuntarily to the closed door at the top of the wooden platform.

'This was the stables. There's an attic flat above,' said Julia. 'But Freddie and Rowena prefer to live in the house. It's nearer to the kitchen. Well, what do you think of it? The kiln is outside. A bit basic. But it's in excellent order according to a potter who lived with us before the war.'

'It's wonderful. So much space.' Esther thought of Christopher's tiny studio at The Folly.

'I knew you'd like it. It could have been made for you.'

Esther, disquieted by Julia's insistence on linking her with The Dovecote, wanted to protest again that she was only a visitor there.

Julia gave her a half-smile, as if concealing some conviction or knowledge that she might or might not wish to share. 'We have classes here twice a week. A few local people attend. Most come from Lyme or Axminster. In the summer we get more. They join in whatever's happening. Rowena does her best in the pottery, but a demonstration class from you would be very much appreciated. As I said, I'll pay you. Oh – why won't you even consider it?'

'I didn't say I wouldn't—' Esther looked round at the studio, at the tubs of clay and slip and realised to her astonishment that she was tempted.

'The Dovecote is partly funded by our courses.' Julia sat on one of the

17

tables, leaning forward and smiling, swinging her legs with an expression of delight in herself and her achievement. 'It's so exciting, Esther, to see people drawn to the community and then to watch them flower. A proportion of everyone's income here is ploughed back into running The Dovecote, and everyone gives classes. We work for a higher purpose than mere monetary gain. However – we do believe that style and skill should be properly rewarded.' She got down from the table. 'Let's find Joseph.'

They went outside. Esther felt the sun beat up from the pavement. The cat she had seen earlier came towards them and rubbed itself round her legs. She could hear the crooning of doves in the outer courtyard, and the tranquillity of the place stole over her. She turned to Julia. 'All right. I'll do it.'

'I knew you would.' Julia's eyes flashed with an intense delight. 'Now, tell me what you were remembering when you said that food could be an art form.'

Esther was startled. A moment earlier she would have been angered by the intrusion. 'Christopher. I was thinking of Christopher.'

They walked slowly along the pavement. 'Joseph was in the war too, and on the Somme right from the beginning,' Julia said after a while. They approached one of the barns. Esther smelled the pungent aroma of sawn timber: huge tree trunks, cut into planking and separated with layers of sticks, were stacked to dry under an open shed. 'It was a particular hell for him. He pretends he doesn't want to remember, but he had an awful time. Meg called him temperamental, and he can be. But the others haven't been as close to his nightmares as I have.'

They entered the double doors of the barn. The floor was littered with chips of wood and shavings. There was a heady smell – a mixture of wood and turpentine and linseed oil. A few pieces of furniture in various stages of assembly stood around the stone workshop and the walls were lined with tools. In the centre of the barn, the light streaming from a skylight on to his hair, a young man in shirt sleeves was working with a plane, smoothing a plank of timber. His hair fell over his eyes and it was not until he turned to her and straightened that Esther recognised him.

'Meet Joseph Kilburn,' said Julia.

He looked at Esther and his eyes lit briefly and then emptied of expression as Julia looked from one to the other. He held out his hand. 'Hello. I believe we've already met.'

Chapter Two

'You've met?' There was a strange quality to Julia's expression, an element of scrutiny and also of unease, as Esther and Joseph Kilburn shook hands with one another.

'I got into difficulties while swimming this morning,' Esther explained. 'Mr Kilburn saw what was happening and came to help me.' It occurred to her that Julia had wanted to introduce her star protégé with a flourish. It was Esther's first realisation of how much Julia needed to direct events, to set the stage and place her characters where she wanted them; she watched with a mixture of amusement and sympathy as Julia rounded on Joseph.

'Why didn't you tell me?' Again there was something odd about her reaction, something studied, even artificial. 'You mean to say you saved her from drowning and you never even said anything!'

'I didn't know it was important.' Joseph threw Esther a brief smile.

'I didn't thank you properly. If you hadn't seen me I really think I would have drowned.' Esther remembered her crazy conviction that Christopher had come to save her. It was no exaggeration to say that she owed Joseph Kilburn her life.

'Forget about it. I've dried out.'

Esther, conscious that Julia was still sulking, turned to include her as she asked, 'May I look round the workshop?'

Joseph continued planing the piece of wood on which he had been working. Through a doorway an assistant in a long apron was fitting an arm-rest to a chair that stood on a workbench; the man was engrossed in his task and did not look up as Esther moved from piece to piece of half-finished furniture. Even in its raw, unfinished state the lines were clean and delicate, she thought. True beauty always had an element of mystery. There was a sense of something hidden that one couldn't quite comprehend, though it made one want to possess an object with an almost physical longing. It had been the same with Christopher's pots. To see them was to adore their strength and grace and subtlety. She allowed herself to wonder whether, if Christopher's work had been commonplace, she would have admired him so much. Suppose his skill as a potter had been less marked and he had merely made pretty pots? It was a new idea to her, that her love had been conditional, and she thrust it from her with distaste.

'The lines are very clean, very austere,' she said at last, sensing that

19

Joseph was waiting for her opinion on his furniture.

'That's how I see things.'

'I like your style. There's no fuss or clutter.'

'Esther is a potter,' Julia said. 'She's going to take some of the outside classes.'

'When do you start?' he asked without any sign of surprise.

'I really don't know.'

'Tomorrow?' suggested Julia.

'It seems my holiday has been taken over.'

'Don't let Julia bully you,' Joseph told her with heavy emphasis as Julia took her by the arm.

'We are going to let The Dovecote work its magic on her,' Julia replied.

There *was* an air of magic about The Dovecote, Esther acknowledged as she set out a deckchair in the tiny walled garden of the holiday cottage, scarcely able to believe now that she had agreed to Julia's request. She dozed in the afternoon sun with a book open in her lap. It was seductive, to let the drone of bees and distant sound of the sea wash over her, to let her mind drift into a state of non-thinking. A sudden pang of guilt, a memory of her readiness that morning to turn her child into an orphan, made her leap up suddenly. She must telephone, make sure that Cassie was all right. What if she was being difficult, or was missing her, or what if she were ill?

Esther locked up the cottage and hurried down the road to the village.

'How are you settling in?' The woman in the post office smiled at Esther with curiosity. There had been talk about the stranger, speculation as to why she was there so early in the season. The woman glanced at the ring on Esther's wedding finger. 'A bit lonely up there for you, isn't it? We don't generally get holiday folk before June.'

'I expect the tourists disrupt life for you in the summer.' Esther moved pointedly to the telephone in the corner, avoiding the woman's probing questions, feeling a resentment against well-meaning strangers, a habit since her widowhood.

'I'll connect you.' The woman hurried along behind the counter and reached for the telephone set. Esther gave her the number. 'Summer visitors are good for trade now we're getting back to normal. I'm used to people coming and going. There's that lot up at The Dovecote all year round, for a start. *And* all through the war.'

'Mrs Brassington's house.'

'*Miss* Brassington,' the woman corrected with a sniff of disapproval. 'You've met her then?'

'Yes. She seems very friendly.'

'Oh, she does. It's all *too* friendly, if you ask me – come in and have a cup of coffee and join a painting class, or anything else if you've a mind to

20

it.' She lowered her voice and covered the telephone mouthpiece confidentially. 'Won't be a jiffy. Soon have you through.'

'Do you object to people being artistic?'

'Well, no.' The woman, sensing Esther's note of contention, began to retract. 'And, I'm not one to gossip. But they're a rum lot. Who's to know what doesn't go on up there?'

'It all seemed very quiet to me.'

'*Seeming* quiet's one thing. A word to the wise. I should keep well away from them if I was you.' The woman handed Esther the telephone. 'Your connection's through.'

Her mother's voice sounded strained. 'How lovely to hear you, darling...'

Esther glanced at the postmistress and, with studied reluctance, the woman moved away. 'Hello, Mummy. Is Cassie all right...?'

'Of course she is. You really mustn't fuss. Everything's fine. How about you? How *are* you?' The emphasis was there, the pressure to acknowledge her continued vulnerability, to admit they had been right to suggest she go away for a while.

'I've been here less than twenty-four hours. I'm still settling in.'

'Is it clean?'

'Yes. Spotless.'

'Is it far from the sea?'

'About twenty minutes on foot. Winmouth is a pretty place. There's a war memorial and a church – and there's a house with a dovecote.' Esther glanced at the postmistress who looked quickly away and began to busy herself with a pile of forms. 'A woman called Julia lives there.'

'Are you *all right*, Esther?'

'Yes, of course I'm all right.' Esther forced a necessary brightness into her voice. 'I've been for a swim.'

There was a pause. 'That's good.'

'I haven't swum since Christopher and I—'

'Esther, is it wise, right now, to talk about him? I'll fetch Cassie to the telephone for you.'

Esther heard the telephone being laid carefully on the hall table. She pictured its dark polished surface, the bowl of flowers on a crocheted mat, conforming to her mother's ideas of artistry, the coatstand with her father's trilby hat and the umbrellas and walking canes. I need to talk about Christopher, she said silently. That's what was wrong. You wouldn't let me talk about him. Everyone assumed, because I didn't say anything, that I was all right. She heard the sound of running feet, imagined Cassie's flushed face, her dark hair and dark-fringed eyes.

'Cassie?'

'Hello? Mummy? I've painted some pictures for you.'

So, that explained her own mother's note of strain. Esther remembered the ritual spreading of old sheets on the kitchen floor, the voluminous grey pinafore from her childhood, the scrubbing of fingernails and washing out of jam-jars until they shone afterwards. Her

21

mother hated mess. 'You'll keep the pictures for me, won't you?'

'They're of The Folly. Except I can't remember everything properly. When are you coming home again? When are we going back to The Folly?'

'Soon. When I've done lots of walking and sitting about in the sunshine.'

'Granny says we can stay in Birmingham with her and Granpy when you're better, instead of going home.'

Esther drew in her breath sharply. 'I don't think so, Cassie.'

'Granny says, if we live with her and Granpy for a bit longer I can go to a proper school and have a pony.'

A pause. Esther sensed the conflict of interests going on in Cassie's mind and she swore silently. 'Put Granny back on the telephone, please. I want to talk to her again.'

She heard the defensive note in her mother's voice: 'Well, I think that's all for now . . .'

'What have you been saying?'

'Esther, you know it makes sense. We want to do the best for you. Christopher left you unprovided for – and you surely can't expect to go back to living on your widow's pension. You weren't eating properly. No wonder you made yourself ill.'

'I have my work, Mummy,' Esther said, prompted by the memory of Julia Brassington's observation that people wanted beautiful things again. 'I can sell pots.'

'That was all very well when Christopher was alive. You can hardly do it on your own. Besides – you have Cassie to think of now.'

'I *am* thinking of Cassie. And the sooner I get back home and start leading a normal life again, the better.'

'I would hardly call living at The Folly a normal life.' Her mother's voice trembled with the constraint of stifling her old prejudices. No proper upbringing for a child. Living like gypsies in the middle of nowhere. Why did you have to marry a potter? Moneyed or not – he was practically an *artisan*!

'Oh, I can't argue with you like this over the telephone.' Esther was conscious of the woman behind the counter, busily stamping forms and listening unashamedly to every word.

Her mother agreed calmly, as if it were she and not Esther who had decided the matter. 'No. You mustn't upset yourself. We'll talk about it when you get home.'

'Home is The Folly, Mummy! Christopher's cottage is my home.' Esther rang up the receiver with a violent 'Clop!' The woman had stopped banging the rubber stamp on the counter and, in the silence that settled, Esther realised she had been shouting.

She avoided the woman's expression, which betrayed too great an eagerness to discuss relationships between mothers and daughters, and, after paying for the call, made her way back up the hill. She went into the small kitchen of the cottage, filled the kettle viciously at the single cold

22

tap and banged it down on the hob, then stood with her arms folded tightly as she waited for the water to boil.

Esther knew with a sinking heart that in this instance her mother was right. If she continued to struggle on her pension she would have to go on denying Cassie all the comfort and advantages she herself had known as a child. She had spoken blithely of selling pots again. Could she? Christopher hadn't produced anything at the pottery after the start of the war and during the four years of emergency studio work had not been wanted. She remembered Julia's words: People want beauty and colour . . .

Esther poured tea into a mug and sipped the scalding liquid, hearing Christopher's voice again, 'We're a crack team, you and I. We can take on the world.'

'It's all very well for you,' she said aloud. 'Why did you have to die and leave me to take on the world alone? It's all very fine being one of the glorious dead. You can be a hero, become a legend, but I have to go on living.'

The next day Esther decided to walk to The Dovecote across country instead of along the road. She set out early for the pottery class and entered the field opposite the cottage. She began mentally to prepare the lesson, picturing the well-equipped workshop, the tubs of pugged clay waiting for use, the clean kick-wheels, sinks and tables. She contrasted it with Christopher's studio, the cramped workbench and tiny, clay-spattered window. The Dovecote studio was a potter's dream. 'It could have been made for you,' Julia had commented with that peculiar note of intimacy. What else had she said . . . ? 'When people come here, they don't ever want to leave.'

Esther pictured the beautiful house and the rambling garden and recalled the quiet atmosphere of purpose there. She swept her hand across the heads of green standing corn as she skirted the farmland, and it occurred to her that she had at last begun to feel alive after two and a half years of feeling nothing at all.

She reached the coastal path and halted. She had come upon a portion of the cliff that was higher than the rest. Below her, to the east and inland, she could see the village of Winmouth and the course of the stream from which it took its name. The beach was visible, though the bulk of it was hidden below the cliff.

From where she stood Esther had a clear view of The Dovecote. The house and its outbuildings, the yard stacked with timber for the workshops, the green lawns and the trees and flower borders were laid out neatly below her. The grounds stopped short of the cliff, their boundary marked by a paling fence, weaving among gorse bushes along the cliff path. A stone hut stood within its limits; it was low, like a shepherd's bothy, and Esther might have dismissed it as such, or as a garden outhouse, had a wisp of smoke not risen from a chimney in its roof.

She set off down the slope of the cliff, keeping her eye on the building; it disappeared from time to time as the path plunged between high banks of gorse. At last she came upon The Dovecote boundary. A gate in the fence and a well-trodden path brought her from the cliff walk into the grounds.

The path led close by the building she had seen. The door was open, propped with a heavy chunk of wood. Esther halted, her curiosity roused by the smoke. 'Is anyone there?' There was no response and she stepped up to the door and peeped inside.

The bleak interior reinforced her initial impression of a bothy. A smoky fire burned in a low grate. A table, a single wooden chair, and an army camp bed covered with a blanket, were the only items of furniture in the room. Esther's attention came to rest on a pullover and a pair of binoculars, slung from a peg on the wall opposite the bed. With a start she recognised the pullover as Joseph Kilburn's. She stared at the binoculars, remembering the figure among the trees, the flash of the sun's reflection. Was this his cottage? Had he been watching her swim? It would account for his reaching her so quickly. Esther turned from the door with a sense of having intruded, but also with a strong feeling of disquiet.

She followed the path towards the trees and entered a shady walk, dry and hard under foot, a tunnel, at the end of which glowed sunlit lawns. She emerged from deep shade into the garden, and the view of The Dovecote made her draw in her breath with a shock of pleasure.

It was so tranquil, so lovely. She could hear the sea and the whisper of the wind in the trees behind her – and another sound, growing louder as she crossed the lawn, breaking the tranquillity, the rattle of machinery from the furniture workshop. Esther was tempted for a moment to confront Joseph Kilburn about the binoculars. If he had watched her, did he know how close she had been to suicide? Was that why he had appeared so quickly? She hesitated, then turned to the house instead of the barns.

Esther followed the sound of voices. Peter and Meg were with Rowena in the large kitchen. Rowena, in her overall, moved between the kitchen table and the stove, tending saucepans. Meg was sitting on the table, swinging her legs and listening to Peter talk; he sat in a chair by the fire and looked up as Esther tapped on the open door. 'Esther – come in. Have some coffee.' Rowena poured coffee into a mug from a jug on the stove.

Peter continued talking as Esther sipped the scalding drink. He was reminiscing about Budapest while Meg listened to him with sad, possessive murmurs of endorsement. 'That is how it was for him. Can you imagine – to be a child of seven and have no mother or father; no one at all to care for you?'

Rowena was making goulash for the evening dinner. 'You need plenty of paprika.' She turned to Peter. 'Aren't I right? Isn't that where people always go wrong? They're too cautious with the paprika?'

Peter smiled silently and nodded.

Rowena flashed a smile at Esther. 'I'll come with you to the pottery when I've set the goulash simmering. I'll introduce you to our regulars and let you know what we've been doing.'

Esther sat in a window-seat with her coffee. They all seemed more relaxed than on the previous day. It was as if they had decided to warm to her.

After a while Freddie came in from the garden. He sat on the seat beside Esther and flirted – first with Esther, then Meg and, from time to time, with his wife. Rowena ignored him until, having set the stew under a tight lid on the stove, she peeled off her apron and threw it at him. 'Leave the women alone. They're not impressed. Come on, Esther. Let's go and meet the potters.'

Rowena was in a talkative mood as they crossed the garden. 'We've not advanced much beyond coil pots, I'm afraid. I'd far rather take a cookery class, but Julia won't hear of it unless it's vegetarian or something to do with herbal cures. Freddie and I are experimenting with herbs,' she added. 'Julia knows an awful lot about healing. She's teaching me about homeopathy – that means treating like with like. Julia's a great believer in water. Everyone should drink lots of water every day. It flushes out the impurities.'

Esther breathed in the subtle scents of the garden, listening to Rowena with half an ear. 'It's all so peaceful.' She turned and scanned the upstairs windows of the house. 'Does anyone else live here? I imagined there would be more of you. Such a big house . . .'

'People come and go. When one person leaves, someone else always seems to take their place. We get more outsiders in the summer – for the courses.'

'Courses on what?'

'Oh, all sorts. Art, philosophy.' Rowena seemed evasive. 'Of course, Freddie and I are fairly new to it all. Peter and Meg have been with Julia since before the war.'

'And Joseph?' Esther glanced towards the worksheds.

'Joseph has been coming here since he was a boy. His parents knew Julia's parents. It's a sort of second home to him. So it's natural I suppose that he came back here. Julia is his refuge.'

'His refuge?' Esther queried, for the description sounded over-dramatic.

'The Dovecote has been a refuge at one time or another for everyone that lives here. Freddie and I came after his mother died last summer.' Rowena smiled with an expression of tenderness that contrasted oddly with her hard, bright face. 'When you're feeling low and unable to cope with life, The Dovecote is the place to come. Julia offers everyone so much kindness – only she calls it love.'

Esther was still thinking about Rowena's use of the word 'refuge' in connection with Joseph Kilburn. She remembered then that Julia had said he had suffered more than most during the war. 'I passed a cottage just inside the grounds. Is that where Joseph lives?'

'Sort of. It's very spartan.'

'Why doesn't he live at the house with the rest of you?'

'He has a room in the house, but he prefers not to disturb us at night.' Rowena saw Esther's look of non-comprehension. 'He has the most ghastly nightmares.'

They were close to the pottery studio where a small crowd of fewer than a dozen women were gathering outside the doors. Esther's thoughts on Joseph Kilburn were cut short by the sudden realisation that she had agreed to face them – not only face them but help Rowena teach them to make pots. The women came from Winmouth and the nearby villages, Rowena was telling Esther. A trio of them attended nearly all the classes. 'Like the three wise monkeys, they can't function without each other,' she said in a low voice.

Esther felt an icy anxiety descend on her. What if she could not do it? What if the memories of working with Christopher were too close and she found herself weeping again?

'They were expecting me to take the class today,' Rowena said. 'Let's hope they are in for a nice surprise.'

Rowena introduced the women in turn and they proudly showed Esther the thumb and coil pots they had made. It was clear that Rowena's knowledge was limited. Esther decided to develop on the basic skills the class had already learned. She set them to kneading clay and moved among them, lending a hand here and there. She remembered the stores of clay, the wood for firing and the backlog of Christopher's unglazed pots at The Folly, and she found herself echoing Christopher's ideas. 'A piece of pottery – just like any other form of art – is an expression of the person who makes it.' When she showed the women how to handle the clay she heard Christopher's emphasis in her voice. 'It's important to get the texture of the clay exactly right. It's the state of the clay that defines the final character of the pot.'

Could she work alone? Her role had seemed redundant after Christopher had gone. She had never questioned his superior craftsmanship: he had been the master and had produced the artistic forms; she had supplied the decoration subordinate to them. His job had been to create, hers only to harmonise. She remembered how dictatorial Christopher had been at first, heard him say again, 'Why is it that schools of art turn out such nincompoops when it comes to the practicalities, with not even the most basic knowledge of clays and pigments and glazes?' She had been resentful of his criticism, but she had learned quickly under his tuition. The form of a pot was of prime importance, he had said, caressing the belly and shoulder of a finished vase. 'Curves are always female. Angles are male. I prefer my pots to be female.'

She had rebelled a little, had questioned his assumption that form must always be superior to decoration, saying, 'The most well-shaped pot can look horrible, finished with the wrong glaze or painted badly, but

26

a beautiful decoration can redeem a badly made pot.' He had said that she was talking rubbish, and that disguising a badly made pot was in any case dishonest.

Honesty had been his creed. A pot had to be sincere. A craftsman – never woman, she remembered – owed it to himself to be true to his ideals. She had not been able to make him agree with her on much – except her conviction that they should be self-reliant. And after a while his arrogance had not mattered, for by then she had recognised his superior craftsmanship. And she had fallen hopelessly in love with him.

She heard his voice in her head and the clay under her hands was smooth and firm and plastic, and it was as if she were back in the studio at The Folly.

'Get a feel for how much life there is in the clay,' she told the class, as Christopher had once told her. 'How sticky it is, how plastic it becomes as you knead it.' She felt quite calm as she worked and knew that she would not begin weeping.

'I've seen you about in the village.' Violet, the girl who had spoken, was tall, with bobbed dark hair and heavy, almost masculine features. 'You're on holiday,' the girl continued eagerly. 'You're not here to stay like the others.'

'No. Julia asked me to take a few classes for Rowena.'

'You're better at it than Rowena,' Violet said in a barely successful stage-whisper. She leaned back in her chair to let Esther demonstrate how to work the clay, watching her rotate the ball and knead it with the palm of her hand. 'You'd think you'd need to be strong to do it properly, but you've hardly got a bit of flesh on you.' Violet displayed her own broad arms, as if to compare them. Esther remembered that Julia had said Violet helped with the household jobs at The Dovecote.

'It's more a question of technique – like making bread. Here, you try it.' Esther watched the girl hold the ball of clay and press it with her hands. 'Put a bit more aggression into it.'

Violet laughed. 'Now you sound like Julia. She says things like that.'

'I don't think we should be aggressive,' said one of the other women. 'It goes against my nature.'

'Then you'll never make a potter,' Esther said.

Violet looked round with a grin and, picking up her ball of clay, slammed it on to the table with a violence that made the others laugh.

'Have you been to many of Julia's classes?' Esther asked, sitting beside her.

'Nearly all of them. I did painting. I did making book-covers. I did embroidery – that was boring, like being at school.'

'What else?' Esther felt a curiosity to know more about the community and Julia.

Violet looked at her, as if searching for the answer to some question. She glanced at Rowena, then looked away. 'Oh, this and that.'

'Some people in the village seem to disapprove of what Julia is doing at The Dovecote.'

27

'They're daft. They don't know what they're talking about. If they took the trouble to find out what she's really like, they'd think different.'

'You're fond of her.'

'She's one of the best. Julia's got all that money, but she doesn't spend it on herself like most rich people do. She likes to help people. She really cares about them and what goes on in their heads. She helps them in all sorts of ways. Julia is a wonderful woman.'

Surprised by this declaration almost of love, Esther looked from Violet to Rowena, who merely nodded confirmation and turned on her that oddly gentle smile.

Esther had hoped that Julia would look in on the class. She would have liked her to have witnessed Violet's zeal, to see Rowena's 'three wise monkeys' instilled with a little aggression as they learned to throw pots, to hear the women's laughter as their attempts to centre the clay failed; and to see the triumph of the few who mastered a steady central spin, shaping a recognisable pot before the afternoon was over.

When the women had gone, Rowena helped Esther to tidy the studio; afterwards they walked across the lawn in the lengthening shadows of the afternoon. Julia came to meet them from the house, dressed in a long green cardigan splashed with paint. 'How did it go?' she said as she reached them. She linked her arms through Esther's and Rowena's and the three of them went indoors.

'It was all very jolly,' said Rowena. 'She's made a hit. Why don't you stay to dinner, Esther?'

'Of course she must stay to dinner. But first, Esther, you must come and see my paintings.'

Julia's studio was at the top of the house. A bright square of red oriental carpet covered part of the floor and another length of carpet hung on the end wall from ceiling to floor. A few chairs and artist's props – a stack of drapery, a jardinière on a Corinthian column – were stowed in one corner.

Esther walked the length of the room and looked at the finished and half-finished paintings, portraits of people she did not know, one of Peter and one – a startlingly intimate, brooding picture – of Joseph. From the windows in the sloping ceiling Esther could see the doves sitting on the barns, nestling against the mossy tiles. 'I'm so glad you asked me to take the pottery class.'

'I knew you would be. I hope, in time, we can help you to find yourself again.'

Esther sighed, no longer irritated by Julia's way of behaving as if she knew all about her, nor surprised that she understood the crisis of grief she had been through.

'Have they been talking about us?' Julia said. 'I'm sure they have – in the post office, in the general store?'

Esther was embarrassed. 'A little.'

'All of us here have known sorrow. We are all healing ourselves from within, rediscovering an *inner* source. It's sad – don't you think? – that so many people have lost contact with the spiritual aspect of their being?'

'It's very hard to feel one is a spiritual being when the suffering was on such a huge scale,' Esther said, thinking of the years of the war, the thousands now who were unemployed and the disabled survivors, a living rebuke to those in government who gave out such platitudes as 'A Land Fit for Heroes'.

'You're wrong.' Julia came to stand beside her. 'Our material suffering and our physical being is really very unimportant. Inside – that's where we live. In a world of thought and feeling. It's the part of us which makes us what we are – ' she paused – 'and what we continue to be after we are dead.'

Julia's eyes shone with conviction. Her expression was compelling, so that Esther felt as if she couldn't pull her own gaze away.

'It's the same with your husband,' Julia said. 'It's his spirit that's important now. Why do you keep him so much to yourself?'

'My parents are uncomfortable about his death. My brother was killed too. If I talk about either of them my mother changes the subject. She thinks it's time I remarried – they didn't really get on with Christopher, you see.'

'They've someone else in mind for you?'

Esther did not answer. Then, suddenly, she found herself talking about the Fieldings' New Year's Day party. 'Giles has always been a good friend. I knew him before I knew Christopher. Only I didn't realise what everyone had been thinking . . .'

They had all stood there, smiling, expecting it, and Giles had begun to make a speech – about how they had been friends since childhood, how they had become closer during the past year and how he hoped that one day they would marry.

'I couldn't believe it. He was proposing in front of them all.'

'It must have been a shock.' Again there was a surprising gentleness in Julia's eyes.

'I don't know why I didn't realise what was happening. Giles had been so good, you see, during the war. He was injured in France early on and couldn't go back to the Front. He used to drive down and visit me and Cassie. And when my brother, and then Christopher was killed, I suppose I saw him as a prop.'

'Poor Giles.'

'He was devastated. I can't remember exactly what I said. I think I swore – you know, like in *Pygmalion*. "Not bloody likely." Only it wasn't very funny.'

Esther remembered the awful silence, everyone staring at her in horror and the sense that she had entered a nightmare in which she knew she was dreaming but couldn't wake herself up. Then the more terrifying nightmare had begun: the faces – her family, Giles, his parents, people she had known for years – had begun to leer at her, the room to spin and dissolve and her head had filled with the gathering roar of the disintegration of her self-control.

'They told me I cried for days. My parents couldn't understand and nor can I really. Why then? Why so long afterwards? I didn't cry at all when I got the news that Christopher was killed. I couldn't. I felt so hard and dry inside.'

'It had to happen sooner or later. It always does.'

'I talk to him,' Esther said. 'All the time, I talk to him. I know he's dead, but it's as if he's right there beside me sometimes.'

'Where's the harm in talking to him? You spoke to him when he was alive.'

'I heard him yesterday when I was swimming.'

Julia moved away from the attic window. After a moment she said, 'Why does that seem strange?' She turned to Esther and again her eyes shone with some inner confidence. 'Why do you think you were brought to The Dovecote, Esther? We are going to help you to live again. You will create beautiful things. Christopher's spirit will be your inspiration.'

Perhaps it was true, thought Esther. Perhaps Christopher was with her 'in spirit' and his memory would give her the strength to go on alone. She had been at ease that afternoon in the pottery studio. It had seemed natural to work with clay, as if Christopher was there beside her.

'I should like to paint you one day,' Julia said suddenly.

'There isn't time. I shall have to go home in a little while.'

'Not now, maybe. But there will be time. Plenty of time.' Julia crossed to her easel and removed a piece of sacking to reveal a painting of a sea nymph riding a fish; it was fanciful and surreal. 'Art should flow from you,' Julia said. 'It should pour in a torrent of excitement that will not be stopped. Come and see Peter's pictures. Peter has learned what I mean.'

Peter's paintings were stacked in the adjacent attic. The scope and number of them were overwhelming and their subject matter shocked Esther when she saw them. His style was that of the Expressionists. The paintings were all, without exception, of the doves in the courtyard: dark, nightmarish pictures of flurries of wings, movement everywhere and a suggestion of violence in them.

'Are you surprised?' Julia said, watching Esther closely. 'But aren't they *good*! You see what I mean? Peter is in touch with his inner self!'

Esther thought about the paintings during dinner. She looked at the man who had painted them, reluctant to believe that they had been executed by Peter's gentle and sensitive hands.

Julia was proud of Peter's paintings. 'When he came to us he was rigid with painful memories,' she told Esther. 'I have drawn him out. I have fed his soul.'

Peter nodded, smiling with a placid air of self-deprecation. 'It's true. It's all true.'

Esther wondered about the others – Meg and Rowena – and was the glib Freddie also in touch with his soul? Freddie was talking about the healing effect of water, encouraged by Rowena. 'Looking at water is wonderful when you feel depressed,' he said. 'Imagine you are parcelling up all your troubles and letting them float off on the tide.' But Esther couldn't tell whether he was serious or whether he was gently mocking Julia.

She wondered why Joseph Kilburn hadn't joined them for dinner and after a while she asked Julia, 'Does Joseph eat alone in his cottage?'

'Sometimes.' Julia's expression became guarded and she turned abruptly to talk to Peter.

'He's gone to Exeter,' Meg said to Esther in a low voice.

'Isn't that rather a long way?'

'Not when you have a Bentley and drive very fast.'

'Joseph likes to live it up a bit,' Rowena said more loudly.

'He goes to a dance club where they play infernal jazz music until ungodly hours in the morning. I think he has friends there – people he met in the war,' Freddie explained.

Esther remembered with a vivid sense of nostalgia dancing the foxtrot and the Chocolate Soldier waltz, Christopher winding up the gramophone, laughing. He would have loved the new Dixieland music.

'Joseph is a loner,' said Julia suddenly, and the others fell silent, expectantly. 'I've tried to impress on him his need for others, that we are here to offer help and understanding ... but if he wants to ignore the hand that's held out to him, what can I do?' She looked up, and Esther saw that Julia's eyes had suddenly brimmed with tears. Peter sought in his pocket for a packet of cigarettes and opened it. Julia took one with a shaking hand and Peter lit it for her, placing a comforting arm round her shoulder. Julia puffed at the cigarette. 'I have so much to *give*,' she said after a while.

The others watched her sympathetically and Rowena stood and began quietly to clear the table. Eventually Julia recovered. 'I don't like to fail, Esther,' she said, as if in explanation. 'I will *not* accept failure.' And, though she smiled, there was a passionate intensity in her words.

Esther found herself drawn repeatedly to The Dovecote. The simplicity of the life there was welcoming and the undemanding, unquestioning company of the community restful. On the afternoons when she was not teaching the pottery group, Esther would sit in the kitchen and talk to the others or walk alone in the garden, where even the silence was healing.

There was a shallow, formal pool in the garden. Jets of water spouted from the mouths of three dolphins forming a fountain at its centre; their jaws were flattened to its base, their tails arched upwards to support a shallow basin, where a high jet of water rose and splashed down again, falling in whichever direction the breeze took it.

Esther sat there one afternoon, several days after she had taken the first pottery class: the women were progressing well – and so was she, Esther told herself. Do you mind? she asked Christopher silently. Was it a betrayal to make new friends and to begin to feel at peace? A light mist cooled her face when the wind blew in her direction. She remembered Freddie and Rowena's therapeutic claims for water. It was true: the constant fall of the fountain was soothing and musical, like the sound of a stream running over rocks.

She heard the more energetic sound of a motor car and, after a while, saw Joseph Kilburn come across the lawn towards her from the courtyard. She had not spoken to him since the day he had rescued her. He appeared to spend very little time with the others, she thought. And yet it seemed as if he was crossing the lawn purposely to speak to her. He looked relaxed, boyish, and today reminded her only faintly of Christopher – in the set of the head, the line of his body. He wore a light-coloured suit with a white motoring scarf and a pair of white shoes with coloured toe caps – the kind her father said were worn only by lounge lizards and cads. He pulled off his motoring gloves as he approached her and raised his hat, smiling. 'I was wondering about you. How are you getting on?'

Esther moved along the seat to make room for him and he sat down beside her. 'I'm being lazy,' she said.

'Good.' He leaned back with his hands in his pockets, digging his heels into the grass. 'There's nothing like it. Though I should rather laze about on the cliff or the beach than in a formal garden.'

'It isn't really formal though, is it? There's a lovely wildness about it.'

He looked at her. 'You're looking better.'

'You mean better than when you dragged me out of the sea?'

'Something like that.'

'I haven't seen you around much,' Esther said. 'Rowena says you like to drive fast.' Christopher had loved motoring, she remembered. His parents had bought him a bull-nosed Morris one birthday before the war, and he had taught her to drive. He had been like a child with a new toy. They had acquired all the motoring paraphernalia: goggles, dust-coats, motor-caps. She had his motoring gloves still and wore them when she used the Morris. She had loved taking the wheel in those days, but driving brought back too many memories for it to be enjoyable any more.

Joseph said, 'Some people drink, some people drive fast cars. I have friends in Exeter – I needed to get away for a few days. It can be very claustrophobic here.'

'I don't think it's claustrophobic. I think it's very peaceful.'

'You'll be going back to your little girl soon.' It was a statement rather than a question, for, of course, there was no doubt that she had to return to the Midlands. Yet the very phrase 'going back' sounded sterile, Esther thought. Her mother's voice on the telephone was always bright with a forced cheerfulness these days. When she had told her about the pottery classes her mother had said, 'You seem to have fallen in love with these people and forgotten all about us.' The choices of phrase had jarred: again the words had suggested notions of betrayal. Cassie sounded plaintive when she spoke to her on the telephone, and always with the

32

same question, 'When are you coming home, Mummy?'

'Soon,' Esther had promised, realising that – though she missed Cassie – she was reluctant to return to her. Life with her daughter would resurrect old memories; it was so beguiling to remain at The Dovecote, where almost nothing disturbed the serenity. She was afraid of going back, Esther realised.

She turned to Joseph. 'I never intended this to be more than a holiday. I had been ill before I came here. I had a nervous collapse. This has been a recuperation.'

He didn't seem surprised. Had Julia already told the others – or had he guessed that day on the beach?

'Has it worked?'

'I think so.' The fact was, she supposed, that human nature didn't relish being depressed; the need to grieve became secondary in the end to a need to survive. 'The day when I almost drowned, I'd been tempted to end everything, to keep on going and swim out to sea and never come back.' She looked at him, remembering the flash of binoculars from the garden. She had reasoned – after discovering his cottage and the binoculars – that Joseph Kilburn didn't look like a snooper, that he must have found her in his view by accident that day. 'I'm so glad you saw me. I was prepared to do battle when I realised someone was watching me through binoculars. I thought you were a peeping tom. But the grim truth is I don't know what I'd have done – except drown – if you hadn't been on the cliff that day.'

She couldn't tell what he was thinking. The smile had faded from his mouth when she said she'd been tempted to swim out to sea. Now his expression altered again and a coldness seemed to cast itself in his eyes.

'I wasn't watching you through binoculars.'

Esther's smile faltered. 'You needn't be embarrassed. I didn't really think you were a snooper. I'm grateful you appeared so quickly.'

'I happened to come down the cliff path. I wasn't watching you swim,' he repeated. 'If I *had* seen you and had known you had suicide on your mind, you can be sure I'd have got there much sooner.'

Joseph knew she didn't believe him. He considered the irony of what he had done and asked himself again how he could have swum out to rescue her, when the idea of drowning so terrified him?

He remembered when Julia had brought Esther into his workshop, wondering, did you form a bond with someone merely because you had saved their life? He had watched her and, with a slight catch at his heart, he had seen that she appreciated the striving for perfection that lay behind everything he made. He saw at the same time how lovely she was; he remembered now that she had also been lovely naked. He wondered what her pottery was like. Very graceful, yet with a hint of strength he decided.

He sensed that Esther was pretending to forget about the binoculars, telling herself it was nothing to her if he had lied. But she would be puzzling it over in her head, putting him down for a devious rotter.

Joseph sensed too that Esther had been serious about drowning herself: she wasn't the sort to say something like that lightly. He remembered that he too had once contemplated suicide. The coward's way out, people said in a high moral tone, but was it more cowardly to end it all than to drift on from day to day?

He looked at the fountain. There were water lilies in the pond, flat, gleaming plates, fleshy and exotic, with here and there a pink lily bud breaking the surface of the water with its phallic head. Tiny ripples spread from the landing place of each jet of water. The sound was soothing. He could see that Esther, in her innocence, would find The Dovecote tranquil. He looked at her. She had confided in him about her illness. She was vulnerable. Should he warn her?

'Julia is very unusual,' Esther mused. 'She seems to care about people very much. Violet – the girl from the village who helps out in the house – called her a wonderful woman.'

'She is,' Joseph said dryly. 'I owe her more than you can imagine.'

'And yet she seems to think you don't want her help.'

Joseph shifted restlessly, leaning forward with his arms resting on his knees and turning the brim of his hat in his hands. 'She's my patron. Of course I've accepted her help.' He turned to look at her. 'Julia talks a lot of nonsense sometimes. Don't get too close to her. She can be a bit overpowering.'

'She didn't seem to mean you'd rejected her help as a patron.'

He continued to look at her, his face devoid of expression, as if debating whether to tell her something. Then he sighed. 'There's one thing you ought to know. You'll find it out anyway, I expect . . . Julia is a healer and spirit medium. She's held seances at The Dovecote since the war.'

Esther stared at him open-mouthed.

He smiled wryly. 'You see? Now you think she's potty. But she's not. Not all mediums are charlatans or cranks. Violet's right – Julia is a wonderful woman. She genuinely wants to help people come to terms with their loss.'

'I never guessed.' Esther remembered Rowena telling her that they had come here after Freddie's mother had died. She remembered Julia's talk about Christopher's spirit becoming her inspiration. Thoughts of table-rapping, ectoplasm, voices and levitations flitted wildly through Esther's mind. Her understanding of Julia and The Dovecote and its inmates seemed threatened. Did Peter and Meg, Rowena and Freddie attend the seances? And Joseph too?

He smiled. 'If you're wondering. No. I prefer not to get involved.'

'Why do you stay at The Dovecote?'

'It feels right for me here. My family used to visit Winmouth every summer when I was a boy. My father was a furniture-maker in the Arts and Crafts tradition. He knew Julia's family. The Brassingtons were very wealthy and always appreciated the arts and beautiful furniture. Julia let me set up my workshop here and she's commissioned a lot of my work.

34

She's travelled widely in Europe since she was a child and has useful – earthly rather than spiritual – contacts who also need beautiful furniture for their homes.'

'But a spirit medium! No wonder everyone in the village gossips about The Dovecote.'

'Oh, come on. There's nothing very new about spiritualism. And people have grown tired of traditional religion because of the war. It let them down. All the old ways of thinking and doing let people down. Besides, who wouldn't want to believe that all those millions weren't simply wiped from the face of the earth but are floating around in the ether waiting to make contact with us again? Julia knows what she's doing. Nobody's obliged to take in all the mumbo-jumbo if they don't want to. The way of life here is very conducive to producing good work. All I want to do is to make beautiful furniture. Julia has given me that opportunity.'

'You mean you're using her.'

He stood up. 'If you like. But no more than Julia uses people. She *needs* people to be dependent on her. Why do you think she feels rejected if people don't play her game? She feeds off their gratitude, their devotion – call it what you will. You'll find out before long.'

Esther shook her head, absorbing what Joseph had told her. 'No, I won't. I'm going back home. I've already stayed here too long.'

He looked at her with an odd, half-ironic smile. 'Do you think it's as easy as that to get away from Julia?'

Esther crossed the lawn. The afternoon sun was low in the sky. Julia stood in the porch and watched her walk towards her.

'Was that Joseph I saw with you?' There was a strained casualness in the question.

'Yes. He was telling me that he used to visit The Dovecote when he was a child.'

'Joseph and I have known each other for a long time. He's very dear to me. But then – all my doves are dear to me.' She smiled and they went indoors. 'Are you staying to supper?'

'No. I won't stay.' Esther hesitated. A shaft of sunlight struck down the stairs and lit the Rossetti print, giving the figure a ghostly prominence.

'You still don't like it, do you?' Julia said. 'You will. Give it time.'

'I've been thinking that the time has come for me to say goodbye to you all.'

Julia's smile faded. 'You can't mean it – already? Has Joseph said something to upset you?'

'I've been here nearly two weeks, Julia. My daughter is missing me and I've things to sort out at home.'

Julia studied her for a moment, twisting her mouth in thought. 'We shall all miss you,' she said at last. 'Your pottery class was a success, don't you think?'

'It hasn't all been one-sided. I'm grateful to you for being so understanding.'

Julia turned suddenly and led the way to the kitchen. 'Well then. Come and say goodbye to my doves.'

'This Giles Fielding. Are you sure you don't want him?' Julia said after Esther had said goodbye to the others and she walked with her towards the outside gates.

'I don't want anyone. How could I? Being with Christopher was so perfect. I know it could never be like that with anyone else.'

'Life goes on.'

Esther turned to Julia. After what Joseph had told her she was surprised that Julia could have made such an earthbound remark.

'I mean, Esther, we can choose to live in the past, or we can let the past into our lives in such a way that it helps us to move on.' Julia held Esther's hands in both her own and looked into her eyes with an expression of compassion. 'I want to help you. I wish you had decided to stay longer with us.'

Esther felt a sudden compulsion to be honest with her. 'Julia – I know that you're a medium.'

Julia's gaze did not falter. 'Does it make any difference?'

'Why didn't you tell me?'

Julia dropped her hands. 'One is always cautious at first. My gift frightens some people. They imagine a lot of nonsense. But I believe the dead want to comfort those they've left behind. Christopher still loves you, Esther. Death hasn't altered the love between you, but perhaps he has plans for you that you don't know about.'

'Like marrying Giles?' Esther wondered how much Julia really believed of what she was saying.

Julia shrugged. 'Who can tell?'

'Christopher didn't even like Giles very much. If I remember, he once called him a chump.'

Julia laughed. 'I think I should have liked your husband. I know I should like to meet him in the spirit world.' She hesitated, then caught Esther's hand again. 'Stay with us. Why not bring Cassie here? Come and live with us at The Dovecote.'

They had reached the courtyard. Esther shook her head and kissed Julia on the cheek. 'Thank you. But that isn't possible.'

'Then write to me. Keep in touch. I know you've begun on a process of healing while you've been here.'

Esther was left with an impression of Julia's tall figure framed in the archway, silhouetted against the garden. The doves were calling to one another in the courtyard. She could still hear them as she walked away up the hill.

Chapter Three

'Where's Cassie?' Esther glanced up the stairs, expecting at any moment to hear the thud of feet and see Cassie's face peer over the banisters.

'She's at the Fieldings' house. They've a young cousin staying there – Daphne, such a pretty name, and she's a pretty girl. The two of them are getting along really well; I thought Cassie might as well stay until teatime. Giles has said he will bring her back.' Her mother spoke quickly, nervous of her decision to send Cassie away now that Esther was there to challenge its logic.

Esther felt a wave of disappointment and anger. Disappointment because, after the long train journey, she had been looking forward to seeing Cassie. Anger because she realised that in her mother's eyes Giles was still in the running in the marital stakes; she might never have gone through the trauma of the past few months as far as her parents were concerned. 'Didn't you tell her I was coming?'

'We thought it would be a nice surprise for Cassie to find you here – after you've settled in and we three have had a chance to talk.'

Esther sensed a weightiness to the word 'talk'. Her suspicions were confirmed when her mother, ignoring her 'What about?' bustled her into the sitting room and her father swung her suitcase up the stairs. 'Soon have this in your room and I'll be back to join you ladies.'

Esther sat on the sofa. She kicked off her shoes, aware of her mother's wince of disapproval, and tucked her stockinged feet under her, resting her arm on the rough moquette, tapping her fingers on it. The room smelled of polish, a testimony to loving care and cleanliness. A vast pot stood in the bay window with its crisp lace curtains – the only item of pottery her mother had ever accepted from Christopher. It contained a flourishing aspidistra. Esther glanced at the mirror over the mantel with the shelves on either side filled with knick-knacks – jars of spills for lighting her father's pipe, vases with flowers painted on them, candlesticks, a heavy ebony clock. She remembered the day Christopher had stood there to ask her father for his daughter's hand in marriage and she had sat on the sofa, as she did now, trying not to laugh or catch his eye . . .

'What did you mean, "after we've had a chance to talk"?'

Her mother glanced towards the door as if for assistance and, since none was to be immediately forthcoming, said lamely, 'Oh, you know. Telling us about what sort of holiday you've had.'

'You've been plotting.'

'When your father comes down we'll talk properly.'

Esther threw back her head. 'Well, seeing as you asked – I've been doing a bit of teaching.'

'Teaching.' Her mother's expression was a mixture of disbelief and anxiety. 'What do you mean? You know you're not a teacher.'

'I told you about the people I met at The Dovecote. Julia asked me to take a pottery class. The house is a sort of artists' community. Some artists live there, other people, mostly amateurs, come once or twice a week to attend various classes.'

'It sounds very peculiar to me.'

Esther thought of Joseph's revelation about Julia being a medium, peculiar indeed in her mother's eyes, but she realised that in her own mind she had already rationalised and accepted it. Joseph was right – there were all kinds of ways of helping people over pain and loss, and Julia was not necessarily a fraud. 'Well, yes. The Dovecote is unusual—'

'Just the sort of Bohemian friends Christopher would have encouraged.'

Esther doubted it but said, 'Oh, you're always so intolerant, Mummy.'

'No, I'm not. We accepted Christopher, didn't we?'

'Only because he came from a *good* family. You thought I was going up in the world, marrying into the Norbrooks.'

'Yes, well, we were deceived on that score. The mother a poet! No wonder Christopher had peculiar ideas.'

'He made pots, Mummy, and so did I. That's not having peculiar ideas.'

'He didn't look after you properly, making you decorate his pots while he sat around in a smoking cap all day.'

Esther let out a gasp of laughter. 'He never in his life wore a smoking cap. And he worked very hard.'

'Well, you know what I mean.'

Her father came into the room. 'Have you told her?' he said with a jocular air.

'Told me what?'

Her mother, gaining confidence said, 'We've decided that you and Cassie should give up The Folly and come to live with us permanently.'

Her father stood by the empty fireplace, his feet astride, his chest squared as if addressing a meeting. 'In the light of your recent illness, your mother and I think it's for the best.'

'You can have Richard's old room for a nice little sitting room...'

Esther untucked her legs and bent to put on her shoes again. 'How could you? When we can still remember them bringing Richard home!' She knew she was being irrational. Her brother was not the issue.

Her mother bit her lip. 'We can't keep your brother's room like a shrine. Tell her, Eliot.'

38

'Esther,' pleaded her father. 'It's the obvious solution. We can look after you and Cassie here. And she can go to a good school instead of that hobbledy-hoy village effort where she has to mix with farm-workers' children.'

'Oh, heaven forbid she should learn reading, 'riting and 'rithmetic among the labouring classes.' Esther knew she was overreacting, but she was furious with them for trying to organise her, for stage-managing this homecoming and making sure that Cassie was out of the way while they 'reasoned' with her.

'Cassie would have space to play – and a pony,' said her mother.

'A pony!' Esther went to the window, where a view of the long garden included a paddock beyond the fence. 'Oh, yes, the pony. That was underhand, Mummy. That's not playing fair.'

Her father cleared his throat. 'We are not playing a game here, Esther. We only want what's best for you.'

Esther knew it was true. But why couldn't they see that she didn't want their stifling, all-enveloping concern? 'What's best for me is to be independent. It's what Christopher and I always wanted.'

'You and Christopher!' her mother said scornfully. 'He may have come from a good family, but he was a no-good underneath it all.'

Esther felt a shock of pain. 'Oh, this time you've gone too far.' How could anyone who had known him not have recognised Christopher's brilliance, nor seen that he had striven for truth in every aspect of his life? She remembered his creed: an artist must, above all, always be sincere.

'Where are you going?'

Esther paused by the sitting-room door. 'Out! To the Fieldings' to fetch Cassie. We're going back to The Folly!'

Cassie chatted to Giles as he drove her home from the Fieldings. He didn't seem to be listening until she cried, 'Oh, look! Look, it's Mummy!' as his motor car swung in through the gates of her grandparents' home in Larch Hill.

Giles brought the car to a halt with a scrunch of tyres and muttered something Cassie could not hear. She saw her mother, who had flung open the front door of the house, rush out on to the step, and Cassie's heart lurched, swinging from delight to consternation. Everyone had said her mother would be well when she came back from Dorset, but Esther's face looked tight and shrivelled, as if she were going to cry. She had cried a great deal when she was ill, Cassie remembered. She felt her heart begin its fluttering, like birds' wings inside her chest, seeing again her mother lying upstairs in bed, or staring for hours on end out of the window. The crying had made her look ugly; it had frightened Cassie, for she wanted her mother always to be beautiful.

Giles climbed from the car and opened the rear door. Esther smiled and waved, and Cassie, with a cry of relief, jumped from the running-board.

The hard ropes of Cassie's pigtails dug against Esther's ribs. She held Cassie away from her, making an effort to be jolly. 'Let me look at you. My goodness, you've grown. I really believe you've grown in the space of a fortnight. I'm sure your legs are longer. Your dress is almost over your knees.' Her gaze took in Cassie's plaits, scraped up so hard that they showed her scalp. 'We shall soon have those curls back,' she said under her breath.

Esther looked at Giles over Cassie's head – poor, dogged Giles, solid and Brylcreemed. His expression was wary, questioning. She realised that the hurt she had dealt him in front of everyone at the New Year's Day party was going to take longer than a few months to heal.

'How are you?' He walked towards her.

'In the middle of a row with the parents. You timed your arrival pretty well. I was about to depart in a temper.'

He smiled. 'I'm sorry.'

'Oh, it doesn't matter now.' Esther turned again to Cassie and hugged her more closely. 'Have you missed me as much as I've missed you?'

'Heaps.' Cassie wriggled free. 'I'm glad you're back.' And then, with all the tact of a ten-year-old, '*Can* I have a pony?'

Esther looked at Giles again. 'The parents have been plotting. It's a bad case of bribery and corruption.'

'I would go along with anything they have in mind,' Giles said in a low voice, 'if it meant it would keep you here.'

Esther, pretending not to hear, turned to her mother, who stood in the front porch, her face puckered with anxiety. She called, 'I don't suppose I shall be going anywhere yet – it looks as if the cavalry has arrived.'

Esther's mother drew her back into the protection of the house. 'That's better. Don't be hasty. I admit I shouldn't have been so rude about Christopher,' smothering now with her concern, touching Esther's hair, patting her arm, trying to smooth over the fact they had quarrelled.

'But you meant it,' Esther said. 'And that's what counts.'

Cassie, looking from one to the other, tried to work out what the quarrel had been about. She felt her heart contract after they said goodbye to Giles, sensing her mother's suffocation as they went inside the house.

The house in Larch Hill had a way of enveloping people. It was always so tidy that Cassie hardly dared to sit on the sofa for fear of leaving some evidence, a dent in the cushions or sticky fingermarks behind. There were pictures and china ornaments everywhere, and always flowers in the hearth, but the windows were rarely thrown open to the garden for fear of admitting flies. Cassie's grandmother had learned some years earlier that flies bred germs – a relatively modern phenomenon in her eyes. She had adopted a pseudo-scientific phraseology when talking about them. Germs 'contaminated' things. They 'bred'. The cleaning cupboard was stocked with various brands of disinfectant and yellow household soap and Martha the housemaid had been given lengthy instructions about how and where to use them.

Esther went to Cassie's room that evening and told her they were to leave Larch Hill the next morning.

'Do we have to go?' Cassie asked, her own longing to return to The Folly clouded by the thought of the pony she had been promised.

'I thought you wanted to go back,' Esther said in exasperation. 'You don't want to live with Granny and Granpy all the time, do you?'

Cassie was silent, then said wistfully, 'I do like Granny and Granpy and Giles and Mrs Fielding – and Daphne.' The Fieldings' cousin, younger than Cassie, had been the sort of child she could bully into doing more or less anything she pleased; as a result she had grown quite attached to her. 'Daphne was my friend.'

'You only knew her for a few weeks.' Esther sat on Cassie's bed. She realised she was being drawn into a futile argument of the kind in which Cassie excelled; with encouragement, she could keep it going for hours.

'You only knew *your* friends for a few weeks. You said you liked the people at The Dovecote.'

'Yes, and now I've said goodbye to them. That's how it is sometimes with friends you've only known for a little while.'

'You said goodbye to Giles. And you've known him for always.'

'That's different, Cassie.' Esther had forgotten how awkward her daughter could be. She remembered the serenity of The Dovecote, and a mental picture of Julia in her long ragged cardigan, smoking nervously, telling her she had begun a process of healing, was oddly comforting.

'You would have liked The Dovecote,' Esther said the next day as they drove in Christopher's battered, bull-nosed Morris to The Folly. 'There's a house on stone pillars for the doves to live in, and creeper growing all over the walls of the big house where the people live, and the most beautiful garden you ever saw.'

'Do the doves like living there instead of flying around in the trees?' Cassie was beginning to enjoy hearing about The Dovecote. It seemed to her to be a magical place, somewhere between a fairy story and heaven – and she believed firmly in heaven; her grandmother had told her all about it: it was where her Uncle Richard had gone, and her father too, to dwell with the heavenly hosts in a house where there were lots of mansions. Cassie had adopted many of her grandparents' ideas during the time that Esther had abandoned her to their care. She knew that the war had been 'necessary', that strikes, women in parliament, film actors and jazz music were bad things and chewing gum was 'common'. Sunday school, rice pudding and behaving properly in public were 'good'. She didn't always agree with her grandmother, but it was good policy to pretend that she did, and some of her grandmother's prejudices had stuck – although Cassie couldn't agree that everyone in films was immoral, for she had laughed and laughed at Charlie Chaplin when Giles took her and Daphne to a cinema, and she adored the newspaper pictures of Douglas Fairbanks and Mary Pickford when they got married. It must be so romantic, Cassie thought, to be in films and be called 'the world's sweetheart'.

'The doves would fly away if they didn't like living there, wouldn't they?' Esther said, in answer to Cassie's question. 'But they're so happy they sit about on the roof tiles and coo and sing to one another all day long.'

Cassie was silent, then she said, 'I should like it if The Dovecote is near the sea.'

'It's close to the edge of a cliff and you can hear the waves on the beach below.'

'Did you swim?'

Esther did not answer immediately, for she was remembering, not the Dorset coast, but the Côte Sauvage and the heat of the sun. A longing for Christopher swept over her with an unexpectedness that brought a hard lump into her throat.

'Mummy – did you swim?'

'Yes, I swam. I swam out too far and a man had to rescue me. What do you think of that?'

Cassie considered the idea. It sounded like an adventure, the sort where Douglas Fairbanks might have acted the part of her mother's rescuer, but she said primly, 'I think you must have been dreaming or you would have seen that you had swum too far.'

Esther looked down at her. 'Perhaps I was. I should have been more careful.' She turned off the main road and a feeling of welcome lay in the familiar landmarks of hedgerow and farm. 'Not far now. We're nearly home.'

She and Christopher had chosen the tiny cottage near Bath because it had an outside staircase that led to a studio in the roof space – and because Esther had fallen in love with the ivy growing all over its walls. 'It's almost completely hidden,' she had said as they peered under the curtain of ivy where the outside stair formed an arch. The space beneath ran back into dripping, echoing darkness where once had turned a water-wheel.

'It's like a Gothic folly,' Christopher had said. The name had stuck and the cottage had become 'The Folly'. It had seemed to sum up their reckless existence.

'What do you mean, "He's a potter"? A manufacturer?' Esther remembered her father asking suspiciously. One of us? A gleam of hope that was quickly dashed. 'How is he going to support you?' he had stormed when he had learned that Christopher's manufactory was a one-man band.

'We shall manage,' Esther had answered blithely. And somehow they had. The one thing she and Christopher had been determined on was to be independent of everyone else. It would have been so easy to let Christopher's parents' wealth subsidise the pottery in the early days, but, after the gift of the Morris car, resisting an advancing tide of generosity, they had fiercely renewed their vow to manage without any more help from his family. Esther's mother had thrown up her hands in despair, but the lease on the cottage had been paid, along with everything else, in Christopher's own sweeping, chaotic way. Bills would disappear after lying around on the kitchen dresser for weeks, and Christopher would open a bottle of wine and announce airily, in response to her delighted, 'You've sold something?' that she wasn't to bother her head about the financial side of things; her role in the business was to be decorative.

It was with the same devil-may-care attitude and a shrug that Christopher had put on uniform. The shrug had summed up his philosophy for life: if things were a bit rough, grin and bear it; when times were good, live life to the full. And he would laugh as if to ridicule the idea that he should live by any philosophy at all.

Esther unlocked the front door and pushed it open. A small pile of letters lay on the mat; the house smelled musty and Cassie wrinkled her nose.

'Shall I go and look for mice in the traps?'

Cassie went through the sitting room to the kitchen scullery as Esther said distractedly, 'If you like.'

Esther picked up the letters from the mat and sank into a chair with them in her lap. She felt the familiar knot of pain in her chest as she looked round the room, seeing Christopher's tennis racket in the corner, some of the pots they had made, the Japanese screen that had cost them a small fortune, the rug where they had first made love. Her gaze took in the photographs on the sideboard – of Christopher in tennis flannels, one taken sitting on the running board of the Morris, and another in his uniform ... Her glance came to rest on the letters and bills in her lap, and a note from Christopher's parents: 'Come and see us as soon as you're home.' Esther smiled at the apparent imperiousness of the command, for it was so like them, and yet no one could have been less despotic than Marjorie and Hugh. There was an envelope addressed to her in a hand she did not recognise. Esther turned it in her lap, and then, with a leap of pleasure, realised that it came from Julia. She must have written soon after she had left.

The letter was mostly gossip. Rowena had burned her hand and they were going to treat it with homeopathic remedies. Esther's interest sharpened as she read that Julia had discovered that Meg had taken some of Peter's paintings to an exhibition without telling anyone.

'The exhibition will be very good for Peter, of course,' Julia wrote. 'But it was quite unethical of Meg.' She had heavily underlined 'quite unethical', and Esther sensed a restrained anger behind Julia's words. 'We shall miss you ...' the letter continued '... and not only because of

43

the pottery class. So write to us soon and let us hear all your news.'

She would write, Esther decided, putting the letter back in its envelope, for Julia and The Dovecote had set her on the road to recovery in a way that none of the doctors had done. She scanned one of the bills, estimating with relief that the money Julia had paid her for the pottery classes would cover the arrears at the grocer's. The winter coal bill was not overwhelming, for she and Cassie had spent few of the winter months at The Folly. If she talked to the coal merchant, paid in instalments . . .

Esther opened another envelope containing, as she had expected, a notice about the lease for The Folly: Christopher had made the original agreement with the landlord and during the war he had dealt with the annual rent when he was on leave; shortly before he was killed he had paid right up to the four-yearly renewal of the lease, 'Just in case anything should go wrong, old thing.'

Esther stared at the unfamiliar jargon about the agreement. She remembered what Christopher had told her when he had first rented the cottage – that they had got it 'for a song' – and her eyes fixed on the figures in growing disbelief.

At that moment Cassie came in from the scullery. 'Look what I've found.' She held a shrivelled mouse by its tail and touched the tiny stiffened limbs experimentally, as if to see whether they would drop off, or to be sure that no breath of life still stirred in them.

Esther jumped to her feet and cried out in horror, 'For goodness' sake, Cassie!'

Cassie regarded her with an expression of puzzled expectation. 'But you said that I should look.'

'I didn't mean pick it up!' Esther opened the window and, taking the dried and mummified mouse, flung it out into a flowerbed. 'Now go and wash your hands!'

Cassie went into the kitchen and ran the tap at the sink in silence. She began to wash her hands obediently, afraid that her clumsy 'Look what I've found' had stirred some dreadful image in her mother's mind. A vague image of a full-sized, human body, desiccated like that of the mouse, slid before her eyes.

Esther took the soap from her and washed as well, then took her daughter's hands in her own and dried them gently with a clean towel. 'I'm sorry. I shouldn't have shouted like that.'

'Was it because it was dead? Are you going to be ill again?'

Esther saw the connection Cassie had made. Few explanations had been offered about her illness: they had told Cassie she was 'tired', she had been working too hard and needed a long rest, but Cassie was ten; they should have realised how much she understood. Esther held her tightly.

'No. I wasn't upset because it was dead, but mice are vermin.'

'They breed *germs*.' Cassie rolled her eyes, echoing one of her grandmother's maxims.

44

'Even more so when they've gone brown and rotten,' Esther said.

They returned to the sitting room and stared out of the window through which the offending mouse had been cast. 'Do dead people go rotten and breed germs?' Cassie said.

Esther blanched, overwhelmed by a picture of the thousands of bodies buried in the mud after Passchendaele. She did not know what was going on in Cassie's mind and found it hard to answer her. 'Of course,' she said at last. 'But when that happens, the person who was inside is no longer there.' She sat in the chair again and pulled Cassie down beside her. 'When someone dies, the person we once knew and loved has gone. You understand, don't you, what I'm saying? When your father was dead...' She could not go on.

'You mean, when Daddy died he went to heaven. So it doesn't matter that his body stayed behind.'

Esther pressed her face against Cassie's hair, remembering Christopher's flesh, the warmth of his beautiful body. 'Yes, that's what I mean.' She realised that she was weeping.

'I wish I could remember him more clearly.' Cassie pulled her mother's face round towards her and panic again filled her eyes. 'You're crying. You're not going to be ill again?'

'No,' Esther said gently. 'I'm not going to be ill. I'm crying because I remember him so very well. I can't bear to think of him when he was dead and all those others with him.'

'Then we'll only think of how he was when he was alive,' Cassie said, taking charge of the situation. 'Will you be all right if I go into the garden?'

Esther nodded and watched her go. She blew her nose and looked at the letter about the rent, staring at the figure the landlord had quoted; it bore no relation to the 'song' Christopher had originally agreed. She would have to drive into Bath to see the man after the weekend. She went to the window and looked out to where Christopher had strung a wooden swing from one of the apple trees. Since the war his father had sent one of his grooms to shorten the ropes for Cassie; but Cassie was not playing on the swing. Esther watched her dig a hole in the flowerbed where the dead mouse had landed. She watched as Cassie pushed the corpse into a shoebox with the blade of the spade, then placed the box in the shallow hole and stood with her hands folded piously and her eyes closed. Esther did not stop her. She recognised in the grim expression on Cassie's face as she filled in the hole with soil that the task was one that had to be done.

Esther drove the five miles to see Christopher's parents the next day. The long approach road through cattle fields always reminded her of the first time she had visited Christopher's family home. She had been so nervous about meeting his parents. Christopher had laughed at her misgivings saying, 'You don't know what you're in for. Just you wait.'

Esther smiled at the memory of her first impression of Hugh and

Marjorie. Hugh had been seated at a pianola, laughing his huge laugh and waving his arms to show that there was nothing up his sleeves as the keys bobbed up and down as if played by unseen hands. The sound of a gramophone had floated down the stairs and the soaring notes of Caruso had merged with the cacophony of Tchaikovsky's *Humoresque* on the pianola, and Marjorie, waving a long cigarette-holder and dressed like a Russian ballet dancer, had stood at the top of the staircase saying, 'Chris, darling – what do you think of Hugh's latest? Isn't it a scream!'

'Marjorie – what do you look like!' Christopher had treated his mother with a familiarity that had startled Esther at first.

'Everyone's going Russian, darling. Have you seen Nijinsky, Esther? He's absolutely divine. Oh, you must! I'll take you.'

Marjorie had been true to her word. She had travelled with Esther and Christopher to Paris one weekend to see Diaghilev's ballet company, and Esther and Marjorie had pretended to swoon over Nijinsky. Another year, Marjorie had been crazy about the Russian opera. 'My parents have fads,' Christopher had said on that first visit. 'Lord knows what it's going to be next.'

'I'm *glad* we're going to see Hugh and Marjorie,' Cassie said.

Esther glanced down at her, seated beside her in the car. Cassie was wearing a string of amber beads that Marjorie had once given her, and a dressing-up hat of eccentric proportions because, Cassie explained very seriously, 'Marjorie likes girls and ladies to wear hats.'

Esther too wore a hat, one that Christopher had once chosen for her, a light blue straw with a large brim, and a pale blue ankle-length dress that had been one of his favourites.

'I'm glad you're glad,' laughed Esther. She saw the house and felt her spirits lift as they did unfailingly whenever she visited Hugh and Marjorie. The place invoked a sense of exhilaration and joy and the whole unruly ethos that had always surrounded Christopher and his family.

'Esther! You're back!' Marjorie came running across the forecourt to meet her. 'I saw the motor car from my sitting-room window. I was writing a poem about flying. You'll never believe it – Hugh has bought an aeroplane! You interrupted the Muse, darlings, and I shan't ever forgive you. Oh, my little one! We have *so* missed your visits.' She swept Cassie into her arms, waving a cigarette in its holder in her free hand, and looked at Esther over Cassie's head. 'When did you get back?'

'Yesterday.'

'Are you well, Esther?' Marjorie straightened and watched Cassie run into the house. 'I mean, are you over it – really over it now?'

'I shall never be over him, Marjorie. You know that. And neither shall you.'

'That's true, darling. But it's different for me. I lost a son, not a lover.'

They walked together up the shallow steps of the house and in through the front entrance. Esther relaxed as they crossed the wide, chequered hall. She always had the sense of entering a Dutch painting when she stepped into Norbrook House, for the floors were tiled in black and white and one could see right through the house from the front door in a long perspective, from room to room.

'I'm glad you came straight over,' Marjorie said. 'Hugh and I want to talk to you. We feel we should discuss the matter of . . . ah, here he is.' She broke off as her husband came across the hall carrying Cassie on his back. Marjorie lowered her voice to an exaggerated whisper. 'Let's talk about boring old money later on.'

Hugh Norbrook was a giant of a man, flat-faced and with a broad chest and waist. He pulled Esther into his arms, making Cassie on his back shriek and fling her arms and legs more tightly round him. 'And how's my favourite daughter-in-law? Fighting fit again, I hope?'

'I think so, Hugh.'

'That's more like it. That's more like the Esther we know.' He released her and they walked through the interconnecting rooms of the house, furnished in earth-toned William Morris chintzes and scented with huge bowls of flowers, until they came to a conservatory. The doors were open to the garden and Cassie slipped from her grandfather's shoulders and ran out to the terrace.

It always seemed as if they had arrived at a different exterior from the one at the front of the house – somehow brighter, more vital – thought Esther as she sank into a wicker basket-chair in the conservatory and looked out across the garden. She tossed her hat on the table beside her. 'I love it at Norbrook.' She was tempted to tell Marjorie about The Dovecote, but contented herself with saying, 'Sometimes I think I might just possibly love houses more than I do people.'

Marjorie sighed. 'I know exactly what you mean.'

Hugh Norbrook stood near the conservatory doors with his hands in his pockets, watching Cassie. He turned to them. 'I won't beat about the bush, Esther. We want to set up a trust fund for Cassie.' He interrupted Esther's protest and came to sit beside her. 'I've had our solicitor draw up all the details. He'll let you see a copy. It's all very straightforward; she'll inherit when she's twenty-one. It's no good looking like that. We're determined to do it. Christopher would have expected it, and if anything should ever happen to you, or to us – well, we want to be certain that Cassie would be taken care of.'

Esther nodded. 'All right.'

'Good girl.'

'But only because it's for Cassie and because Christopher would have wanted it that way.'

'I'll arrange an appointment for you with Williams next week.'

Marjorie had fixed her attention on the garden, watching Cassie turn cartwheels on the lawn, as if she had not been a party to the conversation. Marjorie belonged to a generation and class where women did not soil their reputations by discussing money, and an inbuilt prejudice still lingered. 'Cassie's grown since we saw her at Christmas,' Marjorie said. 'It's been a long time, Esther.' There was a hint of reproach in the remark. They hadn't really understood her collapse, Esther realised. They expected her to be well. They couldn't cope with weakness; they only understood the strong, the hale and hearty. In Hugh and Marjorie's circle you did not show grief, talk seriously of death or illness, or discuss your problems in detail. It was a way of thinking that Christopher had grown up with, and the way he too had lived. And yet, Esther thought, following Marjorie's gaze to where Cassie turned circles on the grass, life was not one long, jolly picnic. There was sadness, there were problems that couldn't be dealt with by a wave of the Norbrook magic wand.

Hugh looked at his wife. 'Now for the other little matter.'

Esther looked at him with a lift of her eyebrows.

'Christopher left you, as you know, without a bean. The fact is, he never made two halfpennies to rub together from his pottery . . .' Esther opened her mouth to challenge him but he interrupted her. 'And he wouldn't have come into any of the Norbrook money until we were dead and gone. We realise your lease is due for renewal, so . . .'

'Oh, do get on with it, Hugh,' said Marjorie, breaking with her taboo. 'The fact is, Esther, you're a penniless widow and we want you to have what's due to you.' She raised her hands in a gesture of apology and, bending to kiss her husband, turned to flash a smile at them both and went down the steps of the terrace to join Cassie.

'I've had Williams draw up the legalities,' Hugh said. 'We shall pay the lease on The Folly and the estate will provide you with an income of thirty pounds a month.'

Esther watched Marjorie, her dark hair beautifully styled, slender in a grey silk, calf-length dress, swing Cassie round and round on the lawn. The Norbrooks had always been able to use the solution of money to cushion the blows. It was one of the reasons why she had so admired Christopher for resisting the easy way out of everything. Marjorie waved. Her laughing nonchalance said, Take your share of our providence and you will never have to struggle or worry again.

Esther turned to Hugh. 'No.'

Hugh reddened. 'Oh, come on, Esther. Don't be difficult. It's hardly a fortune. We realise how difficult things must have been for you.'

It was another loving snare, thought Esther. If anything it was more subtle than the one in which her own parents wanted to imprison her, for it was baited with the assumption that Christopher would have wanted her to accept.

'No,' she repeated. She leaned forward. 'Do what you like for Cassie. But not for me. Don't you see that if I let you do this I'll be betraying the way Christopher and I always lived? We promised each other we would make a go of it without anyone's help.'

'I know that's the way *you* feel, and Marjorie made me keep out of it until the lease for The Folly was up. But now, after your illness . . .'

'There's always been the easy option of falling back on Norbrook money. Christopher knew you would back us when he started the pottery, but he didn't want that. It went against all he stood for, and it goes against all I believe in too.'

Hugh's glance shifted from hers and he stared out across the lawn to the figure of his wife. 'I wish I could persuade you.'

'Well, you can't. There *is* something you can do, though.' Esther opened her bag and pulled out the letter from the landlord. 'Will you read that and tell me what you think? I wrote to the man some time ago to ask for the new agreement to be based on a monthly sum, instead of renewing the lease again for a four-year term, but I know Christopher didn't pay anything like that sort of rent all these years. Do you think I should tackle the landlord again or see a solicitor?'

Hugh scanned the document briefly. He folded it. 'I'll ask my solicitor to sort it out for you if you like. I expect there's been a mistake.'

'I'd be grateful.'

'Meanwhile – think about what I've said.'

'I've thought.' Esther stood and went to him and kissed him. 'It's very generous of you, and I appreciate the love behind it, but, for Christopher's sake – and mine – I have to be independent.'

'Esther . . .'

She put a finger to her lips in a gesture of silence and, ignoring his distress, walked across the terrace and down the steps to the lawn.

Cassie was performing more ambitious acrobatics, with her skirt tucked into the legs of her knickers. She renewed her efforts, calling, 'Watch me, Mummy. You're not watching,' as Esther walked towards Marjorie.

'I hope you're going to be sensible,' Marjorie said without turning her head to look at her.

'I always am. It's what Christopher said he found the most maddening thing about me.'

Marjorie turned to look at her. Her eyes searched Esther's. 'You've turned us down!'

Esther suddenly felt sorry for her. Marjorie and Hugh, like Christopher, had always been used to getting their own way. They were quickly hurt, unable to comprehend if anyone opposed them. 'You must have known I wouldn't accept.'

'You silly girl. How are you going to live?'

'I'll think of something. There's my pension. I can find work. It'll sort itself out.' They were Christopher's words, she realised. 'After all, Christopher's been dead more than two years and I've managed so far.'

'Mummy! Watch me.'

Esther turned to watch Cassie perform a handstand.

'Oh, yes, you managed,' Marjorie said in a voice totally unlike her. 'Just like you wanted to *manage* before the war.' She added in a lower tone so that Cassie should not overhear, 'With dreams and crackpot ideals. Well, dreaming doesn't pay the bills, Esther. You're going to have to come down to earth this time.'

'If I can just sort out the business over the rent. The figures seem all wrong. Hugh is going to ask his solicitor to look into it for me.'

Marjorie gave a short laugh. 'I'm not surprised if the figures seem wrong to you. Christopher was right all those years ago to call the cottage a Folly.'

'I don't understand.'

Marjorie turned to look at her. 'We promised Christopher we would never let you know. But now he's gone, and if it will make you see reason . . .'

'What?' Esther's heart lurched. What were they keeping from her?

'Christopher couldn't afford the lease on The Folly out of the income from the pottery. He barely made enough to keep you both, and then when Cassie came along . . .'

'But he told me the lease was very cheap – just what we could afford.'

'Well, it wasn't. It was damned exorbitant.'

Esther laughed in disbelief. 'The Folly is tiny. It's damp and has mice.'

'Norbrook House has mice. And cockroaches too, come to that, but it costs a fortune to keep up. Hugh has always paid the lease on The Folly.' She smiled ruefully at Esther's dismay. 'He didn't want you to find out. We knew how you felt about that sort of thing. Hugh has this thing about preserving your innocence.'

'How we both felt!' Esther felt a hard knot close her throat. 'We both believed it was so important to be independent.'

'And it was important too that you lived where you wanted. The Folly was such a *romantic* place for you to start married life. Christopher wanted The Folly badly. I could see why you both fell in love with it.'

'We could have lived somewhere else. It wasn't that important.' Esther swallowed the constriction in her throat.

'We never begrudged the money. You mustn't think that for a minute.' Marjorie put an arm round her. 'I would never have told you. But you must see now that it makes sense to let Hugh take care of everything. You'll have a regular income, no coming to us every time there's a bill. Oh, it will all be so much tidier.'

'The bills . . . ?' Esther pulled away. 'Did you pay our other bills as well?'

'Not all of them. The poor boy had some pride.'

Esther remembered the bottles of wine to celebrate, another cheque – not from the pottery commissions but from Hugh and Marjorie. Why hadn't she realised? Why hadn't she worked it out for herself? And then, How could he? she thought. How could he have deceived her all those years and still talked about independence and integrity?

'Hugh saw it as an investment,' Marjorie was saying. 'We knew it was only a matter of time before the pottery would build into a bigger business. But, until then . . .'

'If you don't mind, Marjorie, I think Cassie and I will go home.' Esther called to Cassie and began walking towards the house.

Marjorie hurried after her. 'Esther! Don't be silly. What difference does it make?'

Esther shook her head. 'Leave me alone. I have to think.'

'I have been praying for Esther.'

Julia was seated between Peter and Joseph in the taxi carrying them to a dinner party, given by Julia's friends the Vaudoyers. Julia had arranged a visit to London for her two favourite doves, to pick up on gossip, she said, and to keep in touch: Gerard Vaudoyer, a buyer for Galeries Lafayette in Paris, collected modern artists and had influential friends.

'I pray for you too, Joseph,' Julia added. 'It's true. Peter will tell you.'

Peter, uncomfortable in a dinner suit and smelling strongly of the hair preparation he had used, nodded gravely. 'You should come to a seance some day, Joseph.'

Joseph did not a reply. Instinctively he moved from the tender pressure of Julia's hand against his cheek.

She leaned back in the taxi with a sigh. 'You think you can manage without me, darling. But you can't.'

Joseph looked restlessly out of the window. The visit to London in search of commissions was proof enough of Julia's last statement.

'I think Esther will come back to us one day.' Julia continued. 'I have a feeling about her.'

'In that case, she's bound to return,' Peter said with a smile.

'What do *you* think? Should she? Can we help her?' Julia persisted, turning to Joseph and restraining his arm as the taxi slowed to a halt. He opened the door, releasing his arm temporarily from Julia's grasp, and offering it to her again as he reached the pavement. Julia stepped out beside him and Peter stumbled after her, straightening his waistcoat and running a hand through his flattened hair.

'I really don't know if she'll come back,' Joseph said. 'Esther seemed to have a mind of her own.' Unlike the rest of us, he thought, looking up at the stuccoed and balustraded façade of the block of apartments. Or why else are we here?

More guests were drawing up outside the entrance to the building. The glitter of lights in the lobby streamed on to the pavement, making the spring evening seem drab and chilly.

Joseph turned to Julia. 'Besides, Esther was a seasonal visitor. We hardly know her.'

'A visitor *out* of season,' Peter prompted.

'Out of nowhere and temporarily lost,' Julia murmured. 'She was sent to us. I'm sure of it.'

Was there some truth in Julia's claim? Joseph wondered, for he too had found Esther's arrival significant. Why had he saved her from drowning? Why had he been on the cliff at that precise moment? It seemed symbolic even that she had been naked, like some sort of mythological sea nymph, or one of Julia's spirits.

Julia moved away to greet old friends as they joined the dozen or more dinner guests entering the building, laughing and talking, making their way up the stairs. If Julia wanted to start playing at being God again, that was up to her, Joseph told himself. He supposed a grieving widow was a deserving cause. He was surprised by his own cynicism and reminded himself that he had Julia to thank for the fact that he had not ended up in some institution instead of at The Dovecote. He thought of his friends in Exeter, who had given up altogether, lost their grip on normal living and seized with both hands the comfort of the whisky bottle. There but for the grace of Julia . . . Had he lost all sense of gratitude? he wondered.

Joseph watched Julia as she removed her cloak to reveal a black-beaded evening dress; her hair was hidden by a matching turban and she looked like an eastern princess. He remembered how, a long time before the war, when he was a child and green and innocent, he had thought Julia bewitching. She had not lost her fascination. In a glamorous light and with glittering plumage Julia had a fierce, hawkish attraction. There had been a time, he remembered, when she had always been there for him. She hadn't shrunk from his nightmares and he would for ever be in her debt because of it. But he knew now he had to break the dependency or he might never be able to let go. And Julia knew it too, he realised.

He greeted the Vaudoyers, who treated him as if he were Julia's favoured son – kisses pecking at cheeks, reminiscences of the last time they had met. They introduced him to people – including the Marchesa di Malfi, 'a dear friend from Italy'. Yes, work was going well. A table? But, of course he would make a table for them. Madame Vaudoyer described the measurements she had envisaged. Julia said they must discuss them – later. He took a glass of champagne from the tray offered to him and moved around the fringes of the room to stand by one of the curtained windows and sip the tepid champagne, his back to the wall . . . Keep the noise at bay.

Sometimes he wondered whether all links with his real emotions had gone. There were times when he thought he would go mad again, like the poor fellows whose nerves had been permanently shot to pieces. And, even now the nightmares still came, the sudden attacks of terror when he would wake screaming in the night. There were other, waking dreams in broad daylight, lying on the cliff top, hearing the gulls wail and cry overhead and looking down at the sea, when he would feel himself falling . . .

Julia was there at his side again. 'You're not mingling, darling. I can't believe you're shy like Peter, and even he is being sociable tonight.' They smiled as they heard Peter's hoarse laugh above the murmurs of conversation.

'Are you all right, darling?' She stroked his cheek, her eyes dark in their sockets with concern.

'Yes, I'm fine,' Joseph nodded.

'I can't help worrying about Esther now she's gone. I've written to her.' Julia paused. 'You know – I think she was suicidal.'

Joseph stared at Julia, shocked by the blandness of the statement. Had Esther confided in Julia as she had in him? If so, he should have warned her more strongly that it was a mistake to admit one's vulnerability.

He pictured Esther by the fountain the day he had come back from Exeter, hearing her confess that she had been tempted to swim out to sea. He had been shocked, because she had meant it, but the idea of suicide *was* seductive. They often talked about it – Colin and Tim and the others in Exeter, the spongers, the freaks and hangers-on, not all of them war veterans, who drifted in and out of the drink-sodden hospitality of Colin's house.

There seemed to Joseph to be a personal justice in such an end, but how would he go about it? Off a cliff one night? By drowning? He shrank from the horror of it. Cutting one's throat? He had seen it and it was messy. Most ways of dying were unpleasant. He thought of the men of his platoon and knew he could never contemplate anything that was not swift. If he had his service revolver still . . . but he had few relics of the war: his uniform, his Sam Browne belt, an army knapsack.

He straightened as he saw that people were drifting into the adjoining room, making their way to their places for dinner.

'If Esther was – if she did consider suicide, I think she soon put the idea behind her.' Joseph swallowed the dregs of his champagne and did not look at Julia as he spoke, feeling an odd anxiety for Esther, whom he had met only briefly, but who had made such a strong impression on him. 'I don't think you need worry about her any more.'

He was separated from Julia at dinner and was glad, feeling a sense of freedom as he watched her at the far end of the table, surrounded by old friends. Who wasn't Julia's old friend? he wondered. How different she was, here among society, from when she drifted about in her old painting clothes at The Dovecote. He recognised again that fascination she possessed, the sexual aura she carried around with her. He let his thoughts wander and remembered another dinner party and the girl he had once, in another life, believed he would marry.

She had not been one of Julia's doves. Diana would have found the whole concept of The Dovecote amazing. She had given him a white feather, he remembered. The girls had all handed the boys white feathers. They had sat back with challenging, provocative smiles. It had been a joke. They had all laughed, but they had not been able to ignore the gesture. 'So that's the way the wind blows is it?' Joseph had said, tucking the feather in her hair. 'Well, my girl. I'll show you.' And he had joined up the next day, had lied about his age and got away with it, because the Army needed boys and men with that sort of initiative. He had been ecstatic, he remembered, because it had been so damnably easy, and because Diana had been so proud to see him in uniform.

He had not heard from her since she told him she would never marry him. And he realised he no longer wanted to see her. The future she had envisaged – a hero of a husband, a beautiful home, a family – had not included the wreck who came back from the trenches. There was no question in his own mind of her having jilted him – and, in any case, they had considered themselves too young for a formal engagement. She had done her bit in the war, driven an ambulance in France, seen bad cases. She knew very well what she would have been in for, and she wasn't prepared to take it on. Joseph did not blame her. He wouldn't have expected her to suffer with him.

'You are very absorbed by your thoughts – or is it the salmon that makes you contemplative?' said the Italian marchesa, seated beside him.

'No. The salmon is very good. And I apologise if I have been boorish.'

The woman shrugged, saying in a mocking tone, 'Of course your great age gives you much to be contemplative about.'

He smiled, and apologised again.

The marchesa said she did not know Julia, but she had met the Vaudoyers many years ago, before the war. 'They tell me you are a furniture designer. You know – I have been contemplative too. I have been contemplating making many changes to my villa in Italy. I shall need someone to design the fittings. They say you are clever as well as a handsome young man, that your work is very stylish, very contemporary. I love to surround myself with beautiful modern things. I hate baroque. If something is ugly, even if it is centuries old and extremely valuable, I won't have it in my house.'

Joseph glanced at Julia, who had heard nothing of this conversation. Peter was deep in animated discussion with Madame Vaudoyer, talking about a commission for a painting. Later, Julia would bring up the subject of the table Joseph had promised to make for the Vaudoyers; Gerard Vaudoyer had already sketched out a design: the dimensions were very precise. It was the sort of commission Joseph disliked because of its restrictions and because of its premise that the customer knew best.

'Tell me about your villa.' He turned again to the marchesa.

'If you are interested you would come to Italy, of course?' she said after they had discussed the styles of furniture that suited her taste.

'Of course.' Joseph's heart began to beat erratically and he felt the palms of his hands begin to sweat. Was this his chance to break the dependency? He imagined the Channel crossing, the overland journey through Europe, and felt a pressure begin to mount in his head.

'Next year,' the marchesa said, dismissing the intervening months with a wave of her hand. 'There is much first to organise.' She cocked her head on one side, as if examining him to see if he would do. 'You like the idea? May I get in touch with you when the time comes?'

'Yes,' Joseph said. 'I like the idea.' He glanced at Julia again and it occurred to him that she must not hear about the marchesa's offer.

It seemed to Cassie that they had only been back at The Folly for a short while before her mother set to with an unprecedented fury and got the kiln in the garden going. Cassie learned later, because Marjorie told her, that Esther was angry because she felt Christopher had 'let her down over money'.

Cassie had few memories of her father. She was only five when he had joined up in 1915, and she had seen little of him between then and the day, just over two years later, when she learned that he wouldn't be returning to them from Flanders, though he had promised that he would. She remembered that he had been a tall man, angular, with fair hair. She had a strong memory of him in the garden at The Folly, of being lifted in his arms and held high in the air so that she could see the sky through the leaves of the apple tree. He had held her there, and she had grasped one of the branches of the tree and scrambled into the fork of the trunk. She had looked down at them, the tall, handsome man and her mother. He was in uniform, romantic in his Sam Browne belt; she wore a kimono, her hair loose on her shoulders, and the man in uniform was not looking at Cassie but at her mother, who was laughing as he said her name very softly, 'Esther.'

Esther had not wept at all in the beginning, when Cassie's father failed to return from Flanders, but she had talked about him often, saying she didn't want Cassie to forget him. She had stressed how handsome he was and how talented he had been as a craft potter. She loved beautiful things and beautiful people.

Esther did not weep now either, and Cassie recognised in her expression a determination to survive with dignity, whatever fate might deal her. But it was a determination that bordered on inflexibility. Cassie sensed an obsession in her, as Esther worked for days, lining up the pots that had been stored in the attic studio and painting them with strong, powerful designs in crude, bright colours, such as Cassie had never seen her use before.

Marjorie and Hugh came to visit once, but when they saw Esther in her old skirt and blouse with a scarf wrapped round her head, heaving the pots on to the saggars and packing the kiln, they obeyed her polite but firm observation that they really couldn't do anything to help and were only getting in the way.

When Cassie tried to talk to her mother, Esther looked at her with a preoccupied expression and said, quite gently, 'Leave me alone, Cassie. I have to work and I have to think.' Cassie doubted privately that Esther could think at all, with all the fuss and physical energy that went into getting the kiln to temperature. The wood for the furnace was stacked in a shed and had to be wheeled in barrows for stoking the furnace until it glowed to a red heat. Once the final process had begun, Esther could not leave the kiln, but stoked and watched it constantly until, exhausted, she fell asleep in the kitchen – only to wake with a start when Cassie came home from school, then bite her nails and pace the garden until the kiln had cooled.

When she saw that the pots were almost perfect, Esther did not shout for joy but said calmly, 'We are going to leave The Folly now, Cassie. We have something to sell.'

Esther realised, as she surveyed her work, that her real love had always been in the final stages of a pot rather than in the making. It was Christopher who had always talked of the importance of 'form', who had stressed the subordinate nature of decoration. But these pots were hers. The colours of the designs, painted in clear reds and browns, glowed like the heat of the flame of her anger. The flow of the design on the pots seemed to swallow and consume their shape, as if to render the form irrelevant. With a brief insight into the future, she understood how much her own pottery would come to mean to her.

Esther and Cassie left The Folly early in June, when the irises were in bloom and the apple trees, in full leaf, were at their greenest. Esther left without a backward glance, for to look back might have weakened her conviction that the only choice open to her was to move on.

Cassie had helped her to pack up the finished pots into wooden boxes. She understood that they couldn't stay at The Folly because they didn't have enough money. Cassie even understood that they couldn't stay because Esther wouldn't live on Hugh and Marjorie's charity – though Hugh had begged her. Only in later years did Cassie understand that it had not merely been a matter of Esther's pride, nor even disappointment in the illusion she had built around her dead husband. She had needed permission to leave The Folly, and now that Christopher had let her down, she had it. She was free.

Esther did not tell Cassie that their departure had anything to do with Christopher. She talked about him hardly at all after that. Had she stopped loving him that afternoon, when Marjorie told her the truth about their life together, that their so-called financial independence had been founded on a lie? Perhaps not. But she knew that a little piece of her love had been destroyed: its brilliance had gone for ever.

'We have to do things for ourselves. We are going to be strong and independent,' she told Cassie as they watched the boxes of pots being taken away to the railway station on the carrier's wagon. She ignored Cassie's tears. 'We are two women on our own, and we're not going to be lonely or miserable, because we shall always have each other.'

Paradoxically Esther realised that being independent meant returning to Larch Hill at first, while she looked for work and somewhere to live and tried to sell her pots. After that, she told Cassie, the commissions would come rolling in and they would live on their own, in a proper house with a studio.

Cassie slept for most of the journey in the car, only waking when they reached Birmingham. The streets were noisy with home-going commuters and the sound of traffic, and the buildings were dark with soot. Cassie thought of the gloomy house in Larch Hill, listening to her grandmother play and sing 'Alice Where Art Thou?' on the piano, and being pressed to her black silk bosom, and she longed with all her heart to be back at The Folly, with its apple trees, and the swing in the garden, and the fields all around where she had played on her way home from school.

'I shall tell you stories,' Esther said, sensing Cassie's mood as they neared Larch Hill.

'What about?' Cassie could not hide a spark of interest.

'About places that are light and beautiful and don't smell of soot, where you and I shall live when I've made enough money.'

'Like Hugh and Marjorie's house?'

'Not as grand as Hugh and Marjorie's.'

'Like The Folly?' Cassie said hopefully, a wave of homesickness quickly returning.

'Not as full of memories as The Folly.' Esther, seeing Cassie's enthusiasm begin to fade, continued hurriedly, 'Somewhere new, where we can start a proper life together. And one day I shall have my own pottery and make beautiful pots that people will want to buy.'

'Instead of going to work?'

'Oh, it will still be work – but it will be *my* work, Cassie. All my own.'

Chapter Four

'You're doing what!'

'I've got a job at Ansfield's pottery factory,' Esther said, taking off her hat and coat and flinging herself down on the sofa. She felt pleased with herself. She had only been in Birmingham three days and already she had found herself work and somewhere to live.

'Are you out of your mind?' her father said. 'We understood it was some sort of teaching you were going to do.'

'At least teaching is a *profession*,' wailed her mother.

'Don't you mean, at least it was something you could tell them about in Larch Hill?'

'Oh, that's so unfair, Esther. And you've misled us. We never thought you would entertain the notion of working at a factory. And as for having all those boxes of pots brought here with you! Where are we supposed to put them all?'

'Pottery is my trade, Mummy. I shall look for a buyer for the pots and, meanwhile, the factory work will put money in my hand, the same as teaching would do.'

'You don't need money in your hand. You're our daughter. We can look after you,' said her father. 'Why are you always so darned obstinate?'

'Perhaps I take after you,' Esther said heatedly.

Her father's anger subsided. 'Perhaps you do.' He turned away and took his tobacco from the mantelshelf, taking his time lighting his pipe. 'Well, I suppose, if it's done, it's done. You know your mother is more than happy to look after Cassie.'

Esther hesitated. 'That's another thing. We shan't be living here. It wouldn't work. I'd drive you both mad, making the place untidy and getting in your way. I've found somewhere for me and Cassie to live.' She went on quickly, 'The rent's quite cheap and it's only half an hour away. We shall come and visit you – much more often than when we were living at The Folly.'

'But we wanted Cassie to go to school here,' wailed her mother.

'She can still go to Heather Park. She can catch the tram every morning.'

'Women with families should be at home,' her mother protested. 'And you've been ill. How are you going to look after yourself, never mind Cassie!'

'Cassie is ten. Quite grown-up. She'll be at school all day and I shall be there in the evenings for her.'

Mrs Mortimer, temporarily beaten, fell silent.

'Well.' It was her father's nature, having once given way over an issue, to be seen to do so graciously. 'I suppose you'd better tell us all about this factory. I've met Ansfield once or twice at civic receptions. A bachelor. Lives with his sister. Ansfield's is a family firm. I must say, he seems a decent enough chap.'

'Is it clean?' said her mother, diverted briefly. 'Are they – you know – *nice* people.'

How did Esther tell them about her first impressions of the factory – dark, rambling, filthy, with its huge bottle kilns – a world away from her mother's if not her father's experience? Esther had been shown into the painting room, where the women sat, four to a bench decorating stacks of plates and dishes, talking and joking about a way of life that was unheard of at Larch Hill. Esther thought up an elevated version of the experience and described the pots the factory made: it was 'good' everyday crockery, she said – the sort her mother would have on her own breakfast table.

George Ansfield had interviewed her. When she had told him about working with Christopher, he had looked at her with just a trace of a curl to his lip. 'Why do you want to waste your talents working as a paintress after you've been an artist potter?'

'Because I need the money,' she had said crisply.

'Aren't you Mortimer's daughter – the bicycle manufacturer?'

Esther had stiffened. 'I don't see what that's got to do with it.'

'Simply that I wouldn't have thought . . .' He had shrugged. 'There are plenty of men and women round here could do with a job.'

Esther had gathered her gloves and prepared to leave. 'Then employ them if that's how you feel.'

Ansfield had smiled. 'Calm down. I'm not saying I won't take you on.'

'I don't see that who I am, or who my father is, or the fact that this country has a tide of unemployed has anything to do with it,' Esther had said, regarding him coolly. He was a man of less than forty, amiable, pleasant-featured, a bit old-fashioned. He wore a bow-tie and a good suit with a gold watch-chain across his waistcoat. She had noticed that his shoes were highly polished and didn't seem to have picked up the dust and dirt of the works. Or perhaps he kept a duster in his office especially for cleaning them, she had speculated, noting he had a kind, rather serious face that crinkled at the eye corners when he smiled.

She had sat down again, had decided that she liked him; she knew he had a reputation for fairness, that his father had started as a Staffordshire potter and that he had himself done a stint at the Royal College of Art. He had seemed unnerved by her steady way of regarding him, and had dropped his own gaze.

60

'I pay about eighteen shillings a week. Piece-work. It's not much.'
'You're right. It's not. But it will do.'

He had narrowed his eyes, pressing the tips of his fingers together. 'Very well. Start on Monday. See how you get on. If you stick to it, we'll see about moving you up.'

'I don't want any special treatment.'

He had smiled again. 'I promise you. You won't get it.'

Giles Fielding came to see Esther while she was at Larch Hill.

'Take Giles into the garden,' said her mother. 'The roses are lovely just now.'

Esther led Giles through the hall where Martha, having washed up the dishes from Sunday lunch, and ready for her Sunday afternoon and evening off, was putting on her hat. Giles complimented her on the hat. Martha blushed; and it occurred to Esther for the first time that Giles was attractive to women. He had solid good looks, a steady income from the solicitors' practice where he was a junior partner; people were probably telling one another that she was a fool to have turned him down. They walked across the lawn, side by side, awkward with one another. They had not met since the day Esther had returned from Dorset and The Dovecote.

'You are looking well,' he said. 'I'm glad.'

'It must be my mother's cooking.' Esther smiled ruefully. 'I treat her rather badly, you know. And she's done so much for me. It's a good thing I'm moving out.'

'You'd grown very thin. You had us all worried about you.'

Esther paused to smell the heady scent of one of the roses and, aware that Giles was watching her, walked on. 'There was no need. It was obvious I would recover. People don't die from self-pity.'

'May I come and see you when you're settled into your flat?'

Esther imagined Giles visiting the poky rooms she had found to rent in Handsworth and hesitated.

'I shan't make a nuisance of myself.' Giles's colour had deepened, and immediately Esther told herself she was an ungrateful wretch.

'Yes, of course you must come and see us. But it's not very grand, I'm afraid.'

'I think you're right to break away from here. It's right for *you*. I can see that now and I admire you for it.'

They had reached the fence at the end of the garden, and the scent of the roses drifted down the lawn towards them. The meadow grass in the paddock was long and full of tall buttercups and meadowsweet.

Giles's speech had caused a further awkwardness between them and he tried to lighten it. 'You know, a pony for Cassie still might not be a bad idea.' He leant on the fence. 'It would keep the grass down and Cassie would love it when she comes to visit your parents.'

'You're right. But it's become a matter of principle with me.'

He looked at her. 'How very stubborn you always are.'

'Perhaps.' Esther felt that she could confide in him. She had always been able to talk to him easily, especially when Christopher had been alive. She hated the sense of strain that had come between them more recently. Why had he spoiled everything with that idiotic pronouncement at the New Year party? She looked at him. 'I think the stubbornness comes from a fear that if I'm not careful I shall lose myself under the managing pressures of others.'

'Did I make you feel like that?'

'Yes, Giles. You did.'

'Your illness – I felt very responsible.'

'Well you mustn't. It would probably have happened sooner or later. New Year was simply a trigger.' Esther remembered that Julia had said something of the sort to her when she had stood in her studio at The Dovecote. Julia had also talked of Christopher being her spiritual guide. And yet Christopher had suddenly become a stranger to her. He had kept things from her when he was alive. How could she trust him now, when he was dead? How far it seemed she had come since going to stay in Dorset.

'All the same,' Giles persisted. 'I should have been more perceptive. I shouldn't have rushed things the way I did.'

Esther saw with a sinking heart that he had not given up hopes of marriage. She could not bring herself deliberately to wound him again and said nothing.

He looked away. 'I hear you're going to work at Ansfield's pottery factory.'

She laughed. 'Yes. It's not art, but it's a means to an end.' She looked at him again, trying to decide how much to tell him of her plans. 'I've brought a stack of pots from The Folly. As soon as I've earned enough money from Ansfield's to get me started, I shall find buyers, rent a workshop, and set up my own small pottery again. It's all in the future, but I mean to tour the Birmingham department stores and, if I can find a market for my designs...' No longer Christopher's designs, she thought, but her own.

Her mother was calling and they walked back slowly towards the house. Esther did not finish outlining her plans and Giles seemed deep in contemplation.

Esther's mother had set out tea things in the sitting room. Her father stood by the fireplace and discussed the impartiality of the law – about which he knew nothing – with Giles, who, being a solicitor, knew a little more. Esther smiled at Giles as he listened with his usual diplomatic restraint to her father's opinions.

Cassie had returned from her Sunday School class, clutching her Bible in gloves that had been white at the start of the day and now were smudged with black. She was telling her grandmother the story of the foolish and the wise man, one having built his house on sand, the other on foundations of rock. She turned to Esther. 'I told the vicar I know about a dovecote built on stone pillars, like you told me.'

'What did he say to that?' said Esther.

'He said houses with doves in them didn't count.'

'I'm sure they do,' laughed Giles. 'After all, the dove is a symbol of the Holy Ghost. It's a very Christian bird.'

'A symbol of peace and harmony,' Esther said, remembering the tranquillity of the house by the sea and the little community of artists. '*O that I had wings like a dove* . . .' How did the verse go on, something about flying away and being at rest? She felt a strong desire to see The Dovecote again and to let its stillness soothe her.

Esther went with Giles to his motor car and watched him climb into the driver's seat. She had been glad he had come today, she realised. She remembered all the times during the war when he had driven patiently to The Folly, bringing eggs, coal and potatoes and flour when food was short. 'Life goes on,' Julia had said. And it was true. On an impulse she leaned on the top of the car door. 'Do come and see us in Handsworth, Giles, won't you? It's been good to see you again and to talk.'

He looked at her. 'I feel there's something different about you. Something's changed, but I can't tell what.'

'It's the prospect of working at Ansfield's,' she laughed.

He shook his head. 'No. It's to do with Christopher.'

She straightened. 'Perhaps.'

'I think perhaps you're letting go.'

She did not answer, but stood with her arms folded, watching the car as he drove away.

Was she at last letting go? Esther remembered Giles's observation as she wrote to Julia from the house in Tamarisk Street in Handsworth. There was not a tamarisk, nor any other tree in sight, but the hum of distant trams and the noise from the railway line forced their presence on the small apartment. Her rooms were on the first floor. The ground floor was occupied by the owner of the house, Mrs Plowman, with whom Esther shared a front door, a scullery and the outside lavatory. There was no bathroom. Esther, with Cassie's help, had to drag a zinc hip-bath and jugs of water from the wash-house up the stairs when they wanted a bath, as they did the coal for the small stove. Baths were frowned on by Mrs Plowman, afraid of spillages, carpets spoiling, ceilings coming down. But she was not unkind, for she kept an eye and an ear open for Cassie on school days until Esther got home in the evening.

'What do you do when you discover the man you loved was less than perfect?' Esther wrote to Julia. 'Do you stop loving him . . . ?'

She lifted her head and looked out of the window of the living room. The curtains were drawn in the windows of the house opposite, and the evening sun sent long, melancholy shadows slanting along the sooty red-brick walls. Esther wished blank windows didn't always look so sad. She had placed geraniums in pots on her own windowsills, to brighten them, though it had been more than she could readily afford.

She remembered how Christopher had joked about fame and fortune, telling her he loved her, that they were a team. How could he have deceived her so complacently, while all the time he had let his father shoulder the boring business of subsidising their existence? How could she have been so wrong about a man she had known so intimately? And yet, she still missed him. The pain was still there. She recalled someone once saying that deep sorrow never went away: one learned to live with the emptiness, but for the rest of one's life every moment of joy would be tinged with a sense of loss.

The sun struck the corner of the windowsill and lighted one of the geranium petals. The splash of bright colour, combined with the light and shade on the house walls opposite, brought back one of those flashes of memory that came from time to time with a vivid intensity. A sudden noise, a certain smell, the sound of a tram gathering speed in the next street – there wasn't always any logic about them, but they had the power to halt her in her tracks. And now a geranium and red-brick walls. She remembered his laughter. Was that what she remembered most about him – mocking her, teasing her? Was he here in the room? 'Come on, Esther. Grow up. Did you really expect perfect harmony and to know my every thought?'

She turned from the window. Did Christopher really come to her in those moments when she felt so intensely low? She knew that the power of the mind was strong – she had heard it said enough times by the doctors who had treated her: 'Only tell yourself you are whole and it will be true.' Did it follow that if she told herself Christopher was there her imagination could make him appear? His voice and his presence always seemed so real, as if she had only to turn her head and she would see him, smiling into her eyes, shrugging a little in that dismissive way of his. Why do you make such a mountain of things? Accept what there is and be happy.

The room was empty. She could hear Cassie singing to herself gently as she did her homework in the bedroom. Cassie had settled quickly at Heather Park and without complaining that she missed the easy-going life of a country school, though sometimes Esther wondered . . .

She returned to her letter to Julia. '. . . I have found work, painting pots in a factory. I dab on leaves with a brush, while the girl next to me does flower-buds and talks all the time about anything that comes into her head. It's a million miles from what I have been used to, Julia. And even further away from The Dovecote . . .'

The hooter was sounding as Esther saw the factory chimneys. She ran the last few yards until, when she rounded the street corner, the high wall and wooden factory gates came into view. It was early morning, but the day was already warm. Esther shrugged off her coat as she ran. Her footsteps echoed from the walls of the red-brick, three-storey buildings around the cobbled yard and her breath was harsh in her chest.

The drone of machinery became muted as she entered the narrow alley that led to the decorating shop. Here the sounds were of men whistling, the trundle of trolleys laden with saggars of pots, the clatter and crash of trolleys being loaded and unloaded. Esther released a gasp of frustration as she saw Shawcroft, the works manager, come out from his office with his pocket-watch.

'One minute and thirty seconds past eight, Mrs Norbrook.' He wiped the face of the watch with the flat of his thumb as if the action might help him to see the time more precisely. 'It's not the first time you've been late...'

'I know. I'm sorry, Mr Shawcroft. I promise it won't happen again.'

A smile crept over his fleshy mouth. 'Problems at home? Your little girl? I hope she's well.'

'She's quite well,' Esther said, understanding why the other women called Shawcroft 'Mr Toad' among themselves. 'I can't pin the blame on my daughter.'

'You should set your alarm clock, my dear.' His smile had hardened.

Esther stepped past him and reached for the peg that held her working apron. 'I'll do that.' She slipped her coat on the peg and the apron over her head. He leaned with his arm against the wall, watching her tie the strings behind her waist. He did not move when she had finished and Esther stood with her arms folded, waiting for him to let her pass. At last he eased himself from the wall and moved forward, at the same time as Esther ducked past him. 'You needn't think you should get different treatment from the rest, on account of Mr Ansfield's taken a shine to you.'

Esther turned on him in surprise. 'I wouldn't expect it, Mr Shawcroft. Not on account of anything. Ansfield's hasn't got that sort of reputation.'

'Your father knows Mr Ansfield, doesn't he?'

'They might have met. I really don't know.'

'Oh, I think you do.' He paused. 'The girls don't like favouritism. They can get very spiteful. A crowd of girls can be very nasty-tongued.'

'Well, I'm sure you've had first-hand experience of that, Mr Shawcroft,' Esther murmured, walking on past him and into the decorating shop.

She sat down at her place at the table, blowing out her cheeks.

'Just had a fight with Mr Toad?' said Miriam, seated next to her.

'I can't seem to shake him off. I think I've snubbed him and the next day he pops up again with his oily grin.'

'He tries it on with everybody for a while.' Miriam pushed a plate towards her. 'He'll give up when he finds another poor sucker.'

Esther looked down at the plate, resenting the idea that she should be considered fair game. It was stuffy in the decorating shop where there was no relief from the heat, for the drying ovens and kilns affected every corner of the factory buildings. The women rolled up their sleeves at their workbenches and joked with the men who came through from the yard, wiping the sweat from their foreheads as they pushed the heavy trolleys.

Esther's plate was decorated with evenly spaced pink flowers curling round its rim, each part of the design having been applied individually by one of the girls who occupied the table. George Ansfield's sister, a Royal College graduate, had designed the standard range of tableware. Though dull, it was good, Esther acknowledged as she dipped her brush in the paint and deftly applied a spear-shaped leaf.

She thought about Shawcroft's comments, surprised at the jibe about her father, and she wondered whether Shawcroft's accusation of favouritism could have any foundation. Had Ansfield only employed her because he knew about her background?

She looked at Miriam, patiently applying petals while she talked non-stop to the silent Irene, who dipped her brush with rhythmic regularity, her tongue between her teeth. Louie, on a stool next to her, set a plate on her turntable and, with a fluid movement, finished it with a blue rim. Louie was the oldest of the team; she had worked at Ansfield's 'banding' plates for thirty years. Esther wanted to ask her, Haven't you ever wanted to design plates of your own, to let your mind devise new shapes and patterns and take you where it will? The ambition of most of the women was concentrated in becoming a paintress of such proficiency that she would be moved from piece-work to doing 'fancies' and executing complete designs. The élite among the ceramic painters sat at individual stands; they had pots of brushes and dishes of colour to hand and saw a design through from start to finish, their minds lost in concentration, their brush hand steadied against the pot. Esther watched Miss Lassingham, a thin, delicate woman with tiny hands, painting the fine veining on a rose. Miriam nudged Esther and pushed her next plate to her, and Esther saw that Shawcroft had come into the decorating shop and was walking between the rows of benches.

'Nothing to do, Mrs Norbrook?' He halted by her table. She bent her head over her work, but he did not move away and Esther looked up, her brush poised. 'Mr Ansfield wants a word with you,' he said with a faintly vindictive smile. 'He's in the design office.'

Esther laid down her brush and slipped from her stool, conscious of the women's curiosity as she left the decorating shop.

She climbed the stairs slowly. So Shawcroft had complained of her poor time-keeping to Mr Ansfield. He would have to sack her, of course. Esther felt sick. If she couldn't hold down a job for more than a few weeks, how was she ever going to raise the money for a workshop of her own? A more immediate fear sent a panic sweeping through her. Where else would she find work when employment was so scarce? She reached the first-floor offices and tapped on the door of the design office.

George Ansfield was leaning over a high desk, a design book open in front of him. His chin rested in one hand as if he had been deep in concentration. 'Come in, Esther. Come here. I want to talk to you.'

Esther felt her spirits lift again. He didn't look like a man about to dismiss one of his employees. She walked across the office and saw that he was looking at a set of his sister's designs. She glanced at the other occupant of the room, an elderly man who had been a designer at Ansfield's for years and had moved with the company from Staffordshire; Swales turned to glance at Esther over his spectacles, then swivelled his chair back to his desk.

Esther turned her attention to the design book. Ursula Ansfield worked from home on the factory's luxury ware. It was rumoured that she was an invalid, though the exact nature of her illness wasn't known. The women in the decorating shop spoke of her with a kind of awe, because of the contrast between her physical delicacy and her prodigious talent.

'Some of my sister's newest patterns. I'd be glad of your opinion on this one,' George Ansfield said. The design was for a teapot. A pair of climbing roses twined themselves delicately round the spout and handle. Ansfield stepped back and watched over Esther's shoulder as she studied it. 'What do you think? Will it work?'

'Up to a point.' Esther was reluctant to voice her criticisms that the roses were two-dimensional, that the design failed to take into account the shape of the pot. She thought of Christopher's insistence that form was all important and her own argument, that good form could be ruined by bad design.

'You're not happy with it?'

'Mr Ansfield,' she said in embarrassment. 'I'm a paintress here. It's not my job to be unhappy about the designs.'

He leaned against the wall and folded his arms. 'Never mind all that, Esther. I've been hearing things about the pots you and your husband used to make. I want you to speak your mind. I'm expecting you to share your ideas with us.'

'All right then.' She pointed to the spout and handle. 'You see here – and here? The stems don't flow with the pot. The design looks awkward to me. It turns corners. It seems to be forced unnaturally into following the lines of the spout and the handle.'

'How would you adjust it?'

'I couldn't. It would mean redesigning the shape of the teapot from the beginning or else finding a more compatible design. The painting and the shape of the pot should sweep and twist together up from the base.'

'Ah.'

'You see? I shouldn't have said anything.'

'No. I wanted your opinion.'

'And I'd make the flowers bolder,' Esther said recklessly, now that she had begun. 'They are too . . . pretty.'

Ansfield looked down and fiddled with the pages of his sister's new designs which, in Esther's opinion – had she spoken her mind more openly – were poor. 'Yes,' he said. 'I think you're right.'

She felt angry because he had drawn the criticism from her and sorry for him at the same time, sensing the conflict of loyalties in him. She stared at a photograph on the wall, of the factory employees on a charabanc outing. They were laughing and smiling and their employer, dressed in tweed knickerbockers and golfing socks and smoking a pipe, stood beside the driver.

'Do you have any of your own designs here in Birmingham?' he said suddenly.

'Yes. I have pages of Christopher's designs.' She hesitated. 'And there are several finished pots.'

'May I see them?'

'There are quite a lot of the pots. But they are stored in my parents' garage. You would have to see them there.'

'Do you think now would be a convenient time?'

Esther imagined her mother's face. 'Well – I could telephone.' She felt excitement begin to rise in her.

'Good.' He closed the book of patterns and turned to Swales with a look almost of conspiracy. 'Good. Let's go and telephone from my office.'

'Swales is leaving us soon,' George Ansfield said as he drove out of the factory yard with Esther beside him. 'He told me this morning that he wants to retire. He's come into a small nest-egg, wants to go back to Staffordshire. The thing is, I shall be needing another designer. If I like your pots, and I think I shall . . .' He looked out of the car window and did not finish the sentence.

Esther had already begun to guess at something of the kind. The position of assistant designer would mean more money. It would still be routine, she told herself, trying to subdue her eagerness. Swales hadn't been given much freedom, nor had he seized any in the years he had been with the firm. She looked at George Ansfield surreptitiously. Like most factory owners he would have his own interests rather than hers at heart, and she couldn't imagine that her promotion would mean any radical changes at Ansfield's. But it would be a step nearer to saving for her own workshop. She too would be looking after her own interests.

Esther leaned back against the soft dull leather of the bench-seat of the Ford. She might even be able to afford to drive Christopher's car again. She had begun to miss the Morris, garaged at Larch Hill. She rested her arm on the door, smiling at the driver of a horse and cart as they passed, and, forgetting all caution, she let a wave of optimism sweep over her.

Esther's mother was flustered at the sight of George Ansfield in his polished motor car and highly polished shoes. 'You didn't tell me he was young,' she hissed, as Esther directed him towards the garage. He's not, Esther protested mentally. But there again, neither was he ancient.

She threw a mental prayer heavenward that her mother would not divert her energies from promoting Giles – whom she could deal with – to Ansfield, of whom she was less sure, as a prospective marriage candidate.

The pots were stored in boxes at the back of the garage behind the car. Esther lifted one from its wrapping of brown paper – a bowl, with a vivid swirl of abstract red and yellow flame-like shapes banded in black. George Ansfield took the piece from her and turned it in his hands. He was silent for a long time then said, 'It's not at all what I was expecting.'

'It's not the sort of decoration I did when my husband was alive,' Esther said defensively, and remembered her need to assert her own identity, the fury of energy that had gone into the final firing at The Folly. She unwrapped a second pot with a sinking heart. Ansfield didn't like her style. He had said he had spoken to people about the Norbrook Pottery. He would have expected to see Christopher's work and her own elegantly subdued glazes that allowed, above all, the 'form' of the pot to shine through. Esther took the pots from him and folded them again into their wrapping.

'You've got flair.' He reached past her into the packing case and pulled out another sample; he unwrapped it and stroked the red and brown flame design, holding the dish to the light. 'They are so original.' He looked at her and Esther's heart leaped, seeing the admiration in his eyes.

'You like them?'

'I think they are wonderful. Strong. Unique.'

Esther laughed. 'Then I've got the job?'

'You didn't really think I would waste your talents in the decorating shop for much longer, did you?' he said.

Word spread quickly round the decorating shop that Esther had been moved 'upstairs'. Esther was aware of the resentment. Shawcroft watched her sullenly when she arrived in the mornings and hung up her coat. Whispers of favouritism and worse began to circulate, and Esther guessed that much of the envy and gossip originated from Shawcroft. This worked in Esther's favour. The women at Ansfield's disliked the manager more than they resented Esther's advancement. Besides, they knew Mr Ansfield. The boss was 'straight as a die'. He had an invalid sister and his family were Quakers. The talk soon died. Some even said that Esther deserved her good fortune: they had known from the start she was out of the ordinary.

Esther returned to Larch Hill that weekend. She unwrapped several of her pots and stood them on the running-board of the car.

She had believed Christopher's art beautiful and had always accepted that her own was subordinate to it. She had believed that Christopher's superior craftsmanship and his integrity as an artist must shine through the finished article; but if Christopher, the man, had not been sincere, how could his art have had any real integrity? The honesty of her own designs blazed forth; though they used the form and shape of the pot, they had totally effaced its importance, and Esther realised that in her rage she had created something more truly 'beautiful' than anything Christopher had ever done. She remembered that George Ansfield had called the pots unique, and she felt a glow of pleasure. He had suggested that, if she were to put her ideas about the Climbing Rose design on paper, it might be fruitful for his sister to look at them. Then he had shifted his glance. 'We have to tread carefully, Esther. I hope you understand that your ideas must fit with our own. They must suit Ansfield's name.'

In other words, thought Esther, he and his sister would have the last word. She mustn't expect that working as a designer for Ansfield's would give her the freedom to develop her own designs – George Ansfield had made it clear that their ranges of tableware would change hardly at all as a result of her promotion. Nevertheless, he had given Esther the confidence she had been waiting for. She would start to show her own pots to buyers. She wrapped a selection and packed them up to take back to Tamarisk Street.

Esther shut the front door and called out to let Cassie upstairs and Mrs Plowman downstairs know that she was home. It was all she could do to drag the box of pots up the stairs and her wrist ached from the weight of the vegetables, carried from the market in the shopping-net in her hand.

Esther put the box down on the small landing and went into the living room, where she lifted the net of vegetables on to the table and sank into a chair. Cassie came out from the bedroom and stood in the doorway. She regarded Esther without speaking, then said gently, 'I'll make you a cup of tea.'

'What have I done to you?' Esther thought out loud as Cassie went downstairs to fill the kettle. Cassie seemed to have grown up too quickly in the past weeks, taking on responsibilities that were accepted as normal for a ten-year-old in Tamarisk Street – running errands, carrying water and coal and helping to heave washing down to the yard; gone was the idyllic childhood of The Folly. Was this what was meant by letting go of the past, bringing up her child to a life of hardship in a street with no trees?

Cassie came back into the living room and put the kettle on the fire-hob. 'I like it here,' she said. 'I really do.'

Cassie did not mind having to grow up quickly so much as she had minded leaving The Folly, but Cassie was not unhappy. Though she saw less of her mother since Esther had gone to work at Ansfield's, she had never felt so close to her as she did now, living in Tamarisk Street. And the street was not so bad. The rooms they rented were bright with geraniums. Cassie liked the shape of their petals against the light in the morning. She liked the red and cream pattern of the linoleum on the bedroom floor, the way the sun striped the wall through the broad wooden bars at the foot of the high double bed that she shared with her mother, and the sound of trams when she went to sleep at night. There was a wash-house outside in the yard and a strip of threadbare grass where she could kick stones around – until she broke the wash-house window one day and Esther had to pay for it. The wash-house was next to the lavatory and smelled of old soap and drains. Mrs Plowman did all the washing in a big copper with a wooden lid, Esther's and Cassie's as well as her own. She would preside over it, red-faced; and the perspiration running down her cheeks and the condensation running down the wash-house walls seemed to Cassie to be inextricably linked.

Mrs Plowman had befriended Cassie. She told her stories about the time when her husband was alive, which Cassie found vaguely romantic and exciting. How he used to come home drunk and throw his dinner at the wall, and how he could quote the Bible, word-perfect, when he was 'sozzled'. Mrs Plowman approved of Cassie's interest in Bible stories, but she did not, she said, approve of drinking.

People behaved strangely in the Bible too, Cassie had discovered. They had romantic names and went about slaughtering one another and wreaking vengeance. She read her Bible every day since her grandmother had first made it obligatory, puzzling over the moral complexities of the Old Testament. She attended a Sunday School, attached to a High Anglican Church three streets away. She became very keen on going to church, enjoying the mystic rituals, the priest's robes, the haloes of candles, the chanting and singing and the gleam of silver altar-pieces.

Tamarisk Street was close to a railway line, which smelled of soot, and a timber yard smelling more pleasantly of resin, and there was a sweet-shop on the corner that sold aniseed and liquorice and halfpenny sherbet dabs. Cassie liked walking past the woodyard. She would linger by the fence and peer through at the honey-coloured planks and beams, stacked outside the sheds. The smell of the wood was not a city smell, and it made her long to be back at the little village school in the country, where she had run wild in the fields with her friends.

In the next street, where the trams ran, there were a few scrawny sycamores growing from squares in the pavement. Cassie would pick up the winged seeds and fly them on her way to school. Her grandparents had managed to persuade Esther that Heather Park, where she attended, was a 'good school', but Cassie had strong doubts about it when she was ten. In later, fonder memory, its more progressive, even liberal qualities were destined to impress her, but these were tempered by memories of playing lacrosse with frozen fingers, learning whole chunks of *Hiawatha* by heart, and dates of battles and successions of kings and queens. Heather Park girls dressed in navy gym-slips and long fawn socks with elastic garters. They wore panama hats in the summer and navy felt hats with yellow striped bands in winter. All of this marked the pupils as belonging to Heather Park and therefore superior. Cassie stuffed her hat in her satchel when she neared

Tamarisk Street, where that kind of superiority was looked on with derision. At school, however, she was treated with derision because she came from Tamarisk Street.

She made a nativity scene for Christmas, built and carved from scraps of wood that she had found inside the gates of the timber yard. It won her a school prize, but the other girls in the class looked at her as if she had done something outlandish, because their attempts were made of pipe cleaners and felt and discarded stockings stuffed with cotton wool. Cassie was made to understand that only boys would have attempted anything in wood.

Such necessary conventions were impressed on her by a girl called Janet Massingham-Browne, who had managed to discover where Cassie lived. She was also the first to learn – and to spread the information around – that Cassie didn't have a father. She said this meant that Cassie was a 'bastard'.

Cassie was not sure what the word meant, but she knew from the shocked expressions on the other girls' faces that a 'bastard' must be something terrible. 'I *have* got a father,' she shouted, feeling her face flush hotly. 'But he's dead, because he fought for his country in the Great War.'

'I don't believe you,' the other girl said with a confident smirk. 'Anyway, you're still second-rate because your mother works in a pot bank.'

Cassie did not know whether it was true that she was a bastard, but she would have defended her mother to the last, and this second taunt seemed to be the more provocative of the two. She hit Janet Massingham-Browne with her fist and the other girl crumpled in a heap on the ground before her astonished and delighted eyes.

This act of barbarism brought her to the immediate attention of the teacher on duty, who threatened to send her to the headmistress – which, as everyone knew, meant almost certain expulsion. Cassie explained she had felled her victim because she had called her a bastard. She could not bring herself to repeat the terrible claim that Esther was second-rate. The woman's expression altered. She took Cassie aside into her own teaching domain, the art room, and closed the door.

Miss Collins sat on one of the art tables and regarded Cassie kindly. 'We have to learn to ignore people who deliberately try to wound us, Cassie. Tell yourself, "Sticks and stones..." But don't react.'

Cassie said that people in the Bible were not so passive about injustices done. 'I had to hit her. It was a matter of vengeance.'

'No, you did not,' said Miss Collins sharply. 'And if you do anything like that again, your mother will have to take you away from this school. Perhaps you should be reading the New Testament rather than the Old.'

The threat that Esther might be told sobered Cassie at once. She adopted the conventional attitude under punishment – a submissive air of penitence – and Miss Collins told her that the girl who had taunted

72

her was all the poorer in spirit because of the things she had said.

'If she calls me a bastard again I shall turn the other cheek,' Cassie promised with heavy piety.

'Do that. And, while we're on the subject, young ladies don't use words like "bastard" – not even in private. And anyway, you're not one,' Miss Collins added.

Miss Collins became Cassie's idol after that, and art her favourite subject. Having someone to worship helped to make life at Heather Park more tolerable, but she could not tell her mother about the incident. Cassie made a solemn vow that when her mother owned her own pottery works and became 'first-rate', everyone would know about it.

In the evenings Cassie sat at the table in the window of the living room and did her homework, watching for Esther to come home, dreaming about the time when she would be able to leave Heather Park and she and her mother would live in the country again. The table was covered in an oil-cloth, and Esther sat there too until late in the evening, sketching out new designs, ready for when they would become women on their own in a proper house with a studio. Esther's pots were kept in boxes around the living room and in the garage at Larch Hill. From time to time she would take some with her on the tram on a Saturday afternoon to assail the various retailers of the Midlands, only to return at the end of the day, disillusioned and exhausted.

When letters from The Dovecote arrived they would always make Esther feel unsettled. She had written to tell Julia about her promotion at Ansfield's, and Julia had written back saying, 'Forget all about the ghastly factory works. Come and make your pots here. We can all help look after Cassie and you can turn the pottery studio into a little production works. I know so many people who would jump at the chance to buy your designs. It's the perfect answer . . .'

Julia's energy suffused every line. Was it the 'perfect answer'? The temptation to imagine herself at The Dovecote was strong. Esther looked back on those brief weeks with the community in Dorset as the first genuinely happy time since Christopher had died. But it was impossible, inconceivable that she should accept Julia's patronage. Julia's offer was yet another snare.

Yet, when she lay in bed and told Cassie stories about the house where they would one day live, it was always The Dovecote Esther turned to as a source of inspiration. The house would be 'covered in wisteria'. It would have a red roof and be very beautiful.

'And it will be near the sea,' Cassie prompted. 'You said it would be near the sea.'

'So that we can hear the waves crashing in,' Esther promised. 'I shall make pots and you shall look for shells and make seaweed necklaces all day.'

'And daisy chains.' Cassie sighed, tucking her arms behind her head on the pillow. 'On an enormous lawn.'

'A lawn with flower borders and cedar trees and doves sitting on the roof.'

'Just like at The Dovecote.' This was how their fantasy always finished.

'Just like The Dovecote,' Esther agreed. It had become a ritual. Where was the harm in acknowledging that such a dream-house really existed?

Chapter Five

'Esther *must* come here. It's the obvious answer for her.'

Julia had called a meeting in the sitting room at The Dovecote. She stood by the window, leaning against the sill with her back to the light and with Esther's most recent letter in her hand. 'Does she really think she's going to flourish as an artist, designing for a mass-producer like this man Ansfield, or hawking her wares round Birmingham like some dreadful commercial traveller? No. She must come and live here at The Dovecote.'

'*Must*, Julia?' Joseph sat on the arm of one of the chairs near the door, drawn unwillingly to the meeting, only waiting for a chance when he might leave. He felt uneasy when Julia summoned them together. Her pretence at democracy was growing paper-thin.

Meg glanced at Joseph with one of her swift, dry smiles and murmured, 'Whatever happened to free will and liberty?'

Julia waved a hand impatiently. 'Esther is confused. She doesn't realise what designing for a manufacturer means. She'll be swamped by Ansfield's preoccupation with sales and dividends, and her art will become rigid, stale, mechanical. I've been praying for her. I pray often, night and day, for Esther and her daughter. I think we should put her case to a spirit meeting and ask our Spirit Guide for help.'

'Oh, for goodness' sake, Julia,' said Meg. 'Is that what this is all about?'

The others were silent, aware that antagonism between Julia and Meg was slowly approaching boiling point. Joseph regarded the down-turn of Julia's mouth. She fingered it restlessly, as if she were in need of a cigarette. He realised that he was tired of her: disillusioned with her love and harmony, her management of her 'doves' and her barely concealed autocracy.

'I find your attitude strange, Meg,' Julia was saying. 'You know that we always ask the spirits about anything very important to us.'

'I don't find this issue very important,' Meg said, with a secret containment that, Joseph knew, always drove Julia mad, for Julia had never been able to influence Meg very deeply and she hated nothing more than failure. Not an overwhelming failure, for Meg was not a favoured dove, and Julia only tolerated her because of Peter. If she lost Peter . . . Now that would be a catastrophe. She had done so much with Peter.

Joseph watched as Julia lit a cigarette with trembling fingers. 'You seem to think very little is of importance, Meg,' she said, drawing in smoke with a hiss of breath. 'So much so, that you didn't even bother to consult the rest of us about selling Peter's pictures.'

'Oh, that old chestnut.' Meg turned away in mild exasperation.

'Yes. Your arrogance over Peter's pictures,' Julia said petulantly, and Joseph saw Rowena grip Freddie's hand with a look of intense involvement on her face.

Freddie looked bored, Joseph thought, reflecting that Freddie would have been a decent chap if he hadn't got so hooked up on Julia's spiritualism. Strange, how the death of a parent affected some people. The death of his own parents had not been in any way traumatic, for it seemed comforting to him to know that they had died without witnessing the war. On the other hand, Freddie had been in the trenches, and yet the experience seemed to have affected him hardly at all.

'You've caused disharmony among us, Meg, and that makes me sad,' Julia said. 'In fact, I have to say that I find your presence at The Dovecote very negative . . .'

The others waited breathlessly, wondering if Julia would force the issue.

'And I find yours increasingly dictatorial,' said Meg. 'I came here because I believed The Dovecote was a warm and tolerant community. Since then I've watched people come and go under your patronage, and I wonder how much liberty we really have.'

Julia's face was in shadow. Her hand holding the cigarette was pressed hard against her cheek and the smoke slowly coiled upwards against the light from the window. 'I wonder, Meg, if you too should leave.'

There was an audible gasp from Rowena.

'If Meg goes, so do I,' said Peter quietly.

The remark was followed by a heavy silence and Julia went white. She seemed to shift, as if temporarily off-balance. Had she really not supposed that Peter would support Meg? Joseph wondered. And, more importantly, if Julia thought she had such a hold on Peter, how much more confident would she be that he too was under her control?

Julia stubbed out her cigarette in an ashtray behind her and, thrusting herself past Joseph, she stalked from the room. The rest of those gathered in the sitting room broke out in a babble of argument, Rowena telling Meg that she shouldn't have been so damned high-handed and Meg trying to behave as if nothing had happened.

Joseph left them to it and went after Julia, but she was not in the hall and he guessed she had fled up to her studio. He resisted the sense of duty that made him feel he should follow her, and he went upstairs to the room he seldom used except as a dressing room. He lit the oil-lamp, for although it was still late afternoon, it was already getting dark. It would soon be Christmas.

What about Esther? Joseph wondered as he sat on the narrow bed with his arms resting on his knees. If Esther came to Julia it would be a good move for her career. She would make money, as he had, to buy the kind of freedom that mattered. And in the end that was all that mattered, to be able to work singlemindedly.

He stared at his fingers, stained with oil and glue, the nails short and broken, and they reminded him of his father's hands. He tried to imagine telling Julia he was leaving. You remember last summer, the Marchesa di Malfi: I met her at the Vaudoyers' dinner party . . . ? He had no idea how she would react. Would she be glad when he told her he had a firm offer to discuss the Italian commission – deceived that he was at last confident of going abroad and travelling through France? Somehow he didn't think so.

He got up to change for dinner. The wardrobe door had swung open and the clothes on their hangers looked dry and dusty – like old books propped loosely in a row, each with its story: a blazer from his school cricketing days, a black silk dinner suit next to the khaki of his old army uniform. He stared at the uniform. Why did the marchesa's offer have such overpowering implications of escape?

Rowena was nervous at dinner that evening. She knew she was talking too much, enthusing about mushrooms, swearing they had aphrodisiac properties if you cooked them with the right herbs. She was talking too much and drinking too much and she knew she was a little bit tight, but she always got so nervous when Julia was in one of her moods. She looked at Freddie to help her out but, as usual, he was hopeless, behaving as if nothing had happened. No one mentioned the argument that afternoon, but Julia was making a point of not speaking to Meg. She was talking about holding a seance, as if no one had disputed that they should consult her Spirit Guide about Esther. Well, Rowena thought, she had no objection to Esther coming here so long as she didn't set her sights on Freddie, and it might be good for them to have a child about the place. Therapeutic, Freddie would say. Take her mind off little Barbara . . . Rowena stood unsteadily, remembering when they had brought the baby to her, wrapped tightly in a shawl, the yellow face so tiny and troubled. She cleared the plates on to the sideboard with Freddie and he touched her arm, knowing instinctively what was on her mind. He was a good man. She ought to appreciate him more. She knew he loved her in spite of his flirting, and she loved him – golly, how she loved him. What would she have done without him?

'All right, old thing?'

Rowena nodded, blinking back her tears, and went to fetch the coffee. The painting of Dante's Beatrice seemed to glow in the semi-darkness of the hall. Rowena felt comforted. She knew the spirits would want Esther to come. They always wanted to help Julia. They knew how much love she wanted to share with everyone. Sometimes Freddie and Meg pretended not to take the seances seriously – even though Freddie's mother had spoken through Julia, and Meg had once wept to hear her sister – but Rowena adored the seances without reservation. They made living at The Dovecote even more special. She liked the secret society atmosphere of it all, and the sense of no longer being alone as soon as she entered the meeting room upstairs. She loved the thrill of anticipation when Julia stood poised to receive her Spirit Guide, the hope that little Barbara would speak to her, and the wonderful sense of calm when Julia said that Barbara had come through – that she was happy and well cared-for in the spirit world.

Violet was washing up at the sink. The kitchen was bathed in the gentle light from the oil-lamps, its table strewn with the debris of recent cooking. It seemed to be her own private world when Rowena came here alone and the others were in the dining room. Violet's large hunched figure, her forearms deep in soap suds, didn't intrude on it as the others did.

Violet turned a shining face towards her. 'Julia's going to call a special seance!'

'Yes. I know.'

'It will be nice for Julia if the spirits think the lady that came here last spring should come back to run the pottery.'

'Nice for me too,' Rowena said. It occurred to her as she picked up the coffee pot and crossed the hall that she would be able to leave the pottery alone at last and concentrate on cooking.

Rowena poured the coffee for everyone and sat down next to Joseph, who was talking with Peter. She listened for a while without really hearing what was being said, noticing that Joseph looked troubled again. He was brooding about something, she thought. Then she remembered the Armistice anniversary the next day. She hoped it didn't mean they were in for a bad time, yells in the night, back to the beginning again. Rowena thought of the girl who had jilted Joseph and took a swallow of wine. The bitch – though somehow you couldn't blame her. Rowena was glad Freddie didn't get the screaming ab-dabs, ruining her beauty sleep night after night. It was strange, but the war had affected Freddie hardly at all in that way. She looked at Joseph, apparently so normal most of the time. You could hardly call it 'shell-shock', not when you thought of some. She supposed it took men in different ways, but it was so sad that Joseph resisted coming to the spirit meetings.

Julia had finished her coffee. She seemed to be about to make a speech. She glanced directly at Peter and said, out of the blue, 'Very well, Meg may stay.'

Rowena breathed a sigh of relief. So that little unpleasantness was over and they could all be friends again.

'But from now on I shall not speak to her,' Julia added, talking as if Meg were not there. 'If Meg won't accept the ways of The Dovecote, she is no longer one of my doves.'

Rowena was the first to speak, feeling the burden fall on her to make light of the matter. 'Oh, Julia. You don't really mean that. You know you don't mean it . . .'

'Be quiet,' Julia said quite harshly. 'You must let me be the judge about things. The matter's closed. I want us to vote now about putting Esther's future to the next spirit meeting.'

The others looked at one another. You could tell everyone was very shocked about Meg being ostracised – especially Peter, thought Rowena – but the subject was dropped and the question of Esther assumed its proper importance. Rowena voted with the others about whether they should ask Julia's Spirit Guide to help bring Esther back into the care of The Dovecote. And of course – because Julia wanted it – the verdict was in favour.

At The Dovecote they had observed two minutes' silence for the dead, and had held a seance to enlist the help of Julia's Spirit Guide in returning Esther to them. In London the King had unveiled the new memorial in Whitehall.

Joseph lay unable to sleep on the night of the Armistice anniversary. When he did sleep it was to wake at the door of his cottage, hearing the cries of his platoon in his head and his own screams ringing through the darkness and snatched away on the wind.

He crouched on the floor in the open doorway. Had he been going to them? He had heard them so clearly – Richmond, Stubbs, Cartwright . . . He remembered every one of them by name. He sat on the step and leaned his head back against the doorpost, wrapping his arms round his knees to stop their shaking. His face was wet with tears.

He could hear the sea crashing against the pebbles below the cliff, like the slow, pounding roar of a steam train. The clouds were thick, scudding great billows of smoke across the night sky. They had brought him home by night, he remembered. People had stared at him on the station, strapped to a stretcher even though there wasn't a mark of injury on him.

He started. A figure in a long coat was coming through the trees in the darkness. It was how Death would come. There was a time when he would have welcomed the arrival – and *would* welcome it one day – but not now. He did not want Death to come for him right now. He could not bear to see their faces, Richmond, Stubbs, Cartwright: accusing, pleading, sorrowful. Or worse – forgiving, when he could not yet forgive himself.

Joseph backed against the doorpost, still confused by his dream as Death drew closer, now distinct, tall and stately in the moonlight, now shadowy and monstrous as the clouds scudded across the sky. The figure was upon him. He covered his face with his arms and began to scream. 'Get away! Get away!'

He felt a gentle warmth rather than a touch. Not the heat of the fiery

79

furnace, but a kind heat from healing hands, like the warmth of summer on his brow, a glow of sunlight behind closed eyes, a sense of becoming whole again under fingers exerting a firm pressure, convincing more than words that there was nothing, after all, to fear – and then a voice, repeating, 'It's over. It's over now.'

'Julia?'

She was beside him, kneeling in the doorway, her arms around him, her hand stroking his face. 'I heard you. I was awake. I was so afraid something might happen today. If only you had come to the seance this afternoon.'

Returning to his senses, ashamed of his infirmity, Joseph pulled away from her, saying quietly, 'For Christ's sake, Julia! Why should I want to come to a seance?'

She was silent, and suddenly he began to weep again remembering his dream. 'They were there. They were screaming for us to help them.'

'Hush. It's over. It's over now.'

'I should have gone to them.'

'No. It was not your fault.'

After a while Julia stood and, stepping across his feet into the cottage, she went to the table and lit the lamp. 'Do you want me to stay with you?' She adjusted the wick and fitted the shade.

He looked up and saw that she was wrapped in a long greatcoat over her nightgown. She thrust her hands deep into the pockets and her face was calm, madonna-like in the glow of the lamp.

Slowly he stood up and crossed the room to sit on the bed and Julia came to sit beside him, pulling a packet of cigarettes from her pocket. He accepted the cigarette she offered but did not light it; he put it on the blanket beside him and sat with his head in his hands. 'Sometimes I wish I could end everything. Sometimes, when I'm driving in the Bentley, the temptation comes to go faster and faster and head straight for a wall or a tree.'

'What stops you?' Julia said calmly.

'I don't know. An instinct to stay alive? Cowardice? The same instinct that held me back when they called for me to go to them.'

'Come to the next spirit meeting, Joseph,' Julia said.

He shook his head wearily. 'No. That's not the answer.'

'I know it would help. You would see that they forgive you.'

He was afraid, Joseph thought. Afraid of meeting the dead – really meeting them face to face outside his dream: Richmond, Stubbs, Cartwright, Jackson with the buck tooth and violent grin. He imagined the grin slipping under the mud. Garrett, older than the rest, with his, 'Yes, sir', a touch of insolence in the eyes as if to say he knew Joseph was still only a kid, but very correct as he brought the hand smartly to a salute. He saw Garrett's hand grasping the air and remembered Nash, who had come to him before the battle. 'Sir, if I should cop it, tell my wife . . .' Was it Nash who had called out the last of all? 'Sir . . . Help me, help me, sir.'

Joseph had began to shiver and Julia wrapped a blanket round him. 'We have been praying again for Esther. *Do* you think she should come to us?' she said after a while.

Joseph began to pay attention to the question. There seemed to be a tension in Julia as she waited for him to answer, and he was aware of a feeling of portent about the moment. He glanced across the room, seeing his binoculars hanging on the wall, and realised that there was a particular obsessiveness in Julia over this one.

His unwillingness to reply angered her. 'It's obvious she has to come,' she said impatiently. 'I could find her far more influential customers than a few retail outlets in Birmingham.'

'I know that. You're a very good patron, Julia.'

'I believe in my doves. I love you all – even Meg, the foolish, silly woman. I want your art to shine from each one of you with a shattering radiance.'

Joseph picked up the cigarette from the bed, but his hands still shook and Julia went to the mantelshelf for matches and lit the cigarette for him, drawing deeply before handing it back. 'Do you want me to stay tonight?' she said again.

In the afterglow of healing, Joseph's flesh was attuned to her, alert to every movement she made. He wanted her in his bed, he realised, remembering the sinuous skill of her touch and the generosity of her body – another kind of healing. But there was a danger about Julia. Her love was overpowering as well as generous.

'No,' he said. 'I don't want you to stay.' He would read until daylight to prevent himself from returning to his dreams and to keep at bay the darkness that dredged up the lost men of his platoon.

Julia bent and kissed him, but he could see that he had hurt her. 'You need me,' she said gently. 'Don't reject me too often. Remember that frightened boy who came back from France? We have come so far, darling Joseph – but you still need me.'

Could he manage his nightmares without her? He asked himself, and thought again of the Italian commission.

What about Esther? Should he write to warn her? He was aware of the dangers for her if she accepted Julia's offer. No, he wouldn't write. Esther must make up her own mind.

He sighed. 'I know how much you've done for me, Julia. Whatever happens – don't ever accuse me of ingratitude.'

'Are you calm now?'

'Yes.'

Julia went to the door. 'You didn't ask.' She paused. 'You didn't ask what my Spirit Guide said about Esther. You're a sceptic, Joseph. You shouldn't be. Why should those who have passed over not want to guide those of us who are left behind?'

'What did your Spirit Guide say?' he said patiently.

Julia smiled. 'He's going to contact her dead husband. The spirits have promised me that she will come.'

* * *

Esther, reading Julia's letter, found it hard to believe that the rest of
The Dovecote had been as enthusiastic about her having the pottery
studio as Julia said, and yet how like Julia to talk of it as if the matter was
already decided.

'. . . As for Cassie – you know in your heart that she would love it
here. We could turn the rooms above your pottery studio into a
comfortable flat for you both. Cassie would fit in with the community –
we would get a tutor for her schooling – and she could help out by
feeding the doves, trapping snails for Freddie, collecting vegetables.
I've always believed children should pay their way. Seriously, Esther.
You would be silly to refuse. Everybody – even Joseph – agrees with
me. You say you need to be independent of other people, but you're
wrong, for I believe we are put on this earth to give help and support to
one another.'

Esther read the lines again, her thoughts dwelling briefly on the
comment 'even Joseph agrees with me'. She searched her memory for
something Joseph had said to her about it being hard to get away from
Julia. If he had meant to warn her that Julia was neurotic, did he really
now mean to encourage her to go back? Did he think she should accept
Julia's offer on the terms he had himself adopted, making use of her
generosity for the sake of producing beautiful pots?

What did it matter what any of them felt? Esther thought, and she
wrote back at once, again refusing Julia's offer.

Yet hopes of ever producing designs of her own were fast beginning
to fade, for, since she had begun showing her pot samples to buyers,
Esther had met with little success. Christopher had always done the
selling in the past and she had assumed that it was easy. She had not
been prepared for cool receptions, nor for being told all that was wrong
with her pots.

'I have "no idea of the demands of the market". They are "too
esoteric". They are "not *pretty* enough",' she told Giles Fielding one
Sunday before Christmas when they had gone to church with Cassie. 'I
feel so unworldly and naïve.'

'They've no right to treat your work like that,' he said as they entered
the church porch.

'But they've every right. And it's true. I have no idea of the demands
of the market – except that I now know that I don't want to conform to
it.'

'You couldn't make *pretty* pots if you tried,' said Giles as they found a
seat in the church. 'That's definitely not your style.'

Esther smothered a laugh and Cassie, sitting primly between them
under a large knitted beret, and with her gloved hands clasped piously,
turned to them and said, 'Mummy! You're in *church*.'

'Seriously though. Why should I expect everyone to leap for joy when
they see my work?' Esther said later as they walked back to Tamarisk
Street after the service. She watched Cassie skip ahead of them along

the pavement, her natural high spirits at last given their freedom. 'These people don't see themselves as a charity for aspiring artists, and I should have been more business-like. Do you know, I hadn't even worked out a proper costing?'

'Well, I think your pots are lovely.'

They had reached the house. Cassie had gone ahead indoors and Esther waited on the stairs for Giles to shut the front door behind them.

'They're unusual perhaps,' she acknowledged, remembering with a sense of satisfaction that George Ansfield had called them unique.

'I mean it.' Giles rested a hand on her arm and she did not move. 'Esther, it's been nearly a year since I asked you to marry me. You must know how I still feel about you.' His look was questioning and Esther's heart began to beat quickly as she felt the old pressures on her return.

She avoided his eyes. 'Yes. I know.'

'I want to look after you and Cassie.'

He had, unwittingly, given her the escape she needed. 'We don't need any looking after,' Esther said coldly. 'Surely you can see that? Or all that I'm doing – the pots, Ansfield's – counts for nothing.'

'Don't avoid what I'm saying,' Giles said harshly.

Esther was surprised by his anger. She had never seen him anything but patient and cautious. She realised, to her surprise, that she cared how he felt and that his anger had moved her.

'I don't mean I'm offering myself as a protector,' he said. 'I'm no more a charity than the shops where you show your pottery – though, my God, I feel like one of the virtues sometimes. If not Charity, then Patience. Oh yes, and the others – what is it – Faith and Hope?'

He took her arm once more and she said, 'Shh – Mrs Plowman will hear us.' But she had moved towards him instinctively, understanding his hurt and wanting to expel it. Giles bent his head and pulled her close as she raised her face to speak again.

The kiss frightened her, for it stirred old sensations of betrayal as she remembered all that she had shared with Christopher. She resisted an immediate instinct to hold Giles more closely and, stiffening in his arms, she waited for him to let her go.

'You care. I know you care,' he said fiercely.

Esther shook her head. 'I'm not sure.'

'You can't live like a nun for the rest of your life. People marry again. Christopher wouldn't have expected you to stay . . .'

She interrupted him. 'Giles, I need time.'

He nodded, ashamed because he had presumed to know a dead man's wishes.

'I promise I'll think about it.'

'Thank you,' he said. 'That's all I ask.'

That night Esther lay awake, turning over in her mind the scene with

Giles and asking herself whether she should accept him. It wouldn't be the kind of marriage she had known with Christopher, but perhaps there were marriages that could be just as fulfilling in their own way. And Giles was straightforward, decent; there would be no unexpected breaches of faith. She thought of his kiss and remembered the way Christopher had kissed her, remembered it – not in a vague way, but *exactly* the way he had kissed her: the warmth of his mouth, the touch of his face. She remembered the way a kiss had almost always led to their love-making, passion rising swiftly between them.

Esther turned her head on the pillow, felt his breath on her cheek, heard him say, Do you remember?

'You know I remember,' she whispered.

Do you still love me?

Esther lay, staring at the wall. The question seemed to swim in the darkness and she could not answer it.

Mr Swales had left Ansfield's and Esther had been working alone for some weeks in the design office when George Ansfield said to her one morning, 'I should like you to come home one day and meet my sister.'

Esther, remembering the changes she had made to Ursula Ansfield's Climbing Rose design, felt a qualm of uncertainty.

'I want you to see her. I think, then, you might understand my position a little better.'

George came into the office the next day. 'Ursula would like you to come to tea on Saturday. Is that convenient for you?'

Esther turned to him. 'Yes. But—'

'Good.' He waved a hand before she could say anything else and was gone.

Esther caught a bus to Edgbaston and walked slowly to the road where the Ansfields lived, a grander version of Larch Hill, where she had left Cassie with her grandparents for the afternoon. She approached the large gabled house, surprised to discover that she was nervous about meeting Ursula Ansfield. She imagined a pretty, ailing woman, with fine hands and face, rather like Miss Lassingham in the decorating shop.

She was right on the first point, Esther noted, having been shown upstairs by a maid into an uncomfortably warm sitting room, where a huge fire burned in the grate. Ursula Ansfield was very pale and delicately featured. But in all else she was a surprise, as George Ansfield led her towards the woman seated in a wheelchair near the fireplace. 'Esther, meet Ursula, my sister.'

Esther had not expected that his sister would be so old. She glanced from one to the other and guessed that ten or fifteen years must separate them.

Ursula held out her hand as Esther came towards her. Her illness showed in her face, in the dark-shadowed and heavy-lidded eyes, the mauve lips and the drawn, papery flesh. Esther noted the thin and hunched shoulders and the fine, but surprisingly strong hands.

'My brother has told me all about you.' Ursula turned to him. 'George, shall we have tea up here? It's so cold downstairs. Though I'm sure Esther doesn't feel the cold. She looks like an out-of-doors kind of person. Not like me, Esther,' she added, turning to her. 'I'm afraid I spend too many hours shut up here in my room.'

George bent over the wheelchair. Esther watched as he pushed it closer to the fire and wrapped a rug more firmly round his sister's knees, though the air in the room was stifling. He pulled up a chair for Esther and one for himself and they sat, making polite conversation until a maid in a starched cap and black dress brought a tray of tea and scones.

'I hear you've joined the firm to replace Swales as our assistant designer,' Ursula said when the maid had gone. 'George is quite thrilled to have found a creature with so much imaginative talent.'

Esther looked at George, surprised that he should have spoken of her in such glowing terms to his sister, remembering he had said she must tread carefully when they were altering Ursula's designs.

'Oh, yes,' Ursula laughed, a light, faltering sound that brought a spasm of pain to her face. 'My brother has an eye on the future. I shan't be able to work for much longer, Esther. I'm going stale in more senses than one. We're going to need a successor.' She glanced at her brother. '*George* is going to need a successor for me.'

'Do you like scones, Esther?' George said quickly.

'Yes, Esther, have a scone,' smiled Ursula. 'Have you a hearty appetite? I'm sure you have.' She frowned, pushing an uneaten scone around on her plate and shaking her head when her brother offered to take it away for her. 'I had an appetite once,' she said, as if talking to herself. 'I had an appetite for life.'

George, covering up for his sister's sudden withdrawal from the conversation, talked to Esther about the Climbing Rose range of tableware, trying from time to time to coax Ursula back into the discussion. 'Perhaps Esther could help with the next range of ware from the outset,' he suggested. 'You could mull over some ideas together. We'll talk about it after Christmas.'

'Just as you like,' Ursula said, without any apparent interest.

'You don't mind?' Esther could not hide her surprise.

Ursula threw her a burning look and for an instant a vitality flashed in her eyes. 'Of course I mind. I mind sitting here in a bath-chair all day. I mind someone else taking my place. I mind the fact that I can no longer summon up the energy to put things right when I know they are wrong.'

They sat in silence, then George picked up the conversation for a time and, after a while, Esther said that she must leave.

'I'm sorry. I can be very rude sometimes,' Ursula said without looking at her. 'The doctor tells me it's part of my affliction.'

'She is dying,' George said as he went with Esther downstairs to the door.

'Yes. I realise that. And I'm very sorry.'

'It's so sad, you know, to watch someone's talent fade. That more than anything. When she was suddenly condemned to life in a wheelchair, I was reluctant to admit that other things had changed besides the obvious, physical changes.' He looked at her. 'Especially when everyone else she knew took fright over her illness.'

'I'm sorry,' Esther said again, wishing she knew what else to say.

'She's very angry about her illness. I have to let her down gently. You do see . . . ?'

'I understand.'

His eyes met hers and he said gravely, 'I do apologise if Ursula has upset you.'

'Of course not,' said Esther automatically; but she felt unsettled, as if she had been – or was being used. She looked at her employer and saw the sadness in his eyes and forgave him for expecting her to help him steer the situation along an easy path. 'I've raged at Fate myself,' she said as he opened the door for her. Though there was no one there to let me down gently, Esther thought.

'After your husband died . . . ? Am I right in thinking he was killed in the war?'

'Haven't I told you?'

He shook his head. 'You've told me next to nothing about yourself, Esther. I only know that you are a widow, that you have a child, that your father is Mortimer of Mortimer's bicycles.' He smiled. 'You've been very cagey about your personal life.'

She did not answer. A widow. What dried-up, shadowy images were summoned by the word: old ladies dressed in black, ailing women like Ursula; the smell of camphor, a memory of a visit to a lace-capped aunt, of sitting on a little footstool in a red-draped parlour, the sound of hushed voices and the slow tick of a grandfather clock. When she was a child, widows had always been old, yet her own daughter would grow up, seeing nothing extraordinary about a generation of women who, in their mid-twenties, had lost husbands and lovers.

'I knew that you had an anger inside you,' George said.

'It's fading,' she said quickly. 'But I do understand a little of how Ursula feels.'

'Death seems so unjust.' He ran a hand through his hair. 'How dismal we are. The problem is – what to do about Ursula's work? You've seen how her designs have deteriorated with the illness. And you were right – her style is too pretty. It always was.'

'She's been a pretty woman.'

'Yes. She was that.' He looked at her. 'Your style is so different, Esther – I was stunned when I saw your pots. They are daring, bold. It's the way things are going. People are tired of being depressed; they want bright colours, pots that are functional, but powerful and beautiful as well.' He fell into a troubled thought. Then smiled suddenly. 'But, we must see. We shan't be so gloomy on Monday – and thank you, Esther. Thank you for coming.'

Esther puzzled over the encounter as she left the house. What had it all been about? Did Ansfield really mean her to replace his sister as the company's principal designer one day? Ursula certainly seemed to think so. Had he taken her to see Ursula as a way of saying: be patient – this is what I have in mind for you but I can't offer it to you just yet?

Esther's parents had asked her and Cassie to stay with them for a few days at Easter. They no longer pestered her to come back to live with them, and Esther found herself looking forward to a few days at the house in Larch Hill after the relative discomfort of Tamarisk Street.

Her parents had regarded her move to the design office at Ansfield's with suspicion at first, then with a growing sense of pride. Perhaps they had been wrong, her father conceded. Perhaps women could, with the right guidance – for Ansfield was clearly a responsible sort of fellow – achieve a modest level of success. Women were doing all sorts of odd things these days, even getting into Parliament.

Esther's mother had begun to show a grudging respect for Esther's independence, but it was tempered by her age-old preoccupation. 'Why don't we ask Mr Ansfield to come over to a little dinner party?' she said one day. 'We ought to get to know him.'

Esther relayed the invitation to George, confident that he would have to refuse because of Ursula, but to her surprise he seemed overwhelmed with pleasure at having been asked, and said that Ursula was going into a nursing home over Easter, to give her own nurse a brief holiday. He would be delighted to join them.

Too late to prevent it, Esther learned that her mother had invited the Fieldings to the dinner party as well.

Much later – when the party had filled the house and Esther was moving among the guests – she saw that Giles and George Ansfield had taken on the positions of rivals in her mother's eyes. Worse, they seemed to be living up to their roles. Giles was regarding George with a sour suspicion, and the two men seemed to be circling and avoiding one another.

Christopher had enjoyed this sort of intrigue, Esther remembered. He would have found the situation amusing; but she felt as if she were a prize at a spring bazaar and that everyone was speculating on the outcome. The sound of laughter and talking was too loud in the restricted space of the sitting room. The Fieldings seemed to be watching her every move. How much had Giles confided to his parents about still wanting to marry her? Esther felt a sudden wave of panic engulf her as she remembered her breakdown at the Fieldings' party. Was it all going to happen again? Suddenly she heard Cassie's voice, telling Giles about The Dovecote, saying that Julia wanted them to go and live with her. A picture of The Dovecote came into her mind and Esther felt her panic recede. She saw the green lawns and cedar trees, the barns with their workshops, and the doves fluttering about the courtyard, and a voice – Julia's? – seemed to say to her that there was nothing to fear, she could escape whenever she wanted to.

'Julia wants me to go and live at The Dovecote just to feed her doves and trap the snails,' Cassie was saying scornfully.

'That woman!' Mrs Mortimer had overheard. 'Heaven knows why you still keep in touch with her, Esther. Nor why you fill Cassie's head with all sorts of nonsense about living in a house on a cliff one day. The child really believes it. She was talking yesterday about feeding the birds and swimming in the sea. I should have thought you would have more sense.'

'Cassie knows it's only a game.'

Her mother laughed in disbelief. 'Mark my words, you're storing up trouble for yourself.'

Was it true? Esther wondered. Had she been enticing Cassie with stories into a fantasy world that would never come to anything? And was her dream of independence as a potter part of that foolish fantasy? She thought of the fact that no one had shown any interest in her work except George Ansfield. What if he really did anticipate offering her a position as his chief designer? To work on Ansfield's designs at all had been progress undreamed of when she thought of her life a year ago, but she had no illusions about it, the work at the pottery would always be on George's terms. Could she go on conforming to the needs of a mass-produced product? She thought of Julia's letters. If she went to The Dovecote she could live out her dream – her own studio, a patron, beautiful pots with her name on the base.

George Ansfield was coming towards her across the sitting room. 'I have to leave early, I'm afraid. I promised my sister I would telephone when I got home. She's not been at all well . . .'

Esther, seeing Giles glower at her across the room felt a sense of relief. At least she could relax a little, with one of them out of the way. She went with George to the door and felt almost lighthearted as she said goodnight.

Giles was with Cassie when she returned to the sitting room. He was showing her a trick with lighted matches and an empty matchbox and everyone else was smiling and laughing. Esther tried to imagine life with Giles, to picture Cassie with Giles as a father. Cassie was fond of him, it was true, but would she accept him as a stepfather and call him 'Daddy'? And, even if Cassie accepted that situation, was it what she wanted, Esther asked herself? To be a solicitor's wife with a business of her own? She imagined where they would live, pictured a replica of the house at Larch Hill, and knew instinctively that it was what Giles would expect. Would her pottery enterprise add or detract from Giles's prestige, she wondered? She realised that she had unconsciously adopted the yardstick Giles himself might use. She pictured a small factory somewhere on the edge of the city, with herself in charge and, almost at once, the image was replaced by a more seductive one – a memory of the studio at The Dovecote.

* * *

'There's a letter for you,' Cassie said when Esther reached home one evening in May.

'From Julia?'

Esther looked at the letter lying on the table as she took off her coat. It was from Denholm's, one of the Birmingham department stores. She had been showing her pots to shops and galleries for months now without success. Esther took the letter into the bedroom and put it, unopened, on the dressing table, reluctant to face another rejection. She took off her work clothes and lay on the bed in her petticoat.

There was a tap on the door, and Cassie came into the room. Esther felt a spasm of guilt, for she spent so little time with Cassie these days. She realised that her influence over her was being subtly eroded. It showed in Cassie's reluctance to talk about Heather Park, in the air of self-sufficiency with which she surrounded herself, and in her continuing preoccupation with religion.

Cassie went to the dressing table. 'You haven't opened your letter. Is it from The Dovecote?'

'No, it's not from Julia,' Esther said, studying the thin figure by the dressing table. Cassie was eleven now, soft and dark with large eyes. She was growing up. 'Perhaps we shouldn't talk so much about The Dovecote, Cassie.'

'Why?' In dismay Cassie turned to face her.

How direct children were, how difficult to distract with subterfuge. 'Because it's a long way away and we have to get along with life here, as it is now.' She beckoned to her. 'How are you liking it now at school?'

Cassie came to stand beside her, twisting the counterpane in her fingers. 'It's all right.'

'Only all right? You are happy at Heather Park?'

'Miss Collins is a good sort and so are some of the girls.'

'But . . . ?'

'But nothing,' Cassie said brightly, turning away again.

'Cassie?' Esther coaxed.

'You still haven't opened your letter.' Cassie went to the dressing table and brought the letter to her, watching Esther slit the envelope with her finger and scan it, then give a little cry of excitement. 'What does it say? What's it about?'

Esther looked at Cassie in wonder. 'It's about my pots. It says they want to act as a retail outlet – that means they want to buy them. They want to see some more. They say, when can I start production?'

'They want to place an order for three hundred assorted items of tableware, and I have absolutely no possibility of fulfilling it,' Esther told Giles the following Sunday on their way back from church.

'You'll have to rent a workshop. That was what you've always planned.'

89

'But it's all happening too quickly. I haven't raised any money. And then there's George – Mr Ansfield. I can't leave him in the lurch.'

'But you knew this might happen. You must have thought things through.'

'No,' Esther admitted in panic. 'I don't think I did. I don't think I really expected anyone would want to buy in such numbers at first.'

Giles's voice was harsh and he seemed irritated with her. 'Esther. You can't play at life for ever. People want to take you seriously – Denholm's, Ansfield's.' He gave a short laugh. 'Even me. You have to decide what it is you want.'

'Yes. I suppose you're right.' She knew they were not only talking about her pottery.

He was silent. He stared ahead at Cassie's figure, disappearing into the house. 'Look – I'll lend you the money, if it will help.'

'No. I can't. I won't be obliged—'

He interrupted her and again his voice was harsh. 'You "won't be obliged"? You *are* obliged – every way you turn. What's more, everyone's glad to oblige you. It's all very well, wanting to be independent, but you're not alone. You don't have to be alone. We care about you. We want to help.'

His words echoed Julia's letters, but Giles's intensity of feeling touched a deeper nerve in her, and Esther was moved by the memory of their long friendship, remembering how close they had once been, long before she met Christopher.

'All right – don't be obliged.' He drew in his breath slowly. 'Esther – marry me instead. We'll go into partnership, a two-fold alliance on a proper financial basis.'

Esther was silent.

'Esther? Did you hear me?'

'Yes, Giles. I heard you.'

'Well – will you?'

She shivered. A cart went past in the street. She felt a pressure descend upon her and from far away a voice seemed to be calling her again, offering her a way of escape. 'Give me a few days to think about it, please, Giles. Will you?'

He hesitated. 'I'd better not stay for lunch. I'll stay away until I hear from you.'

'I'll let you know by next weekend. Once and for all. I promise.'

He nodded and strode away.

Esther went inside and shut the door and sank back against the wall, then slid down to sit on the stairs. Did she mean it? Would she give a final yes or no to marrying him? Esther tried to search her heart. Did she love Giles? If she put aside all other considerations – their mutual friendship, Cassie's fondness for him, the convenience of marrying a man who would support her desire for independence – did she love him?

You have to decide what it is you want, Giles had said. Esther searched her heart. What was her most enduring desire? What, besides her pottery, had contributed to her rehabilitation? What did she want? To design pots for George Ansfield? A marriage of convenience? Or a chance to prove herself on her own? A voice, more persistent now, seemed to echo through her head. Come to The Dovecote. Leave them all behind.

Giles's proposal hounded her all the next morning until the factory hooter signalled the lunch-hour and she went along the corridor to George Ansfield's office. George had formed a habit of asking her to join him at lunchtimes, when they would talk over the current designs and share their sandwiches.

He did not look up at first when she knocked and walked into the office that morning, and when he did it was with a preoccupied expression. Esther ignored it, assuming that he was absorbed by something to do with the business; she sat down at the desk and offered him a sandwich and he took it. They ate in silence for a few minutes.

After a while George said, 'Esther – I have to tell you. I heard some disquieting news this morning.' There was a coolness in his expression which, Esther realised now, had been there all the time. She saw that she had displeased him in some way. She smiled, confident she could bully him out of his bad temper. 'Are you going to tell me about it?'

'Oh, I intend to.'

She laughed. 'Whatever is the matter?'

'You tell me.' He slammed down the sandwich he had been eating and, pushing back his chair, began to pace the floor. 'You tell me,' he repeated more deliberately.

Esther watched him, still convinced that the matter would be trivial, but troubled by his strange mood. George Ansfield was a plain man with few pretensions; he had no sense of snobbery, didn't care whether people called him 'jumped up' or whether they admired him for having made a mint of money. He was what he was. His life was in pots and he enjoyed what he did, making a profit, doing business, making things tick along to everyone's satisfaction. Esther realised that she liked and admired him. She did not want to see him so upset. 'Well, I will try to help if you let me know what it's all about,' she said more kindly.

'I had a phone call from Denholm's today.' His voice was unsteady. 'I heard that you have been offering them your designs.'

'That's true.'

He stared at her. 'But they are our designs. You design for Ansfield's. You have promised your pots to me.'

'I haven't promised anything.' She laughed in disbelief.

'It was understood between us. We had talked about the future. In my world that sort of agreement stands for something. You don't go behind my back and sell your designs to one of our customers. You don't, while working for me, set yourself up as a rival.'

'But I didn't.' Esther paused. 'Did I?' Had she? She saw suddenly how it must look from his point of view. 'But this is so silly,' she said. 'I never meant to upset you. And in any case,' she added angrily, '*you* hadn't promised anything either. My future here was all very vague – because of your sister . . .'

'Ursula is dying,' he said angrily. 'I mean – she's *dying*. The doctor said she can't last more than another month or two at the most.'

'Oh, George – I'm so sorry.'

He brushed aside her hand. 'I don't want you to be sorry. I want it to be over with, for my sake as well as hers. Why should she go on suffering? And why should I be forced into this dreadful position of having to wait, month after month, for her to die? How can I offer any sort of life to anyone with an invalid sister to care for?'

Esther stared at him.

'Does that sound selfish? Am I a devil?'

'I don't understand.'

'Don't you see? I love you.' He stopped pacing and took a deep breath. 'I've loved you for months – since before last Christmas. You were to become my partner. I've had it all planned.'

Esther felt her heart beat with swift anger. George had been waiting for his sister to die so that he could ask her to marry him? It was ugly – horrible. She pushed aside her sandwiches and said quietly, 'I think I had better leave.'

He came to the desk. 'No. No, Esther. We'll work something out about the designs. I'll ring Denholm's – I'll tell them it was a mistake. You were acting on our behalf when you showed them your pots.'

'But I wasn't,' she said coldly.

'Esther, you don't know how I feel about you, how I've suffered these past months.'

She stepped away from him. 'Don't. Don't come near me, Mr Ansfield, please—'

He held on to the desk and nodded, taking a grip on himself at last. 'I'm sorry. You need time to think about this.'

'No,' Esther said, picking up her things and backing towards the door. 'I don't need any time at all. I'm leaving.'

Giles took Esther's reply to his own proposal of marriage in the way she would have expected of him. Unlike George Ansfield, he made no fuss. 'I had hoped . . .' he began, and then said nothing.

They stood for a while in the Fieldings' porch in silence, their hands pushed into their coat pockets, Esther wishing she could make it easier for him.

'Well – thank you for taking the trouble to come here and tell me to my face,' Giles said at last.

'Oh, Giles. As if I didn't care about you enough at least for that.'

'No. Of course. I'm sorry.' He cleared his throat. 'Will you come in perhaps? My mother . . .'

'No. I think I'd better not.'

He nodded.

'George Ansfield proposed to me too this afternoon,' Esther said suddenly.

He stared at her in indignation. 'My God! The scoundrel!'

'I rejected him of course. And I can't work there after this. But I wish now I'd been rather more charitable towards him. He's not as cold-blooded as I made him seem.'

'Well, I suppose I shouldn't feel too badly,' Giles said with an attempt at humour. 'There's some comfort in numbers.'

She turned to him. 'Oh, Giles. Poor Giles. I do care for you. But I can't marry you. Somehow, I don't think I shall ever marry.'

'Because of Christopher,' he said miserably.

'Perhaps. Perhaps it's still too soon. What we had was perfect.' She thought of the bills, paid by Hugh and Marjorie. 'Well – almost perfect.'

'So, what will you do now – leave Birmingham?'

'I really don't know.'

Giles hesitated. 'Come and see me again, won't you – if you should decide to go to The Dovecote?'

'Oh – I don't expect I shall do that,' Esther said lightly. And yet she had thought of nothing but The Dovecote since leaving George Ansfield's office that morning. It was as if the soft murmuring cry of the doves was on the summer air. She could almost hear the rush of the sea and the wind in the trees, and a voice, very persuasive – it was there even as she walked away from Giles – reminding her that The Dovecote was the one place where she had found peace of mind, calling to her, drawing her back.

PART TWO

Chapter Six

Cassie was never to forget her first journey to The Dovecote. It was June, the air was dusty and sleepy and the haymakers were in the fields. As they neared the coast, the road ran for a few straight miles through an avenue of beech trees, and it was as if they were entering a long and airy tunnel; the light was cool and green and the drive for those two or three miles was magical.

There was a place nearby, Esther said, where primitive people had long ago come to worship and be buried; not in a Christian way, in church-going hats and gloves, but in the open air, close to the earth and the trees and to the gods of nature they held in reverence.

The branches, reaching up like sinewed grey arms to hold the canopy of leaves, evoked images of heavy, naked limbs. Cassie saw the people of old, brutal, uncivilised, echoed in the knotted shapes of the trees; and she could understand why men and women had once worshipped the gods of nature.

Minutes later and the magic was gone. The car rattled along the road and Esther said, 'Soon we shall see the sea and then we shall be there.' Cassie sensed the suppressed excitement in her mother's voice, in the tight grip of her hands on the steering wheel and in the way she glanced at everything they passed as if remembering it from long ago. At last they bowled down a hill. 'There's the cottage where I stayed a year ago,' Esther called and Cassie, turning her head quickly, saw a pretty whitewashed house beside the road. 'And there is the sea.' Ahead, in the cleft of the valley, was a triangle of blue. 'And there—' As they turned a corner of the road, Esther pulled the car to a sudden halt, drawing in her breath with a sharp intake of air. 'There, Cassie, is The Dovecote.'

Cassie saw a long garden wall that seemed to follow the road for ever. She could see the roofs and gables of some buildings, hidden behind the wall, but nothing more, and she could not hide her disappointment. Where was the beautiful, wistaria-covered house on the edge of the cliff? Where was the sound of the breakers crashing on the shore below? She peered out of the car at the jumble of red-tiled roofs. It was nothing more than a house like any other house. She couldn't even see the doves that lived in their famous home on stone pillars.

'Now, close your eyes,' Esther ordered. 'And don't open them until I tell you.'

Cassie shut her eyes in obedience. She heard her mother put the car into gear and they moved forward, rolling downhill alongside the blank brick wall, until at last, after what seemed an eternity, she felt the car come to a halt and Esther said with a bubble of gaiety in her voice, 'Now you can open your eyes again.'

Cassie looked through a pair of high, black iron gates into a courtyard, and there was the most wonderful sight she had ever seen. She scrambled out and ran to the gates, pressing her face against them. The sound of cooing filled the air, punctuated by the intermittent clatter and whir of wings as birds took off, then landed again in a flurry of movement. Doves, hundreds of them – or so it seemed to Cassie – fluttered, rested, strutted and billed and cooed on and around the peculiar house on stilts. Their feathers shone white in the low, evening sunlight. Their black eyes winked and closed. Their little beaks pecked and preened and they tucked their heads under their wings.

Esther had joined her. 'Isn't it exactly like I told you?'

'Better. Much better.' Cassie could not take her eyes from the dovecote and its fascinating occupants.

'Open the gates and I'll drive in.'

Cassie unlatched the gates, pushing them back against the wall. She climbed on to the running board as her mother drove into the courtyard to pull up near one of the garages. Meanwhile Cassie had jumped off and crossed the yard to the arched gate at one corner, and there, as Esther had described it, was the wistaria-covered house and the vast green lawn and the long terraces of flowers.

A woman, dressed in a baggy skirt and cardigan, was coming towards them from the house. She was very tall and she swung her arms as she walked – or rather strode, for she moved so quickly that no sooner had Cassie seen her by the house, it seemed, than she was looming large before her, smiling and holding out her arms. The embrace was not for Cassie, but for Esther who had joined Cassie in the gateway. 'At last!' the woman said in a low, excited voice. 'Didn't I say you would be back?'

Esther turned to Cassie and pulled her forward. 'My daughter – Cassie, this is my friend, Julia!'

Cassie held out her hand and Julia shook it, stepping aside to observe her critically, taking in the thin figure and the childish awkwardness. Cassie threw back her head to scrutinise the woman in return, and she knew at once – she had sensed it as soon as she saw the way the woman looked at her mother – that, if this was Julia, she did not like her.

Esther walked into the kitchen and it was as if nothing at all had changed. Rowena, dressed in an apron, stood at the stove; Peter sat at the table nursing a mug of tea; Freddie, scrubbing potatoes at the sink, his sleeves rolled to his elbows, turned and grinned at her. 'We knew you wouldn't be able to keep away.'

'I pictured you all, exactly like this, when I thought of you all this time.' Esther laughed, feeling a surge of affection for them. She had only known them for a short time, and yet it was as if she had come home to old friends.

'You took a year to think about it?' said Peter. 'How could you wait that long?'

'I said you'd be back. I've told everyone it's my fatal charm.' Freddie came forward to kiss her. 'My hands are wet. I've put potato water on your coat.' He picked up a towel and wiped her collar, then stepped back to look at Esther with an air of restored satisfaction.

'Are you going to finish those potatoes?' Rowena cast a quarrelsome look at her husband. She seemed to notice Cassie and her expression softened.

'This is Cassandra,' said Julia, following Rowena's gaze. She took hold of Cassie by the shoulders and propelled her towards the centre of the kitchen. 'Beloved of the sun-god Apollo, and endowed with the gift of prophecy.' She laughed as if she had said something very clever.

'My name's Cassie, not Cassandra,' Cassie said emphatically. She had no idea what Julia was talking about. 'And I haven't got a gift of prophecy. Moses was a prophet and he is in the Bible.'

'Cassandra was a bit of a clever boots, too, if I remember.' Julia raised her eyebrows. 'She had an annoying way of always being right.'

'Ah, Cassie obviously has more than a little of the Cassandra in her,' said Freddie, laughing.

Cassie smiled at him, knowing he was teasing her. She thought her mother's friends were very glamorous, like American film actors and actresses. Especially Rowena, who wore a lot of make-up and had dark, glossy hair, and Freddie, who looked like Rudolph Valentino. She felt a little in awe of Peter. He seemed very old, like her grandfather, but he had more hair and a strange accent and he wore very shabby clothes, splashed with paint like Julia's.

Rowena left the stove, smoothing her hands on her apron. 'Would you like to take off your coat and hat and let your mother settle your things in the studio flat, Cassie? Then you can come back here and help me decide what magic ingredients should go into the dinner?'

Cassie nodded and decided that she liked Rowena best so far. Freddie was obviously a tease and Peter seemed too old and silent and watchful to be an immediate ally.

'Where is Meg?' Esther asked, buoyant with happiness as she turned with Cassie to the door. The others looked at one another uneasily, and Esther noticed Peter's embarrassment, his quick glance in Julia's direction.

It was Julia who spoke first. She stood watching them all, touching her mouth restlessly with her fingers flat to her lips, a habit when she was not smoking a cigarette. She said quickly and without answering Esther's question, 'Can you manage on your own at the studio, Esther? You know the way. It's all prepared.' She brushed past her and hurried away along the corridor.

Esther looked at the others in the silence that fell around the sound of Julia's footsteps on the stairs. 'Whatever was all that about?'

Peter muttered something about Meg probably being in the garden. Freddie turned away with an exaggerated lift of his eyebrows. 'Tell you later,' mouthed Rowena.

There was no sign of Meg in the garden as they crossed the lawn again.

'Who else haven't I met?' Cassie asked, puzzling over the peculiar strain to the scene they had left in the kitchen, wondering why no one wanted to talk about Meg.

Esther looked at the barns. 'Joseph. You haven't met Joseph.' There was no sound of activity from the workshops and she saw that the doors to Joseph's workshop were closed and padlocked. In contrast, the door to the pottery studio was wide open to the evening sunshine, propped with a chunk of broken pot. Esther stepped inside and surveyed the tidy benches, the throwing wheels and the rows of clean shelves.

'It's bigger than at The Folly,' Cassie noted approvingly. If her mother was going to become a first-rate potter, she would need the right surroundings. Cassie had decided already that The Dovecote was the right setting. 'Is this where you're going to work?' She wandered between the benches, running her hand along them. 'Will you employ people, like Mr Ansfield does in Birmingham?'

'It won't be a factory,' Esther said distractedly, not really listening. She went to the stairs and climbed them slowly, pausing at the top of the flight. She had never seen inside the flat. She imagined a dark attic, packing cases stacked in corners, an attempt at comfort perhaps with rugs scattered on wooden boards, a few sticks of furniture. She opened the door and Cassie ran up the staircase after her.

Light flooded the room from two sky-lights that were propped open to the warm evening air. A second room led off the first and this too was filled with light. A cool draught brushed Esther's face. The wooden floorboards – clearly recently sanded and varnished, for they were very smooth – were partly covered by a large fringed carpet in shades of red and gold, the colours of Esther's pots. Her glance wandered over the furniture – a sofa bed, a low table, two armchairs, a dresser against the end wall.

Cassie did not know that her mother was recognising Joseph's touch in the furniture – unmistakable in the simple lines – but she too saw that there was something superior about the dresser and tables. 'Come and look at my bedroom.' She had wandered into the adjoining room and at once claimed it for her own.

Esther followed more slowly, surveying the bed and chest of drawers and a small desk and a chair that stood under the skylight; again, they were all beautifully made.

'A desk. My own desk,' Cassie cried out, bending over the table under the window and laying her cheek against its smooth surface.

'How kind of him,' Esther murmured.

100

Freddie had brought their suitcases from the car. He clattered up the stairs and stood in the doorway smiling.

Esther turned to him. 'Freddie, where is Meg?'

'She'll be in her room, painting. I'd better warn you, before you put your foot in it – she and Julia have quarrelled. Meg keeps a low profile for Peter's sake. She'll come down for dinner and be polite and normal, but Julia will pretend she's not there.'

'But why?' Esther said in dismay, perturbed by the shift in her memory of The Dovecote as a centre of love and harmony. 'What's gone wrong?'

Freddie told her how there had been a row over Meg exhibiting Peter's paintings, and that Julia had asked her to leave The Dovecote. 'Julia really got into a panic when Peter threatened to go too. She hates losing anyone. He's doing *awfully* well though – commissions left right and centre, and of course it's all Meg's doing.'

'But that's wonderful.'

'No, it's not. Julia is the one who discovered him, and she's furious with Meg for interfering.' Freddie glanced at Cassie, who was pretending not to listen as she stood on a chair to peer out of the window. He lowered his voice, 'Meg isn't the only one to have crossed Julia. I'll tell you the rest later.'

'You can see the house from here,' Cassie said, when Freddie had gone. 'And the garden, and all the way as far as the sea. There's a little stone cottage near the cliff. Is that where Joseph lives?'

The grounds, spread out below her, seemed to Cassie to be a wonderful foreign island with blue sea beyond its shores and secretive paths and groves of trees. Only one thing was missing. 'I can't see the doves.'

'You can hear them though, if you keep very quiet,' Esther said.

It was true. The soft, vibrating murmur throbbed through the evening air. It sounded faintly mournful, like the mooing of distant cattle or the sound of someone grieving.

Cassie jumped down, pulling off her coat and hat and laying them on the patchwork counterpane on the bed.

'Rowena will be waiting,' Esther said. 'Why don't you go and help her in the kitchen?'

Cassie sensed that her mother wanted to be on her own. But she did not mind. She was already clattering down the stairs. Esther began removing clothes from the suitcases and putting them away in the chest of drawers. She paused by the sloping window and watched Cassie run across the lawn. She was already at home here, Esther thought. The Dovecote was working its charm on Cassie as well. She glanced down and stroked the silken finish of the desk, moved by the fact that Joseph had furnished the flat for them. Had he made some of the pieces especially?

She glanced again from the window. The horizon shimmered in the evening sunlight; in the near distance she could see the belt of trees and shrubs that separated the garden from the cliff. She could glimpse the boundary fence and, among the gorse bushes, the cottage where Joseph lived in voluntary seclusion. She felt a strong desire to talk to him, to ask him what Freddie had meant about other people crossing Julia, to let him know she was back and thank him for the furniture.

Esther finished unpacking quickly; leaving the studio, she crossed the garden and entered the tunnelled walk leading to the cliff path. She reached the stone cottage and saw to her surprise that it was shut up like Joseph's workshop. She felt an irrational sinking of her spirits as she returned the way she had come.

Meg was walking towards her across the lawn.

'Esther! The others have only just told me you're here.' Meg embraced her with her usual slight reserve. 'I expect you're looking for Joseph.'

'His cottage and workshop are shut up. Is he away? Is he in Exeter?'

'Joseph has gone to Italy. He met some Italian woman last year – a marchesa, and she wants him to furnish a whole house. Can you imagine? An Italian villa?' Meg smiled distantly. 'Julia is horribly jealous. She'll never forgive him for this one.'

Esther laughed, swallowing her disappointment. 'Jealous of a rich Italian woman? Meg, *I* am jealous. Never mind Julia.'

'No – it's more than that. Julia is jealous of anyone who interferes with her doves. You know, of course, that Joseph is special to her – her "injured dove"? It's because he had such a bad time in the war. There was a girl. She wouldn't have anything to do with him when he came back. I sometimes wonder whether it made him hate all women. We are all Julia's little tame birds,' Meg sighed. 'And woe betide anyone who feeds us without Julia's permission or if we flutter our own wings too vigorously. That's why she's been so cross with me over Peter. We need you, Esther. We need you to help us combat the forces of tyranny that have begun to work here lately.'

Esther stifled a laugh, and was shocked as she realised that Meg was serious.

'I mean it. She's getting worse.'

'Surely you're exaggerating,' Esther murmured. She decided that the quarrel with Julia must have unhinged Meg a little. She looked older, Esther noted.

Meg looked at her in surprise. 'How can anyone exaggerate where Julia is concerned? She's an exaggeration in herself. You'd better understand now, if you're going to stay – Julia feeds off our devotion. She is vain, controlling and obsessive.'

'But I like her,' Esther protested. She turned to Meg. 'Don't you?'

Meg considered. 'Like her? I hadn't thought about it. We all love her. We all depend on her for some reason or other. But that's a different matter.'

Julia ignored Meg during the evening dinner. It was as Freddie had said: on the surface everything seemed normal and the members of the community chatted with one another and made a point of making Cassie feel at home. Peter sat next to Meg and was attentive, passing dishes to her, drawing her into conversation with Esther and Cassie. Yet, as far as Julia was concerned, Meg might as well not have been at the table.

No one mentioned Peter's pictures. Esther was longing to ask him about his recent successes; she had decided to put an end to the silly squabble between Julia and Meg by raising the subject over dinner, but now that the time had come she could not bring herself to speak about the paintings. Things had changed, she realised. The reserve Esther had first observed in Meg had become something stronger while she had been away. It could better be described as a steeliness. And Julia's face frequently expressed an air of hurt, as if she were sustaining a deep injury. Esther recalled Joseph saying that Julia needed people to be dependent on her, that she felt rejected if they strayed. Something in the extraordinary atmosphere – of a routine having been accepted by the rest of the community – something in Meg's grimness and in the set of Julia's mouth weakened Esther's resolve to shake them all up.

'So, Esther,' Julia said. 'We must make plans for your pottery. We shall visit the clay pits tomorrow and make sure they have the kind of clay you need. And then we must talk about helpers and where and how you will sell.'

'May I come with you to the clay pits?' said Cassie.

Julia turned to her with a frown of displeasure at the interruption. 'You shouldn't talk when others are talking, Cassandra. Don't you know it's not good manners?'

Cassie flushed scarlet and looked swiftly down at her plate. Esther, who always made a point of scolding Cassie in private when it was necessary, felt a flash of resentment against Julia.

'There's no need to hang your head in shame,' Julia said. 'Look me in the eye and tell me you're very sorry and you'll see that all is forgiven.'

Cassie raised her head and, still scarlet-cheeked, said, 'I'm sorry for interrupting.'

Julia leaned towards her a little and smiled gently. 'Well done. You and I shall be the best of friends at that rate. Of course you may come with us. You and I shall sit in the car and talk, while your mother sloshes about in the mud in her rubber boots.'

'What shall we talk about?' Cassie said quickly.

'We shall talk about what you have learned at your previous school and discuss the tutor we are going to employ to teach you. We shall decide together whether you should learn French and Greek and what the future holds in store for you, young Cassandra.'

Cassie frowned. 'I should rather you called me Cassie.' She hesitated, looking Julia in the eye and adding, 'If you please.' She turned to Esther and said in a low voice. 'Do I *have* to have a tutor? Can't I go to a proper school?'

Esther laid down her knife and fork. She felt as if she had been forced into an extraordinary and unprecedented impotence by the exchange between Julia and Cassie. She sensed Julia's manipulative power, remembering Meg's seriousness when she had said that Julia was becoming a tyrant. Julia's enthusiasm for organising everyone seemed all at once to be less innocent and amusing. Esther saw that – in this case at least – it was a force to be resisted from the start. 'I should prefer Cassie to go to the local high school. It's not good for a child always to be in the company of adults.'

'Nonsense. That's how I was brought up,' said Julia. 'My father and mother taught me everything I know and took me all over Europe with them. They were both brilliant individuals. I really couldn't have had a better schooling.'

Esther sensed a tension round the table as the others waited to see if she would hold her stand.

'For you, perhaps, to be taught at home was a sensible solution thirty or forty years ago. But times have changed. Besides, I know Cassie. She has spent a long time with grandparents. She's an only child without benefit of a father, and she will have the best of both worlds in going to a school outside and absorbing everything the community can teach her here. But she *needs* the company of children of her own age.' She held Julia's gaze, to let her know that the discussion was closed.

'Esther,' Julia said in a mollifying tone that contrasted oddly with the glitter – almost of hostility – in her eyes. 'Don't let's quarrel about this on your first evening.'

'I'm not quarrelling,' said Esther in surprise. She felt the tension still in the others; the sensation of being watched, at the centre of a contest, was not pleasant. She looked across the table and met Meg's glance. A ghost of a smile flickered at Meg's mouth and then was gone as she bent her head. 'We won't quarrel. You'll see,' Esther said, turning to Julia. 'How can I quarrel with you when you've been so good to us?' She saw Julia's expression relax, the hostility fade from her eyes. 'But I must insist on one thing while I'm here,' Esther added. 'I shall be the one who decides on Cassie's upbringing.'

There was a moment's silence. Esther could feel the others hold their collective breath while Julia absorbed the pronouncement. Then she saw the expression on Julia's face soften further. 'Of course. And, after all, we have all the summer to talk about it.'

'Tell me about Joseph,' Esther said, determined, having taken the upper hand, that she would break the foolish awe with which the others were treating Julia. She would talk about Joseph's good fortune in finding a client abroad. She would talk about Peter's paintings too, she thought. How feeble they all were to be so frightened of upsetting Julia over such ordinary matters.

'What do you want to know about Joseph?' Julia said coldly. She selected an orange from a bowl of fruit at the centre of the table.

Meg spoke. It was the first time she had addressed Julia directly during the meal. 'I told Esther that Joseph is in Italy.'

There was a silence, then Julia, with a thoughtful twist of her knife into the orange said, 'They used to put to death the bearers of news in Rome, I believe.'

Really, this was too ridiculous, thought Esther. Julia was behaving like a prima donna. 'I thought the Romans only put their messengers to death if the news was bad.' She smiled at Meg. 'And this was such good news, that I'm sure everyone must be really pleased for Joseph ... I couldn't help seeing his influence in the studio flat. I'm only sorry I can't thank him for furnishing it for us.'

'Isn't it lovely?' said Rowena quickly, trying to lighten the atmosphere. 'Julia asked him to choose some pieces before he went.'

'I wanted you to have the best,' Julia said. 'You and Cassie.' She turned to Esther and her eyes were full of tenderness. 'I do feel for you all, you know? I care what happens to you. Already I feel as if you and Cassie are part of my family. I love you all.' She spread her hands as if to embrace everyone at the table and the gesture, briefly, included even Meg.

'We know that,' said Rowena softly, with a swift glance at the others.

'I have unusual gifts, I know, but I'm a normal woman with normal emotions. I feel hurt when I'm rejected and angry when I'm treated badly. If I seem selfish, sometimes unwilling to share you – it's because it's I who have nurtured your talents. I *know* what is best for you. I'm afraid of entrepreneurs – people like this Italian woman – who only want beautiful things so that they can tell their friends they have paid a lot of money for fine furniture or good paintings.' She threw a look at Meg. 'And who don't care tuppence for the artist.'

'When did Joseph go?' Esther asked.

Julia turned on her a look of sad reproach. 'Esther, this kind of questioning is very painful for me.'

'I'm sorry.'

'At Christmas,' said Freddie.

Julia's eyes were moist with emotion. 'The saddest Christmas we have ever had.'

Freddie fetched Esther's boxes of pots from the railway station the next morning. Everyone came to the studio to watch and exclaim as she unpacked them. Julia surveyed the pots, her fingers nervously stroking her mouth; she said very little, but there was a light of excitement in her eyes.

'I wish you would heal this rift with Meg,' Esther said to her as she drove with Julia to the clay pits. They headed away from the coast. Julia drove, as she did everything else, with erratic enthusiasm. The dust flew from the wheels of The Dovecote's large communal Ford as they wove from bend to bend on the country lane and Cassie bounced about on the back seat.

'Meg shouldn't have taken so much upon herself,' Julia said. 'I've always been the one who directed Peter's career.'

'She cares about him as much as you do,' Esther said. 'Whatever she did, however underhand it might seem to you, she did it out of love for Peter.'

'Perhaps.'

'What other motive could she have?'

Julia looked at her. 'Don't you know? Meg resents my control. She will do anything she can to break it.'

'Isn't *that* really the reason why you have quarrelled with her?' Esther said gently. 'Because she won't do as you say?'

'She was looking for a way to challenge me. I find her difficult. I thought, when she first came here and I invited her to join The Dovecote, that she would be responsive to guidance. It's only by revealing ourselves that we can produce true art, Esther, but Meg is not sure that I will bring out of her the side she wants to reveal, and so she paints in water-colour – restrained, pretty pictures that will never amount to anything. There we are. Sometimes people disappoint me.' She looked at Esther. 'But, if it would make you happy, I shall mend the quarrel.'

'You will?'

Julia nodded. They swerved as they came to the main road. 'It's gone on long enough. And it's been very awkward communicating over the everyday household matters. I shall tell her tonight. I shall tell her we are speaking again because you wanted us to.'

Esther said she was glad, yet she sensed that the decision was not without its qualifications, that she was now in some way indebted to Julia. Her instinct seemed to be confirmed when Julia turned to her and said with a smile, 'You won't disappoint me, Esther. I know you won't. I sensed it when I first saw you. You came to us with your heart on your sleeve, demanding that we love you. Your hunger for love and healing was painful to me. It tore at my senses. If someone is grieving, my instinct is to reach out to them, to comfort them and heal. Christopher too wants to reach out to you.'

Esther felt a shock of unease. She said, 'Julia – Christopher is dead.'

'He still loves you.'

'He's dead. How can he? Besides – he wasn't honest with me. I feel as if I didn't really know him very well.' She told Julia again about the lease on The Folly, briefly, conscious of Cassie within hearing range on the back seat, and about Hugh and Marjorie's offer to go on paying the lease for her, stressing her belief in self-reliance.

'Love doesn't die because you discover people are flawed,' Julia said. 'I love all my doves. I know they're not perfect. And where is the virtue in self-reliance, if you deny others the pleasure of helping you? You still love Christopher, Esther. And he loves you and wants to guide you. Now that you've come back and I've seen your pots, I'm certain that you are heading for greatness.'

106

They drove for a while in silence.

'Are we nearly there?' Cassie said, reminding them of her presence after a while.

'Another ten minutes,' sang out Julia cheerfully. 'And then we shall watch your mother put on her boots while you and I sit in comfort and discuss the state of the world, like the doves do on the roof of the dovecote.'

'I love the doves,' Cassie said. 'They're so beautiful.'

'And so do I, Cassie,' said Julia. She smiled at Esther. 'I love them all.'

They drew up at the entrance to the clay pit. Esther walked through the mud to the site office, a determined figure in a long green coat and a hat pulled down over her ears. The workings covered a wide area, a grey landscape of mud and heaps of clay piled in the open to weather. Workers were cutting clay from the base of the steep-sided pit and carting it away in wheelbarrows.

Esther thought about what Julia had said about Christopher wanting to guide her. Julia had meant it in a figurative way of course, she reassured herself. Yet something in Julia's expression, her air of utter conviction, told Esther otherwise. She tried to recall something else that had struck her as odd, something someone had said the previous day. She remembered it as she reached the site office: Rowena had said that Julia had asked Joseph to furnish the flat before he left, but Joseph had left for Italy at Christmas, long before Esther had made the decision to live at The Dovecote. How could Julia have been so sure last autumn that she would come?

Julia watched Esther knock at the door of the office and go inside.

'It's very muddy. You wouldn't think you could make pots out of it,' Cassie remarked, seeing Julia watch her mother.

'All truly beautiful things come from modest beginnings,' Julia told her, still staring at the point where Esther had been. She turned in her seat to view Cassie. 'And now, we shall talk about your future, Cassie. How do you feel about becoming a painter?'

Cassie answered politely that she had enjoyed her painting classes at school with Miss Collins, but that this did not necessarily mean she was going to be a painter.

Cassie felt a sense of indignation when, summoned to Julia's studio a few days later, she was told that she was to have her first painting lesson. Her mother had agreed that she showed promise. Julia and Esther were of one mind, that painting was a skill to be encouraged. It was made clear to Cassie that Julia was being very generous with her time and that the hourly lesson, to follow each week, was something for which she should be grateful. Julia said she wanted to nurture her talents and draw out the artistic streak in her.

Cassie recognised a danger in Julia's generosity. She was determined to resist her nurturing from the start and, although she really did love painting, she was deliberately obtuse and clumsy during the first painting lesson. She watched Julia demonstrate how to paint, noticing that she worked in the same way as she spoke and moved, with a nervous energy and quick, dashing brush-strokes. 'The Dovecote is so beautiful that almost by itself it turns people into artists,' Julia said as she painted. 'I should know. I have lived here since I was much younger than you.'

'Before the war?' said Cassie, for whom the war seemed to provide a demarcation line between the distant past and the present.

'Of course before the war,' Julia said scornfully and with an expression that implied some doubt about her pupil's intelligence. 'When Queen Victoria was alive.' This indeed seemed to Cassie to be ancient history. 'I lived here with my parents and then with my mother until she died.'

'When did she die?' Cassie asked her curiously, finding it impossible to imagine that this tall, exotic woman had ever been a child like herself, with a mother who told her to 'go to bed' or 'stop talking nonsense'. 'Did she die in the war – like my father?'

'Thank goodness Mummy never lived to see the war,' Julia said. 'She would have thought the world had gone mad – which, of course, it had,' she added, as if forgetting that Cassie was there.

'Do you miss her?' Cassie felt an unexpected flow of pity towards Julia, trying to imagine how she would feel if her own mother had died at the same time as her father.

'I miss her and Daddy dreadfully,' Julia said with tears in her eyes. 'We all need someone to love, don't we? It's our only purpose in life. I'm sure of it. Nothing else really matters – only love.'

Cassie stared at her, considering this pronouncement and revising her opinions of Julia a little. 'Why didn't you ever get married?' she said at last. It seemed to be a logical question. People loved one another and then got married. It happened all the time in movies, she thought, remembering Mary Pickford and Douglas Fairbanks.

'I was looking after Mummy,' Julia said simply. 'And then—' She frowned, and Cassie guessed that she was thinking about someone. 'Oh, well. I've never met a man who came up to my expectations. Men are so dreadfully selfish, Cassie. They *need* us, but they take what they need and give nothing back. At least, that's how I see it. Perhaps it was different for your mother. And the war put a different complexion on everything, of course. It turned those who died into paragons.'

Cassie did not answer, reflecting on her mother's loss. She knew what a paragon was, and she supposed that her father had been one, even though he had done something to do with the lease of The Folly to make her mother disappointed with him. But Cassie was learning quickly that one didn't expect people to be perfect.

For all Julia's preaching about love and harmony and its atmosphere of tranquillity, The Dovecote was undermined by the inevitable flaws in human nature. Petty jealousies and suspicions – sometimes built on nothing at all – smouldered in the small community, and Cassie observed them all that summer.

She liked Rowena, even when she understood her failings – of which her jealousy over Freddie was only one. Rowena taught Cassie to cook and let her use her make-up and treated her like an adult instead of a child. Rowena confided in her one day that she had lost a child at birth. It was her secret tragedy that she would never have another. Cassie grieved for her and for Freddie too. She watched Freddie flirt with her mother and with the summer visitors who came to the classes at The Dovecote and saw Rowena watch him too, with a tight, peculiar fury, that broke sometimes – even when everyone was listening – into a torrent of violent accusations. But Cassie knew that Freddie and Rowena loved one another. They were one of those couples who, though they bickered constantly, would have been hopelessly miserable apart.

The same jealousy affected Meg over Peter, though with Meg, as in everything else, the notion of jealousy was hinted at, rather than demonstrated in loud bursts of anger. Meg did not take much notice of Cassie, but Cassie soon realised that there was nothing personal about her indifference; Meg didn't care much for children and simply wasn't interested. She seemed to Cassie to be like an inferior sort of schoolmistress, dull and precise; she always wore very fine silk stockings and lace blouses and wore spectacles on a chain round her neck or pushed up into her silver hair. She seemed to live around the hallway where the telephone was installed.

Meg would come upon Esther in Peter's studio sometimes, and Cassie would see her throw her mother sidelong looks, weighted with an air of suspicion because Peter was paying her too much attention; so that, after a while, growing uncomfortable, Esther would feel obliged to leave.

Cassie felt sorry for her mother because she didn't have a husband. Although Esther had made friends with the people at The Dovecote, neither Rowena nor Meg were women with whom one could make alliances; there was the barrier imposed by their jealousy of Freddie and Peter, but, more significantly, there was Julia.

Cassie soon learned that it was a mistake to confide anything to Rowena that one didn't want Julia to know. She had been helping Freddie one day in his workshed: he had noticed her interest in wood and had given her a small bowl to finish with beeswax and turpentine. Cassie told Rowena about it afterwards, enthusing about the grain, showing off her new-found wisdom about the pith of the wood running through the centre of the bowl, the importance of the seasoning, the pitfalls of using timber that was too 'green'. 'A proper little know-it-all, aren't we?' Rowena said with that touch of asperity that always crept into her voice when Cassie had been too long with one of the other members of the community instead of helping her in the kitchen.

'I'm going to work with wood when I'm older,' Cassie told her blithely.

'Julia has you for a painter,' Rowena said.

'I don't care about that. Julia can't decide things for me.'

'Can't she now?' Rowena answered with a strange expression, and Cassie felt uncomfortable. She felt a deep sense of betrayal later, when Julia said that her attention had been drawn to the fact that Cassie's talents were being 'led down unproductive alleys'. Cassie knew then that Rowena had told her about her ambition to be a woodworker.

She had learned a lesson that day, recognising that she must be wary of her mother's friends and that no one at The Dovecote made alliances against Julia, however much they might grumble about her among themselves.

After that Cassie withdrew a little into herself. There were few children in the village to play with. As the summer drew on she tended to roam the garden, the beach and the cliffs in search of her entertainment. She turned to the courtyard with its dovecote for company, rather than to the adults who inhabited her new home.

The first time Esther had seen Freddie at work alone at his lathe, she had been surprised by the dedication in him. She had imagined teapot stands, a few rolling pins, items for the tourist trade, perhaps. Instead she had found his workshop filled with craft pieces of the highest quality.

'These are very beautiful, you know,' she said one day, picking up a turned bowl, polished with beeswax to a dull sheen.

'What did you expect?' He gave her a wry smile and flicked his attention back to his work.

'Do you mind – that everyone thinks of you as the gardener?'

'Not really. Who needs a lot of fuss if you're happy about what you do? It's in here it matters.' He paused and tapped his forehead. 'Anyway, I don't look down on gardening. There's almost as much pleasure in coaxing something from the soil as there is in shaping a block of wood. Each piece of wood is a challenge. It's not the kind of work Joseph does. Joseph thinks he's a cut above. He sees the limitations in turning – the restrictions and the small range of tools – but that's what I like about it. I like puzzling out the problems and then seeing things work as you want them to.' He laughed. 'Or sometimes not.'

'Why did you leave London, Freddie?' Esther sat on a stool and watched as he started up the treadle again.

'I wanted to do something real. And Rowena thought it would be jolly, something to tell her friends about. She saw The Dovecote as a holiday retreat at first. Then she got interested in the cooking and we've stayed.' He looked at her. 'And there were other reasons.'

'You had lost your mother.'

'And a child. Rowena and I lost our only child within a few hours of the birth.' He smiled. 'Julia is a great comfort to us. But on an artistic level she's rather disappointed in Rowena because she can't make anything of her.'

'And you?' Esther said. 'What has Julia planned for you?'

'She saw my bowls at a craft exhibition when we first met. She said she could sell for me through her contacts in Europe.' He unscrewed the bowl from the headstock and examined it. 'I thought she was joking, but she wasn't. Julia has a knack. She recognises when people have talent.' He threw her another glance. 'Why else do you think she picked on you?'

'I don't know. She hadn't even seen my work when I first came here.'

'That's what I mean by a knack. She sees beyond what other people see. She understands what goes on in your head. She knew at once that you needed her. And if you open yourself to the possibilities here, she will help you, Esther. We feel frustrated by the way she bosses us about sometimes, but Julia has a lot of love to give.'

He returned the bowl to the lathe and began treadling again. 'You ought to come to one of the seances. I'm surprised Julia hasn't suggested it yet.'

Esther laughed. 'Grown men and women listening to knockings from the other side? Levitations?'

'It's not like you think.' He paused. 'And Julia's no fake. Meg and I sometimes mock, but something happens when we all get together. It's very spiritual.'

'I'd rather not,' Esther said abruptly, remembering Julia saying that Christopher wanted to reach out to her, to guide her. At a seance? Was that what she had meant? She remembered Joseph's scepticism about Julia and, glancing across the timber yard to the padlocked barn, she was sorry he had gone. She would have liked to feel there was someone at The Dovecote, besides Cassie, who was on the side of common sense.

She watched Freddie for a while longer, seeing his strong hands manipulate the blade of the gouge against the bowl. Its long wooden handle was pressed against his thigh. The lathe made a gentle soughing noise like the sea casting pebbles on the beach. His body and hands moved to a rolling rhythm and, watching his absorption and love for his work, Esther understood why Julia had invited him to The Dovecote.

Esther had been with Cassie to the beach. There were several holiday-makers on the shore. Esther could hear their distant shouts and laughter behind her as she climbed the cliff path after Cassie, who, reaching the top quickly, waved to her and disappeared. Esther continued up the path alone. The sounds from the shore made her feel isolated, a little melancholy. She halted and, looking up, saw that Julia was above her on the path. 'I thought I would walk down to meet you.' Julia waited for her to catch her up.

They went in single file at first, Julia's long-legged figure striding ahead, until, on the cliff top, they were able to walk side by side. Julia caught Esther's hand and swung it in step with their walking. 'You still think about him, don't you?' she said after a while.

Esther looked away at the sea. It was true, she had been thinking about Christopher. The sun, flecking the crests of the waves, had brought back the French coast with all the old intensity. She wondered whether it would ever fade completely, and she realised that she had accepted, if not forgiven, his deception about renting The Folly. She rationalised it, seeing now that he had done it to protect her. He knew her need for beautiful surroundings, and he had wanted her to live somewhere that was special. How could they have lived there and brought up a child without Hugh and Marjorie's help? It had been she who had been irresponsible.

'You know I can help you,' Julia said quietly as they passed Joseph's cottage and entered the tree-walk.

Esther turned to her and Julia's face was mysterious in the deep, leaf-scented shade of the trees. She felt the pressure of Julia's hand on hers and slowly she eased her own hand away. 'You have helped me so much already, by inviting us to come here, and by putting the pottery at my disposal. As soon as it's up and running I shall pay my way. I'm aware that I'm not making much of a contribution yet—'

'I mean that I can restore your inner life,' Julia interrupted. 'The studio will only be a framework, a space where the healing may take place. Anyone could do that for you.'

They walked a few paces in silence. Then Julia spoke, so quietly that Esther almost did not hear her, though Julia's voice carried inside her head. 'I can put you in touch with him.'

Esther felt her heart beat quickly and she began to tremble. Julia was not looking at her now, but walked a pace or two ahead.

'He's dead, Julia,' Esther called after her. 'The others might be able to convince themselves, but I know there's no comfort after death – except in memories.'

'I mean it,' Julia repeated. 'I can put you in touch with him.' She halted and swung round to face her, and Esther saw from her expression that she was very serious.

Did Julia really believe that she was in touch with the dead? Was she so involved with her seance performances that she had begun to believe it herself? Esther felt a chill creep at the back of her neck. 'No,' she said quietly. 'I don't think so.' She walked past Julia and into the sunlight of the lawn.

'I think you're afraid.'

'I just don't think it's a sensible thing to do.'

'Is it sensible to spend all your life grieving?'

Esther did not answer but walked away from her towards the house. Was Julia mad? she wondered, her heart still beating swiftly as she crossed the lawn. If there was a possibility that Julia was even the slightest bit crazy, how could she have contemplated bringing Cassie here? Because she had fallen in love with a pretty house in a romantic setting? Because the doves in their dovecote were calling to her. Was *she* too still a little bit crazy?

Yet, what if Julia were right? What if Christopher was in some way watching over her, guiding her? Esther thought back to the previous spring when she had first seen The Dovecote. There had seemed to be a predetermination about the way things had happened: arriving when she was at her lowest ebb and when Christopher had seemed so close to her, meeting Julia in the courtyard, Joseph's appearance at the moment when she might otherwise have drowned. It was Julia who had first suggested she had been guided to The Dovecote. By Christopher?

Joseph had been watching her through binoculars, Esther reminded herself – for she hadn't for a moment believed his denial; there had been plenty of time to see that she was in difficulties. A thought struck her and sent a shiver, almost a tremor of fear coursing through her. Was it coincidence that Joseph looked so much like her dead husband? Even she had thought it was Christopher who had swum to rescue her at first. What if . . . Esther cut off her train of thought. She told herself not to be so ridiculous.

Meg was in the hall. 'Cassie has gone to help Rowena make the dinner,' she said without looking up from the accounts book she was checking.

'Julia has suggested I go to a seance.' Esther, still trembling, cleared a space among the plimsolls and hats and sat on the bench in the hall.

Meg looked up briefly, then continued checking through the book. 'She's right. I think you should.'

'Meg – surely *you* don't believe in it?'

Meg avoided her eyes. 'Don't condemn what you don't understand.'

'But you always seem so practical and down-to-earth.'

Meg considered the statement for a moment, then she closed the book and, signalling that Esther should follow, started up the stairs to the gallery above.

Esther went along the bedroom corridor to Meg's pretty room. A desk, set out with tubes and pots and jars of brushes, was set precisely under the window, with a view across the garden to the barns. There was no other evidence of Meg's work, except for a stack of sketchbooks on the floor beside the desk. Meg went to a set of bookshelves beside the bed. Pulling out a photograph album, she sat on the bed and opened the album on her lap.

There were four or five photographs of Meg and of a prettier, younger woman. In one of the pictures the younger woman was wearing the buttoned uniform jacket and felt hat of the Red Cross, and she was smiling directly into the camera.

'My sister,' Meg said after a while, looking down at the photograph. 'She was driving an ambulance when it hit a land-mine. I've often thought how unfair it was. She had so much life before her, while I had lived most of mine. She was so keen to do her bit.' Meg closed the album slowly. 'I don't know if she really speaks to me, but when Julia contacts the spirits I feel she's there. It helps. It really does. Peter has found the seances healing too.' Meg pushed the album back into the bookshelf. 'There's something you don't know.' She turned to Esther, hesitating, then went on in a rush, 'Peter once killed a man. You must understand – he was young, they were bad times in Hungary and – oh, it was a long time ago.' She twisted her hands together in distress, and Esther remembered the violence of the doves in Peter's paintings, beginning to understand what Julia had meant when she said that Peter had found his inner self.

'Most of Peter's memories are of the dead,' Meg went on. 'Julia has talked with the spirits and Peter has found forgiveness. It's very *comforting*, Esther. The others will tell you.'

Esther shook her head, not wanting to be part of it. She remembered Joseph's cynicism about Julia's spiritualism, calling it mumbo-jumbo. 'Joseph wouldn't say it was comforting. He told me about Julia. He has bad memories too, but he has resisted Julia's seances.'

Meg glanced up with a shrewd look. 'Don't you understand, Esther? Joseph is terrified of Julia's gift.'

The dinner gong sounded downstairs and Meg stood up. She smiled sympathetically. 'It's so sad. If he would only let Julia help him, Joseph could find forgiveness too.'

Chapter Seven

In the cloying heat of a July evening, Joseph walked through the piazza of the little town; its rose-coloured walls and medieval towers echoed those of Siena not many miles distant.

When Joseph had arrived in Italy the previous winter he had told himself it was the biggest mistake of his life to have left The Dovecote. The sea crossing in the depths of December, the overland journey through Europe had brought back too many memories of bleak landscapes and of that final sea crossing in the winter of 1916 when they had brought him home, muffled in blankets and lashed to a stretcher. Nineteen years old, babbling and raving, and – when he saw the sea – terrified of drowning.

'Nerves', they had called it. 'Exhaustion.' 'Too long a spell at the Front.' July to November on the Somme had been hard on everybody, and there was nothing very exceptional about shell-shock, except that it put the fear of God into those who were still hanging by a thread to their sanity.

They had packed him off to a hospital in Devon. Everyone had been prepared to forget about him since he had no family to claim him, and then Julia – the sister and mother from his lost youth – had, out of the blue, come to see him and had taken him home to The Dovecote.

The healing process had begun. Distant memories of an idyllic Edwardian childhood – of women in frothy dresses carrying sunshades, plimsolls gritty with sand, and staying out on the beach until sunset – had joined with the roll of the sea and the beauty of The Dovecote; and, in the end, the passage of time had dragged him out of the hell of his more recent memories. The moment had come when he could take up his work again, and there was a solace to be found in wood. Only his nightmares had remained, lest he forget the horror of it and delude himself that he was whole.

The sun struck his face, throwing long shadows between the buildings. He remembered another July day and the madness of going over the top. How could anyone have believed they would make any impression on the German front line, let alone take Bapaume across that wasteland? Men had looked forward to the attack, with no idea of the hell that waited for them. Joseph looked round at the knots of people who had come out into the piazza to stroll and take the evening air. Why him – when so many had been wiped out? Sixty thousand in the first day. And then on and on, the merciless slaughter and not a flat stretch of earth anywhere, nothing but shell-holes and death.

He no longer regretted coming to Italy, he thought as he absorbed the southern heat, the sound of Italian voices, the ancient atmosphere of streets and flaking buildings that seemed to be welded to the landscape. In the streets of the small shabby town the sense of history itself seemed more important than whether the buildings were handsome – and some were distinctly unlovely. One felt that people here had come through centuries of sorrows, had known tragedies as great as his own. There was a feeling of perspective – that life combined pain and joy in its proper measure. He had not been aware before of such a sense of continuity, except when walking on the cliffs at Winmouth, observing the erosion of the land by the sea and, in a similarly philosophical mood, reflecting on the sweep of time.

He climbed the narrow streets beyond the piazza and left the town by the Firenze gate, walking a little way along the white road to the walls of the estate of the Villa Rosa. The noise of the town below him grew fainter, sounded for an instant like wounded men calling – but no, they were Italian voices, foreign, happy, squabbling, enjoying the summer evening. Here perhaps he could at last hope to forget. Joseph turned his key in the small side-gate of the wall and closed it behind him, and the sounds of the outside world faded.

The Marchesa di Malfi was sitting in the courtyard under the shade of a fig tree. She waved to him and he walked slowly along paths through the formal rose garden towards the tranquil brown walls of the villa, streaked gently with bars of light and shade.

'I have invited some people for dinner,' the marchesa said in English as soon as he was within hearing. 'I want them to see the changes you have made here.' She tapped the arm of a chair beside her, inviting him to sit down. 'If we are clever, it could lead to another commission for you. If they can afford you,' she added playfully.

For an instant Joseph was reminded of Julia. And yet Maria was nothing like Julia; she was dramatic, forceful – but in a very overt, Italian way. She was not mysterious in the way that Julia was mysterious; her enthusiasms didn't stem from an inner stillness nor any secret intensity, but were all surface. Maria was voluble, she used her hands to express her exhilaration; her beauty too was conspicuous, one didn't have to search to discover it. She made a handsome widow, and she had known many suitors, she was proud of boasting. She flirted constantly, treating him like an unsophisticated schoolboy since their first meeting in London, and Joseph, responding to her playfulness, acted up to the role because he enjoyed her company.

'They are called Luppi,' she said of the prospective dinner guests. 'They are new money. Rather vulgar. They have bought a villa to the north of Siena. It could be interesting for you to pit your wits against a little vulgarity instead of working among such romantic magnificence.' She waved a hand to indicate the Villa Rosa and gave him an ironical smile.

Joseph sat beside her and rested his feet on the plinth of a terracotta statue of a scantily clad maiden carrying an amphora. 'How do you know I might want to accept another commission here in Italy?'

Maria's face became an exaggerated mask of dejection. 'You have been unhappy in my country, Joseph? You do not think I am grateful for the way you have furnished the Villa Rosa?'

He hastened to reassure her that she couldn't have made him more welcome as her guest, nor been more gracious as a client. 'But I'm a foreigner here.' He thought of the difficulties of dealing with local carpenters and suppliers and carriers, for whom tomorrow always meant the next week or the next. His own natural indolence balked at the effort involved. 'I've been away six months. I do have a country of my own.' He realised how much he still thought of The Dovecote as home. He missed its familiarity and its Englishness. He missed Rowena cooking bacon and eggs at breakfast, English newspapers, and the convenience of his Bentley, garaged with Colin and Tim in Exeter, gathering dust – probably covered in empty whisky bottles, he thought as he remembered the last boozy night before he left England. Tim had probably sold it by now to buy more liquor.

He missed Julia, he realised that evening, listening to the Luppis and Maria jabber away in Italian. His grasp of the language was not good enough to keep up in mixed conversation. He missed the sound of English voices. He looked round the hall hung with tapestries and paintings. He missed Julia's voice, her steady reassurance, 'It's over. It was not your fault,' when he woke, like a frightened child in the night. How cavalier he had let himself become about her protection. He remembered the scene at Christmas when she had accused him of ingratitude and betrayal with a fury that had shocked the other inmates of The Dovecote. 'If only people would understand how much I have to give,' she had said to him, tears running down her face. But no one was a saint, Joseph told himself, and Julia, for all her protestations of selflessness, needed her injured doves just as much as they needed her.

He looked at Maria, remembering how she had come to his bed one night, without formality, without warning and had laughed at his very 'English' consternation. She had come to him on other occasions and she had accepted his nightmares with pity but without surprise. When he had cowered and sweated and screamed for Julia, she had held him in her arms; but her hands had not been Julia's hands and they couldn't stop his raving. He had frightened her, so that she had called for the servants to hold him until the dread had passed.

Joseph too was frightened. What if his madness returned? What if he were to wake one last time, raving in the night, and his nightmare didn't fade but gripped more closely, swallowing him in a black dread with the same inexorability as the mud had sucked down his men? Who would call for Julia then, or know that the touch of her hands could push back the blackness and draw out his pain?

117

He had offered to move out of the villa, but Maria would not hear of it, and the household had grown used to his nightmares. If he had been a murderer they would have accepted it, Joseph realised. Maria and her countrymen saw everything in black and white. Their own history was shot through with violence and war. War was horrible, but it was necessary: brutal measures *were* necessary. Maria talked about the new man, Mussolini, as if he were to become the saviour of Italy. The *Fascisti* were defending their country from Bolshevism, she said. One must look to the good of nations, not individuals.

Maria had been right about the Luppis. They were vulgar but pleasant. Signora Luppi, large, dark and noisy, wore a dress trimmed with chinchilla and a broad head-band of pearls. Signor Luppi was fat and bald and sweated profusely. He turned to Joseph and said in Italian, speaking more slowly, 'Signor Kilburn. We are forgetting. Forgive us, please. We have not seen the marchesa for many months, and we have much to tell her about the estate we are buying. So much work to do. We are enchanted with the splendid work you have completed at the Villa Rosa.' The conversation halted and the Luppis paused to reflect with reverence on the splendid dining table from which they were eating and the chairs on which they were sitting.

'We plan a visit to London in the next summer,' Signora Luppi said in broken English. 'We come to visit you. We talk. Yes? You will be in England? We have much to talk about the Villa di Sogni.'

Maria threw Joseph a knowing look of triumph.

'Yes,' he said. 'Yes, I shall be very pleased to meet you then.'

The exchange seemed to settle a question for him. Of course he would be in England the following year. The Italian summer, with its brilliant skies, its olive groves and burning heat was seductive, pleasantly soothing, like falling asleep in a warm bath; but he was rootless here – and there was always the fear at the back of his mind that he was lulling himself into a false security.

Esther had begun to put her pottery into production at The Dovecote. She promised herself that she would give the project six months. If, after that, things were not going well, if Julia's eccentricities seemed at all threatening, if Cassie was unhappy – they would pack up and return to the Midlands.

But Cassie was not unhappy. She had never, since living at The Folly, known such bliss, for during that long summer The Dovecote was even more idyllic for a child than The Folly had been. There was the sea, for a start. Cassie would get up early in the morning, before the holiday-makers arrived in their cars and charabancs to descend on the beach. She roamed the shore before breakfast, searching for ship-wrecked treasures, dead men's bones, messages in brandy bottles, and found washed-up crabs and coloured shells and long strings of seaweed that popped under her plimsolls. She played sometimes with the children of the summer visitors, but in a dispassionate way, quickly

118

growing bored with their limited pleasures of building sandcastles and jumping in and out of oncoming waves.

The dead crabs and spent carcasses of small creatures, discovered on Cassie's expeditions through the garden and on the cliffs, became subjects for elaborate burial ceremonies – perhaps in memory of the dead mouse at The Folly. Or perhaps she was influenced by a curiosity about Julia's seances. For Cassie had learned through Violet that Julia knew how to get in touch with the dead.

Cassie had been aware for some time that Julia opened The Dovecote once a month to people who had been bereaved. She had watched the small groups of outsiders assemble in the courtyard. One could never be sure where they had all come from, but there were always young women among the group, who, Cassie supposed, had lost lovers or husbands in the war. They stood, quietly talking, the murmur of their voices mingling with the cooing of the doves in the dovecote. They waited patiently until Violet – a regular helper at the seances – was sent to usher the visitors across the lawn and into the house.

Cassie had sensed Esther's unease about this aspect of the life of The Dovecote. At first she had not understood that anything strange was going on, and had assumed that the bereaved visitors had arrived for a lecture; Julia ran various classes and lectures – on philosophy, art and homeopathy – all through the summer.

The room for the seance meetings was on the second floor, directly beneath Julia's studio. The door was always kept locked and Cassie had never been inside. Esther kept away too. 'Julia helps people,' she had said on one of the few occasions when Cassie had asked her about the room. 'She uses the meetings to heal their minds.' It was not strictly true, of course, but Esther had convinced herself that Julia's part in the seances was that of a well-meaning if misguided performer: the foray into spiritualism had perhaps started as an experiment and – having discovered that people believed all the artifice, moreover that they benefited in some way from the experience – Julia had expanded her repertoire. Where was the harm in letting people derive comfort from believing they could find their lost loved ones again?

So Esther had persuaded herself of Julia's intrinsic goodness, and she believed that Cassie remained in ignorance about the true nature of the monthly meetings. But she had reckoned without Violet, and Violet's desire to spread the gospel that Julia was a wonderful woman.

Cassie was neither surprised nor shocked, when Violet confided in her about Julia's 'gift', but she knew instinctively that it was something that couldn't be discussed with her mother. 'The spirits talk to her,' Violet said. 'Julia goes into trance and receives messages from her Spirit Guide. It's all very wonderful, but only Julia has the psychic faculty and can see over to the other side, "Where there is no such thing as death."' Violet rolled back her eyes, either to prove the difficulties of seeing into this other dimension, or to imitate the state of trance.

Death had gained an importance for Cassie since burying the mouse at The Folly. She knew, in later years, that those corpses festering on the Western Front would have been infinitely more repellent than anything she could then have imagined, but, in the moment when she had looked at the shrivelled body of the mouse and made the connection with a human corpse, she had been aware, for the first time, that death was something to be feared.

As with religion, such preoccupations had lingered on after moving to The Dovecote. The various ideas had fused; the deaths of her father and of her uncle and all those many thousands who had perished with them in the war became linked with the blood of Christ and with Julia's transportation into the realm of the spirits.

Cassie would find dead voles or sometimes the stiffened body of a bird and perform secret burial ceremonies under the cedar trees, whose branches made an effective church roof. She wrapped a long white and gold evening frock that Rowena had given her for dressing up round her shoulders and intoned prayers she had composed, linked more to the gods of nature than established religion. Sometimes she would stay there, under the shelter of the cedar branches, kneeling on the dry floor of her 'church', invoking the spirit of a dead vole or sparrow, until it was almost dark. At night she would go to the window of her bedroom and open it wide, to lean on the roof and listen to the night sounds, hoping to hear the disembodied squeak of a creature pass by her as it ascended to heaven.

Rowena always feared for Cassie when she wandered off alone or sought company among the visitors' children. She believed in the white slave trade, having seen Valentino in *The Sheik*, and she told fearsome stories, from the time when she and Freddie had lived in London, about young girls who were ripe for kidnapping and who had mysteriously disappeared.

Esther too had begun to recognise that Cassie was growing up. Little by little, as the summer progressed, she realised that she and Cassie were growing apart, but she was too preoccupied with the pottery to try to halt the process of separation. She had begun work on some new designs that summer, based on the flame pattern of the pots she had fired at The Folly, though less crudely executed. Julia would sometimes visit the studio and sit by the window, watching Esther at the wheel or at her design table.

Sometimes, if it was raining, Cassie would sit at the top of the stair and watch her mother as well. The hum of the wheel and the movement of Esther's hands as pots mushroomed from them was hypnotic. Julia always ignored her, concentrating on Esther, as if she were fascinated by her and by her work; she wandered among the rows of finished pots, examining them and commenting on her favourites. Sometimes, if Esther was drawing, Julia would pause at her shoulder and watch her work out a design, and she would suggest a line or a particular colour and then wander off again. Julia was clever, Cassie noted, in that she never got in the way; she never made her presence seem like an intrusion, and she seemed to know the right time to offer praise or to disappear.

'We shall find an outlet in London,' Julia said one day to Esther. 'I shall take you soon to see some people I know. They have contacts at the Galeries Lafayette in Paris.'

'I already have a customer in Birmingham,' Esther told her. 'I've written again to Denholm's the department store. They're prepared to wait until I can recruit enough workers here to produce the number of pots they want.'

Julia pulled a face. 'Birmingham! Why talk of Birmingham when we can reach London and Paris? Your creations should be exclusive, Esther. Small runs of prestigious ware – that's what we should be aiming for.'

'All the same,' Esther said firmly. 'It's the reason why I left poor George Ansfield and I'm not going to let it slip away.'

Julia shrugged. 'Just as you like.' The phrase had become a habitual one; it meant nothing of the sort, Esther realised. It meant, as always, just as Julia liked, after she had used her powers of persuasion. Julia carried people along with her passionate enthusiasms. It wasn't a selfish enthusiasm – she spoke the truth when she said she cared about people – yet there was a hard core at the centre of Julia that troubled Esther a little, for, once set on a goal for one of her doves, Julia would follow it with a singleminded ruthlessness.

Some days later, Julia talked of London and Paris casually, as if she had almost forgotten about Denholm's; she pointed out the very logical reasons for dropping the department store – it was too close to the Midlands potteries, the outlet wasn't challenging enough. But Esther had her own streak of inflexibility, and she had resolved that she would follow up the interest from Denholm's, if only to prove that Julia couldn't influence her. She was growing used to Julia's ways, she told herself. She wasn't in awe of her like the rest of Julia's doves.

Cassie was not in awe of Julia either, though Rowena and Violet were always telling her she ought to be, because Julia was clever and good and because she loved everyone at The Dovecote so much. Cassie detested the painting classes. She remembered with a perverse sense of nostalgia the art classes at Heather Park. Julia often talked about love while they painted. 'Can you feel the love inside yourself, Cassie?' she would say. 'Not just your love for your mother. Feel the love that people here can give to you. Feel the love you have for them. Feel your love for the whole world. You must build yourself out of love.'

Cassie did not take much notice, although – as when her grand-parents had preached against chewing gum and jazz music – she pretended to take it all in. Cassie had already decided that Julia was peculiar, so nothing she said or did surprised her; and yet, Julia made her uneasy. Cassie would watch her, and wonder about Julia's psychic faculties, and her contact with the other side, where there was no such thing as death. She never felt comfortable alone in Julia's company, and she often wondered what Julia wanted from her mother. To help her recover from her grief? To help her become as good a potter as it was possible for her to be? Why did everyone always assume that Julia's motives were of the highest?

Julia had wanted her to have a tutor, but Cassie was relieved when, after the summer was over, her mother had her own way over her schooling. Esther would drive her each day in the Morris, or sometimes Freddie or Rowena, in The Dovecote's heavy old Ford, as far as the next town where Cassie began the autumn term at the local high school.

The weeks passed, and Esther began training Rowena to help her in the pottery. Later, when they made more pots, Violet too would help out; and, later still, she planned to recruit workers from the village; she would bring employment into the area.

After a while Esther was glad she and Cassie did not live with the others in the house. She began to understand why Joseph had preserved his privacy in his cottage on the edge of the cliff. She looked forward to the trip to London with Julia, for there was a claustrophobia in the small community after the summer visitors had gone. The rift between Meg and Julia had almost healed, but there were other small irritations. Rowena's jealousy of Freddie embraced everyone, and she would sulk for a whole evening if he talked too long with Esther or Meg. Esther too became infected by the atmosphere of petty jealousies; she began to resent it if Cassie stayed with Rowena and Freddie when she came home from school, instead of coming straight to the studio: it seemed to Esther that, because they had no children of their own, they were smothering Cassie with their attention in the way her parents had done. Esther shut herself in the pottery studio when she found herself overwhelmed by The Dovecote. By the time she joined the others again at breakfast or dinner, everyone had usually forgotten what they had squabbled about.

When Cassie wanted to escape she could run down to the beach or the village; there were new friends at school; and at The Dovecote she had a wide choice of places to hide. The garden provided numerous 'dens' – there were tunnels and nests in the long grasses, and a tree-house inside an old hedge, where she invented tables and chairs out of tree-stumps. And there was her church under the cedar trees, where she performed her rituals and burial ceremonies and chanted prayers for the dead. Its huge branches swept low to the ground, completely concealing her from the house; it was quiet and gloomy inside and when the wind blew it made a comfortable roaring sound high above her head.

Of all the secret places at The Dovecote, Cassie liked the courtyard with its house on stone pillars the best. She had never lost the sense of fascination she had felt when she first saw the doves. She could happily spend an hour or more, sprawled in a large wheelbarrow under the shelter of one of the barns. She would take a cushion and one of her books and lie there, listening to the murmur of the doves, watching them strut and doze and preen in the sunlight of the courtyard. She liked the way they walked, and, as they walked, jerked their heads backwards and forwards like mechanical toys. Cassie thought at those moments that her life was about as perfect as it could be. She believed that there was no greater happiness ... And then, one Saturday in October, Joseph came back.

The day Joseph drove into the courtyard Esther and Julia had gone to London, leaving Cassie in Meg and Rowena's care. He had not told anyone he was coming.

From her usual hiding place in the wheelbarrow, Cassie watched the stranger climb from the dark green Bentley and look about him at the courtyard with a speculative glance. She sensed he had been there before and knew his way around, but, though her mother had spoken of Joseph, Cassie did not at first know who he was.

She watched him, hugging her invisibility to herself, and decided that the stranger was an exotic creature, even allowing for the unusual nature of The Dovecote. He was very suntanned. His eyes were dark-fringed and gentle, his nose and mouth and chin were well defined, though not harsh, and a half-smile hovered in his expression. His light-coloured suit and hat were expensive and his manner relaxed as he strolled closer to the dovecote. He stood there for a long time with his head tipped back, watching the doves. The longer he stood, without moving, the more Cassie's position in the shelter of the barn seemed to be one of snooping, and at length she plucked up the courage to scramble from the wheelbarrow and walk out across the yard.

'May I show you to the house?' she said, as she had been taught to say when escorting visitors to their classes. 'I'm afraid Julia's not here today. She's in London with my mother. But I can fetch Peter or Freddie, if you like.'

Joseph stared at Cassie with a look of amusement and then said, 'And who, in God's name, are you?'

'Cassie,' she said indignantly.

Joseph frowned and then a look of enlightenment stole across his face. 'Esther's Cassie?'

'Esther's my mother. She's in London—'

'Yes, so you told me. Why are they in London?'

'For my mother to sell her pots for Paris,' Cassie said – she had not yet, at eleven, learned discretion.

Joseph regarded her again for some seconds. 'So, she came back,' he said to himself.

'Do you know my mother?' Cassie asked.

He nodded. Then he held out his hand. 'Well, Cassie. I'm Joseph. I have come back too. And I am very pleased to meet you.'

Chapter Eight

'Everyone wants to meet you,' Julia had said.

But do I want to meet everyone? Esther wondered as they left the revolving doors of the hotel and, ducking under the hotel porter's umbrella, ran to the waiting taxi. It was their third soirée in three days of visiting, of exhibitions and lunching and dining with potential customers.

'Lady Bowers is a good patron of the arts. She could be useful to us in the future. She's terribly influential and an old friend,' Julia said as she flung herself back into the seat of the taxi.

Esther looked out of the window at the rain streaming outside. The street-lamps made pools of light on the pavements, the house and hotel windows glowed with a cosy seduction, turning the motor cars and carts and carriages into dark silhouettes against the buildings. Esther would have given anything to have stayed at the hotel and put up her feet that evening, or to have been back at her flat with Cassie at The Dovecote, listening to the rain on the skylight and sketching out her designs – the designs and samples assembled in her hotel room that they had not yet shown to anyone since they had come to London.

She looked at Julia. 'Is there any point in all this?'

'Whatever do you mean?'

'I mean we seem to have done nothing but wine, dine and listen to some of the most awful bores in London since we arrived.'

'How ungrateful you are, darling.' Julia's mouth twitched in a smile and she pulled the collar of her evening cape round her neck in a gesture of mock high dudgeon. 'I have a wide network of friends, all of whom must be visited.'

'I'm not talking about your friends. But some of the hangers-on – oh, you know what I mean.' Esther smiled too. Julia's enjoyment of everything was infectious, in spite of her own disagreeable mood. It was as if Julia had become a different person since they had arrived in London. She flitted here and there with a vitality that left Esther exhausted. She seemed to be relishing everything – the leaving of cards and gifts of flowers and chocolates and dressing up each evening. She looked happy and charming and fashionable and her dark eyes flashed with exhilaration. She was as far removed from the paint-stained woman in a cardigan who ruled The Dovecote as a bird of paradise was from a dove.

Esther turned to the window. 'I really should have stuck with my own plan to show the new drawings first to Denholm's.'

'Birmingham is too provincial. And too much interested in the ugly utility ware from potteries like your Mr Ansfield's.'

'Utility needn't be ugly,' Esther said. It was a maxim she would come to adopt with more vigour. But for now it stemmed only from a mild resistance to Julia and a suspicion that she and Julia did not have the same goal in mind on this trip to London in search of buyers.

'I've told you – we have to aim at a more exclusive market, Esther,' Julia said. 'People are more than willing to pay for style.'

'I haven't noticed we have aimed ourselves at any market at all. All we do is eat and make idle talk.'

Julia tutted. 'All in good time. We are preparing the ground.'

The cab halted outside a hotel and they climbed out and entered the foyer where an attendant slid their outdoor clothes from their shoulders and whisked them away. Esther followed Julia along highly polished floors, under glittering chandeliers and past potted palms, and she felt the hotel's softly padded luxury steal around her. She glanced again at Julia, gliding ahead, tall and angular in an ankle-length dress of gold lace and chiffon that shimmered as she moved; her black hair was clamped to her head by a circular head-band set with stones, worn low over her brow; long strings of beads were strung from her neck and across her bare shoulders and they swung and rattled as she walked. Julia turned and flashed a gleeful smile at her. It was then, as Esther observed the light in Julia's intense dark eyes and her aristocratic, almost foreign looks, that it occurred to her that Julia really was beautiful. She marvelled a little at this apparent metamorphosis. Was it real or imagined? Was it only the effect of the elegant clothes and sumptuous surroundings, or had Julia subtly changed? She remembered something Julia had said when they had embarked on a buying spree on their first afternoon in London. 'Develop a reputation for eccentricity if you can, Esther. It gives one a kind of freedom with people, and anything goes.' It was the sort of thing Christopher used to say. They had returned to their hotel, laden with dress- and hat-boxes, and Julia had laughed and chatted and Esther had felt like a girl again, remembering Marjorie's extravagant trips to Paris when they had seen *Sheherazade* and pretended to be crazy about Nijinsky. Christopher had been with her then.

Perhaps that was what accounted for her poor humour this evening, Esther thought, for London, like Paris, had been special. She remembered the tea dances, the Café Royal and dinner at the Carlton after the theatre. It seemed so unnatural to relax and enjoy herself when she was not on Christopher's arm, when he wasn't seated opposite her at dinner, when she couldn't talk to him and say look at this or that, and wasn't this fun?

Influenced by memories of *Sheherazade*, Esther had bought an evening dress of cream silk, low at the neck, with wide sleeves decorated with Eastern motifs and an embroidered cummerbund. The skirt brushed her calves as she followed Julia along the gleaming floor of the vestibule to a pair of carved mahogany doors.

Julia waited for her. 'You look divine. They'll all love you,' she whispered as the hotel attendant flung the doors wide and they entered a lounge.

The air was filled with a gaggle of conversation, like the sound of distant flocks of geese, punctuated by the occasional bay of male laughter. A number of people in evening dress, women in shawls decorated with bright flowers and with combs or feathers in their hair, sat around on low sofas. A piano was playing at the far end of the room and a brief silence fell as Julia and Esther entered, making the melody from the piano more noticeable. The lull was followed by a murmur of appreciation; it ran round the room; a number of those who were seated rose, applauding, to greet them. Esther, constantly surprised by the vast number of Julia's London acquaintances and the affection in which she was held among her circle, watched as Julia embraced first one and then another of the guests.

'Now. I shall introduce you to Lady Bowers,' Julia said, steering Esther through the crowd. Everyone began to move towards a dining room, beyond the tinkling piano and a short flight of stairs, where tables were laid with gleaming cutlery, and Julia led the way to a central table.

Lady Bowers, a boisterous woman of fifty or more, was evidently the attraction of the evening. Esther's rising spirits sank a little as she realised that they were to join her party. She turned from the woman's effusive, 'So, you are to be Julia's new great hope,' with a murmur of deprecation as Julia touched her shoulder and drew her closer to the table. A man stood beside his chair, waiting patiently to be introduced. He was small and very neat with a tiny beard and close-cropped hair.

'Gerard Vaudoyer,' Julia said, taking Esther's elbow firmly in a grip clearly meant to indicate that this was to be more than any routine introduction. She had positioned them in such a way that, when the party was seated, it would be natural for Esther to sit beside the Frenchman. 'Gerard and his wife are old family friends,' Julia said. 'Gerard is a buyer for Galeries Lafayette in Paris.'

'Your wife isn't here this evening?' Esther said, when they were seated and the dinner had begun.

'Alas. Monique, my dear wife, is of a delicate disposition,' Gerard Vaudoyer said. 'She finds evening parties too exhausting.' He smiled. 'You will meet her. We shall have luncheon together tomorrow, Esther. May I be presumptuous and call you Esther? And you must call me Gerard. I feel I know you so well. Julia has talked about you on the telephone. We shall lunch with Monique at our apartment tomorrow, after you have shown me your designs.'

Esther glanced at Julia who, seated on Gerard Vaudoyer's left hand, was apparently deep in conversation with Lady Bowers. Julia glanced up briefly and, meeting Esther's gaze, gave the briefest nod of assent. So, everything was being carefully orchestrated, thought Esther. It occurred to her that she had been very naïve to have imagined there was no plan to their visit, for when did Julia not work to a strategy?

'We lost our only son in the war, Esther,' Gerard Vaudoyer said. 'My wife has not been well since his death. It's the same for everyone who suffered. We have a terrible legacy of sorrow in our hearts.' He turned to Julia, who had been listening, and he took her hand. 'Our dear friend has helped us to get over his death. There are the charlatans, and there are people – wonderful people like Julia. She helps others to express their loss.'

'It's only when we accept our sorrow that we can begin to live again,' Julia said, and it seemed to Esther that she had directed the remark at her. 'So many people resist facing their hurt. They try to forget, thinking that by forgetting they will heal themselves. But death isn't an end; it's only a transformation. The spirit that inhabits our physical body goes on to another dimension with all its experience and love. Surely that is a great comfort to those of us who have lost dear ones!' She spoke with fervour and her eyes held Esther's.

Gerard nodded. 'It is true. We must remember them. We must never forget them.'

Lady Bowers, who had not been listening to Julia's impassioned speech, leaned across the table to speak to Esther, her feathered head-dress bobbing energetically. 'Tell me, my dear. How can such a beautiful young woman, with such fine hands, bear to spend all day making pots and putting those hands into clay?'

'Clay is a wonderful substance,' Esther said, relieved to change the subject. 'It's so malleable, so surprising always. You can't tell by looking at the raw material how much life is there. You have to touch it, feel it, get to know it, and then you can make almost anything from it you want.' She heard echoes of Christopher's teaching. The texture of the clay must relate to the finished form. Know it intimately, Esther. First and foremost, visualise the form. Since she had returned to The Dovecote, Christopher's ideas and opinions had seemed to become important again, so that the dominance of the finished shape overshadowed her when she worked at the wheel, and words like nobility and strength ran constantly through her head. She had begun to feel less confident about colour and glazes as she worked on the ideas she had first generated at The Folly, when she had painted and fired every one of Christopher's pots in a fury of self-assertion. Now that her anger was spent she had to override a feeling that she should return to the way she used to work with Christopher.

Lady Bowers nodded wisely at Julia. 'Julia has a wonderful reputation for creating artists out of the air.' She looked at Esther with her head-feathers tilted at a drunken angle, then said to Julia, 'Tell me. Is Joseph still with you?'

Julia frowned. 'I thought everyone knew. Joseph deserted me and went to Italy.'

Lady Bowers said with an air of disappointment and resignation,

'Think of that! To Italy! Well – I'm sorry. He was good.'

'And where will you go, Esther, when you are famous?' said Gerard Vaudoyer gently.

'Esther would not be so ungrateful as to leave me,' Julia said sharply. 'Men are unreliable. I've always found that. Women have more loyalty.'

Esther said nothing, unable to make sense of her own disquiet.

Julia released a slow sigh of satisfaction as she sank back into the taxi seat and they headed towards their hotel. 'I think that went very well. Don't you?'

'Yes. I like Gerard Vaudoyer. I take back all I said about wasting time.' She looked at Julia shrewdly. 'You're very clever, Julia.'

'I wasn't talking about Gerard.' Julia's eyes flashed in the semi-darkness of the taxi. 'I meant Lady Bowers. Her appetite has been whetted. She'll tell all her friends about my protégée being taken up by Galeries Lafayette. She can't bear to be the last to have something special, and she's going to want an exclusive preview of your designs once she's certain your pottery is going to Paris – and it will be. Gerard won't be able to resist them.'

Esther felt Julia's excitement in the confined space of the taxi. It was a game to her, she thought. No, it was more than that, for Julia was in deadly earnest. Esther felt a strange mixture of admiration and resentment, for she saw that she – like Vaudoyer and Lady Bowers – was being manipulated by Julia. It was resentment that prompted her to say, 'I should like to go alone tomorrow to show Gerard my designs.' She felt rather than saw Julia's change of mood in the darkness. 'You've done so much already – preparing the ground,' Esther continued quickly. 'But I have to be really sure of his reaction to my designs. And if – as you say – he won't be able to resist them, there's really no need for you to be there.'

'You're right,' Julia said, adding, as if the idea had been her own, 'I shall do some visiting, spread the word a little. And then I shall go to see dear Monique in time to meet you and Gerard for luncheon.' Julia laughed suddenly, an infectious, bubbling sound. 'Aren't you thrilled, Esther? Don't you feel we're moving forward swiftly?'

Esther said that she was thrilled, and yet she still could not share Julia's excitement. She felt as if she was being carried along on a tide of enthusiasm, but isolated from it, as if she were taking part in a performance. All the correct directions and props and scenery were in place, yet none of what was happening was of her own making. She realised, for the first time since leaving Birmingham, how far she had removed herself from all her former notions of independence.

Esther watched Gerard Vaudoyer look through her portfolio of designs and let her glance roam the mahogany-panelled office with its ground-glass windows, heavy curtains and buttoned leather chaise-longue on which she sat with more of her designs spread about her. She flicked her glance back to the Frenchman as he examined the finished pieces of pottery on his desk. Esther was glad Julia was not with her. Here, at least, she could judge Vaudoyer's opinion for herself. He turned the pages of the portfolio reflectively and then at last removed his spectacles.

'I am very impressed. They are inspired – full of life and colour. They look to the future. That is necessary. Don't you think?'

'You were right when you said yesterday that one must not forget the past,' Esther said. 'But we must also move on. We must be positive about the future.'

He nodded slowly. 'These designs – they are very assertive.' He looked at her. 'Forgive my asking, but is that Julia's influence?'

Esther looked at him in surprise and not a little indignation. She remembered George Ansfield's honest reaction to her designs, when he had called them unique. George hadn't suggested that they were a product of anyone else's creative talent and she had been grateful.

'Forgive me,' Gerard Vaudoyer said again, seeing Esther's dismay. 'Julia is so forceful – a wonderful person but somehow overwhelming. You seem so unlike the turbulent nature of your pottery . . . Restrained, perhaps, as if there were a heaviness on your heart?'

Esther went to the desk and took the book of designs from him. 'I thought Julia would have told you. I lost my husband in the war.'

'Ah.'

'It doesn't hurt any more – not really – but coming to London, remembering Paris – we had such a wonderful time in Paris – it brings it all back.' Esther looked at him earnestly. 'Will we ever get over the war, do you think?'

'As nations? Yours and mine?'

'Oh, I imagine our respective governments will manage to paper over what happened,' Esther said. 'They'll turn it into some glorious piece of history. But I was talking about the rest of us who lived through it. I have a feeling we will never quite recover.' Esther went to the window. She stood for a moment, then turned, a slight figure, oddly vulnerable, Vaudoyer reflected.

'How exactly has Julia helped you?' Esther said suddenly.

Vaudoyer, surprised, said, 'My wife and I have gained great comfort from Julia's gifts as a spirit healer. My wife found it extremely difficult to accept the death of our son – like so many, his body was never found. Monique hoped against hope for so long, but Julia, through her healing powers, was able to take away her pain. She has persuaded her that it is harmful to Marcel's spirit to wish that he were still alive.' He looked at Esther and said sadly, 'Our son *is* dead.'

He beckoned her back to the desk. 'Come. We are here to talk about your designs and they are splendid.' He took the book from her again. 'I shall select the ones I think will best suit the Galeries and let you know my decision before you leave London at the end of the week. But now

130

let us go home to join Monique and Julia for lunch.'

Monique Vaudoyer seemed robust rather than delicate, Esther thought as she watched their hostess eat lobster and salad and talk energetically between mouthfuls.

'We always feel at home when we come to London,' Monique told her. 'England is our second home, of course. We have the two houses, and Gerard spends almost as much time here as he does in France. And I come with him, because we cannot bear to be parted. Is that not so, Gerard?'

Her husband confirmed this amiably. 'We are happy anywhere, so long as we are together.'

'And always, when we are here, we try to see our darling Julia.' Monique placed her hand on Julia's arm with a little sigh of appreciation.

Julia smiled. 'And I'm always so very happy to see you too, Monique.'

'We talk about the old days, when we were all little children, when Julia used to come to visit with her mother and father when they were touring Europe. They were such happy times. We had a grand house – a château – bigger than this entire apartment block, Esther.' Monique paused looking round the palatial dining room and uttered a more positive sigh. 'Such happy times.' She leaned closer towards Julia with a confiding air. 'Julia – will you do something for us before you go? You know what it is I am asking?'

'Oh, Monique—' Julia murmured, glancing swiftly at Esther.

'Please—' Monique coaxed. 'It would mean so much to us. We miss him so.'

Julia hesitated and, still looking at Esther, seemed to come to a decision. 'Very well. But it will have to be the glass.'

A shock ran through Esther as she realised that Monique was asking Julia to hold a seance. She prayed the subject would be forgotten, and, indeed, it was not mentioned again until the meal was over and they had moved into the adjoining room. They sat, Esther beside Gerard Vaudoyer, Monique and Julia opposite them, while a servant poured coffee into gold-banded cups. Esther stared at the table holding the coffee cups and saucers: it was circular and had an inlaid ebony edge and its surface was like polished silk. 'This is Joseph's work,' she said in surprise, stroking the table and looking up with sudden pleasure. The manservant made the long, silent trek across deep-piled carpets to disappear and close the dining-room doors behind him.

'Ah, Joseph,' said Monique. 'Such a beautiful young man. So sad . . .' But Esther could not ask her what was sad; for Monique had risen and was making her way to a display case by the far wall of the room. 'It is time,' she called, and bent to search in the cupboard of fine cut-glass and porcelain. 'Esther – you too will join hands with us?' Esther, who until then had begun to believe the matter of the seance really was forgotten, was about to protest that she would do no such thing, when she caught Julia's warning glance.

Gerard went to help his wife search for a glass and Julia moved swiftly to sit beside Esther. 'You *must* stay,' she said fiercely.

'But I can't. I don't believe in any of it.'

'Can you honestly say that to her? Can you shatter Monique's faith like that?'

'I'm sure it won't make any difference,' Esther hissed.

'And I'm sure it will. I've progressed so far with her, I won't have you spoil it, Esther.' Julia's eyes burned with passion.

'Will this be suitable?' Gerard called from the other end of the room, holding up a goblet.

'A tumbler,' Julia said. 'I prefer a tumbler.'

'I'd really rather not stay,' Esther said in a low voice, making a move to stand. 'I'll find my way back to the hotel.'

Julia caught her arm and held it tightly. 'If you don't believe, where's the harm in it? You're not afraid?'

'No. Of course not.'

'Then help me – for Monique's sake.'

There was a note almost of pleading in Julia's voice. Esther hesitated a moment too long; Monique was returning with the glass tumbler. Gerard, drawing the curtains slowly at each window, called, 'Now, Esther, you will understand a little why we are so indebted to Julia.' He returned, smiling gently, and removed the tray of coffee cups from the polished table.

Esther saw that she could not leave. To go now would mean making a scene, would offend Julia and upset the Vaudoyers, who were their hosts. She would besides perhaps ruin the scheme for selling her pots in Paris, prepared by Julia on her behalf. Esther remained where she was and watched Monique bring a candlestick and set it on a small table beside one of the sofas. Gerard drew the final pair of curtains with a heavy swish of sound, like a breath extinguishing the daylight, then lit the candle.

They sat in the flickering candlelight and Julia pulled a small pack of cards from her bag and began to set them out in a circle around the ring of ebony inlay at the edge of the table. Each card was marked with a letter of the alphabet. The table could have been made for them, Esther thought, for they fitted exactly.

Having laid out the cards, Julia turned the tumbler upside down and set it, silently and very precisely, at the centre of the table before placing her hands in her lap and folding them. 'First we shall meditate,' she said in a low voice.

Esther waited, her thoughts blank, an unreasoning panic making her heart beat painfully against her ribs. Why had she agreed to stay? Why on earth should she want to help Monique, who, she had decided at the outset, was a silly and self-centred woman?

'Place your finger on the glass,' Julia said in a calm and soothing tone.

As if, by staying, Esther had renounced her own free will, she lifted her hand from her lap, moved it to the table with Gerard and Monique, and placed her forefinger on the base of the tumbler.

'If there is anyone there, make yourself known to us,' Julia said, in the same quiet tone as before, adding her own finger to the glass.

Why hadn't she left at once? Esther asked herself again. Why had she let Julia persuade her, when she knew it was all so much hocus-pocus? How could someone like Gerard believe it – or was he only going through the charade because of his silly wife? How could anyone think they could bring back their son by pulling the curtains and lighting a candle? And what of Julia? Esther glanced sideways at Julia, whose eyes were closed, whose long, angular face was shadowed by the candle and no longer looked beautiful, but sphinx-like, peculiar. Did Julia really believe that what she was doing could 'help' people like the Vaudoyers?

Julia spoke again. 'If you are there, make yourself known to us.'

The glass began to move with a determination that made Esther jump as her finger travelled with it. Having reached a card it swung back across the table to spell out the word 'Y – E – S'.

'We wish to contact Marcel Vaudoyer. Is he there?' Julia said, and her voice was now very light and clear.

Esther felt the glass jerk beneath her hand and again it spelled yes.

'Ah – Marcel,' sighed Monique. 'May I speak with him?'

'Tell me what you wish to say,' Julia said gently.

'Tell him we miss him dearly but we hope he is happy.'

Julia spoke. 'Marcel? Do you hear the voice of your mother?'

The glass was still. The room was very quiet and Esther again felt a rising panic. How could Julia do this to them? The Vaudoyers were her friends. They trusted her. The glass began to move, slowly at first, then more rapidly as it spelled out, letter by letter, the words, '*Maman je suis content*', and then was still.

Monique released a sigh. 'My son. He is happy. Does he remember us still?' As she spoke the glass again began its journey across the table. '*Oui maman . . . Toujours.*'

'Are your friends there with you?'

'*Oui*,' responded the glass.

'Then I am happy,' Monique said, and she fell back against the sofa in an attitude of exhaustion.

'Gerard, have you any words for your son?' asked Julia in a low, calm voice.

Gerard shook his head. He spoke for the first time, clearing his throat. 'Tell him only that I love him.'

The glass trembled, then moved to spell one word, '*Papa*'.

Esther, despite her scepticism, despite her anger at being forced to witness the bizarre performance, felt her eyes prick with tears as the Vaudoyers fell silent.

'Is there anyone else who would like to contact us?' Julia said after a while.

The silence deepened. Suddenly the glass moved again to spell out 'Y – E – S'.

Esther felt the darkness of the room surround her. The light from the candle seemed very intense as with great speed the glass sped across the table, spelling each letter with a purpose that seemed almost savage. Esther closed her eyes after the first few letters, tears squeezing from them. She waited until the sound of the glass sliding across the table was over.

'Christopher?' said Monique. 'Who is Christopher?'

'My husband.' Esther took her hand from the glass. 'Stop it. Stop this now.'

The Vaudoyers were looking at her in hurt dismay, and Monique said reproachfully, 'Esther, *chérie*. You must trust Julia. We are all a little frightened at first.'

'Are you frightened, Esther?' said Julia.

Esther looked at her and shook her head. 'No, but I want you to stop this before you regret what you're doing. You've gone far enough.'

'But Julia is doing nothing,' said Monique, looking puzzled. 'Julia is only the vehicle. Trust her, as we do. Tell her, Julia, how it is.'

'I promise you, no harm will come of this.' Julia was looking at Esther intently.

Esther put her finger back on the glass and stared back at her in defiance. 'Very well. I shall trust you. No more messages – not from Christopher.'

'Don't you wish to ask him anything?' prompted Monique.

Esther shook her head.

Julia closed her eyes and said clearly, her head thrown back, 'Esther does not wish to make contact. Has anyone else a message for us?'

Again the glass began to move. Esther watched, feeling powerless as it spelled the word '*love*', then '*peace*' and finally '*trust*' before it was still. Esther removed her hand. She looked at Julia, relieved that at last they could stop the charade, wanting to ask her, Why? Why did you do that to me?

Julia's eyes were still closed. Her head was tipped back, her expression in the candlelight was trance-like, almost one of rapture, and Esther was reminded of the Rossetti painting at The Dovecote. Julia's breathing had become heavy, sonorous, as if she were asleep, then suddenly she began to speak and her voice was deep, commanding, quite unlike her own: 'Let go, Esther. I'm happy here. It makes me sad to see you mourn for me.'

Esther listened in horror. Did Julia suppose that she would think that Christopher was speaking to her?

'I've been watching over your work and I am pleased with it,' the awful parody of a man's voice continued. 'You're doing well. I remember how well we worked together, Esther. We can still work together if you will let me help you. Trust Julia above everyone. She is your friend.' Julia fell silent. She remained with her head thrown back.

Her breath came unevenly for several seconds more; then, as if waking from a deep sleep, she gave a shuddering sigh and her head fell forward. At last she raised it slowly and, looking about her, said in a hoarse whisper, 'May I have some water?'

Gerard left the sofa and was drawing back the curtains. Monique, blowing out the candle, picked up the glass from the table and called to him, 'Fetch Julia some water.'

Esther, who had withdrawn into the corner of the sofa during the last moments of Julia's performance, sat with her arms wrapped about her and her legs drawn under her, but it was not until Julia had been given the glass of water that the others noticed that she was trembling violently.

Monique sat beside her and put her arms around her. 'My poor Esther. It is always a strain the first time. Hard to believe, but so wonderful, don't you think?'

Esther shook her head and could not speak. Her heart was pounding, an ice-cold wave of nausea swept her spine and forehead and she was sure that at any moment she was going to faint.

Gerard brought her a glass of brandy and she drank it down, holding the glass in both hands with trembling fingers.

Julia stood and slowly gathered up the cards. 'We should return to our hotel, I think. Esther needs to rest and so do I.'

Esther said nothing in the taxi as they drove to their hotel. She still felt icy cold. She did not speak when they entered the hotel and she asked for her key at the desk without looking at Julia. She left her in the foyer and, without waiting for the lift, ran up the stairs to her room. Only then, with a deepening rage against Julia, did Esther allow the tears to flow and she flung herself down on the bed.

She had been alone for some ten or fifteen minutes when she heard a gentle knocking at the door. Esther went into the bathroom where she ran the tap and splashed water on her burning eyes and face before she returned to the bedroom and opened the door. Julia came into the room, and Esther turned away again to the bathroom to cool her wrists under a stream of cold water.

'Darling Esther, are you all right? Are you angry with me?'

Esther looked at her in amazement. Did she really not understand how she felt?

Julia's face was pale, as if from fatigue, and her expression was one of puzzlement mixed with hurt. 'Are you angry?' she repeated.

Esther dried her hands. One question pounded through her head. Why had Julia done it? The only charitable explanation was that she had believed it would help her in some way. The sound of the water still running into the basin was the only sound in the room. She turned off the tap and pushed past Julia into the bedroom. 'How could you do that?' she said at last. 'Do you think I was taken in, like the Vaudoyers, by that pathetic performance? Do you really think I believed that

135

saintly well-wisher was Christopher? You knew nothing about him. How *dare* you impersonate him!'

'There was no impersonation,' Julia said calmly.

Esther shook her head in disbelief. 'Either you're mad, or evil, Julia. And, at the moment, I don't know which.'

'I assure you, I did nothing.' Julia went to the window and, folding her arms, stared down at the street. 'I mean it. I'm only a medium through which the spirits speak.' After a moment she turned and her eyes were troubled, her mouth trembled a little. 'Esther, I wouldn't harm you for the world. I never asked for this gift of mine. I never wanted to be different. Whatever happened at the Vaudoyers – and I don't know what happened beyond the moving of the glass – I promise you, I did nothing consciously to hurt you.' She came towards her. 'But if Christopher spoke, you should listen to him. The spirits always know what's best for us—'

'Get out!' Esther shouted. She picked up the nearest thing to hand, a heavy glass ashtray.

Julia looked at her sadly. 'You don't really hate me, Esther. You know I'm your friend.'

'Get out,' Esther repeated more deliberately.

Julia was about to speak again, then she reached out a hand and, taking the ashtray from Esther, set it on the dressing table and, with a regretful smile, left the room.

Esther, still tense with anger, packed her suitcase swiftly and left the hotel without telling Julia that she was going. She returned to Dorset by the evening train and, arriving at the station, telephoned The Dovecote.

Meg answered. 'Esther. Where are you?'

'At the railway station. Julia is still in London. Meg, do you think someone could come to meet me?'

She remained on the station platform, alternately pacing up and down and sitting on one of the benches close to the waiting room. It was a cold evening for October, but she did not go inside the waiting room; she felt a need to breathe deep draughts of the night air.

Her anger was fading. She felt drained and very tired, and she was weakening in her conviction that Julia had meant some evil in what she had done. Perhaps Julia was not so much evil, nor even mad, as merely stupid and misguided.

In the end she was always disappointed in people, Esther realised. She built them up in her mind, expecting them to conform to some sort of excellence of character, or performance, or of artistic integrity – she thought of Christopher – but most people fell short of perfection: some were merely doing their best.

She remembered her first encounter with Julia and the flow of welcome from The Dovecote. One thing was sure. She couldn't stay there after this. She and Cassie would leave the next day; she would

136

pack up her pots, abandon her plans and return at once to the Midlands.

A motor car swept into the station yard and its lights swept the railings. Esther walked towards it expectantly, then realised that it was not The Dovecote's Ford. A man climbed from the car and walked towards the platform. Esther watched him with a mild curiosity at first, then with a growing interest as she noted that the car was a Bentley and recognised, in the darkness, a familiarity in the man's outline.

'Joseph!'

She began to run. As she reached him she fell against him with a gasp of relief – half sob, half laughter – and he held her.

'What on earth's happened? Where's Julia?'

Esther stepped away from him, dazed by the violence of her reaction to him, yet the feeling of relief that had flooded through her when she had recognised him did not fade. 'Oh, heavens – I'm sorry.'

He picked up her suitcase. 'You'd better tell me about it in the car.'

'I can't believe you're here,' she said as they walked towards the Bentley. 'Are you real?'

'Of course I'm real.'

'You'd be surprised,' she said. 'You just might be one of Julia's apparitions.'

He opened the car door for her and swung her case into the boot, then paused. 'You surely haven't been drawn into that?'

She did not answer but climbed into the passenger seat. 'Oh—' She released a groan of frustration. 'I feel so angry.'

He sat beside her and she smiled at him and let her head fall back against the inside of the car hood, feeling her tiredness lift. She knew that it wasn't true – she didn't feel angry, she felt extraordinarily calm. 'At least, I *was* angry,' she corrected.

'Do you want to tell me?'

'Not now. Later. Tell me what you've been doing. When did you get back? Have you made a name for yourself in Italy?'

'I got back to England three days ago. I don't think they will miss me very much.'

'Italy! How wonderful,' Esther said, as he pulled out from the yard. She settled herself in her seat, enjoying the luxury of being driven. 'Did you have the Bentley with you?'

'I left it with some people in Exeter. In any case, the marchesa had a chauffeur.'

'And have you furnished the entire villa to her satisfaction?'

'I think so. She's recommending me to all her friends in Siena and Florence.'

'That sounds familiar,' Esther said, thinking again of Julia. She released her breath in a sigh. 'Oh, how nice it is to be back in the realms of sanity. What did you think of Italy? Did you become acclimatised? Did you jabber away like the natives and eat Italian food – all that pasta?' She turned to him. 'You look very well on it.'

'The food was excellent.'

137

Joseph had forgotten how deeply he had been attracted to Esther, and it came as a shock to discover that he still was. He recalled the day he had first seen her, eighteen months ago, half drowned, recovering from a nervous collapse and very beautiful. She seemed different, more confident and relaxed, in spite of the way she had thrown herself into his arms when she recognised him. He wondered what had happened in London. Was Julia finding her new dove more difficult than she had expected?

'Your daughter is rather like you,' he said.

'You've met Cassie. I hope she's been behaving herself.'

'As much as any lively eleven-year-old. We've been getting on well.' He hesitated. 'I hope you don't object.'

'Why should I object?'

Joseph recognised his slip. Why *should* anyone mind? Because he was a liability? Because he had violent dreams and was not right in the head? He shrugged. 'One gets used to a general feeling of possessiveness at The Dovecote. It hangs over everyone – Rowena and Freddie, Meg and Peter. It's almost a form of curse.'

'So, why did you come back?'

'I've asked myself that, of course.'

'Is there an answer?'

Was there? Had his dependency on Julia made him return, or was it the magic of the place itself, the fact that The Dovecote was the only place where he had worked for a sustained period, before Italy, with any real sense of peace?

'Frankly, I don't know why,' he said. 'And, as far as I can gather, Julia is even more of a tyrant than ever.'

Esther was silent. 'Do you think Julia's motive is always one of love?' she said after a while.

He did not answer her question. 'What happened? Do you want to tell me about it?'

Esther told him how Julia had persuaded her to stay to the seance at the Vaudoyers' apartment, how the cards had spelled out a message from their son Marcel and from Christopher and how Julia had begun to speak with 'Christopher's' voice.

'It was as if she'd gone into a hypnotic trance – but it was horrible. It certainly wasn't Christopher. Julia told me afterwards that she didn't know what had happened. I was so upset I didn't believe her, but now I'm not so sure.'

'Going into trance is part of a medium's repertoire,' he said. 'It's a sort of self-hypnosis. I don't think they always remember what happens.'

'Does she do it at The Dovecote?'

'I don't know about the seances. I told you. I keep well away.' His profile in the semi-darkness was without expression, and Esther remembered that Meg had said that Joseph was afraid of Julia's gift.

'But there is something you're keeping from me – to do with Julia?'

They had reached Winmouth. He drove up the hill and turned into the courtyard, switching off the engine before he answered. 'Yes. There is something.'

'Do you want to tell me?'

He did not answer. How could he tell her? Julia was my mistress. I submitted to her healing. I was a raving lunatic and she brought me home and took care of me. So that now, to all intents and purposes, I seem no different from the rest of you. I can even go to Italy and, for a while, pretend I don't need Julia any more. He leaned across her and opened the door. 'Some other time.'

He carried her cases to the studio and up the stairs. Esther switched on the light and looked around the flat, aware that Joseph was watching her from the doorway. 'By the way. Cassie has persuaded me to a picnic tomorrow on the headland,' he said. 'Is that all right? Will you come too?'

Esther turned to look at him, remembering her decision to leave The Dovecote the next day and go back to the Midlands. She realised that, since meeting Joseph, she had put aside all thoughts of returning to Birmingham. 'Yes. I'd love to come.'

He smiled. 'Goodnight, then.'

'Goodnight, Joseph. Thank you. That's the second time you've come to my rescue.'

She went over to the main house before she unpacked, crossing the lawn in the darkness. She could hear the faint dragging sound of the sea on the shore and saw a light through the trees and thought of Joseph alone in his cottage. She went upstairs, through the house to the bedroom corridor, and to the room where Cassie was sleeping. She opened the door quietly and tiptoed to the bed. Cassie stirred and turned over. 'Mummy?'

'Shhh.' Esther bent to kiss her. 'Yes, I'm home.'

'I wanted to sleep at the studio when I knew you were coming tonight, but Rowena wouldn't let me stay there on my own. Did Joseph fetch you in the Bentley?'

'Yes. It was very kind of him.'

Cassie turned over. 'I like Joseph. Ever so. He's my best friend. We're going for a picnic tomorrow.'

Chapter Nine

Joseph sat on the grass on the cliff top and studied Esther as she watched Cassie gather blueberries. Her hair, under a large velvet beret, was blown back by the wind that had whipped her cheeks to a healthy glow. Her face was in profile.

She must be over thirty, he reminded himself – at least six or seven years older than he was – and yet she looked as vulnerable as Cassie. His heart gave a lurch as she turned suddenly to look at him, as if she were conscious that he had been watching her.

'It's really too cold for a picnic,' she laughed. 'Not like Italy. Do you miss the heat?'

'It was not too warm in winter, but yes, there are some things about Italy I miss.' The ancient landscape, the slow pace of life and the vitality of the people. He even missed Maria a little. 'It was very useful for me. An education. I gained an awful lot in experience from working there.'

'Not to mention the enhancement of your reputation.'

'That too, of course.'

'Which is more than can be said for me. I doubt Gerard Vaudoyer will want my designs when he learns I've disappeared.'

'You'll find other customers.'

'Yes. I shall follow up my own contacts in Birmingham.'

'Julia won't like that.'

'Julia will have to put up with it. She's not my keeper.'

'You're not the tame dove she expected. Julia needs to have complete control. I did once warn you. It's very important to her.'

'Hence the seances and the healing.'

Joseph felt a twinge of disloyalty, remembering the nights when Julia had stayed with him, held him, saying, *Hush. It was not your fault*, and the nights in Italy when it had been Julia he had cried out for and had wanted to come to his bed. He frowned and changed the subject. 'Will you stay at The Dovecote?'

Esther looked away, narrowing her eyes against the wind. 'I don't know. I don't know if I can trust Julia after what happened – and, in any case, she may not forgive me for running off. I was all set to leave last night. I didn't think I could bear to go on living here.' She looked down at her hands and plucked at the short grass. 'Who knows? She might even ask me to go.'

'It would be a pity, just when you've got your workshop into production.'

She looked at him. 'Yes. It would be a pity.'

Cassie came running back, her hands stained purple from the berries. 'May I look through the binoculars? I've seen a kittiwake.'

'I've been telling her how to recognise the seabirds,' Joseph said.

'I'm impressed.'

'Things look ever so close,' Cassie said. 'Nobody else at The Dovecote has binoculars. I've asked Freddie and Peter.'

'Then take good care of them,' Esther called as Cassie wandered along the path with the binoculars to her face. Esther remembered seeing them hang in Joseph's cottage, recalled the flash of their reflection when she was swimming and her certainty that he had lied to her. 'Are they very powerful?'

'Powerful enough,' Joseph said.

'You never owned up to seeing me swimming. Did it embarrass you?'

He looked at her. He had forgotten. 'Do you mean the day I saw you from the cliff path?'

'Yes,' she said evenly. 'I accused you of spying on me from the garden and you denied it.'

'That's because I didn't see you from the garden.'

Esther felt herself begin to blush. 'I saw the reflection of the sun off your binoculars.'

He stood and his face was hidden from her, so that she could not search his expression. 'Shall we go?' he said. 'It's getting cold.'

Esther packed up the picnic basket, annoyed that he should still persist with his denial and feeling rather foolish. She wondered whether, after all, she could have been mistaken – and knew she had not been.

They spent several afternoons together in the days that followed, forced into walks and picnics by Cassie, but drawn in any case to one another's company by a mutual sense of attraction. One late afternoon, at the end of the week of Esther's return, they had descended the cliff path with Cassie who wanted to collect pebbles. It was cold, and the waves crashed with a brutal determination to wear away the shore. The autumn was turning to winter.

Cassie, in gloves and hat and coat, walked ahead with a bucket, halting every now and then to bend and pick out a shell or select a pebble that took her fancy from among all the others.

'I wonder when Julia will come home from London?' Esther said. She was aware that the past few days had formed an island of calm in her mind after the experience in London. She bent down to pick up a shell. 'I feel a little bit nervous. I don't know what I shall say to her.'

'Pretend nothing happened. That seems to be the best way with Julia.'

Esther looked at him, twisting the shell in her hand: it was bleached clean, very white with a faint blush of pink inside. 'You understand her quite well, don't you?'

'Not as well as she understands me.'

'She once said something odd. She said that she had been close to your nightmares.'

'Yes.' He scuffed the pebbles with his foot and walked ahead a little.

Esther followed more slowly.

'What did she mean?' she said as he paused to wait for her.

He did not look at her but out at the sea. His face was expressionless. 'I really don't know. Julia likes to be enigmatic.'

'But she must have meant something.'

He turned and his eyes were cold with distaste. 'Why do women always want to know the ins and outs of everything? If you're going to badger and nose about like Rowena . . .'

Esther held up her hands. 'I'm sorry.' She looked down at the shell in her hand. 'Here. Truce.' She handed him the shell as a peace offering.

He hesitated, then took it with a dismissive laugh. They walked on, but she knew that he was still angry and, only when they caught up with Cassie, did his mood change again.

Cassie showed them the pebbles she had collected. 'I'm going to give you one to keep,' she told Joseph. 'You can choose the one you like best.' Esther wandered away to the edge of the sea, where the waves ebbed, dragging sand and pebbles with them, leaving a pale line of froth on the shore. She glanced up the beach where Joseph and Cassie had spread the collection of pebbles on the flat rock Esther had found when she first came there; they crouched beside the rock and their heads were close together. Esther felt a swirl of emotion like the pull of the receding tide. It was as if these two people – her daughter, and the man who looked so like her dead husband and had plucked her from the sea – were precious to her and, at the same time, a threat, though she could not say why that should be. She turned again to the water. The dying sun glittered off the edges of the waves as far as she could see.

Why had Joseph been so angry about his nightmares? Esther had sensed a moodiness in him, even on their first meeting. She remembered that Meg had accused him of being temperamental, and Julia had leaped to his defence. He *must* have watched her that day, she told herself. Why else had he been so evasive about it? But on the other hand, why should he lie to her? She glanced up at the cliff face. The house and its gardens were invisible from the beach, but the shrubs and gorse on the cliff top were in view. She could even see the corner of Joseph's cottage, though it blended with the rocks and the bushes so that no one would have noticed it if they had not known it was there. Esther let her glance travel along the cliff top to the point where the footpath made its winding descent. She drew in her breath as she saw a woman emerge from the scrub at the top of the cliff. The figure paused and waved to her, and she waved back reluctantly and, leaving the shoreline, returned to Cassie and Joseph. She watched them for a moment longer, then said, 'I've seen Julia. She's back.'

143

Cassie scooped her pebbles into the bucket. 'I'll show her my collection.' She picked up the bucket and began to run along the beach.

Joseph stood up. 'Are you afraid?' He scanned Esther's face and his expression was sympathetic. His angry mood had gone.

'Afraid?' It seemed a strange word to use, and yet, Esther realised that when she had seen Julia she had felt a lurch of something close to fear. 'Yes. I suppose I am, in a way.'

They turned to walk along the beach and, as they did so, Joseph caught her hand and held it briefly, giving it a light squeeze. 'Don't be. She feeds on that as much as she feeds on our devotion.'

Julia was waiting for them on the path. Cassie was already running ahead again, on her way back to the house, bored with showing the uninterested Julia her bucket of pebbles.

'Esther!' Julia embraced her then turned to Joseph. She touched his cheek with the palm of her hand in a half-proprietary, half-reproachful gesture. 'Meg told me you were back. I'm glad. I've been so anxious about you all this time. I can't tell you how glad I am.'

'It's good to be back,' Joseph said stiffly.

'And have you started work again? I've been telephoning people for you. I knew you would want to start work straight away. We should consider another trip to London...' She walked ahead with Joseph when they reached the gate into the grounds, ignoring Esther who followed behind more slowly.

Esther could not establish Julia's mood. Was she trying to pretend that nothing had happened because she was ashamed of her behaviour at the seance? Was she angry because Esther had left London? Was she even ignoring her a little to punish her? But no, Julia turned suddenly and beckoned. Releasing her hand from Joseph's elbow, she put an arm round Esther's waist. 'Gerard liked your pots. I'll tell you which ones he chose tomorrow. We'll go through them together and work out a plan of campaign. You'll be pleased, I think. There are some of your own favourites among them. I made sure of that.'

They walked together through the trees and, as Joseph left them to go to his workshop, Esther briefly caught his eye. He did not smile. His face had that lack of expression she had noticed before; she now recognised it as a way of hiding his thoughts from her.

'I couldn't help noticing a closeness between you and Joseph,' Julia said the next day as they sorted through Esther's designs in her studio. 'Rowena tells me you've been walking out with him almost every day.'

'Is there anything curious about that?'

'Not in itself.' Julia turned the pages of Esther's design book, as if concentrating on their subject matter. She looked up. 'Take care, Esther, won't you? I've known Joseph longer than you have. He's not always as easy-going as he seems.' She hesitated. 'You can't always count on him.'

144

'None of us is quite what we seem. I discovered that in London,' said Esther, suddenly tired of pretending. Julia had said nothing at all about the seance. She had behaved the previous evening as if nothing had happened between them in London. Something needed to be said: either Julia should apologise or they should agree to forget the incident.

'You're talking about my contact with Christopher.'

'If that's what you want to call it,' Esther said angrily.

'It upset you. And I'm more sorry than I can say.' Julia reached across the table and took Esther's hand with a look of compassion. 'Truly. I only want to help. I have a gift. Don't you think we should use the gifts that are given to us? You have your talent for creating your wonderful designs for your pots. I have a talent for healing people's minds.'

'Did you heal Joseph? Is that why he comes back here?'

'Yes.'

'How?'

Julia let go of her hand and returned her attention to the designs. 'When I knew how much he had suffered I brought him here – to the place of his childhood where he would feel secure. He was desperate to forget his experience in the war.'

'And through you he was able to?'

'The nightmares became less frequent. That was the best I could do for him, considering the limited way in which he would let me help him – by laying on hands and taking away a little of his pain. If only he would come to a seance, I know I could progress further. But, like you, he's afraid.'

I'm not afraid, Esther wanted to insist, but, recalling the scene with the Vaudoyers and Julia's strange, trance-like state that day, she was no longer sure that it was true.

'If Joseph were to meet the spirits of those who died,' Julia continued, 'if he would open himself to the forgiveness that is waiting for him, he would be cured of his nightmares. But he's afraid of facing them.' She looked at Esther earnestly. 'He has plenty to fear. Being a soldier – seeing men die – was very difficult for him.'

Esther remembered Christopher coming home on leave, and she thought of how little he had said about his experiences. She recalled his lifetime technique of shrugging off anything unpleasant. But what if you did not have that capacity, what if the horror was so great that it would not be expelled?

'Be careful,' Julia repeated. 'Don't get too close to Joseph. He needs to distance himself. The rest of my doves have learned to respect his distance. I helped him with my healing energy to deal with the nightmares, to keep them at bay, but Joseph will never be –' she hesitated, selecting the most appropriate word – 'he will never be reliable. That's why I was so afraid for him when he went to Italy. He hadn't been on a ship since the war. He hadn't been away from The Dovecote for any length of time.'

145

'You talk about him as if he were mentally unsound,' Esther said angrily.

Julia looked at her in surprise, as if Esther had missed the whole point of what she had been saying. 'Yes. And so he is.'

Esther went for a walk on the cliffs after studying the designs Gerard Vaudoyer had selected. She wanted to blow away the unpleasant feeling Julia's words had left in her mind. She thought of Joseph's anger when she had probed too far about his nightmares. Why couldn't he simply have told her that Julia had helped him with her healing, by talking to him and laying on hands? Did he think of that too as so much mumbo-jumbo? She glanced down at the rocks on the shore and asked herself again why he should have lied about the day he had come to her rescue. Could she have been mistaken about seeing someone in the garden, or had he been spying on her?

Esther swung away from the headland and walked across the fields to the cottage she had rented the first time she came to Winmouth. The house was closed and shuttered; there were no visitors in November. She walked through the overgrown garden and peered through the cracks in the shutters; she could see nothing and she did not know now what she had wanted to find. Had she expected to recapture some of the tranquillity she had known when she first came here? It was gone, she realised. She had not felt at peace since her visit to London with Julia.

She walked back across the fields, intending to return to The Dovecote by the cliff path. She paused at the point where the house lay spread below her, its gardens and outbuildings visible and Joseph's cottage too. She could see that the door of the cottage stood open. As she looked she noticed a movement, a flash of light among the trees. Esther halted, puzzled, then, with a shiver of apprehension, realised that she was again being watched. She began to hurry, running along the path, keeping her eye on the spot where she had seen the watcher until the path plunged among gorse bushes. She came upon Joseph's cottage and saw that the entrance door was closed. Esther walked up to the door and banged the iron knocker. There was no response and she turned the handle.

The room was as she remembered from the first time she had seen it – a table, chair and the bed with its patchwork blanket and, above the bed, slung from a hook on the wall, Joseph's binoculars. She walked to the fireplace and looked around running her hand along the narrow mantelshelf slowly. Had Joseph been watching her? Had he seen her hurry down the path and quickly returned the binoculars to their hook on the wall?

She turned to leave and, glancing at the mantelshelf, saw the pebble Cassie had given to Joseph and, next to it, a seashell. It was the one she had given him – a peace offering.

Esther left the cottage and walked through the tunnel of trees, where the sound of the sea joined with the wind in the trees to create a sense of

146

agitated unease. A figure stepped from the lawn as she reached the end of the tree-walk and Esther halted in fright. 'Julia! How you startled me.'

'The others said you'd gone for a walk. I hoped we could talk some more about your designs for Gerard.'

'Can't it wait? I wanted to talk to Joseph.'

A look of vexation crossed Julia's face. 'This is important, Esther.'

'So is this,' Esther said grimly as she left Julia and crossed the lawn.

She entered the workshop and saw Joseph at his design table. She stood in front of him, leaning her hands on the table. 'Where were you a moment ago?'

He looked up with an expression of bewilderment. 'Here, of course.'

She looked at the sheaves of paper in front of him and the pen in his hand. The work he was doing could easily have been taken up only seconds earlier.

'You weren't spying on me?'

He put down his pen and leaned back in his chair. 'What are you talking about?'

'Someone was spying on me through binoculars.' She felt slightly deflated.

For a second a look of uncertainty clouded his face, then he smiled. 'What, again?' he said lightly. 'I should have thought it was too cold for swimming.'

'This isn't funny, Joseph. Someone was watching from near your cottage.'

His expression became blank. He turned back to the designs on his table. 'Probably Freddie. I said he could borrow the binoculars any time he wanted. Or Cassie.'

'Cassie's at school,' Esther said coldly.

'Freddie then. He doesn't want Rowena to know he's been looking at sea birds. You know how peculiar she can be. She might get the wrong idea. If I were you, I wouldn't challenge him about it. It's supposed to be a secret.'

His reasoning sounded so lame that it might almost be true. Could she believe him? She realised that she very much wanted to trust him, that she didn't believe Julia's claim that Joseph was unstable. 'I'm sorry.'

'That's all right,' he said easily. 'Pax?'

'Pax,' she said quietly and remembered the seashell on his mantelshelf.

'How is the Paris project coming along?'

'Gerard Vaudoyer has asked for the flame designs – the ones I based on the pots I brought with me when I came here.'

'Good. I think they're the best.'

'I should like to start on some new designs before Christmas.' Esther searched his face, wanting to believe the best in him, but unable totally to dismiss her suspicions.

He frowned at the mention of Christmas. 'I'd forgotten it was so near.'

'You don't enjoy Christmas?'

'I don't enjoy the memories it revives.' He gave her a tight-lipped smile.

'Since I came back to The Dovecote, I seem to have been involved more and more with memories,' Esther said. 'And yet I used to think it was The Dovecote that had begun to release me from the past.'

He did not answer.

'I was so angry when Julia forced me into the seance in London, but perhaps I've misjudged her. She probably meant well enough. I think she believed she could help me get over Christopher.' Joseph still did not reply and Esther went on, 'I know that she has helped you too. She's told me about her healing – laying on hands to rid you of your nightmares. Perhaps there's something in it, if the nightmares occur less often than they did, but why didn't you want me to know about it?'

Joseph remained silent for a moment. The only sound was from the apprentice in the next room, the scrape of a plane on wood. Then he said without looking at her, 'Did Julia also tell you that she and I were lovers?'

Esther felt a stab of shock and disbelief run through her. She had heard the story of the girl he had been going to marry and the white feather – but Julia?

'I find it hard to believe it myself sometimes,' he said with a wry smile.

Esther felt as if a wall of uncertainty had come between them again. She thought of the binoculars: if he had lied the first time, why should he be telling the truth today? Was he lying about Julia? Julia had said nothing to her about a love affair. If Joseph was unstable, Esther thought wildly, how could she decide whether to believe anything at all that he said? Then she remembered Julia's proprietary hand on Joseph's arm, her possessiveness, her distress because Joseph had gone to Italy, and she saw with a growing certainty that what he said was true.

Joseph began to speak, quietly, his eyes on hers as he talked. 'I was a wreck straight after the war. I couldn't sleep. I had nightmares. I'd been through nothing more terrible than thousands of others, I'd suffered no external injuries, but inside ... Do you understand? My mind was damaged. Coming back home was like being raised from the dead. I felt as though I should have been dead. Nothing was the same – old relationships, friends. People couldn't comprehend what we had been through and they didn't want to.'

'People like your fiancée?' Esther said.

He hesitated. 'Diana understood only too well. That was why she ditched me. She had been a nurse, had seen enough of what the war could do. Why should she marry someone who would be a constant reminder?' Joseph watched Esther, judging her reaction to what he had said.

148

'Where is she now?' Esther said carefully.

'God knows. It doesn't really matter, does it? In any case we were only kids – but what a selfish so-and-so I would have been, to have expected her to put up with that.'

'If she loved you . . .'

Joseph smashed his fist suddenly against the table, making Esther jump. 'You don't know what you're talking about.' He passed a hand across his mouth and his hand and lips trembled. 'I'm sorry. I didn't mean to frighten you, but you don't know what you're saying. Love doesn't come into it. I'm glad Diana had the sense to see she couldn't cope. I don't blame her. I understand it.'

'But Julia could cope,' Esther said, feeling an irrational resentment against Julia.

'She offered me a workshop. I'd done an apprenticeship with my father before the war. He had a thriving craft workshop, but the business disintegrated after he died. Our families had been very close when I was a child, and it seemed natural that I should come to Julia afterwards. She took away the worst of the horror and we became lovers briefly. She was old enough to be my mother, and yet that too seemed natural. You have to understand, Esther. Julia was the *only* person who could help me at that time.'

Esther looked into his eyes and they were no longer without expression, but exposed his pain. She imagined Julia nursing him back to health, falling in love with him – it would have been so very easy to fall in love with him.

She told herself that whatever Julia said about Joseph being unreliable would be based on the person she remembered after the war – broken by the Somme. 'I can help you too,' she said. 'And so can Cassie. Don't cut yourself off from people as you have in the past.'

He smiled. 'Thank you. I mean that. One needs friendships.'

Was that what she had been offering? Esther wondered as she returned to the house. Friendship? Or, like Julia, was she more than a little in love with Joseph – the older woman falling for vulnerable youth? She was thirty-one, she reminded herself, and he *was* still a boy compared with Christopher – yet she felt oddly lightheaded, as if something important had happened to her. She sat by the fountain with her hands thrust into the pockets of her coat. No water played from the water spouts; the surface of the pool was very still and black. The dolphins, mottled with lichen, gaped at her in an attitude of jeering scepticism. What would Christopher have said? What would Julia say? Esther stared back at the dolphins. Whatever Julia might say, she realised that she believed and trusted Joseph without reserve. It was in her nature to trust him. She could not help herself.

Cassie knew from the very beginning that her mother was falling in love with Joseph. Esther altered when he was near, colour heightened her cheeks, her eyes deepened with animation when she talked about him, and she sang sometimes while she worked at her designs.

In Cassie's eleven-year-old view of things, if her mother had fallen in love again, why shouldn't everything be as perfect as it had been when her father was alive? Yet, from the beginning, from the day she saw him in the courtyard, glamorous, gently preoccupied as he watched the doves, Cassie too had fallen in love.

Sometimes, when Esther was busy in her studio, Cassie had Joseph all to herself. They would go down to the beach, where the sound of the sea was like the slow roar of a steam engine, and the wind cut her face like a knife. Seagulls circled with their mournful cry, and Cassie had to shout to make herself heard as she hunted for driftwood and Joseph roamed along the shore with his hands in his pockets. Sometimes she took off her shoes and stockings and curled her toes in the cold wet sand, or walked in the sea until the water made her feet and ankles ache so badly that Joseph had to rub them to bring them back to life. But he never stopped her from doing things, as her mother did, because they were 'silly' or because she might 'catch cold'.

It was Joseph, rather than Freddie, who showed Cassie how to really understand the nature of wood, its texture, its irregularities and its vigour. He quickly became her friend and her teacher. Even then, before she knew about his nightmares, Cassie recognised in him a sense of great sadness. But Cassie had fallen in love with his vitality, not his legacy of sorrow; she was captivated by the beauty of his furniture and his love of natural things; he had the sort of smile that made her heart turn over inside and it was Cassie who saw him laugh long before her mother ever did.

'Don't ever grow up,' Joseph told her one day. 'Or at least, if you must let nature take its course, hang on to your childish delight in everything.'

They were on the cliff path and he had let her look through the binoculars that he carried round his neck whenever they walked on the cliffs. He had pointed out a pair of cormorants on an outcrop of rock, and Cassie was thrilled to see them, magnified before her eyes; it was as if she could almost have reached out her hand and touched one on its perch.

'I'm not childish,' Cassie retorted, handing back the binoculars. 'And when I grow up I'm going to be just like you.'

'I pray you're not,' he said, the dark side of him quickly returning.

'I'm going to be a furniture-maker.'

'Ah ...' Joseph nodded with a touch of self-mockery. 'A worthy ambition, my dear Cassie. But I shall have to look to my laurels if I'm going to have a rival in my old age.'

Cassie could not think of him growing into old age. While she was not particularly interested in his romantic background – that was a side of him for the adult world to contemplate – she knew a little about him, because she had heard Rowena gossiping. She knew that his fiancée had given him a white feather to make him join up, and that 'the bitch would have nothing to do with him' when the war was over. Cassie did not know then that Julia and Joseph had once been lovers. Had she known such a thing, at the tender age of eleven, she might well have looked upon her hero differently.

Joseph, for his part, was aware of a lightness of heart whenever he was with Cassie. She was one of a new generation. Her youth wasn't blighted by the legacy of the slaughter. Though she had lost a father, she was too young to have been scarred very deeply by the loss and was growing up in a mood of eager optimism for the future. His own and Esther's generation, the hopes of their youth crushed by the war, were trying to come to terms with life again; they found it harder to believe that the future was good. Cassie had no reason to believe it was not.

Joseph went away again that Christmas and did not return until the middle of January. He knew that Julia was always afraid – after Italy – that he would go away for good. But he had only gone to Exeter to spend Christmas with Colin and Tim and other survivors of the war. It was at Christmas the Army had sent him back from France: they had strapped him to a stretcher because he had lost his reason and had tried to strangle a sergeant. Only Julia knew just how crazy he had been – and his fellow inmates at the hospital, who, without a Julia to rescue them, had found their own salvation in whisky.

Esther's range of flame pottery was packed up and ready for Paris. She was already working on a second commission for Gerard Vaudoyer as well as designs for Lady Bowers and more of Julia's friends. She felt in need of a change of scene at Christmas and went with Cassie to visit her parents.

She told them about her work at the pottery. 'I do most of the throwing,' she explained. 'Rowena helps, and I'm teaching Violet to throw and to paint.' Though Violet was large and ungainly, she had shown a surprisingly elegant touch with a brush, and had picked up the techniques almost instinctively. 'Between us we do all the fetching and carrying and looking after the kiln.'

'It doesn't sound very feminine,' her father protested mildly.

'But Esther has some very distinguished customers,' interrupted Mrs Mortimer. Esther imagined her mother telling all her friends about her clients, casually dropping the name of Lady Bowers into the conversation. She felt a pang of guilt about the offer from Denholm's department store; she had let it lapse; seduced by the flow of recent commissions, she had allowed the work on her London and Paris orders to become all-absorbing.

Esther had made her mother promise they wouldn't see anything of the Fieldings while she was staying in Birmingham. 'Giles is walking out with a girl called Margaret Davenport,' her mother said with a significant tilt to her head, as if to say, look how you missed your chance. She added in the hushed tones she generally reserved for the dead, 'Poor Giles. On the rebound, I expect.'

Cassie enjoyed the New Year most of all, when Esther drove with her to Hugh and Marjorie's house near Bath and she was allowed to stay up until past midnight. A neighbour who came 'first-footing' with a piece of coal was dragged to a chair by the roaring fire and given a glass of brandy, and all the party guests linked arms to sing 'Auld Lang Syne'. Everyone laughed a lot and Esther cried a little – not with the awful tearing sobs Cassie remembered from two years earlier, but with laughter still on her lips.

Some time after they had been back at The Dovecote, Joseph too returned. Cassie realised how much her mother had missed him when she heard her singing again one morning. She recognised that the relationship between her mother and Joseph was nothing like her mother's friendship with Giles. There was an unspoken sense of disturbance between them that Cassie did not fully understand. Only later was she able to define it as the sexual magnetism that draws two people together.

It was about this time that a pair of wild pigeons came to live in the dovecote in the courtyard. Cassie discovered them one afternoon when she came home from school. Joseph had driven to pick her up in his car; she was always pleased when he came to meet her and hoped the other girls would see him – for Joseph, dressed in his Oxford bags and driving a Bentley, was undeniably impressive.

'Oh look!' Cassie said as she climbed from the car and saw the pigeons. 'A couple of foreigners have come to stay. Do you think they're male or female?'

It was a heavy February day. The mist had not lifted since the morning and frost still lay on the roofs of the barns at half-past four in the afternoon. The cooing of the doves inside the house was like a low, drawn out lament, and the only birds to brave the weather were the pigeons, grey and white in a grey and white landscape, strutting about on the dovecote platform.

Joseph went to look at them. He stood with his hands in his pockets and crooned to them.

'Julia won't like it. They might breed with the white ones,' Cassie said.

'I don't think so,' Joseph replied. 'Pigeons pair up for life.'

Cassie repeated this piece of information when she went into the kitchen, where Rowena was at the stove and Meg was going through the accounts. She said how pretty the birds had looked in the grey and white scene. 'It was like a photograph.' She was keen on photographs since Hugh and Marjorie had given her a Brownie box-camera for Christmas. She had taken photographs of everyone at The Dovecote. She kept one of Joseph hidden in her gym-slip pocket, to show off to the girls at school.

'Very picturesque,' Meg said in response to Cassie's remark about the pigeons and in her sharp, sarcastic way.

Cassie had discovered some information about dovecotes at school that autumn and she repeated this too: that in the grim days of the middle ages, when the lords of the manor had a taste for squab pie, the owner of a dovecote had kept doves as a sitting supply of fresh meat.

'Think of the poor little squabs waiting to be plucked from their perches,' Cassie said with a shudder, and she imagined Julia doing the same for Rowena to cook up in the kitchen.

Rowena looked at her in horror. 'But that's terrible, if it's true. Did you know that – about the doves – Joseph?' still unable to believe such barbarity had existed.

Joseph, who had been sitting in the window-seat and hardly seemed to be listening to this conversation, said, 'Did I know what?'

'That the owner of a dovecote kept doves for the lean days of winter in case nothing more satisfying presented itself?' Meg said with an ironical tone to her voice.

Joseph gave her a wry smile. 'Sure. We all know that.'

Cassie was looking through Joseph's binoculars from the garden one afternoon. Esther and Joseph were on the cliff path, walking, their hands close together, almost touching, yet with a tension that kept them apart. Through the binoculars Cassie saw Joseph bend down and, picking a flower from a clump of sea-pinks, he gave it to her mother. Their hands met, and Cassie remembered the happy times at The Folly, a voice saying softly, 'Esther', and she knew that if Joseph had been the man in the garden all that time ago, he would have said her mother's name in the same tender way.

Suddenly Julia came out from the bushes. She seemed very angry. 'What are you doing with those binoculars, child? You might break them.'

'Joseph said I might borrow them,' Cassie protested. 'He lets me borrow them any time I like.' She knew that Julia too had seen Esther and Joseph together. Was that why she was so angry? Did she want Esther all to herself?

A moment later, Esther and Joseph came down through the tree walk. They hesitated when they saw Julia, then Joseph murmured something and went quickly to his workshop, as he always did if Julia met them together.

As if it embarrassed him to be seen with her, thought Esther. Or was it to spare Julia's feelings? Was Julia still in love with Joseph? Did she perpetuate the myth that he was unreliable, unsound, an injured dove, because she didn't want to admit that he no longer needed her?

'You should be more careful than to walk with him on the cliff,' Julia said as they progressed slowly towards the garden.

Cassie trailed behind, looking up at the tree canopy through Joseph's binoculars. She wondered what Julia was saying to her mother, but could not be bothered to hurry on and find out. Here in the tree-walk, even on the hottest day, it always felt mysterious and cold. The wind in the tree canopy followed behind, as if to urge a glance over one's shoulder. Cassie liked the delicious feelings of terror it inspired, and the way the sound of the sea blended with the roar of the wind.

Esther said incredulously, 'Not walk with him on the cliff? What do you think he's going to do – push me off?'

Julia threw a look at Cassie, far behind them, and lowered her voice. 'And you shouldn't leave Cassie with him so much when you're working. I told you, Esther. He's unreliable. I know.'

'That might have been true some time ago,' Esther said. 'But his stay in Italy made a difference to him. Joseph is over the war. Why won't you let him alone and stop reminding him about it all the time?'

'And you, are you over your husband?' Julia said, changing the subject.

'I think so. I really feel as if the weight of grieving has gone.'

Julia placed a gentle hand on Esther's arm. 'Are you sure? Don't you remember how upset you were when he spoke to you in London?'

'Julia – he didn't speak to me,' Esther said patiently. 'Please don't expect me to believe for a minute that what happened that afternoon had anything to do with Christopher.'

'If only you weren't so afraid.'

'I'm not afraid. I'm just being – realistic,' Esther said in exasperation.

'You see, it's clear to me that you aren't healed, and that you won't be healed until you speak to him. You should let Christopher release you by coming to a seance.'

Esther was silent. For a moment she was tempted, out of a sense of frustration with Julia, to say that she would go. There were other reasons too why she should perhaps prove that Christopher had 'released' her. She thought of Joseph and knew that she was falling in love again. But was it possible to move on without first cutting her ties with the past? Was it necessary to prove to herself – if not to Julia – that she had at last put Christopher behind her?

Julia looked at her with a sad tenderness in her expression. She stroked a strand of hair from Esther's face and held her chin in the palm of her hand with a gesture Esther had seen her use on others at The Dovecote.

'Come to a seance,' Julia coaxed. 'Come this week.' Her eyes held Esther's compellingly; the pupils were large dark pools of tenderness.

Esther hesitated. Should she go? Should she brave whatever phony spirit performance Julia might think up and prove to herself that it was a lot of nonsense? It was almost as if Julia had issued a challenge, as if, unconsciously, she had said, prove it isn't true that I have you tied, as I have tied the others to The Dovecote.

Esther looked at Julia and came to a decision: she would stand up to her, show her once and for all that she couldn't be bamboozled by spirit voices. She heard herself say, 'All right. I'll come.'

'You must be crazy,' Joseph said when she told him.

'I'm going to make Julia see that I'm not impressed by all her talk about Christopher's spirit watching over me. I'm tired of Julia putting on her psychic look and telling me a lot of hooey. I'll show her I'm not one of her simple-minded doves.'

He turned away. 'You're doing exactly what Julia wants. You think you're acting of your own free will, but you're not. Believe me, I know.'

Esther remembered Joseph saying that Julia understood him, that it had seemed natural they should become lovers, that Julia was the only person who could help him when he came back from France. She felt a surge of jealousy. She thought she had accepted Joseph's affair with Julia – he had been barely twenty, sick, lonely, he had needed someone, she had told herself. And yet, why did Joseph still come back to Julia, now that he was cured?

'Before you realise it she'll have you neatly bound up in her web, ready to suck you dry,' Joseph said.

'Is that what she did with you?' Esther knew the question had been mean-spirited. Feeling ashamed, she turned on her heel and left his workshop.

Chapter Ten

Freddie took Esther's hand as they walked along the corridor to the seance room. 'You're trembling.'

'I'm cold. That's all.'

'There's nothing to be frightened about,' Rowena hissed, hurrying to catch up with them, frowning a warning at Freddie to drop Esther's hand at once, a signal he blithely ignored.

'We were all wary at first,' Peter said. 'Expecting devilish goings-ons. Sacrificial offerings. Naked virgins.'

'Why else do you think Peter and I came?' said Freddie. They entered the meeting room and Esther looked round her in surprise, for it was far less sinister than she had expected. A semi-circle of straight-backed wooden chairs were arranged in front of a low stage, hidden behind heavy brown velvet curtains. The windows too were curtained, and the room was lit simply by three central gas chandeliers hissing gently in the silence.

Freddie waited for Esther and Rowena to sit down before he sat between them, folding his arms and leaning back in his chair, clearly enjoying himself. 'Relax. You'll see. It's going to be all right.' He looked at Esther. 'No *naked women*,' he said with mock significance.

The words and his look penetrated Esther's thoughts and she remembered Joseph saying that he sometimes let Freddie borrow his binoculars. Had it been Freddie who watched her swim, she wondered with a shock? The idea came almost as a relief. Freddie *had* been in the garden that day. Why hadn't it occurred to her before?

She avoided looking at him. Peter was talking to some of the visitors Esther had seen gather in the courtyard; Cassie had once joked about them to Joseph, saying they looked as if they were queuing for a circus. 'A freak-show anyway,' Joseph had said quietly to Esther.

She remembered Joseph's warning about coming to the seance, his look of hurt when she had turned on him. He really shouldn't assume he knew better than she did how to respond to Julia, but she wished now her parting remark could be undone. He had told her she was crazy to give in to Julia. Had she given in? She rejected the idea. No. She had come to the seance to prove that she couldn't be bullied or mesmerised.

Peter sat down heavily, as if he were in church. It was very much like being in church, or at a prayer meeting, thought Esther. She began to feel less anxious and even to wonder what Joseph was doing: she had left

157

Cassie with him; without actually lying to her she had avoided telling Cassie where she was going. She had left them looking at pictures of sea birds in the flat.

Did Joseph still depend on Julia emotionally? Whether he did or not, Julia had helped him to come to terms with his memories of the Somme, and for that Esther knew she should be grateful. The chairs were filling quickly; the atmosphere really was like a church or chapel gathering. At any moment, Esther thought, the Winmouth vicar might appear and declare they were raising funds to preserve the roof, or someone would announce that they were going to sing a hymn.

Instead, Violet appeared from behind the stage curtains, her large face peering out into the congregation. 'Is everybody here?' A murmur of acknowledgement ran round the room. Violet's glance fell upon Esther; she threw her a look of excitement and disappeared from view.

Violet believed wholeheartedly in the seances, Esther remembered; she believed that Julia was a wonderful woman, had raised her almost to the status of a saint – or high priestess at least. Was that how the others saw her? Esther wondered. Did Peter and Meg, Rowena and Freddie – solemn now as the curtains swung back from the platform – really believe Julia had mystic powers?

Julia stood alone. She was dressed in a long, loose-fitting red gown; her hair was held by a jewelled band. There was a padded leather chair beside her and a small round table with a glass of water on it. Behind her a pair of candelabras burned with long candles and made a haze of soft light; beyond lay a thick, almost tangible darkness and, as Esther watched, the gas-lamps in the room flickered and dimmed.

'Welcome, friends,' Julia said in a warm tone, raising her arms, her sleeves falling back to reveal her naked forearms; they were white and smooth, and startlingly youthful in the candlelight. Esther thought of those arms encircling Joseph, of Joseph and Julia together in his cottage. 'Welcome in love, all my friends. Let us join hands and meditate for a few moments. Let us bathe in that energy which, with love and concern for our well-being, opens us to the spirit world.'

Esther sat, her hands gripped on either side by Rowena and Freddie. She forced herself to adopt an uneasy scepticism as she watched Julia, her head thrown back, her eyes closed in the same apparent mystic ecstasy Esther had witnessed at the Vaudoyers'. She looked at Julia, beautiful and mysterious in the candlelight, and Esther understood, with a shock of self-realisation, that she was deeply jealous of her. Julia had once shared Joseph's bed. Erotic images paraded before her and a single thought ran through her head: *Julia and Joseph were lovers.* She supposed, with self-irony, that it was a kind of meditation.

Esther felt sick as she tried to make sense of her emotions. Julia loved everyone – no one could dispute that – and though she might have loved Joseph physically, she loved everyone in her all-embracing way. Love governed everything Julia did. How could one respond to that with petty-minded jealousy?

Julia spoke and the strength of her voice in the silence made Esther jump. 'If I can help a troubled spirit find itself, I shall be very happy today.'

'That's not Julia but her Spirit Guide talking,' Rowena whispered to Esther with her attention fixed on the stage.

'I ask each and every one of you to accept who and what you are,' Julia continued without opening her eyes. Her voice, rich and deep, was the one she had used in London. 'Be certain that you give out love and light. Seek contact with your inner source. Be at peace and find harmony within.'

Did Julia really believe that by coming to the seance she could be healed of her grief? Esther wondered as the voice fell silent. If so, Julia's concern was misplaced; she had spoken the truth when she had told her that the weight of her grieving had gone. The audience was quiet, waiting. Clearly they had all experienced inner harmony many times before, Esther told herself, adopting an exaggerated cynicism to keep at bay a deepening tension within her, a tension which made her heart beat more quickly and held her on the edge of her chair. She jumped violently as Julia's head jerked to one side. Esther felt the hair creep on the back of her neck as Julia's eyes opened and her gaze came to rest on her, for Julia's expression was glazed and unrecognising.

'I sense one among our number who is not at peace.'

Rowena gripped Esther's hand more tightly. 'Don't say anything,' she whispered. 'Just let the energy in.'

'Esther.' The word was spoken softly, lovingly. 'Why are you troubled, daughter? Don't be afraid. Open yourself to us in your mind and heart. Free yourself of negative thoughts and let us in. If you feel our presence here, don't reject it but accept that it is good.'

Julia fell silent. Esther felt the air around her grow lighter. It seemed to her that she couldn't move her hands and arms, nor take her eyes from Julia's.

Again the voice came from Julia's lips: 'Esther. Don't be afraid. Don't resist us, for we have come here to help.'

The longer Esther looked into Julia's eyes, the more helpless she felt and the more the air around her lightened, until it seemed as if the rest of the congregation was in the distance below her. She sat alone on a high place, far away in the open, as though transported to the cliff on a sunny day, with only herself and Julia present. She closed her eyes, and the room and even Julia faded and there was nothing but the voice in her head.

'Will you let us help you?'

'Yes.' She heard her own voice, though she was not conscious that she had spoken. She was floating, as she had once floated between land and sky, when Christopher had seemed so close that she need only swim out as far as the horizon to be reunited with him. She remembered how pleasant it had been to let go of the world in that soothing warmth behind her closed eyes, until she had wakened to the slap of the sea.

'There is someone here who is known to you. He has watched you and is distressed for you. Will you allow him to come through?'

Again Esther heard herself respond. 'Christopher.' A dry sob broke from her.

The voice issuing from Julia was gentle. 'Christopher is distressed, because you have ignored his advice. He has a message for you.' There was a pause, a moment of silence, then the voice continued. 'He is unhappy because you didn't trust our daughter, Julia, who has found harmony and who cares for your well-being. In what way did you not trust her, Esther?'

'I don't know,' Esther faltered, and a memory of the seance in London filtered into her consciousness. She remembered her anger and the feeling that she had been used.

'Because of her judgement of Joseph?' the voice prompted. 'Julia knows that great unhappiness lies in store for you through Joseph. It isn't wise to get close to him . . . Trust her. She is your friend.'

Esther opened her eyes. She felt the sensation of warmth and lightness fade. Something was wrong: Julia's eyes held hers, but they had lost their blank expression and her face no longer seemed to be in trance. A look of recognition passed between the two women – in Julia's eyes a moment of wariness, in Esther's a look of accusation, as she saw that she was being manipulated.

Julia's expression turned to one of disappointment and Esther realised that she had stopped speaking in the ringing tones of her Spirit Guide. She spoke quietly, sadly. 'You are too sceptical, Esther dear. I'm afraid I must ask you to leave the meeting.'

Rowena and Freddie had released Esther's hands and she stood, feeling everyone's eyes upon her. She felt the changed atmosphere in the room as the rest of those present at the meeting regarded her with a mixture of disappointment and pity. Esther walked to the door, opened it and went into the corridor, closing the door firmly behind her.

She leaned against the wall. What had happened? Had she really believed that Julia's 'Spirit Guide' was speaking to her? Oh, Julia was clever, she realised. And – if clever, then scheming and divisive, and she had been foolish to regard her as her friend. She must take Cassie away from this place. At once. That night.

Esther heard a sound, a soft foot-fall, and she eased herself from the wall. The corridor was poorly lit; its windows were curtained like those inside the meeting room and, though the evening sunlight filtered up the stairs, the far end of the passage lay almost in complete darkness.

Esther's heart began to beat painfully against her ribs. A cold wave of fear swept her back and neck as she saw a dark shape at the foot of the attic stair. A man stood there, dressed in army uniform; he reached a hand towards her, then turned and retreated into the darkness.

Christopher? For a moment Esther believed it. She pressed the palm of her hand against her mouth to prevent herself from crying out. A moment later she felt a calm anger displace her fear. She raced along the passage and up the narrow staircase to the corridor above.

A single gas-jet burned dimly outside Julia's studio, and a dirty skylight lit the far end of the attic corridor. The bedrooms here, once servants' quarters, had been knocked through to make the two painting studios – one Peter's, the other Julia's. There were no other rooms at the top of the house: anyone who had entered either of the attics must still be there.

Esther's heart pounded as she flung open the door to Peter's studio and from the corridor surveyed the interior. The evening sunlight flooded the room from the gable lights in the sloping roof, and the paintings of doves, stacked against the walls, were lit as if by two broad spotlights. The birds' wings were spread as though to take flight from the canvas, their wing feathers like knife-blades in the shafts of light.

Esther could see without entering that no one was hiding there. She closed the door softly and moved along the corridor to Julia's room. Her anger had already subsided. Again she felt a chill of fear as she turned the door handle and threw open the door.

Julia's studio too was empty, bathed in a soft, broad light from the continuous run of glass panes let into the roof. The room was tidy. Canvasses were stacked against the walls. There was nowhere at all for anyone to hide.

Esther leaned against the door-post and pressed her hand against her mouth, this time to prevent the tears that threatened to break from her. What? What had she seen? She wondered for a moment whether her experience at the seance had temporarily unbalanced her. But, no – she had seen him. There had been someone – Christopher, or someone – on the stair.

Esther walked back to Peter's room and then to Julia's studio again, as if, by meticulous inspection, an explanation would reveal itself. Julia's easel stood under the central roof-light, its canvas draped in a piece of sacking. A chair was pushed to one side, littered with jam-jars filled with brushes and tubes of paint. Esther had not been to the attic studio for many weeks. Its air of normality, the soft evening sunlight, and the lack of evidence of any further manifestations – either human or supernatural – made her turn her attention to the easel. She felt the revival of ordinary responses, and curiosity made her raise a corner of the sacking. Her interest increasing, she lifted away the cover altogether and stepped backwards with a gasp, for her own face looked back at her from the portrait.

The figure was seated at the wheel in her pottery studio; in her lap she held a vase – one she recognised, a design chosen by Gerard Vaudoyer for Galeries Lafayette. The details of the face were accurate – with a stretch of the imagination she could almost have been gazing into a mirror. More, there was something in the eyes of the portrait that suggested a tenderness between subject and painter. Had Julia done all this from memory – without a sitting? Esther remembered the hours Julia had spent with her in the pottery, apparently doing nothing but observe, chatting idly, offering the odd word of advice. But to execute such a painting from memory suggested an intimate preoccupation with the subject, an intimacy too intense to be comfortable.

Esther draped the sacking over the easel and left the attic. Of all that had happened that evening, this latest surprise seemed more disturbing than the rest.

Cassie was in the flat, drawing. Her bedroom was stamped with her personality: a collection of driftwood, bones, fossils and shells and pebbles littered her desk and the floor. Drawings of furniture and house interiors were pinned around the walls, designs for imaginary rooms with a sense of perspective that had made Joseph seize upon them excitedly one day, saying they were remarkable for her years. They bore none of the crude carelessness typical of the pictures Cassie had painted for Julia – before Julia had given up the lessons, concluding that Cassie's talents didn't lie as an artist after all.

Cassie was happy here, Esther realised, as she stood in the doorway between the two rooms. Her thoughts returned to the seance. Did she really want to take Cassie away from her school and all this freedom? If Joseph could ignore Julia's more outlandish behaviour, couldn't she do the same?

'Cassie – where's Joseph?' Esther said suddenly.

'He had to go away.'

'Away? Do you mean in his car?'

'No. He wouldn't do that. He promised to keep me company, didn't he? He said he had to go over to the house.'

Esther remembered the figure on the stair and her heart beat quickly as she said, keeping her voice calm, 'But why should he do that? Everyone at the house was at Julia's meeting.'

'He said he wanted some food for tonight – or something. Does it matter?' Cassie, absorbed by her drawing, was being exasperatingly vague. 'Or else he was going to his cottage. I've forgotten.'

Esther went into the next room and knelt on the sofa-bed to look out of the window and across the lawn towards Joseph's cottage. The members of the seance meeting were filtering out from the house in twos and threes. Julia stood on the shallow steps of the entrance, still dressed in the long red gown; she raised her hand in a slightly theatrical gesture of farewell and Esther heard people call out affectionate responses. Her attention was caught by another figure; a man was leaving the house by the kitchen entrance; he was hidden from Julia and the others by the herbaceous borders as he skirted the garden and walked quickly towards the tree-walk, but she could see that it was Joseph.

Esther was thankful that Julia had gone back inside the house as she sped across the lawn. She slowed her step when she reached the tree-walk. The wind was in the trees and Joseph did not hear her. From behind he could have been Christopher. She remembered how like him he had seemed that first day on the beach; in uniform they would have looked almost identical. She remembered Julia's warnings: Joseph is unreliable . . . It isn't wise to get close to him . . . Great unhappiness lies in store for you . . . A sob broke from her and Joseph turned at the sound.

His expression was one of profound alarm as he waited for Esther to catch up with him. 'Esther! Good God. What's the matter?'

'What exactly are you up to?' Disappointment and anger filled Esther's throat and choked her words. He was carrying a canvas bag – an old army knapsack. Did it hide his uniform? She snatched the bag from him and threw it on the ground and knelt, tearing at the straps. 'What have you got in there? What are you trying to do to me?' The contents of the bag spilled out on to the ground.

Esther looked at Joseph in bewilderment. She pressed her hand to her mouth then said at last, 'Why were you at the house just now?'

'I wanted some food for tonight.'

Esther stared at the loaf of bread and the tins scattered on the ground. 'I don't believe you.'

'All right. There was another reason. I wanted to make sure you were all right. I went up to the meeting room and hung around a bit outside.'

Esther shook her head. 'I didn't see you . . .' She broke off at the irony of her words. She tried to decide whether he was lying. Why would he want to dress up as her dead husband and frighten her? It didn't make sense – unless he were unstable, as Julia had warned her. But if he had pretended to be Christopher, wouldn't Julia know about it? Were they in league together? Esther felt as if she were going crazy as the suspicions flew round in her head. 'Why do that anyway?' she said with a final attempt to justify her attack. 'Why were you following me around?'

'I don't know. I suddenly felt more unhappy about your going to the meeting. I didn't trust Julia.' Joseph squatted beside her and began to pick up the tins. 'Believe me – I only want to help.'

That's what Julia keeps saying,' Esther said angrily. 'I wish people would stop trying to help me and let me get on with my life.'

'I warned you not to go to the seance. You should have listened. It's obviously upset you.' He jerked his head in the direction of his cottage. 'Do you want to come in and talk about it?'

Esther hesitated, needing to confide in someone about her conviction that she had seen someone in the corridor, tempted for a moment to trust him; then she shook her head. 'No.' She helped him pick up the food. 'I'm sorry. I hope I haven't spoiled anything.' She handed him the bread, and he stood up, hitching the bag over his shoulder.

'What has Julia done?' he said quietly, and his eyes had taken on the peculiar lack of expression that always seemed to set a barrier between them.

'It really doesn't matter now. You were right, I should never have gone to the seance.'

Esther watched him walk on through the trees. The light was dying and his figure became less distinct, a blurred outline. It could so easily have been Christopher in the gathering gloom.

Joseph did not come in to dinner that evening; Meg said he had gone off to Exeter for the night. Esther could not challenge Julia about the seance during dinner; there was an unspoken understanding that the community didn't discuss anything to do with the seances in front of Cassie. The mood at dinner was subdued and, on Esther's part, it simmered with unspoken accusations; but it was not until the following morning, at breakfast, after Cassie had gone to get ready for school, that Esther was able to confront Julia.

'Why didn't you tell me you'd been working on a portrait of me?' she said, keeping her voice steady.

'You've been in my studio?'

'Yesterday. After you asked me to leave the seance.'

Peter and Meg were the only other members of the community still at the table. Peter glanced up with interest. 'I didn't know you had been working on a portrait of Esther. It's something I have thought of doing.'

Meg threw Esther one of her restrained looks, a mixture of veiled resentment and suspicion.

'I was looking for someone in uniform when I went to your studio.' Esther spoke levelly and she watched Julia closely.

'A railway attendant?' suggested Meg.

'A soldier. My dead husband. I thought I saw him on the attic stair.'

'He manifested himself?' Julia said, and her expression was calm.

'Something – or someone did. I followed it to your studio and it disappeared.'

'Esther, dear. Why do you resist so? What are you afraid of?'

'I'm not afraid. I simply want to know what – if anything – is going on.'

'It's rare for a spirit to show itself,' Julia said thoughtfully. 'But it has happened before.' She looked at Esther with compassion. 'Don't you see? Christopher came to warn you. Don't reject him. It isn't wise to go against the advice of the spirits.'

Esther saw that Meg was watching Julia carefully. She seemed to be about to speak, then a frown crossed her face and she looked down at the table.

'Don't you mean, it isn't wise to cross you?' Esther said quietly, thinking of all Joseph – and Meg and Freddie too – had ever said about Julia's need to dominate the community.

Julia stood up. 'We'll pretend you didn't say that, shall we? I'll put your present mood down to your hysterical state of mind. We *can* bring tranquillity to you, Esther. I shan't give up. Meanwhile, I don't think

I'll come with you to the clay pit this morning. Can you manage alone?'

Esther looked at her watch. She felt defeated. 'Yes,' she said distractedly. 'Yes, of course.'

Julia paused by the door. 'I'm sorry you've decided to take this attitude. It makes it so much harder for us to help you. I thought after the meeting you would have realised ... I thought it would be as obvious to you as it is to the rest of us that Christopher is watching over you.'

One thing only was obvious, thought Esther. Julia, for whatever reason – because she genuinely believed Joseph was a threat? – had wanted to convince her at the seance that Christopher disapproved of their friendship. As for the figure on the stairs ... Perhaps Julia was right about her being overwrought. It was possible that her imagination had played tricks on her. It seemed incredible now that she should have gone so far as to suspect Joseph of masquerading as Christopher.

Meg stood, dabbing her lips with a napkin. 'I'm going into Lyme this morning. Would you like me to drive Cassie to school for you?'

'Would you?' said Esther thankfully. 'I'd forgotten all about going to the clay pit.'

Meg gave her a tight smile and left the breakfast room.

Esther slumped in her chair. 'Am I going mad, Peter? Did I really think I saw him?'

Peter poured her another cup of coffee. 'It is possible you imagined something.' He sat beside her, watching her sip it. 'Julia's right though, you know. You shouldn't close your mind to the possibility that Christopher is trying to communicate with you. He was there at the meeting.'

'*You* think so?' Esther said in dismay.

He nodded slowly. 'We all felt it. We talked about it afterwards.'

'But you can't really believe he would want to warn me against Joseph?'

Peter gave a deep sigh and leaned his elbows on the table. He rested his heavy head in his hands and when he looked up his eyes were troubled. 'Joseph was deeply traumatised by the war, Esther. Haven't you seen what happened to some soldiers? They called it shell-shock, fatigue, too long an exposure to too many horrors. Julia has helped him, as she has helped us all when our minds were troubled. Do you know my own history of evil?'

'A little,' Esther said, remembering Meg telling her that Peter had once killed someone.

'I had a great burden of sin, but Julia took it from me. Julia creates an ambience of love that drives out all our bad memories and our fears. She shares the burdens we carry through life with us.' He took Esther's hand and held it to his face. 'Trust her. She is a wonderful person.'

A wonderful person. Violet's phrase again.

'Do you remember the love you felt when you first came to us?' Peter still held her hand and was stroking it absentmindedly. The effect was

165

soothing, reassuring. 'Do you recall that first awareness of tolerance, kindness, stability?'

'It was the most striking thing about The Dovecote. The atmosphere was almost tangible.'

'That hasn't changed. Oh, we might have our differences. But the driving energy of The Dovecote will always be one of love. People come back after they've gone away. They can't forget what they've drawn from this place.' He stroked Esther's hair and she rested her head against his shoulder. They sat for some seconds without moving, without it seeming strange that Peter still held her hand and that her cheek was against his arm.

Meg came into the breakfast room. 'We're off now, but Cassie can't find her homework . . .' She halted when she saw them and her face froze in an expression of disbelief as she saw Esther with her head on Peter's shoulder.

Esther stood. 'I'll help you look.'

Peter began shifting crockery about on the table.

'He's up to his old tricks,' Meg said, her eyes hard and cold as Esther passed her. 'He tried it once before. We had a girl here from Ireland—'

'No, he's not, Meg,' Esther said. 'He was only being kind.'

Meg's pale face flushed scarlet with fury and she gave a harsh, incredulous laugh. 'Are you really such a wide-eyed innocent on every quarter!'

'I wish she had never come here,' Meg said when Esther had left the dining room. 'Do you remember, right at the beginning, Freddie said she would stir us all up? Well, she's done that all right. You. Freddie. Poor Joseph. And Julia! Julia's really gone overboard this time.'

'You think Julia manufactured a sighting?'

'Well, don't you? It wouldn't be the first time Julia's improved on the seances for the sake of the doubting Thomases – the ones who have to have proof.'

'Esther is different.'

'Oh, I know,' Meg said sharply. 'Rowena and I can see she's different by the way you and Freddie behave when she's around.'

'Meg,' Peter said reproachfully. 'That sort of comment isn't worthy of you. And it's not worth disturbing the harmony of The Dovecote. I've never thought of you as being small-minded.'

'Esther's done that to us. Esther brings us all down to size,' Meg said. She looked at him in disgust. 'Men! You're all the same. You can't even see what's happening to you half the time.'

'I thought you liked her.'

'I did like her.' Meg was thoughtful. 'I tried to help her, you know. It was I who first suggested she should come to a seance. I thought she would find the comfort you and I have found. But she's a sceptic, and there's no way to convince the confirmed sceptic. Not even Julia can do that.' Meg went to the door. 'Esther's a bad influence here. But perhaps she's had enough. She nearly left us after she had been to London with Julia. Something happened there too. Perhaps yesterday's seance will be enough to frighten her away.'

'You can't want that to happen?'

'I think perhaps I do. It would be better for everyone – Joseph most of all. Then we could all get back to the way we were before she came.'

Esther waved goodbye as Cassie left with Meg for school. Meg's animosity seemed if anything more intense as she crashed the Ford into gear and swung out of the gates and, for a moment, Esther felt a qualm about letting Cassie go with her.

She was always surprised by Meg's flashes of jealousy. She had come to expect it of Rowena – because of Freddie, even, on occasions, because of Violet's superior skill in the pottery: images of Rowena slamming pans about on the stove were common. 'When I said I would help you in the pottery, I didn't expect you to thank me by sneaking off with my husband,' she had once cried, swinging round from the stove in a fury. 'That's ridiculous,' Esther had gasped; but Rowena's fits of jealousy were never open to reason. 'I won't have it! Go flirt with Peter. Meg might not be as wise to you as I am.'

But neither was Meg immune to suspicion and jealousy, Esther realised. Perhaps Peter's affections, like Freddie's, had more than a touch of lechery in them, enough to stir even the self-contained Meg to fury; but it was because the community was so claustrophobic – it tended to turn in on itself. She remembered Joseph had once talked of a universal possessiveness infecting The Dovecote; he had called it a kind of curse. It was why he had gone to Italy and why, when things got too intense, he took off to Exeter for days and nights on end. Perhaps she should follow his example, take Cassie to see her grandparents for the weekend and clear the air a little. Esther walked away from the courtyard, glancing again at her watch as she entered the studio. She would have to hurry if she was going to get to the clay pits early.

Her most recent range of pottery, a private commission for a friend of Lady Bowers, stood on a shelf inside the doorway. Esther had given Rowena and Violet a few days' holiday but they would start again after the weekend and begin work on some fresh designs; the studio would hum and clatter pleasantly with the sound of the three of them at the wheels and benches and she would forget all about Julia's seance.

Silence in the studio was always pleasant as well, she realised. Shafts of sunlight caught the dust motes, made bright stripes across the floor and lit a bowl of flowers on one of the benches. Thinking that Cassie had put them there, Esther went to examine the flowers. A card with a drawing of a dove on it lay beside the bowl. She picked it up and looked at the quick pencil sketch, recognising Peter's hand, though it had only a trace of the jarring violence of his paintings. Were the flowers an apology from him for the incident at breakfast? If so, Esther was touched by the gesture.

Five minutes later she had left the studio, thrown her boots into the car and was turning the starting handle. The engine groaned and turned over once and then was dead. The same thing happened each time she cranked the handle. The only sound as the engine died was the mocking call of the doves from the roofs of the barn and from inside the dovecote. Esther gave a cry of frustration and shook her fist at a pigeon parading on the platform outside the dovecote, bobbing and turning as it cooed. 'It's all very well for you.'

'Temper, temper. That's not the sound of peace and harmony we like to hear.' She had not seen Joseph come into the courtyard.

'It won't go.' She looked at him. 'I thought you were in Exeter.'

'Well, I'm not. Are you in a hurry?'

'I said I'd be at the quarry at nine. If the site manager's gone off into the clay pits I shall have to trudge all the way over to the quarry face to find him.'

Joseph went to the front of the car and swung the handle with a flourish. He swung it again with no response. 'I'll drive you.'

'But you can't. Your work—'

'It can wait.'

'You'll need boots if you're coming with me.'

'I'll get them.'

'That's marvellous. Thank you.' She hesitated and, remembering that she had suspected him of collaborating with Julia, felt rather foolish. 'I'm sorry for the way I behaved yesterday after Julia's seance – I mean, chasing after you like that.'

'Forget it.'

Esther sat on her car and waited for him to return. The doves' monotonous cooing was no longer a mockery as she turned her face to the sun, letting it soak into her skin, letting the sound of the birds become a murmuring rhythm in her head. A shadow passed in front of her and Esther opened her eyes.

'Are you having trouble?' Julia stood by the dovecote with a basket of grain in her hand; she began scattering it over the cobbles and the birds swooped down from the roofs and began pecking at the scattered seeds.

'It won't start.'

'Are you going to wait for Meg to get back with the Ford – or shall I fetch Freddie to look at it?'

'There's no need.'

Julia shook her head sadly. 'Esther – I don't bear any grudges. When will you learn that quarrels here are soon over. We are like the birds –' she mimicked the crooning of the doves – 'they don't squabble for long.' She turned to her. 'Let me call Freddie.'

'No – I meant, there's no need because Joseph is taking me in the Bentley.'

A frown crossed Julia's face. 'Do you think that's wise after yesterday – after Christopher appeared to you?'

'Julia. This is ridiculous. You must know that isn't true.'

168

Julia's eyes were troubled. 'You don't know what you're saying. You mustn't ridicule the spirits. If Christopher appeared to you, he did so with very good reason.'

Joseph came into the yard and Julia turned to him quickly. 'Joseph, don't take Esther. There are reasons why you shouldn't drive her.'

'Are the portents against it?' Joseph said over his shoulder as he went to his car.

'I'm serious. You mustn't mock. You should neither of you mock the spirits.' Julia's expression was strained, and Esther, again trying to catch her out, to detect a flaw in her sincerity, saw only concern in Julia's eyes. 'Please. For both your sakes. Have I ever asked much from you, Joseph?'

Joseph halted and his face was pinched with suppressed emotion. 'Oh, yes. You've asked too much, Julia. You want a person's soul as well as their love. You're not content with affection, you want slavish, absolute commitment.'

He started up the car and backed out from the barn.

'You were rather pompous with her,' Esther said as they drove away from The Dovecote, surprised by the grimness in his expression.

'We are all too soft with Julia. That's why she's become the tyrant she has.'

'I never really believed it until yesterday.'

He glanced at her. 'Whatever happened at the seance . . . don't feel too harshly about Julia just yet. Tyrant she may be – but tyrants aren't always wicked and corrupt. She means well. Even I know that.'

'It's more difficult to deal with when the tyranny's based on love and wanting what's best for you,' Esther said, remembering her parents and Marjorie and Hugh. She looked at Joseph and, thinking of Julia, wanted to say, But I guess you know that already.

They drove in silence for a while. It had begun to rain, a steady drizzle, and Joseph stopped to put up the hood; the hinges were stiff and Esther climbed out to help him. Joseph walked to the passenger side of the car as she struggled with the catch.

'I'm sorry I doubted you,' Esther said.

'Did you?' He reached round her to adjust the catch and his hand brushed hers.

'Yesterday—' How could she tell him that she had believed he had pretended to be her dead husband? It sounded so absurd.

'Forget about yesterday. You thought you could outwit Julia and you failed. You made a mistake. Don't try to meet her on her own ground next time.' Esther felt the weight of his arm against her waist as she turned from the car and they found themselves in an embrace from which neither of them moved, though the rain had turned to a steady downpour. Joseph hesitated before bending his head under the brim of her hat to kiss her. They parted and he touched her hat with a vague gesture of detachment as he made an attempt to rationalise the situation. 'Esther, these past few weeks with you and Cassie have made

169

me feel human again. I thought we could be friends, but it's not turning out like that.'

'No,' Esther acknowledged.

'And I don't know what to do about it.'

He looked at her and Esther knew that there was no conflict, no need to think of Julia, no guilt or pressures from the past. She smiled. 'We're getting wet. We should be inside, under the hood, not standing out here in the rain.'

Joseph opened the door for her and Esther sat in the passenger seat. An untroubled happiness stole through her. Joseph climbed back into the car and did not drive on straight away but sat for a few seconds with his head bowed against the wheel. Then he looked up and, starting the engine, said with a studied coldness, 'I'm sorry. Forget that happened. I'll try to keep out of your way after today.'

'But why?' Esther said in dismay as the car moved off. She made him look at her. 'Joseph, since I met you, I've started to live again too. I feel happy. I'm glad we could be more than friends.'

'It can't work. I've no right to fall in love. I'm too much of a liability.' He looked at her. 'I don't think you really have any idea what it would be like.'

'How about me? I still see my dead husband at every corner. I hear spirit messages from him. I'm an emotional wreck.'

'Don't joke,' he said. 'You don't know what you're saying.'

'Yes I do. It's taken me more than four years to get over Christopher. I don't know if I'm over him even now, but I know one thing – when you kissed me then I wasn't thinking of anyone else. Ever since you dragged me out of the sea I've been falling in love with you.'

'You thought I was your husband at the time,' he reminded her gently. He looked at her and there was a tenderness in his expression. 'Please, forget what I said. Don't get close to me. I mean it. It would be the worst thing you could do.'

They reached the clay pit and drove into the works entrance. It was still raining and they stared at the water on the windscreen. 'I'll come with you,' Joseph said. He pulled on his boots and raincoat.

'You'll get wet.'

'I can't sit in the car and watch you.'

The pit manager, Kettlewell, had already gone out into the clay workings, and the boy in charge of the office did not understand the delivery concessions Esther had agreed with him. 'Oh, come on,' she said, turning to Joseph, 'we'll have to find him.' Esther set off ahead of him across the muddy yard into the clay pit.

The clay, always soft underfoot, had been turned by the sudden downpour into a landscape of mud, intersected with holes and furrows where the ground had been dug and vehicles had ploughed deep channels. Water lay in pools and runnels of slime, glistening, lifeless; it clung and sucked at their boots, so that every step became an effort.

'Keep to the higher ground,' Esther called. 'It's usually passable at the edges.'

Joseph did not answer. She turned to look at him and saw that his face was pale and sweating.

'Is anything the matter?'

'It's the mud. I should have realised. I'll go back.' He waved a hand to her to go on. 'Don't worry. I'll be fine.'

Esther was puzzled. What did he mean, he should have realised? She watched him turn back towards the yard. She could see Mr Kettlewell at the clay workings, talking to a group of diggers. She hesitated, then, as the manager came towards her, she went on.

'This is no place for a lady,' Kettlewell said.

'I needed to see you. I wanted to ask you to repeat the special order for the clay you sent last time, but I couldn't make the boy in the office understand what I wanted.'

'It comes from a finer seam than the rest. I'll come back with you and we'll get down what you want.' They turned and started back towards the office. 'Still selling abroad?'

'Yes.'

'It's nice to know you're doing well,' Kettlewell said. 'It's good for us to have regular orders locally again.' He broke off. 'Is he with you?'

Esther glanced in the direction where he was pointing. Joseph had left the outer edge of the workings but, instead of making for the yard where the Bentley was parked, he had begun heading towards the part of the pit where the mud was at its thickest.

'What's the silly so-and-so think he's playing at?' Kettlewell broke into a laboured run, his feet splayed for balance, his boots making a sucking, sloppy sound with each step.

Joseph's head jerked up when he heard Kettlewell's shout, and Esther's heart turned cold as she understood what had happened. She saw the clay workings as Joseph saw them – the grey, pock-marked landscape of the battlefield. He waved his arms. His face was strained with terror. 'No! Get back. Get down! Get down!'

'He's a mental case,' muttered Kettlewell.

Esther struggled after him. 'You don't understand. He was on the Somme. He—' She halted as Joseph let out a yell of anguish.

'Can you hear them? God, can't you hear them? I've got to get to them!' His eyes were wild with the horror that gripped him as he stared at Esther but seemed not to see her, seizing Kettlewell's arm and holding him back from the pool of water in front of them. 'Listen!' He held up his hand so that Esther, shaking with tension, strained her ears to hear the sounds that had filled him with such terror.

The cries of the workers at the cutting face, as they laughed and called to one another, drifted across the clay pit. 'Can't you hear them? They're drowning out there.' Joseph turned on them with another cry of anguish.

'You can't help them, old son.' Kettlewell, taking charge of the situation, eased Joseph's fingers from his sleeve and put his own arm round his shoulders. The pit manager's expression was strained, but his voice was almost tender as he coaxed, 'Come on, lad. Let's get back.'

Joseph stared at him, then burst into tears. He wiped his face on his coat sleeve. 'Sorry. Don't know what happened.' He looked at Esther, but his eyes still did not seem to see her. He allowed himself to be led away, trudging through the mud like a sleepwalker with his hands thrust deep into his coat pockets. He obeyed Kettlewell's instruction to get into the passenger seat of the Bentley and sat with his head back against the seat. His face was waxy and glistened with sweat as the clay-pit manager closed the car door.

Kettlewell turned to Esther, and his own face was pale. 'I hoped I'd seen the last of that sort of thing. Poor blighter. Do you want me to telephone for help?'

'No. I can manage him,' Esther said, though she had no idea whether it was true. She saw Kettlewell watch them until they had left the clay-pit site. She drove steadily, glancing from time to time at Joseph, praying that he wasn't still lost in the nightmare world inside his head. He had begun to shake. Sweat poured down his cheek and jaw, and she did not know what to do. Should she halt the car, cover him with a travel rug from the boot, or drive grimly on? After a while she pulled the Bentley into the side of the road. She fetched the rug and wrapped it round him, then knelt on the running-board beside the passenger seat and held him tightly, repeating over and over, 'It's all right. Its all right.'

At last she felt him grow still and his breathing became more even. Esther relaxed her grip and stood up.

'You should have left me there,' Joseph said. 'I wish I was under six feet of mud.'

'No, you don't,' Esther was glad to find some relief in anger. 'Don't talk like that. I can't stand self-pity.'

'I should have died with the rest of them.'

'How can you say that? Christopher died with the rest of them. What use is he to anyone six feet under? You should be thanking God you were left alive.'

He looked at her in disgust. 'You silly bitch. You don't even know what you're talking about.'

Esther hit him. His look was startled as she slammed shut the door and returned to the driving seat. She stared through the windscreen and clenched her hands in her lap, shaking with anger, waiting for him to speak. But he would not look at her. He covered his face with his hands as if to shut her out.

Esther felt a wave of remorse. She turned to him and stroked his hair from his forehead and, pulling away his fingers from his eyes, kissed his face, then his mouth, urging a response. She moved away and they sat, staring at one another.

'I'm sorry,' Esther said. 'I shouldn't have done that. I should never

172

have hit you.' She started the car and they drove on slowly.

After a while Joseph said, 'I lost a whole section.' The self-pitying note had gone from his voice; he spoke levelly and without emotion. 'We went with the first wave on the Somme. I was nineteen. I'd just been put in charge of a section, and I led every one of those poor blighters to their death. Men went down in their thousands in the first wave. They say it was like cutting corn and that they picked off the officers first – but not me. Oh, no. I got a head wound, only a graze, but it was enough to put me out for a few minutes. When I came round I hadn't a clue what was going on. I was terrified, an absolute gibbering idiot. It's a wonder I didn't run round in circles like the rats used to do when they got hysterical: I would have got my head blown off there and then.' Joseph fell silent. Esther drove without looking at him and, after a while, he continued in a flat, exhausted voice. 'Anyway, I eventually came to my senses and managed to crawl back to the lines. Nobody knew I'd been in a funk, but that wasn't the end of it; we could hear them, those who'd pushed on and been hit, calling, out there in No Man's Land, on the wire, in flooded shell-holes. It took some of them more than sixteen hours to die, until we couldn't hear them any more.' He looked at her. 'That was the real hell. Hearing those poor chaps begging us to go to them and we couldn't do anything for them.'

'It wasn't your fault,' Esther said. 'Nobody should have been put through that.'

'But I was. And if it was some sort of test – I failed, Esther. I was one of those who broke under the strain. And then at Christmas – months after it was over – I wept, I fought, I screamed and yelled and they had to tie me down to a stretcher and shove a gag in my mouth. Nervous collapse, they called it. They sent me to the hospital at Étaples and then home to England.'

'Do you want to talk to Julia?' Esther said after a while. 'I mean – do you need her to help you?'

'No. I don't want Julia,' he said as they neared The Dovecote. 'I've run to Julia too often.'

He climbed from the car in the courtyard and opened the door for her. 'I'll be fine now. Don't worry. It used to be happening all the time.'

'Are you sure you're all right?'

He nodded. 'I'll put the car away.' He turned to her. 'What we talked about earlier, about being more than friends. Forget it.' His manner was brusque, almost offhand. 'Don't take things I say like that too seriously. I mean, I'm not consistent, Esther. Julia will tell you. It's all part of the same problem – of not being right in the head.'

Esther watched him climb into the driving seat of the Bentley. He did not look at her again and she turned away. It was as though she had found happiness and lost it again all in one morning. She realised, with a certainty that startled her, that she could have loved Joseph with the same singlemindedness as she had once loved Christopher.

She walked through the archway from the courtyard and crossed the

173

lawn to the kitchen garden to fetch a lettuce for her lunch. Freddie was working among the runner-bean poles. He waved to her and nodded when she pointed to indicate that she was taking a lettuce. She walked back slowly towards the pottery studio, restless after what had happened; she felt little inclination to start packing up the latest commission for London. Again she wondered about going to Birmingham for a few days; it would give her time – Joseph too – to think things over. The rest of the day stretched before her until Cassie came home from school. She knew she would waste it sketching designs that didn't satisfy her, when what she really wanted was to be with Joseph.

Christopher had been one of those who had died, she reminded herself; and yet she felt no resentment because Joseph had survived. She wondered whether Christopher too had cried for help and then been abandoned by his comrades. She closed her mind to the images that crowded it. How much more terrible to picture such scenes from memory.

She sensed that something was wrong before she entered the studio. Had she left the door so far ajar, or the bowl of Peter's flowers in precisely that position on the table near the entrance? Esther walked slowly into the workshop. A number of the pots from the consignment for London lay smashed on the floor behind the door. It was as if a hand had hurled them from the shelf in an explosion of energy. Esther crouched to pick up a broken section of a jug. She held it in her lap and stared at it. The sun shone on the earth floor, hard and thick with clay-dust and foot-prints; but they gave no clue as to who had been there.

The pots couldn't have been knocked from the shelf by accident, Esther reasoned, yet she could not imagine that anyone from The Dovecote would break them deliberately. She remembered Julia's warning about ignoring the spirits – her claim that Christopher was upset by her friendship with Joseph. She stood and looked round the empty studio. Despite the sunshine it felt cold. A swirl of cool air wrapped itself round her and softly swung the door to. At the same time Esther heard a footstep outside and a shadow fell across the gap near the floor. She drew in her breath sharply and, moving forward in one stride, flung open the door.

Chapter Eleven

Joseph stood outside. 'I came over to apologise for being such a pig to you a minute ago.' He stared past her at the broken pots. 'What's happened?'

Esther was trembling. 'I found them like that. You don't think . . . It couldn't have been Christopher?'

He stared at her, then laughed. 'You mean ghosts? Julia *has* got to you.' He bent and picked up a piece of broken pot. 'There's nothing very supernatural about this. What a shame. They were lovely.'

'Julia herself then? It's the sort of thing she might do to persuade me that Christopher is trying to get through to me.'

He looked at her in surprise. 'Well, I wouldn't put it past her.'

'But why – unless she's crazy – or a fraud? You told me she wasn't a fraud,' Esther said accusingly.

'Not in the ordinary sense – but she gets obsessions.' Joseph looked again at the broken crockery. 'She can't stand it when her doves flap their wings too independently – and she definitely feels you've done that. She can manage Rowena and Freddie – they're not very complicated. She can cope with Meg and Peter – Peter is a model dove, a star pupil – though Meg upset her when she sold some of his paintings.'

'And what about you?' Esther said quietly. 'Can she manage you?'

He avoided the challenge in her eyes. 'She was already looking for another deserving cause when you arrived. You fitted the role perfectly: a grief-stricken widow in need of love; talented, ripe for a patron – her new chosen dove.'

Esther shivered. 'I wish you wouldn't keep using that expression. I'm beginning to hate it.'

'You're not one of Julia's doves,' he said. 'You, me and Cassie are like the wild pigeons in the courtyard. Pigeons can come and go as they please. They feed where they want. They are independent.'

At last Esther laughed. 'Tell me – however did I get involved with this place?'

'The same as I did – its magic is seductive.'

Esther found a bucket and began to pick up the pieces of broken pot. Joseph bent to help her.

'What am I going to do about Julia?' Esther said after a while.

'Refuse to be browbeaten. See her games for what they are.'

175

'Is she mad?'

'Perhaps. A little. But who isn't?' He looked at her and Esther knew that he was remembering the clay pit. He stood up and moved away to the window.

'Have lunch with me,' Esther said suddenly. 'I really would like you to have lunch with me – to say thank you for driving me to the clay pit this morning.'

He nodded. 'Yes. I should like to stay.'

They swept up the last of the pottery, then went upstairs to the flat. Esther set out lunch on the coffee table. 'What are you thinking about?' she said, as Joseph stood, leaning against the low ceiling, his hands in his pockets, staring out across the garden through the skylight.

'About what happened – about the men.' He sat beside her on the sofa bed. 'I think of them a lot when I'm alone. Sometimes they sound like sea birds calling. It was like that towards the end – weird after the screaming. A wailing would start up – one would start off another – and we crouched in the mud, listening, helpless.'

'But it's over now.'

'Is it? That's what I thought afterwards. And then, without any warning, my nerve went. Every time I heard a shell I got the shakes. It was as if all hell had been let loose again.' He looked up. 'I'm sorry. Your husband . . . I shouldn't talk about it, but this morning has stirred it all up again.'

'Eat,' Esther said with mock severity, pouring coffee, relieved when he did as she said. 'I never thanked you properly for making the furniture in here.'

'It was Julia's idea. She wanted the best. She knew you would come back.' He paused, remembering how Julia had enlisted the help of the 'spirits' when Esther was in Birmingham. He wondered whether to tell her and make light of it. What was he doing here in her flat? he asked himself, looking round at the furniture he had made, commissioned by Julia with such certainty. He noted the feminine touches Esther had added to the flat: the cushions, plants, a few photographs of Cassie, and others – her family? None, he noticed, of her husband. He remembered the previous day – Julia's words, warning him off: 'You're getting too fond of her. Put a stop to it now, before you both get hurt.'

Joseph knew Julia was right. He shouldn't be getting involved with any woman, least of all one as vulnerable as Esther. But there were times when he wished Julia would leave everyone alone. He remembered Esther coming after him and emptying his knapsack . . . The memory made him uneasy. He turned his thoughts instead to the previous evening in Exeter. For once, it hadn't helped to be with the others – to get away and lose himself in drink and music. They had gone to a dance hall, and he had picked up a girl and danced with her all evening. There was usually a comfort in the soft touch of a woman's clothing, the small hand in his, the smell of cigarette smoke and cheap scent and the light chatter that ran along with the music, so that one need say little, only let the girl do all the talking. It was the music that helped as much as anything, he realised. More than alcohol. It blotted out thought and held at bay the images that lurked, dark and shapeless, in the recesses of his mind, waiting to leap out and identify themselves, to seize him by the throat screaming, 'Remember the death, the noise? Remember how it was?'

'And of course, Joseph Kilburn furniture is the best,' Esther was saying, smiling at him, relaxed now they were having lunch.

'Of course.' Joseph brought himself to with an effort.

'It's true,' Esther said happily. 'I wonder your marchesa let you leave Italy.' She stood and cleared away one of the food plates to a table near the window.

Joseph watched her, feeling a quietness steal over him and reluctant to resist a sense of pleasure at being with her. The memory of the clay pit faded, became unimportant compared with the growing realisation that he was in love and swiftly getting out of his depth. To bathe in this feeling of elation, to let matters take their course was tempting. 'She's not my marchesa,' he said.

'I wish I knew what she was like. Was she very beautiful?'

'You look lovely,' he said suddenly. 'I wish I could paint. I would try a portrait. Like that, with the light on you.'

'Julia has been painting me. I saw the portrait yesterday. I'd no idea she was doing it. I had the strangest feeling about it – as if she had got inside me somehow. It was almost frightening.' Esther remembered why she had gone to Julia's studio – in search of Christopher – and she fell silent. What a strange mood had come over her yesterday, so that she had been ready to listen to Julia's Spirit Guide and to believe that she had seen Christopher in person. '*Why* do we always end up talking about Julia? Tell me about the marchesa.'

'We talk about Julia because, in spite of everything, she gets under our skin.' Joseph felt a sharp sense of anger. For a moment he hated Julia, who was part of his past, who still had a power over him, who could make him feel he was dependent on her and that if he broke away completely he would be lost again. If only they could go far away from The Dovecote, he and Esther and Cassie. Was it possible? Could he forget and start his life again?

Esther came to sit beside him. They looked at one another and Joseph saw that Esther wanted him as much as he wanted her, suddenly, and with a physical rush. She blushed because she knew that it showed in her eyes.

'Come here,' he said. 'I want to kiss you again.'

'Not until you've told me about the marchesa.'

'I didn't have a very serious love affair with Maria. She was a good friend . . . and, yes, I slept with her now and then. Do you mind?'

'No,' Esther lied.

'Perhaps, if I had been older, or she had been younger . . .'

'I am much older than you,' Esther persisted.

'Not enough to put you in your dotage.'

'Julia is even older.' She was teasing, but he saw at once that she had regretted saying it.

Joseph frowned. Julia was different. Julia took away the pain. And he remembered that, even in Italy, the nightmares had come. However far away he went, there would be no escape. He was no good to Esther. Julia was right. Where was the point in pretending he could ever lead a normal life? A shadow clouded his eyes, bringing to them a closed-off expression. He stood and walked restlessly to the window. 'Perhaps we'd better call a halt to this. Nervous strain or stark, raving barmy – it can't work. You have the memories of your dead husband, but I have a living death on my shoulders. I've no right to accept anyone's love.'

Esther went to him and, folding her arms round him, silenced him with her lips on his mouth. 'You've as much right to love as anyone. No. More.' She kissed him again. 'Love me,' she whispered, pity and compassion mingling with desire. Joseph could not hold out against the need that flooded through him; his mouth softened with passion and he drew her to him. His hands gripped hers, released them, grasped her hair, her neck and reached for her waist as he kissed her again. He lifted her and carried her to the sofa and there, on a tide of hunger, they made love.

They lay, still at last together, and the soft afternoon sunlight stole across the room. Now what? Esther wondered. Do we banish all the spectres of the past and live happily ever after? Do we run away together and tell Julia her doves have flown? As if he understood her thoughts, Joseph stirred and said, 'Regrets?'

'No. Have you?'

'I couldn't regret anything just now.' He sat up and rolled over to reach for his clothes.

Esther stroked the line of his back and thigh. 'I do love you. It wasn't just lust, was it? We can make one another happy.'

He did not answer but began to dress, and Esther felt the sense of distance in him return, affecting them both. He turned a face serious with concern towards her. 'You saw what happened to me this morning. That was fairly mild. Sometimes I wake in the night raving like a madman. During the war, when I was in France, I tried to strangle another soldier.'

'That was a long time ago now.'

'How do I know something like that won't ever happen again?' He knelt beside her and took her face in his hands. 'Do you understand? I can't offer you anything except this. The rest is what you saw this morning. I don't sleep at night. I get moods. I go off at a tangent.'

'I could live with that.'

'I can't ask you to. Sometimes Julia knows what she's talking about.'

'What has Julia got to do with it? I love you.'

'And I am almost sure I love you. Which is why . . .'

'Which is why it would work,' she insisted. 'At least give it a chance ... Won't you? I'm not expecting you to ask me to marry you. Let's take one thing at a time.'

Joseph turned away; he finished dressing then came to her. He looked at her long and hard, wanting more than anything to believe her. 'As soon as you've had enough, you'll be honest about it ... ? No pretending?'

'I promise.'

She moved from him and he swung her round, forcing her to look at him. 'I mean it. It's important. We've got to be absolutely honest with one another.'

'I promise,' Esther repeated. 'No pretending.' She felt a momentary stab of unease, for there was in the pledge a distinct echo of another time, another love, when honesty had seemed to be of supreme importance. But Joseph wasn't Christopher, she told herself, dismissing her misgivings. They went downstairs and walked across the lawn to the house, and Esther, seizing Joseph's hand, felt buoyant with happiness. She had no false illusions about there being a 'happy ever after'. There would be wonderful moments of oblivion like those of the past hour, but Joseph would never be miraculously freed from his trauma. Perhaps she would never quite be free of Christopher, but they had both taken a step forward. The next step was to confront Julia.

'We should tell everyone, don't you think?' she said. 'Let Julia see we don't care a straw about the spirits disapproving?'

Joseph smiled. He did not contradict her, but there was less certainty in his own mind that Julia would understand.

The others were having lunch in the kitchen. Rowena presided over the table. Peter was laughing with Julia over something. They glanced up and quickly fell silent when they saw Esther and Joseph come in together. Freddie, munching on a breadstick, let his mouth fall open in an 'o' of surprise.

'Well!' said Meg. 'To what do we owe this pleasure? Joseph has come to lunch.'

Julia said nothing. She looked from Joseph to Esther and back at Joseph, and Esther knew the fact they had recently made love was written all over their faces. She felt a tremor of fear and was glad when Joseph reached for her hand again and held it. She gripped his fingers to steady herself.

'We've had lunch already,' said Joseph. 'We lunched together.'

He laid emphasis on the word 'together', and Julia's eyes flashed and narrowed. She rested her elbows on the table and pressed the fingers of one hand against her lips, surveying Esther, then spoke at last. 'Is this some sort of announcement – the touching hand-clasp, the sweet air of harmony?'

'Isn't harmony what you always aim for, Julia?' murmured Meg.

'Esther, darling, I'm distraught,' cried Freddie, placing his hand flat across his heart. 'How could you reject me and take up with another?'

179

'Oh, shut up,' Rowena scowled at him. 'Can't you see they're serious?' She glanced warily at Julia.

'I need a cigarette.' Julia turned to Freddie. 'Give me a cigarette.'

Freddie picked up a packet of cigarettes from the window-seat and handed one to Julia. Her hand trembled as she lit it and she puffed nervously, blinking her eyes against the smoke. 'Well, you already know my reservations, but I shall try to be happy for you, darlings. You are both very dear to me.' She paused. 'Will you stay here?' throwing a swift glance at Joseph, 'I shouldn't want to think I was going to lose your joint talents.'

'Yes, for now,' Esther said quickly. 'For a little while.' She took a deep breath. 'But I want us to get one thing clear. I don't for a minute think Christopher has been trying to get in touch with me from the other side. Nor do I believe he would object to my friendship with Joseph even if he *could* know about it. And the fact that I walked into my studio when I came back from the clay pit and found my pots smashed on the floor has nothing to do with Christopher either.'

'Your pots are broken? Which ones?' Julia's hand paused in mid-air, her cigarette half-way to her lips. Again she glanced at Joseph. He frowned impatiently under her gaze and, releasing Esther's hand, walked to the window, distancing himself from them all.

'Some of my order for London.'

'But who would do such a thing?' said Peter.

Esther looked at Julia. 'You tell me.'

'Oh, no,' Peter protested. 'You can't accuse Julia. She loves your work. Julia couldn't see it destroyed.'

Julia smiled, then she stood slowly and stubbed out her cigarette on her plate. 'Don't worry, Peter dear. I understand why Esther is behaving like this. She hates to admit that sometimes I am right.'

Esther remembered that Joseph had used almost the same words. *Sometimes Julia knows what she's talking about.* He didn't appear to have noticed, nor even to have heard, but stood with his back to them and his arms folded, looking out at the garden. His figure was in silhouette, and Esther caught her breath as, for an instant, she saw Christopher there. She shook off the impression, feeling angry with him. Why didn't he stand by her and face Julia squarely? Was he so afraid, that the only way he could deal with Julia was by distancing himself?

'We ought to investigate the studio,' said Meg. 'Perhaps the cat...'

'A cat didn't do that,' Esther said coldly.

'I warned you,' Julia said with a dry smile. 'The spirits have a way of telling us what we least want to hear.'

'You mean Christopher?' said Esther. 'Christopher threw a few pots around the studio to let me know he thinks I should stay celibate?' She heard Joseph's swift intake of breath. So he *was* listening. She glanced at him and saw him turn and shake his head with a warning glance. Why didn't he support her? Esther thought wretchedly. They ought to stand up to Julia together.

'Christopher's spirit isn't jealous, Esther,' Julia said. 'How little you understand of what I've been trying to tell you. He still cares about your happiness.'

'So, he shows it by smashing my work?'

Meg said, 'Are you sure you didn't break the pots yourself?' Her pale face flushed scarlet as they all stared at her, and she turned suddenly and walked from the kitchen.

The others let their gaze rest on Esther, the idea clearly taking root in their minds. 'Well, did you?' said Peter sympathetically. 'You've been under a lot of strain lately.'

'No, of course she didn't.' Joseph swung away from the window. He leaned against the wall and lit a cigarette. 'Esther – can't we forget about your pots for now?'

'It could have been any one of us,' said Freddie. 'We've all been here this morning. We're all a little jealous of Esther's talent. It could even have been you, Joseph. Were you with Esther when she found them?'

'Don't you think that's stretching things a bit?' said Esther with an exasperated laugh; but she felt her confidence ebbing as Julia continued to watch her calmly and Joseph made no further attempt to interfere, nor even to defend himself against Freddie's suggestion. He didn't appear to be listening any more, and had turned his head to look out at the garden again.

'Well then – it's one of those mysteries,' said Peter at last, trying to find a way of appeasement for everyone. 'I agree, you should forget it, Esther. It's not the only strange thing to have happened.' He looked at her with a meaningful expression, as if to remind her of the figure she had seen after the seance.

Esther stared at them. They all believed Julia's ridiculous rubbish about spirits – except Joseph, and he seemed to have lost interest altogether. It was as if the closeness they had shared in her flat was being swiftly eroded. The fact that they had made love seemed already to have been lost in the confusion of all the other events: Julia's seance, the figure on the attic stairs, and now the inquest into her broken pots. She wanted Joseph to reassure her that nothing mattered except the fact that they had found one another; but he seemed to have grown too distant to reassure anybody of anything. Esther turned and left the kitchen before the tears that pricked at her eyes could fall.

'Esther!' Freddie called after her placatingly. And Esther heard Rowena, with a familiar edge to her voice say, 'Oh, leave her alone, won't you? You're always trailing around after her.'

Esther went to the flat. Her idea about going to Birmingham for a few days seemed all at once to be sensible and rational. She began to pack a suitcase for herself and Cassie. She heard Joseph enter the studio and call to her. She did not answer and, after a few seconds, he came up the stairs. 'What on earth are you doing?'

'I have to think. I have to get away for a while.'

'From me?'

She looked at him, wanting him to tell her that what had happened between them had meant something – that it was more important to him than Julia, or his 'not very serious' love affair with the Italian marchesa. 'Why should you suppose that I want to get away from you?'

'Second thoughts already, perhaps?'

'No. Though I'm wondering whether you might have. Why did you go so cold on me? It's as if you're another person when Julia's there. I only wanted to get to the bottom of who broke my pots. Freddie had more to offer about it than you did.'

'If you haven't had second thoughts, why are you leaving?'

She returned to her packing: 'I have to work things out about Julia. If *she* didn't break my pots . . . I don't know what to think. If I go away for a few days with Cassie, perhaps everything will click into place somehow. Besides, I haven't seen Mummy and Daddy for months. We owe them a visit.' She came to him. 'It won't be for long – a few days. That's all.'

He kissed her, but without his earlier passion. 'I think perhaps it's a good idea,' he said, his face without expression.

Cassie did not know about the seance, but she knew that something had happened between her mother and Julia. Esther had explained, when she came home from school, that she wanted to sort something out in her mind, so they were going away to visit Granny and Granpy.

Going away. It was her mother's solution to everything. Esther would never have looked on it as *running* away, Cassie was to realise in later years. In Esther's own mind it was a means of coming to grips with a problem. She had to 'think' – but alone, always alone. She had to reach her own solutions without being influenced by anyone else, and, having 'sorted things out' she could continue, stronger than before . . . As she had done over Christopher's deception, when she left The Folly. As she had over George Ansfield and Giles wanting to marry her, when she went to live with Julia. Perhaps it was a good idea to put a distance between herself and Julia after the seance. But to do the same with Joseph, so soon after they had become lovers? Was she unconsciously testing him in some way?

Cassie did not know at first that her mother and Joseph were lovers, though she sensed a change between them when she came home from school that day, and in the rest of the community's attitude towards them. Cassie did not want to leave The Dovecote, nor did she want to leave Joseph; it would soon be the long summer holiday and he had promised to teach her all about woodworking that summer. Cassie was more afraid than she had been at Christmas that, when her mother had sorted things out, she would decide to stay in Birmingham and they would never see Joseph again.

Cassie was aware of an emptiness inside her when she thought of leaving Joseph, and she knew she couldn't bear it. She was twelve that summer. Her own feelings were becoming difficult to understand.

Sometimes, when she saw Joseph walk towards her across the garden or turn to laugh at her, or when he ruffled her hair and said, 'Cassie', in his special teasing way, she felt as if she were melting inside. The thought of losing that beautiful, brilliant creature and never to see him again tore at her heart. More pragmatically, she was afraid that, if they returned to Birmingham and stayed there, she might end up having to go back to Heather Park.

Her grandmother tried to push Esther and Giles together again while Cassie and her mother were in Birmingham. She clearly didn't know about Joseph, thought Cassie, or she wouldn't have wasted her time. The Fieldings came to tea one Sunday and it was all horribly embarrassing. Giles had obviously got over being in love with Esther, and yet her grandmother kept saying how they ought to spend some time together. It would be just like when they were younger. Didn't Mr and Mrs Fielding agree? Esther and Giles made weak excuses about why they couldn't see one another – there wasn't really enough time, they were both rather busy. In the end, Mrs Fielding said pointedly that Giles had been seeing rather a lot of Margaret Davenport lately, so perhaps it wouldn't be very sensible for Giles and Esther to go around together; Margaret might get the wrong idea. Cassie saw Esther and Giles look at one another and then they both began to laugh. She felt extraordinarily happy, for she had always liked Giles; she was glad he wasn't sad any more.

Esther spoke the truth when she had said that she was busy. After the weekend she had gone on a secret mission into Birmingham. Mrs Mortimer thought she was shopping, and Cassie said nothing because Esther had sworn her to secrecy. Esther had begun confiding things in Cassie around this time, and she told her a little about Joseph: she said that he had bad dreams and that sometimes he wasn't well, because of what happened in the war.

Cassie knew already about Joseph's nightmares. They were linked with her secret burial ceremonies under the cedar trees. At night when she leaned out of her bedroom window above the studio, hoping to hear the squeak of a mouse or a vole ascending to heaven, she would distinguish other sounds among the night noises: the screech of an owl, the shriek of a vixen and the stifled moans of the doves from the courtyard. Sometimes more puzzling cries had drifted on the night air. The wail of a soul in torment? The cries of a shipwrecked sailor carried on the wind? They never really frightened her, but they made her curious. When, seeing a light in Joseph's cottage one night, she had realised where the cries had come from, Cassie had ached with sadness and she had wanted to go to comfort him.

Cassie had not connected Joseph's night terrors with the war until her mother talked about them. She knew the war had killed people like her father in great numbers, and that it had made people sick and lopped off their limbs. When they had lived at The Folly a local man had gone away to be a soldier and he had come back with only half a face, the nose obliterated, one eye that watered and the other a shrivelled hole, but he had not frightened her in the way that he frightened the other children. Cassie had once seen a man with shell-shock in a garden near her grandparents' house in Birmingham; he was falling about and shouting and other people in the garden had run to help him. Cassie had walked on, for she had been taught by her grandmother not to stare, and afterwards Esther said the man's odd behaviour had been caused by the constant noise of gunfire in the trenches. That had not frightened Cassie either. So, when Esther said that Joseph had shell-shock Cassie was surprised, but not afraid. Joseph didn't shake his head from side to side or walk with a list, nor did he seem to be physically damaged – so that was all right – but she felt sorry for him about the night terrors.

Cassie heard her mother talking to Joseph on the telephone after her secret mission in Birmingham. It was a hot evening, and she could not sleep, so she was sitting on the stairs. She had often sat at the top of the stairs when Esther had been ill, listening to the sounds of the household below: the slip-slop of Martha the housemaid, going to and fro in her down-at-heel shoes, the rise and fall of her grandparents' voices talking in the sitting room. The ring of the telephone would always provide an element of intrigue as she tried to guess from the one-sided conversation who was on the other end of the line.

Cassie knew at once this time that Esther was talking to Joseph, because she sounded so happy; she said she was missing him and that she wouldn't stay more than a few more days in Birmingham; that she wasn't going to let Julia upset their plans; she said that even if Julia had been behind the broken pots it wasn't important any more; and she told Joseph about her visit to Denholm's the department store in Birmingham – that they still wanted to buy her pots.

'Would you be very unhappy if we left The Dovecote for good, Cassie?' Esther said later, coming to sit on the edge of Cassie's bed.

'So long as Joseph left too.'

'I hope we shall all three be able to live somewhere together, instead of with Julia. Would you mind that very much?'

Cassie hugged her mother, and joy swelled inside her so that she thought she might burst. 'Of course I shan't mind. Joseph's my favourite person.'

'He needs a lot of love,' Esther warned. 'Yours and mine.'

'Then we'll give it to him,' Cassie promised. She set aside her romantic crush on Joseph from that moment; the seeds of adult love, still barely acknowledged, buried themselves deeper in her subconscious. Her mother was happy again. That was all that mattered. Cassie thought for a while about the reality of leaving The Dovecote. 'I shall miss the doves.'

'And so shall I.'

'I shall miss Rowena and Freddie and the others.'

'There's no reason why we shouldn't still visit them sometimes,' Esther said gaily.

'Would I have to go to school at Heather Park?'

'Not if you don't want to.'

So, the future was settled. Esther went to visit the buyer at Denholm's again and began planning the production of an autumn range of pottery. All that remained was to decide with Joseph where they should live and work ... And then, one afternoon, George Ansfield came to see her.

'I heard you were back in Birmingham.'

'Golly, the grapevine works quickly among you businessmen,' Esther said. She led George into the sitting room. Her mother, aware of the potential for romance now that Giles Fielding was out of the running, brought them tea and left the room, closing the door with conspiratorial stealth.

George sat on the opposite side of the fireplace and Esther wished for once that her mother had stayed to make conversation instead of leaving them quite so delicately alone. He was dressed in tweeds, his shoes, as always, highly polished, and he looked fit and confident and somehow altered, as if he were lighter at heart. He sipped his tea and leaned back in the chair and surveyed Esther in a speculative way that increased her anxiety, for she still remembered the last time she had seen him, and his proposal of marriage.

'I was talking to someone at Denholm's. They said you had been there.'

'I was testing the waters.' Esther was cautious.

'Are you here in Birmingham for good?'

'No. Only visiting.'

'That's a pity. I was going to ask whether you're still interested in joining me.'

'What sort of joining you?' Esther said with a wry smile.

George's composure left him briefly and he blushed. 'In the business, of course. Don't worry, I've forgotten all that nonsense.' He toyed with his teaspoon then looked up. 'Ursula died at Christmas.'

'Oh – I'm sorry,' Esther said.

'I badly need a good designer. More than that, I'm thinking of expanding the factory's production to include a more superior ware. If you came to work for me you'd run the luxury ranges of designs.'

Esther shook her head. 'I'm sorry, George. I have my own business now. I've been in production for about six months.'

'I know. That's why I asked you. Your name is getting about. Esther, with your flair and ideas and my business experience, we could make a formidable team. Don't dismiss it out of hand.'

To Esther's surprise she was tempted. George knew his own worth when he said that he was a good businessman. She remembered how well they had once worked together; but it would mean coming to live near Birmingham, and she had no idea what Joseph would feel about setting up his own workshop in the Midlands, nor – she had to admit –

whether he was ready to leave The Dovecote straight away.

'I would want *complete* autonomy over my designs.'

'And you would have it. The warehouses over the road have just come on to the market. We could set up painting rooms for "Esther Norbrook" designs there. The main factory would supply you with the shapes you wanted.'

Esther smiled. 'You seem to have worked it all out.'

'Not really. The idea came to me when I heard you were back in the area.'

Esther stood and went to the window. She folded her arms, looking out at the roses in the garden. It was the dream she had once believed was impossible at Ansfield's. She felt a lift of excitement at the idea of producing her pots on a much larger scale. She would be able to concentrate on designing rather than on production; she would reach a much broader market, being close to retail outlets like Denholm's and other big stores. Instead of small runs of prestigious ware, she would be able to make tableware in imaginative styles that could influence people's taste all over the country. But what about Joseph? 'I'm not sure. It's complicated, George.'

'There's someone else involved.'

'How did you know?'

He laughed. 'It shines out of you. You look radiant. Don't tell me about it. I still feel embarrassed enough about last year for it to be rather painful.'

'I should have to discuss this with him.'

He stood. 'All right. Discuss it. But don't keep me waiting too long.'

Esther rang Joseph when George had gone. Rowena answered the telephone and her tone was guarded, even slightly hostile. 'I think Joseph's in his workshop.'

'Then would you call him?' Esther heard Rowena leave the telephone. After what seemed like hours Joseph came to the phone.

'Esther?' His voice sounded strained.

She told him about George's offer.

'You must take it,' he said at once.

'Just like that?' Esther laughed. 'You wouldn't mind?'

'I think it's the best thing that could have happened for you.'

'You mean you could bear to move your workshop and live in the Midlands?'

He did not answer at first. 'I mean it's your home territory. And you have your family there.'

'But what about you?' Esther persisted.

There was a pause, then he said quietly, 'I think you should forget about me.'

'No!' Esther's throat was dry and she could not swallow. What had happened? Her thoughts flew again to the scene in the kitchen at The Dovecote, remembering how Joseph had distanced himself, as if afraid of provoking Julia. She remembered his saying, 'Sometimes Julia knows what she's talking about.' What had Julia said while she was gone? Why hadn't she realised that she would take the opportunity to intervene?

'Esther – we'll talk about it,' Joseph said quietly. 'But not now. Not over the telephone.'

'Please,' Esther whispered, gripping the phone. She closed her eyes and her heart beat painfully against her ribs. 'Don't make any decisions. I'll be back at the end of the week.'

'Esther—'

'Yes?'

'Nothing. I love you. Whatever happens – believe that.'

Esther heard the click of the telephone. She stood with the handset against her breast, then put it back on the hall table.

It was Esther's mother who brought a letter to her in bed early the following morning. 'The postmark is Dorset,' she said, examining the envelope curiously. 'How very odd. The address is printed – almost as if a child had written it.'

'Mummy!' Esther snatched the letter from her, then frowned as she saw that her mother was correct: the letters were large and badly formed – though they looked as if they had been done by someone who wished to disguise their handwriting, rather than by a child. She slit the envelope and prised it open so that she could see the contents without drawing them out.

'Still peculiar?' her mother inquired, pretending to busy herself with folding Esther's dressing gown at the end of her bed.

'It's nothing – only a note from The Dovecote.' She closed the envelope and gave her mother a brief, dismissive smile. 'It's about going back.'

Esther waited until her mother had left the room. Her hands were trembling with anger as she took out the single sheet of paper and read again the sentence: 'KEEP AWAY FROM THE DOVECOTE.' Esther screwed up the paper and threw it across the room.

It was from Julia, of course. Julia, having thought about it, had decided to try to get rid of her, so that she could keep Joseph where she wanted him; she would rather frighten her away than lose her favourite dove. Well, one thing had become clear, Esther told herself as she dressed quickly and went to telephone Joseph: Julia's obsession with power had finally turned her head. And it must, after all, have been Julia who had broken her pots; like the note, it fitted so well with the bizarre warnings at the seance.

Meg answered the telephone; she said that Joseph wasn't there. No, she couldn't say where he was. Her voice was stiff, unmistakably hostile.

'Then let me talk to Julia,' Esther said.

'Julia isn't here either at the moment. Is anything wrong?'

'No. Nothing's wrong,' Esther said. 'But you can tell Julia to expect me back tonight.' She slammed the telephone receiver on its hook and replaced the set on the table. She returned to her room and, stooping to pick up the scrap of paper, smoothed it out between her fingers. She stared at it for a while, trying to quell a growing feeling of agitation, then put it back in its envelope and began to pack.

Chapter Twelve

The journey to Dorset took all day.

Esther avoided talking about Joseph. She knew Cassie had guessed that something had happened, but she could not confide in her. Cassie was talkative at first, glad to be going back, but after a while even she grew tired of talking to herself. And so they drove almost in silence until, towards dusk, they reached the avenue of beech trees.

The huge shapes towered above them. 'They don't seem so friendly, do they?' Cassie said, tipping back her head to look up into the dark mass of the tree canopy; and Esther felt her unease deepen.

It was almost dark when they reached The Dovecote. Julia came to meet them in the courtyard. There was an air of authority in the way she waited for them to climb from the car, then she came forward with open arms, loving as ever. 'We heard the car. Isn't it strange how one learns to recognise motor-car engines? I said at once, "That is Esther and Cassie returned to us."'

Esther looked at her coldly. She imagined Julia writing the note in her room, narrowing her eyes against the smoke from her cigarette as she leaned back to admire its brevity: KEEP AWAY FROM THE DOVECOTE. Was Julia a hypocrite as well as devious? Esther remembered with a jolt of regret how much she had once admired Julia for her loving generosity. Could she really have been so wrong?

Julia seemed as affectionate and enthusiastic as she always did as she swung their suitcases from the luggage-rack. 'Come on. We'll drop these off in the studio then go over to the house. We have supper waiting for you. You must both be hungry after such a long journey.'

A flicker of doubt weakened Esther's anger as she tried to guess what was going on in the other woman's mind. She scanned the barns as they crossed the lawn. The workshops were in darkness. They entered the pottery studio and Esther lit one of the lamps and swung round to confront Julia. 'Where's Joseph? Meg was cagey on the telephone . . . He's not here – is he?'

Julia put down the cases and placed her arm round Cassie's shoulders as if she hadn't even heard Esther's question. 'Do you know, Cassie? I think you've grown in a matter of days.' She turned to Esther. 'Children always grow much more quickly in the summer, don't you think? It's all the sunshine and fresh air. You must be starving, Cassie. Go to the kitchen and see if Rowena wants any help.'

'Julia, where is Joseph?' Esther repeated as Cassie crossed the lawn.

Julia turned at last to address the question. Her expression seemed to Esther to hold the faintest trace of satisfaction. 'Joseph went to London this morning. He left as soon as he knew you were coming back.'

Esther stared. 'Are you saying he didn't want to see me?'

Julia did not answer at first. She sat at Esther's pottery wheel and made the turntable spin slowly. 'Esther, darling, have you stopped to think what you might do to Joseph if you continue with your relationship? You had a husband who died at Passchendaele. You are a *constant* reminder of Joseph's pain.'

'There are a hundred and one constant reminders. I can help him get over them. I love him.'

Julia smiled gently. 'But so do I love him. We all love him at The Dovecote.'

'That's different. You know it is.'

'Yes, it is, but it's the sort of loving stability he needs. I'm convinced that you will be bad for him. Just as Christopher is convinced that Joseph is a disastrous choice for you.'

'Christopher is *dead*,' Esther said heavily, wearily.

Julia ignored her. 'What are you going to do when Joseph wakes beside you, screaming with fear? Not once, but night after night? Have you even thought of the effect on Cassie?'

'It doesn't frighten me. Nor will it frighten Cassie when she understands. Besides – his terrors come less often than they did.'

Julia looked at her with compassion. 'Esther, don't lie to me. He's told me all about what happened at the clay pit.'

Esther felt a wave of resentment – more potent than the jealousy she had felt when she knew that Joseph and Julia had been lovers. Why had he told Julia about the clay pit? It seemed a betrayal of the intimacy they had shared that day. Had Joseph also told Julia about their closeness when they returned to her flat? Had he discussed their love dispassionately with her, debating whether marriage would be out of the question in the light of his instability?

'We've decided the affair shouldn't be allowed to continue,' Julia said, swinging round on the stool to face her.

Esther gave a gasp of incredulity. So, her conjecture had not been very far wrong. 'We?'

'My doves. Meg, Peter, Rowena, Freddie – everyone here feels the same.'

'Is that why you warned me to stay away?' Esther said angrily, but relieved that Julia had not included Joseph in her quorum of doves. 'Oh, I got your note. Was it a joint effort?' She imagined them conferring, deciding what to write. 'I suppose you thought I would believe the spirits were at work again – Christopher talking to me through the national postal service? It's a bit terrestrial, isn't it?'

Julia frowned. 'Darling – I haven't the faintest idea what you are talking about.'

190

'This!' Esther drew the letter from her bag and thrust it at her.

Julia glanced at it. When she looked up her expression was one of apparent bewilderment. 'Why should I stoop to something so Machiavellian? If I wanted you to leave The Dovecote, I would tell you so. Besides, I don't want you to leave, and you're being very ungracious to imagine that I do; after all the work we've put into your pottery. You know how much I want you here, as much as I want Joseph here. I know this is where you belong. It's where you both work best.'

'Then who sent it?' Esther said in desperation.

'I could hazard an idea, but it wasn't me.' Julia handed the note back to her. 'Don't you believe me?'

Esther shook her head in bewilderment. 'I don't know.' She searched Julia's face, but there was no evidence of deception there, only a look of sympathy. Esther remembered Julia's tenderness towards her, the way she had offered the studio and provided everything she had needed. The love was still there, she realised. Julia's love still shone out from her eyes.

Julia seemed to hesitate. 'Esther, if Meg behaved oddly on the telephone . . . it's because some of the others have tended to blame you for upsetting Joseph. I think you should know that he had a relapse while you were away.'

A chill clutched at Esther's heart. She remembered Joseph's trauma at the quarry and imagined it happening again, in the isolation of his cottage. She saw him wandering on the cliff, lured by the cries of the sea birds, in search of his abandoned men. She should have been there. She shouldn't have been so self-absorbed as to make an issue of the broken pots: it seemed such a trivial matter now.

'I was here.' Julia regarded Esther calmly, as if reading her mind. 'I am always here. He knows he can rely on me. I won't ever abandon him as others have in the past.'

'I love him.' Esther repeated doggedly. 'I can make him happy.'

'That's extremely arrogant of you – and foolish, for it isn't true. Happiness is shortlived with Joseph. It's best he lives quietly. Change is disturbing for him. Remember how worried I was when he went to Italy?'

'Italy was good for him,' Esther insisted. 'He told me he had started to live again. It's this place that drags him down. The Dovecote is smothering – too loving, too demanding on everyone's emotions.'

A flash of uncertainty crossed Julia's face. 'If that's so, why do you both keep coming back? Why do my doves stay here with me?'

'Because you've fed them and tamed them so well that they've forgotten how to fly away.' Esther sat down suddenly on a chair. The realisation that Joseph had gone to London to avoid meeting her sank in. She remembered his strange mood on the telephone, his statement that she should accept George Ansfield's offer and forget all about him, as if already he had divorced himself from the memory of their intimacy.

191

'If only I'd been here.' Esther pictured Joseph in a state of terror. She turned on Julia accusingly. 'What did you say to him? I don't understand why he had a relapse.'

Julia avoided her eyes. She paused, steadying the wheel thoughtfully. 'He had violent dreams after you left. I thought he should talk about what was worrying him. His dreams are often more disturbing when he's worrying about something. In the end he told me about the incident at the clay pit and we talked for a long time about what was best for you both. I have a client interested in him. She's in London and very eager to see his work. We thought he should go away for a few days.'

'*You* thought he should.'

'I told you. I know him.' Julia smiled sadly. 'I did warn you.' She stood and went to the door. 'I'll leave you to calm down a little, but do come over to the house soon. Rowena has gone to a lot of trouble over a meal to welcome you back. We'll start afresh, Esther. All of us. We'll work out a way to live through this and, after a while, you'll see I'm right and you'll learn to forgive a little. It's the way of The Dovecote. These things always blow over.'

Esther took the suitcases up to the flat and began to unpack. She stood by the window with her arms folded tightly, seeing the lights of the house shine across the lawn in the darkness. She went over in her mind the recent scene with Julia, trying to pinpoint a flaw in her sincerity, but there had been none.

She turned from the window and her glance fell on the anonymous note. If Julia hadn't sent it, then who? She surveyed the room as if it might provide a clue, and she remembered the afternoon when she and Joseph had made love. Her heart ached as she contrasted their happiness that day with Joseph's coldness on the telephone. Had *he* sent the note because he wanted to keep her away? She remembered other contradictions in him. Why had he told Julia about the clay pit, after he had said that he didn't want her to know what had happened and that he had run to Julia too often in the past? Esther felt a fresh upsurge of jealousy as she imagined him discussing the situation in Julia's studio or in his cottage, Julia touching his cheek in that devouring way of hers, looking at him with eyes that brimmed with concern.

Esther paced the floor restlessly. If only she could see him face to face, look into his eyes, hold him again, she would know what was in his mind. Or would she? Esther pictured his closed expression when she felt cut off from his thoughts. Could one ever know what was going on in another person's mind? She remembered her gullibility over Christopher and her discovery about The Folly. For all his talk of integrity, had she known Christopher at all? Should she have guessed that he had been relying on Hugh and Marjorie to support them? Had the clues been there and she had missed them? She tried to remember and failed as she returned restlessly to her suitcase, its lid still open on the floor. She lifted it on to the sofa and began to empty it. Joseph was different, she told herself fiercely. She had not been wrong about the pain in him, nor about the love in his eyes when he had said they must always be honest with one another. An idea began to form in her mind and quickly she began to repack.

There was a restrained mood of welcome at dinner. Rowena seemed oddly anxious to please. The others responded dutifully to Julia's efforts to produce a mood of normality as they chatted about the Winmouth summer visitors, the community's courses, the garden, the weather; anything except the fact that Joseph had gone away or had been sent away in order not to see her.

Cassie chatted artlessly with everyone. Her uncomplicated pleasure at being back at The Dovecote helped to ease the tension, but Esther's mind was calculating her strategy for the next day. She guessed that Meg would have booked the hotel for Joseph in London and, laying a hand on her arm, drew her aside as they left the dining room after supper.

'I need to know where Joseph is staying. If I can talk to him without Julia around . . .'

Meg looked at her impassively, then at Julia's figure striding ahead of them to the sitting room. She lowered her voice. 'She won't like it if you go after him. We all agreed, Esther. Joseph's best on his own.'

'Meg – I love him. I really love him. Think how you would feel if it was Peter.'

Meg regarded her and her eyes shifted guiltily. 'All right. Come to my room later this evening.'

Esther wandered round the room. Meg's paint sketches lay on the desk and she glanced at them restlessly.

'You don't have to tell me. They're amateurish,' Meg said, looking up from searching through various notebooks.

'No, they're not. They're very good.'

'But Peter's are better.'

'Peter's *are* special.'

Meg sighed with an air of acceptance. She looked at Esther and hesitated. 'I'm sorry if I've misjudged you. I've been unkind and I feel ashamed of myself . . .'

'No, Meg,' Esther said at once. 'When I was a stranger here you all made me so welcome. I've upset the status quo. There was bound to be some ill-feeling. I understand.'

'No, you don't.' Meg sat very stiffly, her thin hands turning the pages of the notebook in her lap, without looking at them. Suddenly a flush suffused her face. 'It was me who broke your pots.'

Esther stared at her. 'You?'

Meg nodded. 'I saw Peter had taken you some flowers that morning. I was so angry.' She pulled a handkerchief from her sleeve, beginning to cry. 'It's Julia really, I suppose. She makes us behave irrationally, we're

193

all affected by her – even you. We get things out of proportion.'

Relief flooded through Esther. Julia hadn't broken her pots, nor had any ghost, nor – and she realised how fearfully she had considered the possibility – nor had Joseph. 'And the note telling me to keep away from The Dovecote,' Esther said. 'So that was you too?'

Meg dried her eyes and drew in a shuddering breath. She looked at her with a puzzled expression. 'What note?'

Esther's hopes fell again as she realised that Meg had no idea what she was talking about. 'Oh, it doesn't matter.' She glanced again at Meg's painting – a water-colour sketch of the garden. 'Why do you stay here?' she asked curiously.

'Because of Peter. Peter thrives on the intense atmosphere of The Dovecote. He understands the contradictions here, the love that borders on obsession, the fine line between Julia's guidance and her need for power. He owes a lot to Julia. Without her he wouldn't be painting such wonderful pictures.' Meg smiled. 'I do know Julia has nurtured something in him that I could never have brought to the surface. Just think! Peter might never have discovered his true genius. It wouldn't have happened if he hadn't come here.' She paused. 'And Julia did the same for Joseph, you know. She helped him to work again. There's so much suffering in Joseph, a hatred of the war and what it did to him, but also guilt because he survived.'

'It's not the same,' Esther said fiercely. 'Joseph doesn't need Julia any more.'

'Can you really be so sure? You've known him less than a year. He has known Julia for most of his life.'

Esther said impatiently, 'Are you going to help me or not?'

Meg hesitated, then she bent and tore a page from one of the notebooks in her lap.

Esther read the address and telephone number of a London hotel. 'Thank you.'

'What about Cassie?'

'I'll take her with me.'

'Leave her here. She'll be all right, I promise. Rowena and I will see to that. And there will be less of a stir if you slip away on your own.'

Esther told Cassie briefly where she was going.

'Does Julia know?'

'Not yet. But I'm sure Meg will tell Rowena, and Rowena will soon tell Julia. Anyway, it doesn't matter whether she does or not.'

'Will she be cross?'

'I expect so.'

Cassie was thoughtful.

'Don't you want me to go?' Esther said.

Cassie flung her arms round her. 'I don't mind about Julia. So long as you come back with Joseph.'

Esther thought about this exchange as she left the Morris in the station yard and walked towards the railway booking office. How much did Cassie know about the tangle of emotions involved? She realised that, of all of them, Cassie was the least in awe of Julia. She smiled as she remembered the first time Cassie had stood up to her, saying she was not Cassandra, nor was she a prophetess, that the role of prophet was reserved exclusively for characters in the Bible. How long ago it all seemed – since Cassie had left Heather Park, since they had lived in Tamarisk Street and she had worked at Ansfield's.

It had begun to rain and Cassie was confined indoors after Esther had driven away. The hours dragged as she concentrated on avoiding Julia, for she knew that Julia would soon guess where Esther had gone: departures and arrivals at The Dovecote never went unobserved. Cassie was not really afraid of Julia, but she knew she didn't want to witness her anger if she could help it. She sat in the window of the studio flat for a while, listening to the sporadic murmurs of conversation between Rowena and Violet, painting pots in the studio below. She heard Rowena tell Violet that Esther was in London, and she crept to the top of the stairs.

They were discussing Esther and Joseph. 'She ought to leave him alone,' Rowena was saying. 'Stirring him up like that and upsetting Julia – upsetting all of us. Mind you, Freddie was in the war too . . . He didn't go funny in the head because of it. If you ask me, there was something wrong there to begin with – I mean, Joseph's a bit of an odd fish.'

'Yellow,' said Violet. 'That's what my father says about those that got themselves invalided out like that . . .'

Cassie returned to the window of the flat, not wanting to hear anything else bad about Joseph. She wouldn't have it, she told herself fervently, tears stinging her eyes. He wasn't an odd fish and he certainly wasn't a yellow-belly coward. She stared at the rain, beginning to wish it wasn't a holiday, for at least at school the time went quickly and she had company of her own age. Rowena came to see her with a glass of milk at eleven o'clock and Cassie told her stiffly, remembering the conversation with Violet, that she was going to arrange her pebble collection.

'Meg says you're to sleep at the house tonight. Your mother has gone to London.' Rowena regarded Cassie thoughtfully.

'Yes, but you're not to tell Julia.'

Rowena looked apprehensive. 'Julia's sure to wonder where she is.'

'Please,' Cassie said, swallowing her hostility and smiling encouragingly.

'All right. Just for now.' Rowena went away again, suggesting Cassie come downstairs to the studio and that she should help her in the kitchen later, bribing her with the promise of a surprise for lunch. But Cassie did not want Rowena and Violet's company, and she was too wary of meeting Julia to take up the suggestion of helping in the kitchen. She reasoned that if she stayed in the window of her bedroom she would be able to keep an eye on the house, and she would have plenty of warning if Julia decided to come over to the studio. She was not sure what Julia might do to her – Julia rarely shouted and her displeasure was always cold. She knew she would not hurt her and yet, for the first time in her life, without Esther there, Cassie began to feel afraid.

She had drunk the milk and rearranged the pebbles and began to dream up a design for the house she and Esther would share with Joseph, when a movement on the lawn caught Cassie's eye and her heart fluttered under her ribs. Then she saw with relief that Julia wasn't coming to see her, nor the women in the pottery, for she wore her raincoat and carried an umbrella and she had Peter with her as they headed towards the courtyard. After a while Cassie heard the sound of the Ford rattling down the hill.

Cassie put away her things and went downstairs. Esther's pots stood in rows on the shelves: those awaiting decoration on the lower shelves, those that had been completed and were ready for refiring on the top. Rowena looked up and smiled as Cassie passed her, and Violet said, 'What mischief are you up to now?'

Cassie told her scornfully that she was too old for mischief. She had not disliked Violet before today, but now – after the damning accusation against Joseph – she decided that she didn't care for her very much at all. Why had she never noticed how big and awkward Violet was, or that her laugh was always too loud? Besides, Violet thought Julia was a 'wonderful' person: what sort of judge of character was that?

Cassie ran to the house, enjoying the rain on her face and the sharp sensation as it touched the back of her neck and her bare arms. The entrance hall was empty. She could hear Freddie and Meg talking in the sitting room. She had been going to visit Freddie, but now that Meg was with him, and with Julia away from the house, it seemed as if Cassie had the whole of The Dovecote to herself as she went upstairs to the first floor.

The corridors leading to the bedrooms and to the attic studios lay silent and deserted. Cassie wandered to the bedroom next to Rowena and Freddie's room, where she slept when Esther was away. It seemed cold, impersonal; nobody had made up the bed, and the striped flock mattress looked dingy and uninviting. Cassie went to the linen cupboard along the corridor and, fetching sheets and blankets, returned in the direction of her room. The door to Joseph's room was slightly ajar. She was tempted to push it further and peep inside as she walked past.

Cassie surveyed the interior. The room was very dull, like the guest bedrooms, for Joseph hardly used it except as a place to store his things. There were stacks of dusty books in a corner, various boxes and a wardrobe full of his clothes. Cassie rested her bundle of sheets on the bed and walked about; she tried to picture Joseph there, but the small bleak room seemed all wrong for the person she knew. She opened the wardrobe and remembered the pleasant smell of Joseph as it drifted from his clothes. She touched the light-coloured suits and fancy waistcoats and the nice pullovers folded on the shelves. She took the sleeve of one of the cream linen jackets and held it against her face, trying to capture something, though she did not quite know what, and feeling a lump of sadness rise in her throat. Then she saw Joseph's Army uniform, its coarse khaki-coloured jacket, and the shiny leather cross-belt. A peaked hat rested on the shelf above it, and a pair of boots stood on the floor of the wardrobe. The jacket was askew on its wooden hanger, as if it had not been put away very carefully, and Cassie reached up and straightened it. The feel of the khaki against her wrist brought back an immediate flood of memory, and she realised that she was remembering her father, the man in the garden, who had lifted her into the apple tree at The Folly.

The touch of the uniform made Cassie feel uneasy. She shut the wardrobe door quickly and, picking up the sheets and blankets, returned to her temporary bedroom, where she made up the bed, then wandered slowly to the main staircase.

The attic stairs seemed dark and mysterious at the far end of the long corridor. Very little light penetrated that end of the house. Cassie felt a delicious sense of terror as she pictured the possible dangers that might lurk at the top of that dimly lit staircase – evil hobgoblins, a crone at her spinning-wheel, an enchanted, half-ravening beast; for she was well versed in traditional folk-tales. She walked along the corridor, pausing to listen at the door that shut off the room used for Julia's spiritualist meetings. She wondered what went on inside. There was no sound and, reassured that the spirits at least were not out to get her, Cassie walked on and climbed the narrow stairs at the end of the passage.

She looked first into Peter's studio. The pictures of the doves were like images of ghosts, and Cassie slammed the door shut before they could fly up from the canvas and whirl around her head. Next she opened the door to Julia's room. She had not been there since Julia had given up on her painting lessons, saying they should wait until Cassie was a little older when her direction would become more clear.

Cassie walked about the room, pleased with the sound of the rain on the roof-lights, like the rattle of tiny glass beads. She looked at all Julia's paintings, lingering to admire the one of Joseph, but unhappy about the sad look in his eyes, and she knew Julia hadn't painted him accurately. If *she* had done the portrait she would have put a broad grin, or at least a quizzical look on his face, like the one he wore whenever she questioned his judgement or said something to amuse him.

She came to a halt by Julia's easel, covered in a piece of cloth. She lifted the corner carefully and was surprised to see that it concealed a portrait of her mother. It was clever, Cassie acknowledged, pulling the cover back further, but, as with the picture of Joseph, there was something wrong. It was how Julia saw Esther, not how Cassie did.

Bored, she replaced the cloth and glanced about the room. Her attention came to rest on a beautifully coloured oriental tapestry she had always coveted. It was really a rug – there was a similar one on the floor, and others like them in the flat above the pottery studio – but this, Cassie's favourite, was displayed in Julia's studio, attached, top and bottom, to horizontal bars fastened to the wall.

There was something odd about the rug today. The bars that held it rigid seemed to have become detached, so that the rug swung away from the wall. Yet, though it had come loose, the construction seemed to be in no danger of falling down. Cassie touched the rug experimentally and it swung further into the room. Examination revealed that each bar was hinged at one end and was designed to fit invisibly into a catch at the other; because the catches had been left unclicked, the rug was swinging free.

Of more immediate interest to Cassie was the fact that the rug, when flush to the wall, had concealed a door-frame, set up a few inches from the floor. The frame – with rusted hinges but no door attached – led on to a wooden landing, where she could see the top of a staircase leading down into darkness.

Cassie stared at this discovery, feeling pleasantly intrigued, for it had all the possibilities of an adventure. She remembered that the attic studios at The Dovecote had been converted from servants' quarters and realised that this must once have been a service stair – like those at Hugh and Marjorie's house, where servants in black and white uniforms still scuttled up and down corridors and staircases, bearing trays of food and jugs of steaming water for washing.

Confirming that the rug clicked in and out of its catches freely, Cassie slipped through the doorway and pulled the rug to behind her. She reached the foot of the staircase and, exploring a short corridor in semi-darkness, found her way obstructed by a heavy curtain; beyond it lay the wings of what appeared to be a theatre.

Cassie stepped out on to a large stage. More curtains screened the area where, in a proper theatre, one would have expected to see footlights. She peeped through them and saw a plain room, fitted out with a row of chairs.

Cassie's own side of the stage was almost as bare and uninteresting as the room beyond. It held a few candelabras, a leather chair and a table with a jug and water-tumbler on it; and there was a vast, gauzy screen that moved with a rattle of curtain rings along a horizontal pole high above her head. She amused herself by running the screen across the stage and back again, then returned to the wings to explore the corridor hidden behind the folds of curtain. Here, in a corner, she found a packing case filled with various costumes, a megaphone, and a box of musical instruments.

She picked up a little tambourine edged with musical bells and shook it. It made a pleasant tinkling sound. Cassie turned her attention to the dressing-up costumes and pulled out a long white robe and various

198

shawls and veils. She wrapped a silk shawl round her waist and returned to the stage with the tambourine. She had been dancing and 'shimmying' and bowing and curtsying to an imaginary audience for some minutes, when the sound of a door closing in the seance room made her heart leap to her mouth. After a moment Violet's white face peered at her from low down between the stage curtains.

'Lord, Miss Cassie! What are you doing up there?'

Cassie could see Violet's thick brown stockings and garters underneath her coarse cotton skirt as she scrambled between the curtains on to the stage. 'I'm exploring,' she said defiantly, for she was not afraid of Violet.

'Poking your nose in where it's not wanted, more like. How did you get in? The door was locked.'

Cassie saw that Violet held a key. Did she know about the peculiar doorway in Julia's studio, or was it Julia's secret? 'I found a staircase,' Cassie said, then added, since Violet didn't seem surprised by this information, 'why does Julia keep it hidden?'

'So she can come down here and talk to the spirits when she feels like it,' Violet said with an air of importance.

'Is that why you're here now? To talk to the spirits?'

'Julia wouldn't mind.' Violet's reply was rather too hasty to be convincing.

'I bet she would if she knew. You just waited until she went out so that you could come in here and pretend. You wish you were clever like Julia, and could get in touch with the spirits all by yourself, don't you? That's why you go to all the seances.'

Cassie did not know how clearly she had hit on the truth, but Violet looked at her furiously; then her gaze rested on the shawl Cassie was wearing and the tambourine in her hand. She raised her eyes with a frightened stare. 'What do you think Julia would say to this sort of sneaky, nosy-parkering into her business?' she said in a tone that suddenly seemed to hold a note of menace.

Cassie knew that she didn't want Julia to have a chance to say anything at all. 'I don't know,' she stammered, her courage at last beginning to fail her.

'She wouldn't be too pleased, now, would she?' Violet seemed to be gaining in authority as Cassie's position grew weaker.

'We could go out again and not say anything?' Cassie ventured without much faith.

Violet looked at her for a while, puzzling it out and considering her own position, then, to Cassie's amazement, she nodded. 'I think that's a good idea.'

Cassie handed her the shawl and tambourine, and Violet returned them to the box in the corridor. She led the way to the curtains at the front of the stage and parted them, waiting for Cassie to jump down first and then following her. Once they were in the corridor she locked the door, her face red with mental exertion. 'Now then. I shan't tell Julia on you, if you don't tell anyone – not a soul, mind – that you've seen what you've seen.'

'Not about the staircase?' Cassie said.

'Not about the stair, nor them things in the box, nor about me coming after you.'

Cassie nodded.

'Promise you won't, or you'll be for it.' A thought occurred to her and Violet seemed pleased with it. 'The spirits don't like it, you see. They get very angry if they're interfered with by outsiders.'

Cassie promised absolute secrecy, and Violet at last seemed satisfied. They went downstairs in a companionable way, and Violet said she was going back to her painting while Cassie might go to see Rowena, who was getting lunch.

Cassie contrived to forget about the room. After all, there had been nothing very unusual about it, except for its hidden staircase and the box of costumes and musical instruments. She wouldn't tell her mother about it she decided, remembering Violet's caution about the spirits; for – in spite of a feeling in Cassie's mind that she didn't really believe in such things, perhaps not even in her own mystic ceremonies under the cedar trees – she had a sense of foreboding about Violet's warning.

Esther, arriving at the hotel in London, learned that Joseph was staying there, but that he was out.

She booked a room for herself and chose a light summer dress from the selection of clothes she had flung into her suitcase. Then, afraid that she would miss Joseph when he returned to the hotel, she took the lift and sat in a chair at a small table in the lobby and pretended to read a magazine.

It was raining outside. People hurried indoors, shaking umbrellas, laughing at their haste to get out of the wet. After more than an hour, Joseph still had not arrived.

The seductive luxury of the hotel, its muted activity and the self-conscious arrivals in the lobby began to irritate Esther. She resented the way the swish of the revolving doors caused a draught of air to stir the leaves of the potted palm trees inside the entrance, making her start and focus on each revolution. She was distracted by the soft click and shuffle of heels on the black and white tiled floor, the low murmur of voices and occasional explosions of laughter. The hotel was preparing for evening dinner; a faint smell of food drifted from the dining room; she heard the sound of stringed instruments being tuned. Esther ordered a glass of gin and Vermouth to deflect the unwanted attention of the hotel staff, and drank it slowly, sharing her attention between the clock above the hotel desk, the magazine in her lap, and the intermittently revolving doors.

In the end she did not see him arrive. She had allowed herself to become absorbed by her reading when a soft footstep close by made her glance up from the page.

'Esther?'

Esther let the book slip to her lap, dismayed that she had not seen him before he saw her. He wore a coat over his suit and an uncharacteristically muted tie. She noticed that he looked tired as he ran a hand through his hair, wet from the rain.

'Esther, what in heaven's name are you doing here?'

She cleared her throat nervously. 'Looking for you, of course.'

'I've been with a customer all day.'

'I know. On Julia's orders.'

'Not entirely. One has a life outside Julia's orbit. I had a long-standing appointment here.' He sounded defensive.

Esther looked away, disappointed in him. He might at least have been honest with her. 'That's odd. I got the distinct impression you were in London because you had been told to run away.' She gripped the edge of the book in her lap. 'Your customer. Did he or she want to buy?'

Joseph sat beside her. 'I wasn't running away.'

'That's how it looked to me. That's how the others seem to see it too.'

'I would have been back in a couple of days.'

'And then what? Another anonymous note – "get lost" – appearing one morning?'

He shook his head. 'I don't know what you're talking about.'

'An anonymous note. Someone wrote to me in Birmingham to tell me to keep away from The Dovecote. I thought at first it was Julia. But it wasn't.' She searched his expression. 'Do you know who it could have been?'

He lowered his glance. 'Meg? Rowena? They've always been very jealous of you.'

Esther was suddenly overwhelmed by all the uncertainties. 'I don't know. It was Meg who smashed my pots. She told me yesterday. She was jealous of Peter . . .' She tailed off. What did it matter now? What did anything matter, except that she had found him?

'Look. I know we have to talk. I told you on the telephone I want to talk,' Joseph said. He glanced at his watch and when his eyes met hers they were calm, expressionless. 'Can you stay? Will you have dinner with me?'

Esther nodded. 'I've booked in.'

He stood. 'Shall I see you here – say in half an hour?'

She watched him cross the lobby to the lift. He turned at the lift doors and unexpectedly gave her a hesitant wave and her heart gave a sudden lurch, for the distance lent a sadness to the gesture. A fleeting image crossed her mind as she raised her hand in return, of a figure in uniform, in the shadows of the attic stair. She banished it. On an impulse, she took the lift back to her room and bathed and put on make-up. She dressed her hair in a softly sweeping chignon and changed into the evening dress she had brought with her; it was heavily beaded, red and gold, with a deep neckline front and back, and Julia had persuaded her to buy it on her last trip to London. Had she packed it this morning with the unconscious intention of seducing him? Esther wondered. If she had, there was nothing unconscious or subtle about her purpose as she returned to the lobby.

Joseph was waiting for her. When he saw her he did not move, and Esther saw that her attempt to appeal to his senses was too glaring. As she walked towards him, his mood seemed to alter and become angry. 'You don't need to do that.' He took her arm and steered her towards the dining room.

'I thought you might have forgotten you'd made love to me,' Esther said angrily under her breath as a waiter came towards them. She felt a gratification in the swift expression of passion, almost of hatred in Joseph's eyes.

'Don't you know I want to make love to you however you look?'

They did not speak to one another as they were shown to a table, nor while selecting their meal, except to consult over the menu. They did not look at one another until Joseph had ordered.

'I thought you wanted to talk,' Esther said at last.

Joseph frowned and fingered the handle of the knife in front of him. 'If you hadn't come to London – I would have said what I've got to say back at The Dovecote.'

'Well, I've forestalled you.'

'Yes.'

'So, you can forget whatever little speech you had been rehearsing for when you got back.'

'Not entirely. I shall feel the same whatever you say – and whatever you do.' He looked at her, as if to warn her that he wouldn't be moved by any appeal, either to his senses or his emotions. He paused for the waiter to serve them before he spoke again. At last, he voiced the words Esther had dreaded hearing and with a sudden tenderness that pulled the ground from under her. 'Esther, I think you should make this move to Ansfield's, but I honestly think you should make it without me.'

She shook her head. 'No. You don't mean that.'

'Yes, I do. It's providence that Ansfield made the offer, and it's the right thing for you just now. But I shan't be coming with you.'

Panic seized Esther's heart so that she felt as if she couldn't breathe. She broke up the bread roll on her plate steadily, feigning a heavy pragmatism. 'Then I shan't go. Cassie and I will stay at The Dovecote.'

'No. You have to get away from Julia. Don't let her become as much a part of your life as she has mine.'

Esther's control slipped from her and she let the bread fall. She gripped her hands tightly in her lap. 'Joseph, please don't do this to me.'

He toyed with his spoon in the soup, not eating, not looking at her. 'I'm sorry. But it's for the best.'

'Do you love me . . . ? You said you did.'

He did not answer but held the spoon still.

Esther closed her eyes. She opened them and leaned forward, forcing an answer from him. 'Do you love me?' she repeated fiercely. 'Did you mean it?'

'You must *know* I love you. It's because I love you,' he said violently. The people at the next table glanced at them and Joseph lowered his voice. 'What can I offer you and Cassie? Have you stopped to think what living with me might do to her? She's still a child.' Esther heard echoes of Julia in his words and told herself he didn't mean them. 'Don't you know how much I care about Cassie as well?' Joseph fell abruptly silent as a waiter came towards them. He gestured the man away and he veered off at an angle to another table. 'I can't stand this,' he said suddenly. 'Are you hungry?'

Esther shook her head miserably.

'Neither am I. Shall we go?'

They stood, ignoring the curious glances of the diners near their table, and left the restaurant, Joseph waving aside the solicitous concern of the waiters.

It was quiet in the lobby. Most of the hotel guests were at dinner. They were alone with the lift-boy as the ornate glass and wrought-iron cage transported them silently to the first floor. They said nothing, but the space between them was charged with tension until the lift slowed to a halt and the cage door rattled, releasing them into a long, blue-carpeted corridor.

Joseph walked beside Esther as far as her room. She unlocked the door and turned to him, resting a hand on his sleeve. 'Don't go yet – not like this. Julia will only confuse the issue for us if we leave things unresolved until we get back to The Dovecote.'

Joseph hesitated, then reached across her to switch on the light inside the room. Esther felt the shock of his touch; she stood very still, wanting to weep, wanting to cling to him, wanting most of all for him to hold her. She leaned against the wall and began to cry with hard, dry sobs.

'Oh – Esther.' Joseph closed the door behind them.

'We could be so happy,' she wept. 'Why are you making us miserable?'

He pulled her into his arms and they clung to one another until, after a while, Esther's sobs ceased. He held her in his arms a moment longer, then released her, and his expression was one of helplessness.

Esther reached for him again, but he moved away and paced the room restlessly, looking at her clothes strewn across her suitcase, and at last sitting on the bed.

'Soon after you'd gone to Birmingham, I had another fit of the horrors. I was raving – baying at the moon, ready to do murder – or so Julia told me when she came to me . . .' His face twisted at the memory. 'If it had been anyone else who had found me – you or Cassie . . . But Julia calmed me, as she knows how, with the touch of her hands, by bringing me back to reality and then talking about the past. She helps me to face it in a way that's healing. It's a skill – almost like hypnosis, I suppose – but it works. Then she talked about the future. She showed me how impossible it would be for you and me to live together. How selfish I was even to consider it. How unfair it would be on you. How damaging to Cassie – even dangerous.'

Esther watched him, not moving from the door. 'How do you know you were violent if you've only Julia's word for it?' she said obstinately. 'I've told Cassie that you have nightmares. Children are resilient and Cassie more than most. She's growing up quickly. We don't have to wrap her up in cotton wool.'

Joseph rested his elbows on his knees and buried his head in his hands. 'Esther – please. You're not making this easy for me.'

'I don't want to,' she said angrily, crossing the room to sit next to him. She pulled his hands from his face. 'If – just supposing – we marry . . .'

'You really mean it, don't you? You'd tie yourself to a mental cripple.'

'Yes – because I don't believe you are what you say. You're twenty-five. You've got your whole life ahead of you. You said yourself when I first met you that we've got to put the war behind us and get on with what's left.'

He could not tear his eyes from hers, nor from the unreserved love that shone from them.

'Stay with me,' she begged. 'Stay with me tonight. Let me be the judge of what I want.'

For a moment his expression flared with hope. Then – as if she were watching the sun swallowed up by clouds – Esther saw his eyes become familiarly expressionless. 'We can't risk it. You're not judging the situation rationally.'

'You mean, you can't let me take the risk – or you won't risk being hurt?' Esther said harshly. 'Are you really such a coward?'

He flinched visibly. 'Don't use that word.'

'Why? Because to be thought a coward is the worst thing you can think of?'

'Because it's true. If it wasn't true, I wouldn't still be alive when they are dead.'

'You weren't a coward because they died. You couldn't have saved them, you would only have joined them, drowning alongside them in the mud or hanging on the wire. Millions of men died. Christopher died. It happened. But you *are* a coward because you'd rather live in your private misery, looking backwards all the time. You're scared of living normally. You're scared of loving anyone.'

He looked at her, despair in his eyes, helpless against the truth of her accusation.

She placed her hands behind his head and pressed her lips to his. 'Kiss me,' she said fiercely. 'Prove I'm wrong.'

'Oh – Esther. What am I to do?' Joseph felt his senses respond to her and he bent his head to let his mouth brush the skin of her neck and shoulder.

Esther closed her eyes. 'Kiss me,' she whispered, trembling as she felt his breath and lips warm on her neck. His fingers slid round her back and his mouth was on hers. She held his head in her hands, and she was crying again – crying and laughing as their bodies met in a spasm of desire. Their hands locked, parted to release buttons, legs intertwining as they sank into the bed. 'Don't leave me again,' she whispered, and his tenderness made her want to weep again. His flesh against hers roused sensations that seemed unique, without reference to the past, but born of this new love, rapturous, exquisitely sensitive. And then, as they gasped and clung to one another, she said once more, 'Don't leave me again. I couldn't bear it.'

Esther woke first. She lay for a long time and watched him sleeping, adoring the smooth mound of his naked shoulder, moving closer to taste it. His skin was cool.

He did not stir. A tension crossed his brow briefly and she raised herself on one elbow and brushed his forehead with her lips. How intimate it was to watch a lover sleeping. She felt a happiness steal over her, more profound than anything she had known. He was hers. She had wrested him from Julia and they would make it work. A swift fear that still she might lose him again made her slip down beside him and hold him close. Joseph turned in his sleep and wrapped his leg against her. She wanted him again, she thought, resting her cheek against his chest. She wanted him to wake and make love to her. She looked at him, memorising the line of his jaw, as if it was necessary to imprint this moment on her mind. Joseph opened his eyes; for a second an uncertainty clouded them, then he turned his head and smiled at her. 'How long have you been awake?'

'Long enough to stir up a desire for you. You look beautiful.'

He continued to look at her. 'Aren't I supposed to say that sort of thing?' She felt him stir against her. 'And you do,' he added. 'You look wonderful.' He pulled her on top of him. 'I haven't had such a normal night's sleep for years.'

Esther brushed his hair from his face and kissed the lines of strain that still threatened to crease his brow; she bent to kiss the lines round his mouth, then his mouth itself. She rolled back on to her pillow. 'I don't think I can ever have been so happy. I keep telling myself I'm too old for you, people will say I'm cradle-snatching – but the fact is, I don't care.'

He raised himself on one elbow and lay with the length of his body close against her. 'Thank you for being there,' he said softly. 'Thank you for making me feel whole.'

She felt her body respond to the pulse of his flesh. 'I'll always be there,' she said gently, and folded him in her arms.

They went down to breakfast together. They ate enthusiastically, ravenously, laughing a little because they knew that anyone observing them couldn't have mistaken the fact that they were lovers.

'What do you want to do?' Joseph said as they took the lift back to her room. 'Will Cassie be missing you? Do you want to go to Dorset?'

'Not yet.' She seized his hand and pressed it to her lips, knowing they were not yet strong enough to face The Dovecote. 'Let's have one day of freedom.' They left the lift-cage. 'What about you? What are your plans?'

'I've arranged to meet another customer this morning.'

'Is it one of Julia's friends?' Esther said jealously.

'No. They are called Luppi. I met them last year in Italy. Julia knows nothing about it.'

'I shall go to see if Gerard Vaudoyer is in London,' Esther decided. 'I might as well keep some of my customers when I leave Julia.' A feeling of panic made her grasp Joseph's hand again as they reached her door. 'We *will* do this together? No going back on it this time. If I'm going to join Ansfield's, you'll come with me to the Midlands? No matter what Julia says? She can't rule our lives for us.'

'No going back,' he promised.

They arranged to meet again for lunch at the hotel, and parted. Esther telephoned Gerard Vaudoyer's office from the hotel lobby.

'Esther! How marvellous,' Gerard enthused. 'Is Julia there with you?'

Esther felt a pang of guilt. Would Julia see this morning's work as an act of betrayal? And was it? Was she betraying Julia's generosity by going to Gerard behind her back? 'No. I'm in London by chance, Gerard,' she said. 'I wondered if you would have time to see me?'

There was a brief, barely noticeable pause. Esther sensed his apprehension, the unspoken questions in his mind. Why wasn't Julia with her? Why hadn't she given him prior notice of her visit? 'Of course. Eleven thirty? Come to lunch afterwards. Monique will be overjoyed to see you.'

'I'm afraid I already have a luncheon appointment.'

'Ah. Another time perhaps.'

'Is it about the autumn range?' Gerard said when she was seated in his office. 'But how marvellous! Julia didn't think you were ready to show it to us yet.'

'I'm not. Gerard – I'm thinking of leaving The Dovecote. I've had an offer from a manufacturer in Birmingham that will provide me with larger premises.'

Gerard spread his hands in despair. 'You are deserting the Galeries?'

'If I go to Ansfield's, I shall be able to continue producing the same sort of designs. How would you feel about my work for Paris being produced under the auspices of a larger manufacturer?'

Gerard looked doubtful. 'Your designs are special, Esther. Exclusivity is important to our customers. What does Julia say to all this?'

Esther twisted her hands in her lap and could not look him in the eye. 'Julia doesn't know about it yet.'

'Ah—' He looked at her reproachfully.

'You think I'm stabbing her in the back,' Esther said, wishing the remark didn't have such a ring of truth.

Gerard shrugged with an enigmatic, Gallic twist of the mouth. 'You would not be the first.'

'Julia doesn't own her protégés,' Esther said defensively. 'There comes a point when one should move on. I shall always be grateful to her but—' She frowned. 'Things have changed. There are personal reasons why I have to leave The Dovecote.'

'You have fallen in love?'

Esther laughed. 'Trust a Frenchman to think that. But – yes. It's true.'

'You're in love with Mr Ansfield?'

'With George? Good Lord, no,' Esther laughed.

'Whoever he is, he's a lucky man and I am very happy for you. Do you remember we talked once about the sad legacy of the war and how one must look to the future? I'm glad you have found happiness.'

Esther smiled and stood up. 'So, we shall not lose interest in one another?'

'Not at all. I look forward to seeing your autumn range.'

Esther kissed him on both cheeks. 'Give my best wishes to Monique.'

'But of course.'

It was past one o'clock when Esther reached the hotel. She went to her room to change and returned to sit in the lobby, glancing uneasily at the clock over the hotel desk. She had arranged to meet Joseph on the quarter hour and it was already twenty minutes past. She went to the desk and asked if Joseph had checked into his room, then sat at one of the small gilded tables and watched the revolving doors.

A feeling of melancholy crept over her as she recalled her long vigil the previous day. Joseph had run away from her before, she reminded herself. What was to stop him running away again? She willed him to come through the doors, watching every shadowy image that showed through the glass, only to prove to be a complete stranger when it entered the lobby. At last Esther could bear the close atmosphere of the hotel no longer. She went outside to the pavement where she walked up and down the street, scanning the oncoming pedestrians and the lumbering traffic of motor vehicles and carts and carriages, her heart lifting at the approach of every slow-moving motor car and the arrival of every taxi.

She waited until half past one, then allowed him an extra fifteen minutes – the traffic was heavy, he had been delayed, he had had an accident, panic pounded through her. At a quarter to two she walked with dignity into the hotel and made her way to the lift-shaft. Depression seeped through her in the silence of the lift's ascent as she avoided the curious gaze of the lift-boy.

Esther walked slowly along the corridor and unlocked the door of her room. Slowly, mechanically she packed her suitcase and sat on the bed for a while. Then she rang the hotel desk and asked for a porter to carry her case to the lobby. She sat on the bed again, touching the pillow, remembering their night together. At least he couldn't take that away from her.

The porter's rap on the door made her jump. Esther stood slowly and looked round the room, at her suitcase near the door and a last look at the bed before she picked up her coat. A second knock at the door, more insistent, made her cross the room to open it. Joseph, without his hat, a look of desperation on his face, stood in the corridor.

'Thank God you're still here. I thought you'd think the worst.'

Esther fell into his arms. 'How can you do that to me? Where were you?'

He led her to the bed. 'With a customer. I telephoned the desk to speak to you. They couldn't find you in the hotel. I thought . . .' He looked at her and kissed her. 'Never mind. Listen. I have a commission. A *fantastic* commission.'

'But that's wonderful.'

'More than that – the Luppis have more money than sense. After this we'll buy a house somewhere. I've been working it all out – somewhere close to Birmingham, not too far from your work.'

'And I thought you'd left me,' Esther laughed.

A frown crossed his face. 'It would mean some travel first. A few weeks, perhaps a month in Italy to discuss the Luppis' plans. Would you mind?'

Esther shook her head. Happiness filled her up so that she felt she could hardly speak. 'I can't believe this is happening. Tell me – is it really true?'

Their exhilaration lasted the entire train journey to Dorset as they made plans for the weeks and months ahead. Esther was to telephone George Ansfield the next day, arrange to see him, and accept his offer of a partnership. Joseph would prepare for the Italian commission, and they would break the news to Julia – a more sobering thought. They dismissed it and planned their search for a house in the country, the dream house Esther had talked of to Cassie – except that it would be far from the cry of seagulls and the crash of the sea.

Their euphoria ended as they reached the station and drove in Esther's car to The Dovecote. 'I feel extraordinarily guilty,' she admitted as they entered the courtyard in the gathering darkness. 'I feel as if we're criminals – or traitors. I know it's silly, but I can't help it.'

'It's not silly,' Joseph said, climbing from the car. Esther saw that his own expression was grim. 'What about Cassie? Will you tell her straight away?'

'No. She'll be sleeping. Besides, I don't want to go over to the house tonight. Do we have to let anyone know we're here? Can't we wait until tomorrow?' Esther could hear the gentle cooing of the doves in the dovecote; its outline was black against the sky. She felt for Joseph's hand and realised that she was shivering. His hand was cold and she felt the tension in him. 'What if Julia should try to convince you again?' she said. 'Why am I so frightened of her?'

Joseph drew her close to him and kissed her. 'Shall I stay with you tonight?'

'Yes.' Esther said fiercely. 'Now and every night.'

They did not see the silent figure standing in the shadows of the barn, listening, observing, as they moved together from the doors of the garage. Nor did they hear the low moan of despair that joined with the mournful calling of the doves when they had gone.

Chapter Thirteen

Esther woke to a keening sound in the night. She lay for a moment, listening, remembering the hotel in London, and then that she was back in her flat above the studio with Joseph. Joseph! She got out of bed and lit the lamp, flooding the room with light.

Joseph was fully dressed. He sat at the foot of the bed with his knees drawn up and his back against the wall. His head was in his hands, buried between his knees, and his body shook violently as if he were very cold.

Esther went to him, scrambling over the counterpane to reach him. Not again, she pleaded. Everything had been so perfect. Why now? It was this place, this ghastly, smothering atmosphere created by Julia. She wrapped him in her arms. 'Darling, I'm here. It's all right.' She felt him resist her, begin to fight her from him. His fist hit her shoulder and the pain made her reel away. She shouted at him. 'Joseph, it's me, for God's sake! Look . . .' She tried to turn his face towards her. 'It's me. We're in my flat at The Dovecote.'

Still he struggled to escape her arms. His teeth were clenched as he cried out, 'You bastards! You bloody bastards!' Esther released him and sat back on her heels. He turned to her and his eyes were wild with terror.

'Can't you see them? Oh, God! Can't you see?' He cowered against the wall again and, with a cry that brought a cold sickness to Esther's stomach, he screamed out, 'Shells! Get down! Get down!' He lurched forward, pushing her with him, flat to the bed.

The counterpane was soft against Esther's face, smothering her mouth and nose. She struggled to free herself so that she could breathe more easily, but still Joseph held her down on the bed. The grip of his hand on the back of her head was tightening in her hair; he pushed her face into the counterpane and she could not twist her head. The bones in Esther's nose and face felt as though they were being crushed, her throat gagged as she choked for air, and she saw the sergeant Joseph had tried to strangle, his eyes bulging while men tore Joseph away, pinioned his arms and strapped him to a stretcher. She remembered Julia's warnings about Joseph being unreliable as the darkness behind her eyes deepened and the blood drummed in her head.

Suddenly Joseph released her, and gasping, choking for air, Esther rolled on to her side. Joseph had flung his hands over his own head. He was screaming and crying, 'Oh God! Please! No more! God! Oh, God. No more!'

Esther lay and stared at the pale light from the lamp throwing soft shadows at the ceiling. She listened, feeling strangely distant, as Joseph continue to cry and moan beside her. She was afraid to touch him again, afraid that the confining touch of her arms would make him attack her or trigger another horror. She knew that she had never felt so helpless, and tears slid down her face as she watched him. Then she dried her face on the counterpane and began to talk to him quietly.

'Joseph. It's Esther. It's all right.' She did not know whether he could hear her, and she spoke more harshly. 'Joseph, I'm here with you. It's Esther. And I love you. Do you hear me? I love you! The horror has gone. It was terrible, but it's over.' She thought he was growing quieter and she continued, gaining confidence. 'It's over now. Darling, I love you. I'll always be here for you.'

At last Joseph fell silent. For a long time he did not move from where he lay, in a curled, tight ball of tension with his hands locked behind his head. Then, as Esther watched, his fingers slowly loosened their grip, his arms relaxed, he crawled towards her and she drew his head into her lap, bending to kiss the tears from his face, stroking his hair, murmuring words of love. 'I'll always be here,' she said again, until his breathing became more regular and at last he slept.

Esther kept a vigil, lying across the counterpane with Joseph in her arms until the first streaks of dawn began to colour the sky. She watched the clouds grow lighter and the pink and yellow fade to pale grey, and only then did she notice that Joseph's shoes were muddy against the counterpane. She puzzled over where he could have gone in the night – back to his cottage? Had he wandered the cliff in search of his men? She slept a little, then felt him stir and, half fearful again, watched him roll away from her.

Joseph lay staring at the ceiling, trying to remember something, then he turned his head to look at her, his eyes wide with despair. 'It happened again, didn't it?'

'Yes,' she said quietly.

He groaned and turned away from her, then saw that he had dressed in the night. He had no recollection of it, except – he looked at Esther, shocked by the memory that he had fought her from him. 'Did I hurt you?'

Esther shook her head. 'It doesn't matter. It must have happened because you were anxious about us – because of coming back to face Julia. You went for months without dreaming before . . . And in Italy. You've said you hardly dreamed at all in Italy. Once we've left The Dovecote it will get better again. I know it will.'

'What are you – an amateur psychiatrist?' he said coldly. 'Every day, in every way, I'm getting better and better?' After a few seconds he sat up. 'Have I been outside?'

'I don't know. I think you must have been.'

He glanced down at his shoes, then gave a bitter laugh. 'Christ! I don't even know where I've been.'

'Oh, Joseph. It doesn't matter. You came out of it. It's all right.' She reached for him but he moved away.

'It's not *all right*. It's far from *all right*. It's always going to be the same.'

Cassie lay in bed and remembered hearing the sound of her mother's car in the night. She had watched for the bedroom door to open, so that she could pretend to be asleep until Esther reached her pillow, then pull her down in a bear-hug and ask her whether she had brought Joseph back with her; but, though she had waited for a long time, Esther had not come over to the house to see her. A long time later, she remembered, she had heard faint cries in the dark, like the sound of seagulls wailing, or the cries she heard when she knew that Joseph had been having nightmares, or the sound of the doves moaning, deep in their house when they were sad. She supposed she must have drifted back to sleep, for now it was morning and the sun was streaming through her window as she climbed out of bed and dressed.

The house was quiet as Cassie opened the front door. She would go straight to the flat, she decided. But something made her halt and listen on her way across the lawn. At first she could not tell what was different. The sun streamed across the garden, throwing long, early morning shadows. The sound of the sea was gentle, rhythmic. Then she became aware that something was missing. She could not hear the usual cooing of the doves.

Slowly, out of curiosity rather than a sense of misgiving, Cassie walked to the gateway separating the garden from the courtyard. The dovecote was deeply patterned with sunshine and shadow and the courtyard was bathed in a peculiar silence. Then Cassie saw them. All around the dovecote, in a scene of silent carnage, dead birds lay on the cobbles.

She crouched and began to gather the doves, one by one, in her arms. Their necks had been wrung and their heads hung limply; they were cold and stiff and very dead. She could not carry them all as she made her way to the studio. Joseph came to the top of the stair as Cassie reached it, and he stood, looking down at her. He saw the doves at the same time as he saw Cassie and murmured, 'No. Dear God. No.'

'Look,' Cassie sobbed, 'Look, Joseph. Look what someone's done to the doves.' She stared at the birds heaped in her arms and tears poured down her face.

Joseph came to her then, clattering down the staircase. He held her and tried to soothe her as they climbed up to the flat. Cassie crushed the feathered corpses against her breast, and began to weep more deeply.

Esther had been getting dressed. She turned in surprise to face them, hearing Cassie's sobs first of all. 'Darling? Whatever's wrong'

Cassie did not go to her mother; instead she held out her arms to show her the dead doves.

Esther turned pale, and Cassie remembered the mouse at The Folly and her fear that her mother would be ill again. But this was nothing like the mouse – different too from the tiny corpses Cassie had buried at The Dovecote. The look in her mother's eyes was one of anguish, as if she had seen something truly terrible, and her voice was almost a whisper as she raised her hand to her mouth. 'Oh, Joseph. No.'

Joseph stood there, staring at them both. Then he turned back to the door. Cassie looked from one to the other as her mother cried after him, 'Where are you going?' and heard him shout in return, 'Out! Do you still say it will get better!' And with a tremor of horror, remembering the cries in the night, Cassie realised what Esther was thinking.

For a moment she hated her mother for believing such a terrible thing. She dropped the birds on the floor and ran to her bedroom and shouted with all her strength before she slammed the door, 'You're wrong! You're wrong! Joseph wouldn't do that!'

Joseph breathed great gulps of cool air, feeling dirty, wanting to clear all the rubbish out of his head. After a while he went to the house and found Julia in her attic studio where she was painting.

His own portrait was propped against the wall. He did not like it: the eyes were wrong; his pain was too conspicuous. He felt that Julia had bared his soul for the world to view.

She did not look up from the easel as he stood in the doorway. 'Come in,' she said. 'I thought you would turn up sooner or later.'

He moved across the room. A second portrait rested on her easel: it was of Esther and was almost finished; Julia was adding the finishing touches. 'You had a nightmare last night. I heard you,' she said without looking at him.

'It passed.' He tried to rid himself of the image of the doves in Cassie's arms. 'They always pass.'

'Don't deny that you need help, Joseph.'

He threw her a look of despair. 'Do you know about the doves?'

'Yes. I know. I know everything that happens here.' She continued painting for a moment then sat back in her chair, laying her brush aside. 'What do you think of it?'

Joseph stared at the painting. A cruel insight shot through it. Esther's eyes were troubled and they met those of the onlooker with a crude plea for love.

He turned away. 'I think it's hateful. You only see the woman who came to you two years ago. Esther has learned to live again since then – through her work, thanks to you, and through love. The portrait is a lie.'

To Joseph's surprise, he had moved her. He had thought Julia was deeply entrenched in her assumptions, but for a moment a bleak expression crossed her face.

'You don't know her as I do. Esther's grief isn't yet discharged. She's disturbed the spirits and she *has* to let them help her. You'd understand if you submitted to the love of the spirit world yourself.'

Joseph went to the window. He could see the roofs of the barns, strangely blank and empty without the doves fluttering about the tiles. 'Did I kill them?' He forced his fist into the palm of his hand. 'I went out in the night. I must have killed them.'

'No,' Julia said. 'The spirits have sent us a sign.'

Joseph turned in surprise, for a light of conviction burned in Julia's eyes.

'Joseph, I'm going to hold a seance this morning,' she said eagerly. 'You must come. We must talk to the spirits about what happened.'

For a moment Joseph hesitated. Did Julia really believe what she was saying, that some mystic force had killed the doves? Had something finally tipped her over the edge of sanity? Then he shook his head. 'I'm leaving. With or without Esther, I'm leaving here. I've got another commission in Italy. This time I'm going for good.'

Julia hesitated. When she spoke her dark eyes brimmed with tears. 'But you're not ready yet to cast me aside. How will you manage? Who was it gave you life again when they brought you back from the Somme? Who sat with you, night after night, like a mother with her child? Who understands your pain, loves you as no one else can?' She turned her head away, wiping at her eyes with her hand. When she looked at him again she was calm. 'If only you and Esther had listened to me from the beginning. I tried to tell you things would go badly wrong. Instead, pigheaded as always, you thought you knew best.'

'I fell in love, Julia. Can you blame me for that?'

She did not answer at first. 'You call that love, to put Esther's happiness in jeopardy?'

Joseph flinched at the truth of the question. 'Esther was so sure it could work. I really believed she might be happy. I thought I could make her happy...'

'No. With *my* help, Esther can thrive – through her art, through her work – as you have thrived. But together you would be disastrous for one another. You must not be together, Joseph. Her experience – the death of her husband – would be a constant spur to your affliction. The consequences of that are too dangerous for her. You'll harm her – if not physically, then with the constant cycle of reminders that her husband died in the same, terrible way your men died. If you won't think of yourself, think of Esther. And if you won't think of Esther, think of Cassie. What kind of father could you be to her?'

Joseph remembered the doves in Cassie's arms, seeing Cassie's white face and the white feathers against her dress, and he felt again the cold revulsion that had stolen through his veins as he asked himself, was that the reason he had dressed in the night – to set out on a bizarre mission of slaughter? Had his unconscious mind sought out a symbolic gesture to expunge his deeper guilt?

215

He looked at Julia with a sense of despair, for he knew already that she was right, that for their own safety he must forget about Esther and Cassie.

'You must help me, Joseph. You must help me persuade Esther that you and she can never be happy together. The spirits must convince her.'

'What do you want me to do?' he said, feeling a resignation seep through him.

'She has to come to a seance.' Julia held out her hand to him, smiling, coaxing. 'And when she comes – you must be there too.'

The community had congregated in the kitchen, curious to know why Julia had called them together, until they saw the doves laid out in a long row on the table as if in preparation for cooking.

Esther, looking at the birds, noted with a sense of detachment that two of them were pigeons. She searched the faces of everyone gathered there. Peter and Meg solemnly held one another by the hand. Freddie was trying to make light of the matter, though he too was clearly moved by what had happened. Rowena, sobbing, was terrified, as thoughts of witchcraft and black magic coursed through her fertile mind. Julia stood by the stove, smoking a cigarette. She avoided looking at the row of birds.

Only Cassie and Joseph were absent. Esther did not know where Joseph had gone – to the beach or the cliffs? She had left Cassie in the flat, had calmed her, and had lied, saying that of course she knew Joseph hadn't harmed the doves.

Had he? She tried to dismiss the dreadful possibility, remembering their happiness and the brief flowering of freedom in London. She told herself that nothing else mattered: regardless of who had killed the doves, they would soon be away from The Dovecote, and then they could begin a new life. But Joseph had been out in the night, she reminded herself, and he had no recollection of where he had been. She tried not to think about the pressure of his hand on the back of her neck, the feeling of being suffocated, nor to imagine the same hands wringing the necks of the doves.

'I suppose we have to get to the bottom of this,' Meg said, looking at Julia.

'Well, they didn't fall down and die of their own accord,' Freddie said, trying to laugh.

'What are you suggesting?' asked Peter. 'That somebody – one of us – has done this?'

'It could have been an outsider,' Meg suggested hopefully. 'You know how much some people in the village dislike us. Anyone from Winmouth could have got into the courtyard. We don't lock the gates.'

'You can't deny that some of the village wouldn't mind discrediting us,' added Peter. 'They don't like Violet and the others coming to the meetings.'

'What about Joseph?' said Freddie quietly.

'Where is Joseph?' Rowena asked, drying her eyes now that the discussion had taken a more logical turn. They turned to look at Esther.

'I don't know,' she said uneasily. 'He's gone for a walk. I haven't seen him for a while.'

'I have.' Julia broke her silence. 'He came to see me this morning. He had another nightmare last night.'

Esther felt a lurch of jealousy. Joseph had gone straight to Julia and told her about his nightmare? Had he also told her about London? Julia met her gaze, and for a moment a light flamed in her eyes; Esther sensed a white heat in it. Did Julia hate them for uniting against her, without her permission and against all her warnings?

Julia's mood went as swiftly as it had come and her expression softened again.

Julia looked round at them all, stubbing out her cigarette on the stove. 'I don't think this is as simple as one of Joseph's aberrations. There is another possibility. I think the spirits were involved. It's obvious to me that this is a sign – from Christopher.'

'As far as I remember, he didn't go in for killing doves,' said Esther with heavy sarcasm.

'Esther! Don't mock the spirits!' wailed Rowena.

The others fell silent; even their credulity had been tested by Julia's suggestion.

'I think we should hold a meeting, talk to our Spirit Guide, and ask his advice.' Julia looked hard at Esther.'And I think we should all be there.'

Esther left the house and went to Joseph's cottage. Julia's attempts to separate her and Joseph were becoming more and more grotesque. Julia was deranged, she told herself fiercely, and the sooner she and Cassie and Joseph got away from this place the better.

The door to the cottage was open. Joseph lay on his bed, staring at the ceiling and smoking a cigarette. He turned to look at her. 'Is Cassie all right?'

'Where were you?' said Esther. 'Julia called one of her meetings. Meg and Peter think someone from the village killed the doves. Julia thinks it was spirits.'She sat down heavily on the bed. 'Julia's going to hold a seance. She wants everyone to be there in an hour.'

Joseph raised himself on one elbow. He was watching her. He seemed to be steeling himself, then he said, 'Esther – after last night . . .'

'Don't say it.'

'I have to. If you stay with me, it would be like that over and over again. Look how upset Cassie was this morning.'

'That was different. That was because of the doves.'

He did not answer.

'Joseph?'

'Oh, face the facts,' he said impatiently. 'What happened to the doves is all part of the same thing.'

'No, it isn't. Once we are away from Julia and this place . . .'

'We've got to forget about going away together.'

'Is that what Julia says?' Esther said savagely.

'Esther – I'm serious.'

'So am I. Deadly serious. I'm going to put an end to Julia's games once and for all this morning. And then you and I are getting right away from here.'

'You're going to the seance?' he said in alarm.

'I think Julia killed the birds herself. It's all part of her plan to convince me that Christopher is sending messages of doom. She's jealous. She can't bear us to be happy. It's pathetic, and I'm going to expose her for what she is.'

Joseph shook his head. 'It's not as simple as that . . . I went out last night.'

'Yes. And, in a wild, crazy moment, it did occur to me that you had gone to the courtyard and wrung those poor birds' necks one by one. But I know you couldn't have done it.'

'Can you be sure? I can't. Julia says I'm sometimes violent. I know I attacked you last night.'

'Julia says! Julia says! You're completely dominated by her. Why did you go to her this morning? I thought you wanted to be alone.'

'I had to see her – to know what to think about what had happened.'

'And did she tell you? Does she tell you what you can think? What did you say to her – that we made love in London? Does she like all the details?'

'I won't even answer that.'

Esther's eyelids burned with tears. 'Did she say that she killed the doves, or did she spin you a tale that it was Christopher – my *dead* husband?'

'She made me realise we ought to take more notice of what she's been saying. You and I should never have got involved with each other.'

Esther sat on the bed beside him. She took his hand. 'Joseph. Remember London and how happy we were, how simple everything really is? I know it's only Julia makes you say these things.'

Briefly trust flickered in Joseph's eyes before he moved his hand from hers. 'Maybe – but we can't ignore what happened last night.'

Esther stood up. 'You're right, and that's why I'm going to Julia's seance.'

Joseph said slowly, remembering Julia's voice, persuasive, convincing. 'Don't go,' he said. 'I know you mustn't go.'

'Don't tell me you're getting premonitions too now? I thought you were immune from all that?'

He did not answer straight away, then he said sadly, 'If you do go, I know Julia will manage to destroy us. She would rather destroy us than leave us alone.'

Esther hesitated only briefly in the doorway, then she smiled at him and left the cottage.

Esther sat in the meeting room between Peter and Meg. The others spoke in whispers, staring at the closed curtains as if wary of penetrating the quietness.

Peter was trying to be pragmatic. 'Either one of us did go out to the courtyard at dead of night, or there are other forces at work.'

'No one can make me believe it was done by spirits,' said Esther.

Meg seemed the least disturbed by the morning's events. 'Where's Julia? She asked us to be here, and now she hasn't turned up.'

'She was on the telephone for ages,' whispered Rowena. 'I thought she was going to get some more people to come.'

'Perhaps the faithful of Winmouth didn't feel like dashing up from the village for a seance at ten o'clock in the morning,' said Esther, allowing her anger to brew. She realised that she had to plan; she must be ready to outwit Julia when she appeared.

'I can't pretend I'm in the mood.' Freddie was still trying to maintain a lightheartedness. 'These meetings aren't what they used to be.'

'Bad sensations have crept in during the last year,' hissed Rowena. She threw Esther a withering look before turning back to face the stage.

'Because of me?' said Esther loudly.

'You have to admit some odd things have happened since you came to us,' Peter said gently.

Rowena spoke again. 'Look how Meg fell out with Julia. They didn't speak for months.'

'Oh, come on. I don't see how you can blame Esther for that. She wasn't even here . . .' defended Freddie.

'Then you caused friction between me and Freddie.'

'This is ridiculous!' Esther was diverted from the argument as the curtains swung apart. 'Who is working the curtains?'

'Violet,' whispered Meg.

Esther scanned the lighted part of the stage and the shadows, but could see no sign of Violet. She jumped involuntarily as Julia appeared from the deep darkness at the rear of the stage and came forward to stand at the front of the platform. She was dressed in a simple white shift and wore a head-band with a white feather in it. With a sense of horror, Esther fixed her attention on the feather, imagining that it had been plucked from one of the dead doves.

'My dearest friends.' Julia spread her hands as if to embrace them and spoke quietly, affectionately. 'Welcome in love, my dears. We have come together this morning because we have a troubled spirit among us and we wish to appeal to our Spirit Guide for advice.' The light in the room dimmed and Julia raised her arms. 'Let us meditate and call upon the energy within and around us that opens us to the spirit world.'

Esther watched as Julia went into trance and began to speak in the voice of her Spirit Guide. 'Be at peace...' Julia's breathing grew shallow and, after a while, she said, 'There is one here who wishes to make contact.'

Esther stiffened, waiting. What was Julia going to do? She must be ready for her this time; she *must not* let herself be fooled. She remembered Joseph's conviction that she shouldn't come to the seance. He had seemed afraid for himself as well as for her, almost as if he'd known what Julia might be planning. Did he? She thought with a shock. Had Julia confided in him? But, if that was so, wouldn't Joseph have done more than warn her not to come?

A tinkling of bells broke into Esther's thoughts. A light flickered at the rear of the stage. She heard Rowena's gasp of excitement and felt a prickle of fear as Meg's hand grasped her arm.

Julia's voice continued, gentle, kindly. 'Our brother is unhappy, Esther, because you've ignored all our advice. Our only concern is for your happiness. What will it take, he asks, to persuade you that such a close association with Joseph is unwise?'

The light grew brighter and Esther could see now that it shone from behind a translucent curtain. A shadow appeared, moved forward and became more distinct – the silhouette of a soldier in uniform. Esther fought down a crowd of responses, refusing to believe that the phenomenon was anything but human. But who? Who was impersonating Christopher? She closed her mind to the explanation that hammered into her brain, telling herself, as Cassie had done that morning: You're wrong. You're wrong ... Joseph wouldn't do that.

'Christopher is afraid for you,' Julia's voice continued. 'He's displeased because your foolishness might put his daughter Cassie at risk.'

This was only a cheap trick, Esther told herself fiercely. She had to expose Julia. How could she ever have trusted a woman who would stoop to using her love for Cassie in this way? She must get to the platform and reveal the identity of the figure in uniform before it disappeared. But what then? A lethargy held Esther to her chair. What if she discovered it was Joseph? She tried to stand, but it seemed as if her arms and legs would not move.

Julia's voice continued relentlessly. 'A great sadness overwhelms us, for if you resist us, Esther, who can vouch for the safety of Christopher's daughter? Remember the doves...' The figure of the soldier raised its arm slowly and Esther saw with a growing horror that he held one of the doves, the head hanging limply from his hand. Nausea rose in her, and she knew that at any moment she was going to faint. At last she found her strength.

'No! No. This is wicked!' She leaped up and ran to the stage. At the same moment, the figure behind the curtain turned from the sphere of light and disappeared.

Julia did not move. Her head was thrown back and her eyes were closed – Rossetti's painting, *Beata Beatrix* made flesh. Esther began to climb on to the stage. She must discover the identity of the figure in uniform. Suddenly Julia stirred; she cried out in a voice that rose to a shriek. 'No, Esther! Think of Cassie. You must go to Cassie!'

Esther was frozen by indecision. Did Julia know what she was saying or was she really in a trance? Could she be right – that Cassie was in danger? With a sob of terror Esther scrambled from the stage and ran to the door of the seance room. Why had she left Cassie alone?

Cassie was in the pottery studio, sitting at one of the work-benches. She had been crying – Esther saw the screwed-up handkerchief in her hand – but she was safe.

'Where's Joseph?' Esther gasped. 'Has he been in here?'

'Yes. He went away again.'

'When? Where?'

'A long time ago. He said he wanted to be by himself.'

Meg and Rowena had followed her. 'Stay with Cassie,' Esther told them and, leaving the studio, she sped across the lawn to the tree-walk.

Freddie was coming out of the house. 'Esther! Wait for me. I'll come with you.'

Esther ignored him. What had she seen? she asked herself. The blurred figure in uniform appeared over and over in her mind, like a badly executed photographic image – a raised arm, the body of the dove.

Esther halted. 'Freddie – you can't believe that – that theatrical display was my dead husband.'

Freddie was uncomfortable. 'Look. Sometimes, Julia thinks people need a little extra persuasion. It does no harm. Most of us know what's going on. And if it helps people, comforts them to see their loved ones...'

'Comforts them! My God. This time she went too far.' Esther turned away and began to run as she entered the tree-walk.

'What if she's right?' Freddie shouted, hurrying after. 'What if you *are* making a terrible mistake, saddling yourself with Joseph? What if Joseph's sickness, moods, strange behaviour – call it what you like – could harm you and Cassie? Julia is frightened for you. Shouldn't she do everything she can to prevent you from going ahead?'

'Who was it, Freddie?' Esther said. 'Who was that pretending to be Christopher?'

He did not answer.

'You *know*. I'm convinced you know. Was it Joseph? Has Julia made him join in her game of persuasion? How can she have such a hold on you all? What does she do – *hypnotise* everybody?'

'Esther, you're getting this out of proportion.'

'Am I? What about the doves in the courtyard? Was that out of proportion?'

'I admit, that was different. But perhaps it was Joseph who killed them. And even if it was Julia – you know how she cares about us all.

221

She would do anything to protect you. She loves you and she loves Joseph . . .'

They had reached Joseph's cottage. The door stood open but it was empty.

'. . . She understands him,' Freddie said miserably. 'You weren't here when he first came to her. Peter and Meg have told us. You don't know.'

Esther scanned the room. She saw the binoculars on the wall and remembered the times she had accused Joseph of spying on her. She turned to Freddie. 'Why do you borrow Joseph's binoculars? Why don't you get some of your own?'

Freddie stared at her. 'Binoculars? What would I want with binoculars?'

'To watch birds,' Esther said, hysteria rising in her again. Please God. Let Joseph not really have lied to her over this. 'You borrow them from Joseph to watch birds, but you don't let Rowena know in case she gets the wrong idea.'

'Who on earth told you that? I wouldn't know a sparrow from a thrush.'

Esther felt a dragging sense of despair. So, she had been right all that time ago – Joseph had watched her secretly, then lied about it. She saw again the figure in uniform and remembered the first time it had appeared. A trick of the light on the stairs? Had he managed to hide somewhere? Her mind became more lucid as she searched through all the possibilities. She had challenged him in the garden that day, but if he had wanted to hide the Army uniform, would he have taken it to his cottage? Would he do that now? Esther turned from the cottage and began to walk quickly towards the house.

She tried to think back over more recent instances when Joseph had behaved oddly. There was the anonymous note to keep her from The Dovecote – the message was so consistent with his swift changes of mood, it should have been obvious he had sent it. And the latest, the dead doves, after Joseph had been out in the night – her first instinct had been right . . . What was more, he had gone straight to Julia that morning. Whenever anything happened, he went, like a homing pigeon, to Julia.

'Esther,' Freddie called after her helplessly but she ignored him, hearing only the wind in the trees overhead and the distant roar of the sea, mocking her with the memory of the way they had loved one another in London. You thought you knew him. You thought he loved you.

She ran into the house, impatient now to confirm her fears, and took the stairs two at a time. She made for the bedroom corridor and threw open the door to Joseph's room. Only then did she halt and catch her breath.

The room was empty, the wardrobe door wide open, revealing a row of suits and jackets on their hangers. But it was not these that made her draw in her breath with a sob, nor even the Army officer's uniform, hanging askew with its buttons undone, as if it had been put away in a great hurry. Esther stared instead at the wardrobe floor and the stiffened carcass of a dead dove.

A coldness spread and numbed her body and, fighting back a wave of sickness, she stumbled from the room and fell against the wall in the corridor. Proof. It was there, if proof she had needed. She heard a sound and saw Julia coming towards her along the corridor. Esther pressed the back of her hand to her mouth and, gathering her strength, she hurried past her.

'Esther – wait!'

'Don't talk to me!' Esther cried. 'I don't want anything more to do with you – not any of you.'

She remembered Joseph saying that he and she were like the wild pigeons in the courtyard. But it wasn't true. All Julia's doves belonged to her, and every one of them had forgotten how to fly free. She remembered Joseph's own warning: *Do you think it's easy to get away from Julia?* But Julia would never get the chance to tame her as well, Esther vowed as she ran across the lawn to the studio.

Ignoring Meg and Rowena she said to Cassie, 'Pack everything you want to take with you. We're leaving here at once.'

PART THREE

Chapter Fourteen

Joseph walked quickly along the cliff and down the path to the beach. He thought about the seance and wondered whether Esther would still believe that happiness was a simple matter of living together far from The Dovecote.

There were a handful of holiday-makers on the sand: children were making sandcastles, men with their trouser legs rolled up were standing in the water. They ignored him as he passed them, as if he were invisible, intent on the business of enjoying themselves.

A man was swimming several yards out from the shore, his head forming a dark spot bobbing above the waves. Joseph remembered the first time he had seen Esther, how it had seemed as if fate had intervened and sent her to him – naked, exposed by her pain as much as he was, and as vulnerable to Julia. But there was a difference, he reminded himself. Esther had resisted Julia – had taken the hand that was held out to her and then released it. Whereas he – who had always thought it possible to use Julia's help and discard her – had discovered himself tied. By gratitude – or because, in his own way, he loved Julia in return? He had, from the beginning, been mesmerised by her, he remembered. She had been so exotic, so passionate, so ... liberating with her knowledge of healing, and with hands that could banish his horrors.

He walked for a long time and finally left the beach and made his way up to the village. The midday sun glinted on the windows of the houses; the reflections reminded him that Esther had accused him once of watching her. It had been Julia, of course. He had known for some time that Julia took his binoculars to spy on people. Julia was always the same – obsessive, excitable, consumed by her latest 'dove'. Why had he covered up for her even then? Why had he wanted to hide from Esther the fact that Julia's obsessions could verge on madness? He knew he should have warned her long ago, when he had guessed Julia had watched her from the cliff, instead of trying to convince himself there was no real harm in Julia's preoccupation. For – in spite of everything – he could still believe that she meant well. Julia loved too much, that was all. She wanted to protect her doves, guide them, keep them safe so they would not – or, in the end, *could* not fly away.

He saw a figure coming towards him on the road and recognised Violet in a dark coat, with her hair scraped back from her face into a bun, hurrying down the hill from The Dovecote. As he drew nearer he saw that the girl's face was streaked with tears. His thoughts went again to the seance. Of course – she had been there. Had it upset her? Had Julia said something to disturb her? Or was she crying because of the doves? Violet stared at him and, as he approached her, she gave a cry of alarm and rushed on.

Freddie was wandering about, looking distraught, as Joseph entered the grounds of The Dovecote.

'Where is everyone?'

Freddie hesitated, then said, 'Esther and Cassie have left – I mean they've gone for good this time. Julia is in her room. She's very distressed.'

Joseph took in what Freddie had said and felt a slow and deepening emptiness, but hardly any surprise. He allowed himself a brief wallow in regret: if only the doves were still flying around their house in the courtyard, if only Esther had listened to him . . . Then he knew that he should be relieved she had gone without needing explanations or goodbyes. He remembered he had made her promise that as soon as she'd had enough she would be honest about it. He had asked her not to pretend. Well, she had kept her promise.

Freddie looked at him, as if weighing him up. Joseph said nothing. He turned away and went across the lawn to his cottage. He did not want to talk about it. He wanted no questions or analysis. He wanted to think, and to decide what to do – but he did not want to discuss it.

Esther would say nothing about why they were leaving The Dovecote so suddenly, except that she and Joseph had quarrelled. Cassie grieved because Joseph was not coming with them and because her mother had said, without any further explanation, that they would never see him again. She had packed her suitcase obediently, knowing her mother must be very unhappy about it – indeed, Esther seemed to be temporarily crazed that day. Cassie could only suppose the killing of the doves was to blame for everything; it had upset everyone . . . especially Joseph.

He had come back to see her that morning while her mother was at a meeting in the kitchen with the others. He had told her he wasn't going to live with them after all, because sometimes he had nightmares and sometimes he did peculiar things, and because it wasn't fair to her and her mother to have to look after him when that happened. Cassie had cried bitterly. He had dried her eyes with his handkerchief and said she must be brave for her mother's sake. She had given the handkerchief back to him, trying to smile, saying, 'Look how it's crumpled now. You won't look so smart any more.'

'No, I'm not so smart,' he had said, and smiled at her in a sad way that made Cassie's heart turn over, and she had wanted to tell him he would always be the most wonderful person in the world for her.

Joseph had talked a little about the dead birds, explaining that sometimes people did wicked things without knowing why they did them. And then he talked of Julia and said Cassie and her mother mustn't think too badly of her, that sometimes people behaved in a certain way because they thought what they did was necessary and – even though it seemed wrong – they did what they did anyway. Some people had thought the war was necessary, and so men had killed one another even though killing was wrong. But the doves weren't hurting anybody, Cassie protested. No, he agreed. But sometimes innocent creatures got hurt by accident. He thought for a while, then added, '... and sometimes people hurt other people very much without wanting to.'

The incidents of that day had become confused in Cassie's mind with her discovery of the staircase in Julia's studio. Violet had said the spirits wouldn't be pleased because she'd discovered the seance room. Had the spirits taken their revenge on the doves? If she hadn't explored that day, perhaps the birds would still be alive and Joseph and her mother might not have quarrelled about whether they should live together. A conviction grew in Cassie's mind that somehow it had all been her fault.

Esther refused to talk about Joseph after they had left The Dovecote. Cassie did not tell her mother what Joseph had said when he came to see her. Nor did she say anything about the day Violet found her in the seance room – about the staircase from Julia's studio and the boxes of costumes and musical instruments. She was afraid it would cause more trouble. It became a secret, like her hiding places in The Dovecote garden and her ceremonies under the cedar tree, like sitting on the stairs at her grandparents' house to hear the grown-ups talking, or in the wheelbarrow in the barn, listening to the murmur of the doves.

Cassie dreamed about the doves afterwards. She would wake, weeping for the poor dead birds night after night at her grandparents' house, and the doves were mixed up with the loss of Joseph and the pain of first love.

Her grandmother worried about Cassie's dreams. She said that was what came of being involved with a set of peculiar people, and Esther should have had more sense. But Cassie did not blame Esther. She was sorry for her because she had decided to leave The Dovecote and because they weren't going to live with Joseph any more.

Esther had taken nothing with her except her files and pattern books. There had been no time to organise the transport of clay and pots, no time to consider what to do about the unfinished work at the studio. She wrote to Rowena, sending her a cheque and asking her to use the money to send on her pots and pay off the outstanding debts, and she wrote to the various clients, telling them of the move from The Dovecote, asking for their patience until she was settled in new premises. She sent no word to Julia, nor would she write to Joseph – the break must be clean and complete – but she kept in touch with Meg, and she wrote to Violet, because of the pottery, and explained her reason for leaving in terms of a quarrel with Julia. Violet did not reply, and Esther was distressed, for

229

she was unhappy about abandoning so abruptly the work they had begun.

Through Meg, Esther learned that Joseph too had left The Dovecote. Where had he gone? To Exeter? To Italy? She stared at Meg's letter in disbelief, for she had assumed, after what had happened, that Joseph would never leave Julia again. She could not think of him now without seeing the figure in uniform; the image flicked repeatedly across her mind, less distinct now it was translated to memory, like something half glimpsed at the edge of her vision. Only the dove and the uniform remained clear. Why had he agreed to do it? she asked herself, as she had asked herself over and over. Julia might think she could make her believe she had seen or heard Christopher's ghost, but Joseph must have known she wouldn't be taken in. With Joseph it would have been more complicated – a bizarre attempt to make her see he was unstable? You must know I love you. It's because I love you ... he had said in London, trying to convince her that they should part. She had truly believed that nothing could persuade her he was right.

Esther dismissed him. She would not remember the way they had loved, nor the things they had promised one another. She put the love affair with Joseph behind her. She had judged badly and she had been hurt; but the episode was over and there was a lot of work to be done.

She had found rooms to rent near Edgbaston. 'Smarter than Tamarisk Street but no match for Larch Hill,' she told George Ansfield when she went to see him.

They had agreed she should have complete control over the new range of production. They talked all morning, making plans. George had already bought the warehouses across the street from the main factory. 'We'll go over and inspect them in a bit,' he said. 'You can tell me if you approve. But first we'll have some lunch. I took the liberty of ordering a hamper.'

Esther smiled. 'It's an improvement on your sandwiches. Do you remember when we used to share them?'

'Mine were always cheese. Ursula told Cook to make them for me.'

'Do you miss her?' Esther said quietly.

'Oh, yes. But one gets used to things, you know.' He looked at her, unpacking the contents of the hamper on to the desk. 'We move on.'

Esther nodded. The doctrine sounded good. She would adopt it herself.

George opened a bottle of champagne and they drank to the success of their enterprise and a new departure for them both.

'Are the girls still here – Miriam, Irene, Louie?' Esther said suddenly. 'May I see them?'

They went down to the decorating shop, past men carrying boards stacked with plates, who stared at Esther with surprised recognition. As they neared the manager's office at the entrance to the firing shop, Esther saw Shawcroft at his desk. He looked up and stared through the office window at her.

230

'I haven't told anyone about you yet. He thinks he's seen a ghost,' murmured George.

Esther fell silent, remembering The Dovecote, and she felt a wave of misery sweep through her. She had thought she could keep Joseph out of her head, but everything was still vivid – the hotel room in London, the clay pit, and his nightmare in her studio. The contradictions in the man she had loved and the inconsistencies in the way he had behaved still turned themselves over and over in her mind.

'Anything wrong?' George stood, his hand poised on the door of the office.

'Nothing.' Esther smiled at him and squared her shoulders.

'Of course,' George said, misunderstanding. 'You two didn't get on. We'll soon get over that.' He opened the door to Shawcroft's office.

Esther went forward. 'Don't worry, Mr Shawcroft. You're not seeing things.' She held out her hand as the works manager rose from his desk. George explained about her rejoining the company. 'I shall be overseeing the designing and painting over the road,' Esther said. 'I hope we're going to get along just fine.'

'Why, yes—' Shawcroft blushed and looked flustered.

'Fresh blood, Mr Shawcroft,' said George. 'Ansfield's is starting something new.'

The man bowed his head in acknowledgement and tried to look pleased.

They walked on. Esther paused in the door of the decorating shop, recalling the hours she had spent at the work-tables, supplying leaves to Irene's 'centres', Miriam's petals and Louie's banding. Little had changed except that Miss Lassingham looked thinner, and a few of the faces were unfamiliar.

'Good morning to you, girls. Mrs Norbrook is going to bring Ansfield's up to date with her creative lines.'

The women stared as Shawcroft had done. Miriam spoke first. 'We never dreamed you'd come back.'

'Better the devil you know.' Esther threw a smile at George. 'How are you, Miriam – Louie . . . ?' She smiled at them all, feeling a strong comfort in the memory of when they had worked together; there was a sense of welcome in being back at Ansfield's, where, for a time at least, her life had seemed uncomplicated.

'You're going to need a core of experienced paintresses to work on the new lines,' George said as they went outside again to the yard and crossed the street to the new building. 'Had you thought about that?'

'I wish I could have brought one of my helpers from Dorset. She was almost past her apprenticeship.' Esther remembered Violet's enthusiasm, the clean, airy studio, her chatter as she worked; and she contrasted the picture ruefully with the dirty Victorian buildings and cramped offices at Ansfield's.

The new premises across the street were no less antiquated than the main factory. They consisted of a series of small warehouses, linked by

231

narrow passages and staircases; but the upper storeys had the advantage of large windows along the full length. Esther could see that the rooms had the potential for creating two good studios.

'Our ware has always been conservative, traditional – I have to admit it, even pedestrian,' George said. 'And there'll always be a demand for that type of pot. But if we're going to remain competitive, we've got to show some flair.'

Esther looked around the upper floor, visualising benches occupied by pots and paintresses and feeling an unexpected surge of energy and optimism. 'Oh, we'll show some flair.'

'Will you miss your studio in Dorset?'

'I shall miss Rowena and Violet, who worked with me. I feel I left them in the lurch.' She dropped her gaze, not wanting to talk about The Dovecote.

'They'll survive,' he said with uncharacteristic bluntness, and Esther remembered that she had once left George without warning. Had he really forgotten about wanting to marry her? she wondered. And, if he remembered it as well as she did, was he embarrassed by it at all?

'Would you like to take some of the girls from the old decorating shop?' George said, going to the window and looking down on to the street. A coke wagon rumbled by and turned into the yard over the road. Shawcroft crossed the yard to meet it.

'Can you spare them?'

He turned to face her. 'I want us to put every effort we can into your designs.'

'Thank you, George. Then I should like to take the girls I originally worked with – Miriam, Irene and Louie.'

He nodded, then said with a flush of pleasure, 'I'm more delighted than I can say about this, Esther. I'm glad too that you've found personal happiness at last . . .' He tailed off, seeing the change in her expression.

Esther looked at him in confusion. It had not occurred to her that George didn't know the extent to which her plans had changed. To her horror she felt her eyes fill with tears. She said quickly, 'I'm on my own, George. I'm afraid, as far as personal happiness goes, it didn't work out.'

George's face coloured in dismay. 'I'm so sorry—'

'No,' she interrupted. 'I'm sorry. I should have told you sooner, only—' she hesitated. 'Well, it's not easy . . . as you can imagine.'

She heard a note of doubt enter George's voice. 'Are you sure about this – about coming here?'

'I'm more sure than I've been about anything lately. It's the right thing for me to do.' Esther remembered that it was Joseph who had first said so. 'Someone told me your offer was providence, George. And I think perhaps he was right.'

Joseph arrived in Italy in August, a time when people took to the hills to

232

get away from the summer heat. He thought of the Marchesa di Malfi and went to see her for old times' sake. He stayed a week, followed by another . . . and another. The atmosphere of the Villa Rosa and the little hill town near Siena enveloped him with its seduction – of sun and wine; of excitable, voluble voices and a sense of bustle interspersed with endless leisure.

He lay for long afternoons in the shade of the fig tree in the villa courtyard, with a panama hat over his eyes, doing nothing, trying to forget Julia, The Dovecote, Esther and Cassie.

'What is wrong?' Maria asked him one day, sitting down beside him and regarding him shrewdly. 'My friends, the Luppis have telephoned twice, impatient to know when you will begin work at the Villa di Sogni. I cannot believe it is my poor company that is keeping you here so long.'

Joseph lifted his hat and shifted his feet from the plinth of the statue of a Roman virgin. 'There's nothing impoverished about your company, Maria. You're very good for me.'

She raised an eyebrow. 'Don't patronise me. I know something's happened. Have you fallen in love?'

'Yes. And I don't want to talk about it.'

'Work will help.'

'For once work doesn't seem attractive.'

'If you don't work again soon you will lose the commission. The Luppis are not patient people.'

Joseph sighed. 'And you are a bully, darling Maria. I'm going for a walk.'

He left the villa courtyard and, jamming his hat on his head, entered the baking heat of the road beyond the villa walls; almost at once he was surrounded by a crowd of children begging for coins. He shook them off and made his way down the hill towards the town, which bathed in a dazzling haze of Sunday stillness.

He had no sense of purpose except to escape the lethargy that had affected him since leaving The Dovecote. He recalled with a haunting intensity the day he drove away. Julia had sensed this time that she had lost him for ever; she had pleaded with him, her eyes red with crying.

He blotted out the memory and tried to imagine a September Sunday in England, tried to picture Esther and Cassie in Birmingham, but he had to abandon the attempt. It was impossible to envisage the smoky, brick-red chapels and streets of the Midlands against the sights and sounds all around him – the ragged children, the chime of church bells, the tall, sun-soaked houses, and the burning sky above. A cloud of doves flew up into the air as he reached a small piazza fringed by crumbling houses, and at once the clatter of wings evoked memories of The Dovecote.

Esther had said he wasn't capable of killing the doves, but she had believed it at first, he reminded himself, and from the moment when he had seen the dead birds in Cassie's arms he knew his own brief spell of happiness was over. If he could do such a terrible thing, the truth was he would never be cured. Perhaps Esther too, deep down, had finally recognised that she couldn't trust him.

Had Julia's motives been selfless? he wondered. One thing was certain: Julia had made him more unhappy than she could ever have imagined by driving them apart. Maria said that Julia was a witch – he was bewitched, *stregato*, or else why did he always return to The Dovecote? But he knew now that he would never go back. He had made his plans quickly once the decision was made, had left soon after Esther, taking little with him except a vivid picture of Julia's tearful farewell.

'I only did what was best for you,' Julia had cried. 'I love you, Joseph. You know how much I love you.'

He would arrange for his workshop to be dismantled, he decided, put his machines and tools in store. Colin and Tim would house them for him. They had offered to take him in, he remembered, gleeful to say, 'I told you so', when they knew he was leaving Julia – for they had never had much opinion of her. He missed Cassie, he realised. Dear, eager Cassie with her enthusiasm and her interest in wood. Already she had the instinct of a craft-artist, and he could have taught her so much . . . Doves whirled up on to the roof of one of the buildings again, breaking his train of thought.

He halted. A child was running towards him, a young girl with dark hair under a straw hat, in white gloves and stockings and with thin brown arms sticking out from her cotton frock. He drew in his breath sharply because, for an instant, she could have been Cassie. As he paused he saw a crowd, in black Sunday best, gathering at the corner of the street. It was a typical Italian scene, the chime of church bells, the chatter of church-going people . . . But the murmur of the crowd was loud, he realised; the sun cast a harsh glare and deep shadows into the street; and the girl was crying as she ran towards him. '*Signore! Signore!*' She seized his hand and let out a torrent of Italian, from which he could distinguish nothing, except that her *papa* was in trouble.

He allowed the girl to drag him towards the corner, where the crowd of church-goers talked anxiously with one another but did nothing to interfere with what was happening by the church steps. Three men in the black-shirted, quasi-military uniform of a Fascist squad stood over a figure lying on the pavement. As Joseph watched, one of the Blackshirts kicked at the man on the ground, who squirmed away towards the wall and covered his head with his arms.

'Hey!' Joseph released the girl's hand and began to force his way through the crowd. 'Hey! Shame on you! *Basta!*'

Hands held him back, voices jabbered as he tried to push through; one said in English, 'Don't be involved, *signore*. It is not your problem.' But there were others in the crowd who began to echo Joseph's cry. '*Basta!*'

The Blackshirts glanced at one another and looked around as if aware that they were few in number. They shifted away from the man on the pavement and, pausing only to shout a casual threat towards the crowd, walked off. People began to disperse, talking excitedly among themselves. Joseph went to the man on the ground as he groaned and struggled to sit up. The man held his shoulder and groaned again as the child knelt on the pavement beside him; his suit was covered in the dust of the street and his cheek was bleeding from a cut.

'You need a doctor,' Joseph said. '*Il medico?*'

The man shook his head and said in English, 'It was not a bad beating. Only a warning, they said. One moment to rest and I shall be well.'

Joseph sat on the step beside him and the man took his daughter in his arms, soothing her against him. He said in Italian, 'See now. Papa is fine.'

'Why did they attack you?'

'I am a council official, *signore*. A Socialist. I spoke out against the *Fascisti* to people in church last Sunday.' The man picked up his hat and glanced round the square. 'Please, signore. Leave me now. You should not be seen with me. You are English, but no one is secure.'

Shaken, Joseph watched the man move slowly away. The girl held her father's hand and glanced up anxiously at every step, and again the resemblance to Cassie caught at Joseph's heart. He had no stomach now for wandering around the town, and after a while he returned to the villa.

He told Maria about the incident over lunch, saying that the man's only apparent crime had been to criticise the Fascists to fellow members of his church congregation.

'He was a Socialist. Socialism is very bad for Italy,' Maria said. 'It knows of nothing but strikes and violence.'

'Aren't you more worried about the violence from the Fascists?'

'We need a strong movement to shake up the government. Italy was let down after the war, Joseph. Promises were broken. For four years we had made terrible sacrifices and for what? The ordinary man in the street feels he suffered in the war for little reward.'

'This was an ordinary man in the street who was beaten up by his own countrymen. They terrified his child.'

Maria shrugged. 'He was not badly hurt. You said so yourself.' She looked up and smiled sympathetically. 'Don't worry, Joseph. If anyone comes asking questions I shall defend you. I shall soon persuade them you are not a dangerous alien.'

Joseph said coldly that had not been his concern and changed the subject. He did not want to quarrel with Maria after their past association. But, as he lay on his bed during the siesta hour and listened to the crickets in the courtyard below, he knew that before long he and Maria would quarrel. He had sat around at the Villa Rosa for too many weeks doing nothing but dwell on past mistakes. It was time to move on.

235

* * *

Joseph telephoned the Luppis the next day to arrange his accommodation with them. On impulse, returning to his old passion, he bought a car, an Alfa tourer and, saying farewell to Maria, drove to the Villa di Sogni.

The Luppis' estate lay about half an hour's drive to the north of Siena. Oxen paced slowly on the road in front of him, and the land rose in shallow terraces to the hazy cluster of stone buildings forming a village ahead. Rows of dark cypress trees shimmered on the burning skyline as Joseph drove through the vineyards and dry and dusty fields. He slowed the Alfa to a crawl as he reached the high wall surrounding the villa, and swung the car in through the rusted iron gates.

A straight and stony drive led through an avenue of blue-green cypresses, at the end of which stood the Villa di Sogni, long and vast, like an ornate monastery, with a low red roof and narrow rows of shuttered windows in the pale yellow walls. Joseph brought the car to a halt by the steps in front of the entrance, and the Luppis came to meet him as he climbed out. They greeted him as if they were minor nobility and he a long-lost relative they were delighted to indulge a little. A pair of gun-dogs came down the steps behind them, and a valet appeared and hurried to the car to remove Joseph's luggage as the Luppis drew him into the villa with cries of excitement.

The valet's heels rang hollow as he led the way to the worn marble staircase. The rooms, cool and dark after the bright sunlight, were filled with flowers; but the house itself, Joseph noted, as his eyes grew accustomed to the shadows, was in a state of disarray. There was a confusion of dustsheets, timber and ladders in the main hall, and, as they crossed it, he heard and saw workmen in the adjoining rooms, their voices echoing from the walls.

'You will sleep at the Villa di Sogni tonight,' said Signora Luppi with a grand gesture of her hand towards the staircase.

'Tomorrow we show you your *podere* – the farmhouse,' added Signor Luppi. He saw Joseph's frown of uncertainty. 'You prefer to be housed away from the main building, yes?'

'For my work,' said Joseph. 'I shall need complete isolation when I'm not involved with the workmen here at the villa.'

'Of course.' Signora Luppi turned to cast a broad smile on him. Her mouth was large and loose, her face lined by the sun. 'You are an artist. We must respect your needs. But tonight you are our guest and we must entertain you.' She laughed as she saw him glance doubtfully into the dustsheeted rooms off the hall and said in Italian, 'It's chaos. Yes? But, by a miracle, we do live here and we try to entertain our visitors.'

Joseph submitted to their hospitality. He had slept without nightmares since arriving in Italy, and he did not expect the pattern to change in one evening. The guest room they had prepared for him was austere, but someone had placed a bowl of flowers on the table in front of the shutters and the bed looked comfortable. He opened the windows when he was alone and looked out on to the gardens of the villa. His eye followed the network of gravelled walks and avenues of trees, of flowerbeds and steps and balustrades and paving, some areas already established, others in the process of change. A group of gardeners worked at the far end of the garden, wheeling barrow-loads of soil, laying paving, calling to one another. He could hear their garrulous voices. How far removed from the hushed tranquillity of The Dovecote it was. And yet, this place was in its way more tranquil. He felt a sense of calm in the lofty, empty rooms, and the monastic atmosphere of the building – and in its absence of memories.

The Luppis sat with Joseph on the terrace after dinner. The gardeners had gone and the place was still. The sun cast long shadows along the gravelled walks, turning the cypresses an inky green. Signora Luppi explained her plans for the villa, and her husband told stories about their troubles with workmen. The Luppis' grasp of English was better than Joseph's Italian, and he was glad to be spared the effort of translating as he outlined his own immediate impressions of the house and his ideas for the main staircase and the dining room.

'It is a plain house, Signor Kilburn,' Signora Luppi said of the villa. 'It needs much work for our comfort.'

Joseph could visualise a staircase that would accentuate the villa's monastic severity, but he suspected the Luppis didn't share his love of simplicity.

'We shall fill the house with your wonderful furniture,' Signora Luppi said in response to his suggestion of a few pieces.

'The commission was for a staircase and dining room only,' Joseph reminded her.

'Of course! I have plans. We will talk.'

Her husband interrupted. 'In three years we have bought this place and the neighbouring land and farms. We have built, restored the vineyards, begun work on the garden. Now we must make the interior also very fine. We shall have open fires in the bedrooms. You will design the overmantels for us.'

'Have you experienced an Italian winter, Signor Kilburn?' Signora Luppi shivered dramatically.

'It seems I shall be here longer than I expected,' Joseph said, and he remembered with a rush of sadness that he had once promised Esther an absence of a few weeks when he had first told her about the Luppis' commission. Now, he realised, it didn't matter how long he stayed in Italy, nor where he went afterwards. A sweeping sense of loneliness overtook him.

'We have changed all the water pipes and put in new floors and relocated the servants' quarters . . .' Signor Luppi was saying, reverting to his native Italian.

'All to the designs of that frightful architect, Estevez,' interrupted his wife.

237

'We are in the last stages of the rebuilding,' explained Signor Luppi. 'Thank goodness it is over. My wife and Estevez did not get along.'

Signora Luppi threw up her hands. 'The man was an idiot. I had to dismiss him. He did not know the first thing about style. But no more. Now you are here we shall get along splendidly.'

'I hope so,' said Joseph, though he had begun to feel a sneaking sympathy for the dismissed Estevez.

The next day Signor Luppi went with Joseph to show him the house where he would live. The Luppi estate included two farms, he explained. The *podere* where Joseph was to live, had been replaced by a larger, working farm-dwelling, closer to the villa. There was also a lodge and a carpenter's house on the estate. The carpenter would work under Joseph's instruction.

They arrived finally at a small farmhouse lying at a distance of about half a mile from the Villa di Sogni; it was built of stone, with a shallow roof of curving red tiles, and it nestled into the side of the hill. The upper storey had access to the sloping ground behind it, and there was also an outside stair.

'Here is your abode,' Signor Luppi said with a cordial and generous sweep of the hand, as if to include the entire hillside in the gesture. He explained that the ground floor of the building had once been a stable, now converted, for Joseph's use, to a workshop and studio.

The low-ceilinged living room and bedroom above the stable were cool and light; the doors stood open to the air, and the windows overlooked the valley. 'It is very generous accommodation,' Joseph said as they descended the outside stair to the workshop.

'We do not mean you to run away,' said Signor Luppi.

The phrase sent waves of unease through Joseph's mind. Was that what he and Esther had done when they had parted without any explanation? He was struck by a vivid memory of their happiness in London and their return to The Dovecote with such strong plans for the future.

He had closed his mind after Esther had gone from The Dovecote, refused to think about what had happened or even to talk to Julia about what had taken place at the seance. He shut it from his thoughts now too; he must not begin to harbour regrets. He would remember only the slaughter of the doves; everything that had happened afterwards had turned out for the best.

'We want you to feel you are at home here,' Signor Luppi was saying. 'To do good work for us, yes? The Villa di Sogni must be the envy of all Siena.'

'The envy of Florence too?' Joseph joked, shaking off his bleak mood.

'And of Florence – why not?' echoed his host, laughing heartily. 'It is good.'

238

Esther worked on the alterations to the warehouses with George, and the days and weeks passed into autumn. With a sense of piety, as a penance for abandoning the work in Dorset, she refused to draw more than a basic salary until her side of the business was in full production.

To Esther's surprise, Cassie had asked if she might go back to Heather Park. 'I'm going to be a furniture designer when I leave school,' she explained. 'Miss Collins will be able to help me.'

Cassie knew her mother was angry when she said she wanted to be a furniture designer like Joseph. She had told her not to be so ridiculous, and the atmosphere between them was cold for a while. But, in the end, Esther agreed that Cassie should be allowed to attend Heather Park.

Cassie had other reasons for returning: she wanted those girls who had said Esther was second-rate to know that her mother had become a manufacturer. More importantly, Cassie had Joseph's photograph with which to impress them – though she didn't let Esther know she had it. She kept it under her pillow at night, and the corners had become worn and faded.

'She's growing up,' Esther's mother said when Cassie tried on her uniform at her grandparents' house. 'Hardly anything still fits her.'

Esther sat back on her heels, having let down the hem of Cassie's old gym-slip and discovered that it was still well above her knees. 'It's a pity she couldn't have worn her things from the school in Dorset.'

'Oh, but Heather Park has such a *nice* uniform,' her mother said, rubbing the fabric between finger and thumb. 'It's a very superior serge.'

Cassie, standing on a stool and turning slowly so that Esther might fold and pin the hem of the skirt, grinned at her mother and Esther grinned back. Cassie was glad they were friends again. She could hear Martha the housemaid singing in the back scullery. There was a smell of fish, as there always was at the house at Larch Hill on Fridays, and, though she missed Joseph, and was sure her mother missed him too, there was a comfortable sense of everything being right with the world.

'A new gym-slip it is then,' Esther said, taking the pins out of her mouth and packing them back in their box.

'Daddy and I will pay,' her mother said, with a decided note to her voice.

'No, not this time,' Esther said, with an equal air of determination.

Cassie looked from her mother to her grandmother, and her grandmother's sulky expression made her want to smile and hug her at the same time.

'Look – I *am* grateful for the way you've always helped,' Esther said more gently. 'But I can manage on my own.'

'Exactly! On your own!'

Esther stood up and said in a bored tone, 'Now, what's that supposed to mean?'

Cassie's grandfather had come into the room. He cleared his throat. 'Your mother means, you don't seem to be looking for a husband.'

It occurred to Cassie that her grandparents still knew nothing at all about Joseph, and she saw instinctively that her mother would never tell them; it would always remain a secret. She tried – as she had so often tried since leaving The Dovecote – to imagine the parting between Joseph and her mother. Had Esther pleaded with him to live with them? Had Joseph told her his story about it not being fair because he sometimes had nightmares and sometimes he did strange things – and so they had quarrelled? But if that was all they had quarrelled about, why wouldn't her mother even talk about him?

'I *mean* you lost your chance with Giles,' said Mrs Mortimer, still talking about husbands. 'He's going to marry Margaret Davenport at Christmas.'

'But that's wonderful news. I'm very pleased for them,' Esther said.

'Oh!' her mother released an unrefined wail of exasperation.

'Besides,' said Esther. 'I shall soon be as rich as Croesus. So, who needs a husband?'

Esther's pleasure for Giles was genuine. She knew instinctively that, though she had understood him thoroughly, she would not have made Giles very happy. She considered her marriage to Christopher. She had loved him but, after eight years of intimacy, had she known much about him? Her thoughts turned automatically to Joseph. Had she understood him at all? Could she ever have guessed that his dependency on Julia might lead him to do something so cruel as to pretend to be Christopher's ghost?

'You really think you're going to do well out of your alliance with Ansfield then?' her father was saying.

'I'm sure of it. We've got such splendid ideas between us.'

Her mother looked at her, forgetting Giles for a moment. 'You know, people will talk if you don't take care.'

Esther laughed. 'Well, you can't have it all ways, Mummy. At least if they do, they'll assume I have a man in my life.'

'Esther! I don't think there's any cause for you to talk like that!' Esther's mother grew thoughtful. 'Perhaps we should have a dinner party – and invite George Ansfield again.'

'Yes,' Esther said in exasperation. 'That's a splendid idea!'

Esther had not expected her mother to take her at her word when she had added, with more than a touch of sarcasm, 'Why don't you ask Giles and Margaret as well?'

She sat at her mother's table, her elbow close to George's. He had dressed to the occasion, she noted, for he looked fashionable, though slightly ill at ease in a dinner jacket. Margaret Davenport was leaning across the table to talk to them. She was the perfect mate for Giles, Esther conceded: pretty, decorous, with bobbed hair and in a square-necked, expensively simple evening dress.

Esther caught Giles's eye and he blushed, for he had been watching her. Had she dressed too flamboyantly? she wondered with a pang of alarm. She had felt an immature urge to shock her mother. Why did her family always bring out the worst in her? Making her so often revert to sarcasm, and now exhibitionism – for she wore the dress she had worn in London when she had wanted to seduce Joseph. And had succeeded, she remembered, feeling a hollow ache of longing. She still wanted him. Only a few weeks had passed, yet how long ago it seemed since they had loved one another. She remembered the line of his jaw, the little frowns at the corners of his eyes, and the intimacy of waking in a bed with him beside her. Why was it so much easier to remember how much he had attracted her, rather than how badly he had treated her?

'Esther?' George touched her elbow gently, and she realised that they were all looking at her, waiting for her to say something. George prompted her. 'Margaret asked when we can hope to see "Esther Norbrook" ware in the shops?'

'I should think after Christmas.' She turned to George. 'A trial run in some of the Birmingham stores.'

'And then London – Paris?' said Giles.

'Esther already has valuable customers in London and Paris. But, yes. We hope to expand Ansfield's markets abroad.'

'How exciting,' said Margaret. She smiled at Giles with a proprietary air. How much did Giles still care? Esther wondered, for he did not look at her, nor at his fiancée, but toyed with his knife at the side of his plate. Suddenly he looked up and raised his glass. 'To you both. I wish your enterprise every success.'

Some weeks later, George was poring over the morning post in his office. He glanced up with a broad smile as Esther arrived. 'Denholm's like the first batch of "Esther Norbrook". I knew they would. You're in business.'

'That's marvellous,' agreed Esther distractedly. It was, but it was hardly a surprise: she had known already that Denholm's were persuaded. The real challenge would be the larger London stores, which she must tackle without Julia's patronage to boost her name. Besides, she had something else on her mind.

'You seem preoccupied,' George said. 'What is it?'

Esther held an envelope in her hand. She pulled a card from it to show him. 'George. I've been invited to a wedding. Well – we have really. It's Giles and Margaret. They seem to have assumed that we ... that is ... Look. If you don't want to come, I'll understand. I'll explain to them ...'

George beamed. 'I should love to come. There's nothing a confirmed bachelor likes better than a good wedding.'

'You don't mind?'

'Not a bit.' He looked at her, his head on one side. 'I know what you're thinking, but I got over that a long time ago. Besides,' he went back to his correspondence, 'anyone with half an eye can see that your heart's still elsewhere.'

To her surprise, Esther enjoyed the wedding. She felt a lump come to her throat as Giles made his wedding vows, remembering her brother Richard – for the two had been schoolfriends – wishing he had lived long enough to lead a normal, ordinary life, with marriage and a family. She cried a little and threw rice and drank champagne and laughed a lot with Cassie and George. And afterwards George drove them home.

'I'll be glad when you're not too proud to draw a decent salary, and can afford somewhere more salubrious than this,' he said as they watched Cassie run into the house with the keys.

'I like it here,' Esther laughed, for the rooms she rented were comfortable and large; she and Cassie had the use of two floors and a bathroom and there was even a share in a garden at the back of the house. 'It's near Cassie's school and it's cosy. We've made it ours.'

'All the same. After Christmas . . .'

'After Esther Norbrook ware starts to pay its way,' Esther said, silencing him. 'We'll talk about money then.'

'Good.' He placed his hands behind his head, smiling. 'I've enjoyed today.'

'So have I. Thank you for coming with us, George.' She leaned forward and kissed his cheek. 'I'll see you on Monday.' Esther climbed from the car and stepped on to the pavement. She stood in the gateway and waved as George drove away. She had enjoyed his company, she reflected as she turned away from the road. They made a good combination. It was like their early days together, but without the threat that either one of them would get the wrong idea.

There was a letter waiting for her indoors.

'The postmark is Dorset. Is it from Julia?' Cassie asked anxiously.

Esther felt an irrational leap of fear; but the letter was from Meg, not Julia. It was full of news about The Dovecote, the most startling being the fact that the contents of Joseph's workshop had been dismantled and shifted to Exeter some weeks earlier.

'. . . The timber, machinery, everything, lock, stock and barrel was collected in lorries and taken away by some very odd people,' Meg wrote. 'Julia was distraught. We have all suffered, Esther, on your account. But, now that Joseph is in Italy and his things have gone, we really think Julia might get over it. Peter and I have been through it all before. We know that peace will return. It always does.'

Peace – because the wild pigeons had flown, thought Esther, and she was struck by a memory of a line of doves on Rowena's kitchen table, each with the life wrung from it.

'What does the letter say?' Cassie had taken off her wedding clothes and was playing with the brim of the hat, trying not to look too eager for news of Joseph.

'Joseph has had all his things removed from The Dovecote and he's in

Italy,' Esther said, shocked by the news into talking about him, though she had vowed to herself she wouldn't.

Had he left Julia for ever? Esther sat with the letter in her lap and felt a mixture of anxiety and perplexity as she imagined the lorries taking the timber away, dragging out the machinery, transporting it to Exeter. To his friends there? Did Joseph intend returning to live with them after the commission in Italy? She told herself that she did not, must not care. And yet, she could not help wondering how Joseph could have made such a complete break from Julia, when he had not been able to in the past. Esther looked up, thinking aloud, as she said to Cassie, 'I don't understand. It doesn't make sense.'

Chapter Fifteen

The Luppis' plans for the Villa di Sogni turned out to be as elaborate as Joseph had feared. He wondered, in the light of his austere style as a designer, why they had chosen him, until he realised that they had no conception of his work except for what they had seen at the Villa Rosa. He discovered that Signora Luppi had quarrelled with no less than three architects during the estate's conversion. Once word had gone round that they were temperamental, no architect would come near them – even in a land where touchiness was endemic. The Luppis, in desperation, had remembered meeting Joseph. Maria had sung his praises as a model of reasonableness. Their visit to London had done the rest.

Joseph, though no architect, was glad to immerse himself in the work of making changes to the villa. His habit of withdrawal from close company made it easy for him to ignore the day-to-day irritations of his clients and to concentrate instead on the difficulties of organising order out of the chaos. He valued his isolation in the hillside *podere* as much as he had valued his cottage at The Dovecote. He would wake each morning and open the door of his bedroom to watch the sun rise over the hills before planning his work for the day. The servant, an ancient widow, arrived at eight and prepared breakfast for him. The rest of the morning was devoted to work at the villa, to endless discussions with Signora Luppi and laboured conversations with Lorenzo the chief carpenter, who, once he had grasped what was wanted, quickly proved himself sweet-natured and compliant.

Electricity had already been installed in the villa; water and heating were laid on. The main stair was still in its original state of dilapidation. The Luppis had at last managed to secure a local architect to work alongside Joseph for the work of reconstruction, and to complete the rest of the house. Roberto Falzon was very young. He had little authority over the workmen, and Joseph, in spite of his poor grasp of Italian, found himself in charge of the stonemasons as well as the carpenters. But Roberto was a man of inventive ideas and, what was more, he respected Joseph's; they found in each other a valuable accomplice in resisting the more dramatic excesses of the Luppis.

Gradually changes began to take place, and the days fell into a regular pattern. Joseph and Roberto had luncheon at the villa with the Luppis if they were at home, and with the various workmen if they were not.

After lunch everyone disappeared for a siesta, and Joseph would drive to his *podere* to prepare designs and plan materials for the staircase, the dining room, and several other projects at the villa. He would return in the evening for yet more discussions with the Luppis over dinner and, around midnight, drive home and fall into an exhausted and dreamless sleep.

By the end of October, the scaffolding for the main stair was in place and the stone and timber ordered or already cut. 'We shall have a party to celebrate,' declared Signora Luppi one evening during dinner. 'We shall invite the Marchesa di Malfi and our friends from Florence. We must honour you both.'

Roberto, serious and averse to fuss, was clearly embarrassed. He swivelled his wine glass on the table, murmuring that it wasn't necessary. Joseph neither protested nor expressed enthusiasm; as in everything else, his natural indolence made him inclined to go along with whatever plans were being laid; he had no objection to the Luppis' holding a party in his honour. However – remembering her support for Mussolini's Fascists – he did not relish seeing Maria again.

The party turned out to be all that Joseph detested: the artificial voices and opinions, the lavish dress and silly drinks in glasses with sugared edges and pieces of fruit floating in them. The only saving grace was the American jazz – played from a gramophone, since the repertoire of the local musicians fell short of such tunes as 'Whispering' and 'Ain't We Got Fun'. Joseph felt a perverse nostalgia for Colin and Tim's company – when 'Ain't We Got Fun', sung by Colin, his voice slack with emotion, had been the accompaniment to a decent glass of whisky. He surveyed the scene in the hall. The scaffolding had been decorated with bunting and a clamour of Italian voices rose to the vaulted ceiling.

'The Luppis give brilliant parties, apparently,' said a voice in English close to his ear. He turned to look at the woman who had penetrated the general hubbub, and recognised a pretty interior decorator the Luppis were employing to design the soft furnishings for the villa. She wore a gold scarf, wrapped round her hair like a turban, and a scandalously tight, low-necked dress. He was reminded of Esther's attempt to shock him that night when she had come after him in London. He drank down his cocktail and took another, impatient to reach a level of drunkenness that numbed one's mind.

'You're English,' he said, deciding she was a vamp.

'Yes. We English have a certain snob value still.'

He stared at her, surprised by her self-mockery, reassessing his opinion of her. She glanced at the Luppis and said in an undertone, 'The signora is rather a challenge, don't you think?'

'There have been so many changes to be made and so many new things to add to the villa,' Signora Luppi was telling one of the guests in Italian. 'I am overwhelmed by it all.'

Joseph exchanged glances with his companion. 'I feel Signora Luppi would be hard-put to feel overwhelmed by anything. Don't you?'

'Now what are you both smiling about?'

Joseph had not seen Maria arrive. She came towards him, shaking the damp from her clothes, and kissed him on both cheeks. 'What frightful weather out there. Enough to drown us all. Joseph. Introduce me to this divine creature beside you.'

Joseph turned to his companion. 'I'm sorry. I don't—'

'Sally,' the girl said, extending her hand to the marchesa. 'Sally Edmonds. And you must be the Marchesa di Malfi.'

Joseph listened to them begin to discuss the world of interior design. Alcohol had mellowed his ambivalent feelings about Maria. She had been jolly liberal towards him, he remembered – not demanding like Julia, not intractable like Esther. He beckoned and introduced Roberto, who blushed and bowed over the marchesa's hand.

Maria surveyed Roberto with a delicate intensity, and Joseph saw a sexual interest flicker in her eyes. Had she once regarded him with that same evaluation? He remembered how she had flirted and how readily he had responded. Maria was a good sort. But why had he never noticed how predatory she could be?

'I almost forgot. Have you heard?' Maria cried, turning suddenly to call to the Luppis.

Signora Luppi, in a dark pink, tubular dress that reached her ankles, so that she resembled a kind of sausage, said, 'What, Maria darling? What haven't we heard?'

'Why – Mussolini has begun his march to seize Rome. They have Trieste and Venice already – and Florence; I heard it on the way here.'

'It's true,' said one of the guests from Florence. 'The *squadre* were out, assembling in the rain. There is going to be almost no opposition. They say the King will ask Mussolini to form a Cabinet as soon as he goes to Rome.'

Maria turned to Joseph. 'Darling. I forgot. You disapprove. Joseph thinks Mussolini is too boisterous for us.'

'Mussolini will be a strong leader for our country. The English always have to impose their opinions on everyone else,' said one of the guests from Florence with surprising asperity.

'Don't rise to the bait. Don't get involved,' Joseph heard Sally Edmonds murmur, throwing him a restraining glance.

'Aren't we all very much concerned about the future for our country?' said Roberto, blushing furiously at his own recklessness in offering an opinion.

'But you are Italian, Roberto. You understand,' said Signora Luppi.

'The world has grown smaller because of the war,' Joseph said, speaking slowly and gravely, vaguely aware that drink was making him pompous. 'We are all very much involved with one another's affairs.'

'It is because of the war that the English are so arrogant,' said someone. 'The English think they won the war singlehanded. Italy's sacrifices were forgotten when the Allies shared out the spoils.'

Joseph, needled by the sudden chill of hostility round him, said, 'Well, you can't deny, Italy was pretty bloody reluctant to join in before 1915.'

'We could not have stayed neutral,' Roberto said placatingly. 'We had to come in on the Allied side.'

'We?' said Maria with a gentle lift of the eyebrows. 'Weren't you too young for all that, Signor Falzon?'

Roberto blushed and spilled his drink.

'We suffered for joining with the Allies,' said Signora Luppi. 'The Villa di Sogni was taken over by refugees. They wrecked it, and it was left to go to ruin before we bought it.'

'Ah – what is achieved by war, Joseph?' said Maria. She laid a reassuring hand on his arm. He realised that she was remembering his nightmares at the Villa Rosa, and that for his sake she already regretted the turn the conversation had taken.

'There was a lot of anti-English feeling in Florence during the war,' remarked the guest who had objected to Joseph's opinion of Mussolini. 'We did not like the English soldiers' drunken and riotous ways.'

'Soldiers need to drink to forget,' Joseph said harshly.

Maria took his arm and linked her other arm in Roberto's. She drew them away from the conversation as it continued in praise of Mussolini – his remarkable energies, his talent for seizing the moment – the man of the future. 'Come, Joseph, *caro*,' said Maria. 'Show me your plans for this splendid new stair.'

The news about the Fascists' march on Rome had brought back the memory of the man on the pavement and his child, crying for help. Joseph remembered the crowd who had stood by while the Blackshirts administered a beating, and he remembered other cries for help when he had stood by, helpless. That night, after the party, he woke screaming and soaked in sweat as he stared into the darkness. He had heard them again, calling like wild birds at sea. So, it was not over yet.

Would it ever be over? He wondered, remembering how they had tied him to a stretcher, reliving the terror and hopelessness before Julia had come to him. Was he always going to remain crippled, unable to lead a normal life? He remembered being in a trench with his men, a packet of Woodbines passed around, a swallow of brandy for courage. They had only been boys, and so had he, not equipped for that sort of leadership. Over the top, lads. Don't dwell on death. Don't think about lying in agony. He could see each face as if it were yesterday: Richmond, Stubbs, Cartwright... They paraded before him, accusing him with their eyes. He heard their cries. He should have gone to them. Other officers had gone after their men. A sergeant in one of the Australian battalions had gone out time after time into No Man's Land and carried back the wounded until he was shot by a sniper. The age old question ran through his head. Had he been a coward? Had he gone into a funk because he had thought only of preserving his own skin?

He turned and buried his face in his pillow, cold and drenched with sweat. After a while he got up and washed in a bowl by the bed, then went outside and down the stair to his workroom. He lit the oil-lamp and bent over his desk, and began to rework the design for the overmantels at the Villa di Sogni. As he worked, he listened to the crickets and saw the dawn lighten the sky, and he thought of the last time he had seen Julia, her voice harsh with sobbing, pathetic in its plea, 'At least let me explain about the seance.'

'I don't want to know,' he had said. 'Whatever you've said or done to persuade Esther – spirit voices, ghostly warnings – it's not important. That's not the issue for me. And it has nothing to do with my decision to leave.'

He thought of Esther and Cassie far away in England, and told himself the night had proved, if he had needed any proof, that they were better off without him. But he wondered about them, and he wondered whether Esther ever thought about him and what she had told Cassie. He began to wonder too, for the first time, what exactly had happened at Julia's seance that day, when Esther was finally convinced that Julia was right.

Maria stayed with the Luppis for two weeks. After the first week, Roberto confessed to Joseph that he had fallen in love with the marchesa. 'What can I do?' he said desperately. 'She wants me to go back with her and design a bell-tower for the Villa Rosa. But I have Socialist sympathies. The marchesa supports the Fascists. She stands in opposition to everything in which I believe. And yet I adore her.'

Joseph was afraid for his friend Roberto. He knew Maria well enough to believe that she would hurt him. She would be excited at first by the architect's innocent good looks and gullibility. His Socialist tendencies might add a little spice to the relationship, but in the end she would discard him.

'Do you really want my advice?'

Roberto turned an anguished face to him. 'Tell me she is no good for me. Tell me I must listen to my head and not my heart.'

'She's no good for you,' Joseph said. 'And only idiots listen to their hearts.'

Roberto left the next day with Maria. He explained himself in a letter some weeks later:

'. . . *What use is a heart if we do not listen to its beating? You were wrong. Only a fool will choose the easy way rather than love, and I would face any pain for the joy I feel right now.*'

Was Roberto right? Joseph asked himself, reading and rereading the letter. Should one seize love and suffering, however unequal the quantities? What if the suffering involved others? He lay in the room above his workshop and listened to the crickets in the dark. It would soon be Christmas. He wondered what Esther and Cassie would do. How far away an English Christmas seemed – plum pudding, presents round a tree, a roaring fire . . . He remembered walking on the cliff with Cassie, telling her about Italy: he had said that it was a very beautiful country, but that sometimes the endless sunshine made it seem harsh. Cassie had sat on the grass at the edge of the cliff; it had been early autumn, and she had said she thought it would be wonderful to live every day with the sun shining down and to see lizards on the rocks and hear the crickets singing.

'Sometimes it's good to feel the rain falling gently too,' Joseph had told her, sitting beside her, seeing the wind blow her dark hair, aware that she stole little glances at him from time to time. 'And don't you like it when the snow is lying on the ground?' He had actually felt the pleasure of snow as he said it; he had forgotten the winter of 1916 and remembered only the pleasure of snow when he was a child.

'I like Christmas,' Cassie had said, and then, with an insight that had made his heart miss a beat, 'but it must have been terrible to spend Christmas in a foreign country, fighting.'

'Will you go back to Italy again?' she had asked him as she picked blueberries along the path, and he had said that he thought he would not return to Italy unless something drove him away from England.

'I'm glad,' Cassie had said gravely.

Her expression, the blueberry stains round her mouth, and the sheer pleasure of her company had made him laugh with a freedom and warmth he had not known for years. 'And why is that, Cassandra?'

She had grinned at his use of her full name, not minding his teasing. '. . . Because I know nothing could ever drive you away from us. So you'll be around for ever and ever.'

Sally Edmonds had begun work at the villa. She lodged in Siena and drove out to the Villa di Sogni each day. She said she did not dare stay near the Luppis for long, in case she was browbeaten into compromising her talent and accepting Signora Luppi's ideas wholesale.

'I thought you were stout-hearted,' Joseph said, after offering to drive her back to her apartment to collect some materials one day. It was December, but the sun was still warm, more like an English autumn. 'Surely the *signora* doesn't frighten you.'

'Signora Luppi terrifies me,' laughed Sally as they headed for Siena.

'Me too,' Joseph admitted. He glanced sideways at her. She was very pretty, he noticed: her short fair hair was lighter than when he had first met her at the Luppis' party, bleached already by the sun, and the freckles on her nose and cheeks had deepened. She wore a crocheted silk hat pulled low over her ears, which gave her an elfin appearance, and her legs were long and slim in silk stockings. He found himself staring and pulled his attention away.

'What are you doing out here anyway?' he said.

'Escaping a broken love affair,' she said with too much nonchalance for it to be convincing. 'I could ask you the same question.'

'You might get the same answer.'

'Did she throw you over? That's what happened to me. He's married, of course. The bastard ditched me when his wife found out about us.'

'Not exactly.'

'Ah. You ditched *her*.'

'It's more complicated than that.'

'It can't be. Either you love someone, so you stay with them. Or you don't, so you split.'

They reached her apartment and Sally jumped from the car. 'Come inside for a minute.'

Her rooms – above an ironmonger's shop – were large, cool and airy. The shutters were closed; they let in chinks of light as he watched her search among the cushions of the sofa. Swatches of furnishing fabrics lay around on the floor among a muddle of plates and coffee cups. The apartment was very untidy, he noticed. She went into the adjoining room and Joseph glimpsed a disordered bed with a high wooden headboard, and clothes and yet more fabric samples on the floor. She bent and searched through these and then returned with a pile of swatches, smiling triumphantly. 'Found them. Have some coffee?'

He sat and watched her as she brewed the coffee, chatting all the while as she stood by the stove. She came from the Midlands, she said. Her parents lived in Nottingham. She had brothers and sisters who would miss her at Christmas. She said it almost made one want to go home. 'Do you think you'll stay in Italy after your work for the Luppis is finished?' she asked him.

'I don't know. I don't like what is happening in this country. At least in England, no one anticipates a dictatorship to follow after Lloyd George.'

They went out to the narrow street again, where the wall opposite her apartment was pasted with peeling advertisements; one was for a political rally. Mussolini's popularity was increasing now that he was Prime Minister. People talked of him as *Il Duce*, but with affection, as if he was some kind of genial uncle rather than a new Caesar. Meeting Sally had stirred all kinds of nostalgia for England, Joseph realised, not least for an absence of political violence.

He stood on the cobbles and waited, looking in the window of the dusty, crumbling store below the apartment, while Sally locked the street door with its large iron key. The shop was crammed with objects; amongst the candles and hip-baths and iron cooking pots, the gardening forks, wooden clothes pegs and wicker clothes baskets – a polished box, laid out with a hand-set of woodworking tools, caught Joseph's eye. It contained a tenon saw, a hammer, a rule and spirit level, a screwdriver and various boxes of nails and screws. The set was exquisitely presented and incongruous in the squalid setting of the street. He rested his forehead against the glass and was overwhelmed by a sentimental memory of Cassie, leaning over his workbench with her chin in her hands, renewing her vow that one day she would be a furniture designer.

'You look like a little boy seeing a toy in the window and wishing your parents could afford it,' Sally said coming to stand beside him.

He looked at her. 'Is it possible, do you think, to send parcels to England in time for Christmas?'

'I don't know . . .' She shook her head, smiling, for Joseph was already on his way into the shop.

He watched as the storekeeper took the tool-set from the window and wrapped it for him. He began to sweat. Had he gone mad? Was it sheer self-indulgence? He saw Sally's curious gaze through the doorway as she waited in the street, and she raised her eyebrows in a question when he came out from the shop with the parcel under his arm.

Joseph smiled ruefully. 'I told you it was complicated.'

Cassie often dreamed about Joseph's workshop. She would wake with the aroma of resin and French polish still in her head and a memory of him saying, 'Smell this. Isn't it wonderful?' She missed him, and she knew her mother missed him too, though Esther never mentioned Joseph's name any more. If ever Cassie talked about him or expressed disappointment because they were not going to live together, her mother would look at her with a sad reproof and say, 'We are not going to think about that any more.'

But Cassie thought about Joseph in secret. She thought about him all the time, and she tried to puzzle out why it was so impossible for them all to be together, and why, because someone had nightmares, she should be persuaded that she had stop loving him.

It did not sound particularly Christian to Cassie. For, since returning to Birmingham, she had become very religious again. Her sense of Christian goodwill did not extend to Julia, however. Not even at Christmas, when a large, flat parcel arrived at their door.

Esther dragged the parcel into the sitting room. She propped it against the table and sat on the sofa, staring at it.

'Aren't you going to open it?' Cassie said in exasperation, fetching a pair of scissors from the sideboard drawer.

'I think I already know what it is.' Esther took the scissors and reluctantly cut the string.

The brown paper fell away to reveal Julia's portrait of Esther. Cassie stared at the picture in silence, remembering the day she had first seen it in Julia's studio; she remembered the seance room too, and Violet's warning about the spirits being displeased; and with a knot of pain in her chest she thought of the morning when she had found the dead doves. 'What are you going to do with it?' she said at last.

'I never liked it.'

'I wonder why she sent it to you.' Cassie picked up a note that had fallen from the wrapping and handed it to her mother.

Esther read it, then let it fall to the carpet. She stood and wrapped the portrait vigorously in its paper again and heaved it into her bedroom.

Cassie could hear her pushing it behind the wardrobe.

The piece of paper with Julia's writing on it lay on the floor. There were only a few lines and Cassie could read them clearly. *'Believe me I never did anything with intent to cause you pain, only to save you suffering – out of love. I have lost Joseph. Do I have to lose you as well?'*

Esther returned to the sitting room. She bent to pick up Julia's letter and, screwing it into a tight ball, she dropped it on to the fire.

George had asked them to spend Christmas with him. He came to fetch Esther and Cassie after church. He had set up a big fir tree in the hall of his house – much larger than the one at Cassie's grandparents' home – with coloured electric lights and baubles, and there was a little stack of presents on the carpet underneath it.

George's housekeeper had cooked a chicken, and they pulled crêpe-paper Christmas crackers with trinkets hidden inside them. Cassie's was a racing car and Esther's a charm for a bracelet; George laughed because his was a wooden puzzle which he could not work out until Cassie showed him how. George laughed and joked a lot and Esther too seemed happy.

Cassie had known for some time that George was in love with her mother. She had known from the way he had looked at her, as long ago as Giles's wedding, and she saw it on those occasions when they went to a concert or the cinema together and George drove her mother home in his car. Cassie would sit in the window of the flat and watch them draw up to the kerb outside. Her mother would sit in George's car for a while and they would talk, and then George would climb out and open the door for her and stand on the pavement until Esther had gone inside the house. He didn't know that Cassie was watching him, that she could see every shade of his expression under the light from the street-lamp. There was something about the way he looked at Esther that always made Cassie feel sad, for she realised he would never reach her mother's heart in the way her father and Joseph had done. Cassie knew too that she didn't want George to reach Esther's heart in the same way as Joseph – for Joseph had been special.

After dinner that Christmas everyone opened the presents under the tree. George sat in an armchair with a glass of sherry, looking pleased with himself, while Cassie and her mother exclaimed as they opened the pile of parcels. And then, to Cassie's surprise, her mother produced a present for George, a long woollen scarf, which he said looked 'dashed smart' and that he would wear it the next time he went motoring.

He had given Esther a silver brooch. She sat looking at it for a few seconds after she had opened the box in which it lay on a bed of cotton wool. It was in the shape of a little bird on a branch and, without thinking, as she leaned over her mother's shoulder, Cassie said, 'Oh, it looks just like one of the doves.'

'Yes.' Her mother did not move or take out the brooch, but held the open box in her hand.

George looked troubled. 'Have I done something to upset you?'

'No. It's lovely,' Esther said, and repeated – as she had done with all the presents he had given them – 'You shouldn't have.'

George pinned the brooch to her dress and Esther smiled; but Cassie felt sick with remorse because she had said it looked like one of the doves. She could see that George still knew something was wrong.

He had bought Cassie a doll. It was too childish a thing – a fussy, prissy-looking creature with a frilly dress and petticoats and real lace pantaloons and eyes that opened and shut with a click of its stiff black eyelashes. Cassie knew George had meant to be kind, so she thanked him as if was the best present in the world, and she hugged him, because she didn't want to see the look in his eyes that would make her feel sorry for him again.

Esther took off the brooch as soon as they reached home that evening. She put it in its box and Cassie never saw her wear it again.

That night Esther cried. Cassie could hear her from the next room, and the sound was the same as the sound she had made when she had wept all that time after Cassie's father was killed. But Cassie knew that this time Esther was thinking of Joseph. Her mother's pain joined with her own hurt, and Cassie remembered walking on the cliffs; she heard Joseph telling her how to recognise cormorants and to tell kittiwakes from common gulls; she saw his workshop again, saw his hands lovingly shape a piece of wood as he told her which joints were used for strength, that the accuracy of joints was the key to perfection . . . she pictured his smile, and Cassie reached for the dog-eared photograph under her pillow and wept silently, so that her mother should not hear.

Joseph put away the tool-set for Cassie under a shelf in his workshop and told himself he should never have bought it: the gesture had been a sentimental mistake. And yet, in buying the present and putting it away, it was as if he had cleared something from his past: he could relegate Cassie and Esther, with the box, to a shelf somewhere in the recesses of his mind, so they no longer dominated every vacant moment, every quiet thought.

He often went to Sally's apartment after that. He liked its untidy atmosphere and the luxury of speaking English without reserve, her easy acceptance of him, her lack of curiosity about his past and the endless cups of coffee.

One afternoon she offered him more than coffee. 'There are no strings attached,' she promised. 'I know your life is complicated. And I'm still in love with that bastard who wrecked my life for me. But – I get so lonely sometimes. And to be truthful, I miss the physical side of it all.'

Her honesty made him laugh. 'That's good,' she said. 'I haven't seen you smile much.' And, still laughing, they fell on her untidy bed together.

She asked him to spend Christmas with her, but Joseph refused without saying why. The Luppis thought he was staying with friends, and Sally thought he had gone to stay with Maria. But he went to a hotel in Florence and joined the crowds of anonymous revellers, and, nostalgic for Colin and Tim's squalid hospitality in Exeter, he numbed old memories with cognac.

The Luppis' plans for the Villa di Sogni were growing more lavish; they had long since exceeded Joseph's original commission and payment was becoming a matter of embarrassment. Squabbles between the Luppis were frequent. 'The extravagance of the house is all her wish,' Signor Luppi confided one day, when Joseph had reminded him of several bills still outstanding. 'Why did we buy the place? Because *she* fell in love with it. *She* had to have it. I shall sell it! I shall lease it to some mad American for thousands of dollars.'

'I like my surroundings to be luxurious,' Signora Luppi confided when Joseph suggested she should consult her husband over yet another innovation. 'I cannot live without luxury,' she protested.

'And I cannot work without money,' Joseph said. 'So if I am to design panelling for all the bedrooms as well as the overmantels, Signor Luppi must be consulted. It is work that will take weeks, even months. I must know you are both in agreement and that the money will be forthcoming.'

'I shall sell everything – the furniture, everything – and go and live in a hotel,' Signor Luppi threatened that evening at dinner, when the question of refurbishing all fourteen bedrooms was raised. 'I have no more money. It is all her fault! She wants to spend money, money all the time. Everything has to be perfect – which means it must cost.'

'Yes, it's true I like money,' Signora Luppi shouted. 'For inviting our friends here. For food and wine. We cannot give them beans and salami! We need money to make the house comfortable for them and to make the gardens sympathetic. I want comfort,' she explained. 'Nothing more than that. A little beauty – yes. But not extravagance.'

Her husband threw down his napkin and left the dining room and Joseph was alone with the signora Luppi.

'I am so depressed, Giuseppe' – she had taken to calling Joseph by an Italian version of his name when they were alone, for she said she thought of him as their adopted son. 'It is a big responsibility to remake the house and the garden. And there is the estate to run, the visitors – so near Florence there are many people one must see. Then I am called to talk to Miss Edmonds about curtains, or to look at the staircase or to talk about the garden – some trees arrive, a stonemason wishes to rebuild the wall – so many interruptions. All morning. While *him* – he goes to the farms and looks at the vineyards all day and does nothing!'

'You manage very well,' Joseph said soothingly, despairingly, seeing himself drawn into their squabbling with no means of extricating himself. 'But, you know, your husband has a point . . .'

'Oh, my husband! My husband! I am sick of him and his caution. I am sick of the house too. You know? Oh yes. You think it is easy – Roberto running away to Maria, workmen everywhere you look, the smell of glue and paint, strangers living in the house, telling me I have no good taste? Oh, I know how you talk about me, you and Miss Edmonds. The signora Luppi is a Philistine. She don't know about beautiful things.'

Joseph looked at her puffy features, the mouth turned petulantly down and he felt a dislike mixed with a sense of fatigue. 'Perhaps the time has come for a parting of the ways,' he said quietly. 'After the stair is finished . . .'

'Yes. We part the ways,' Signora Luppi cried. 'Is time. Get out! Get out!'

The next morning, Signor Luppi met Joseph when he arrived at the villa. He came down the steps from the main entrance and waited for him to climb from the car. 'Please—' he spread his hands. 'Forgive. I pay you what we owe.'

'Your wife wants me to leave. I shall go at the end of the month – the stair is almost completed.'

'No, no. She doesn't want you to leave us like Roberto. You are like a son to us, Joseph. You do good work for us. You make the Villa di Sogni the envy of Florence – but it must be finished *properly*. It is a beautiful house. It deserves beautiful design of furniture. We will go ahead with the bedrooms.'

'We must discuss a price,' Joseph said reluctantly. He imagined several more months of living with the Luppis, of listening to their wrangling and all the irritations of pitting his convictions about the needs of the house against their expectations. And yet he was tempted to stay, he realised. Signor Luppi did not exaggerate when he said the Villa di Sogni was a beautiful house; Joseph felt as if he knew it intimately, had begun to absorb its atmosphere; he could already visualise the panelling to the upstairs rooms.

'The money – is no problem. I frighten my wife a little, that is all. Come – you will stay?'

Joseph nodded. 'OK. I will stay.'

'Why did I do it?' Joseph lay on Sally's bed while she flitted about the room in her underslip. 'They are cutting down in all sorts of ways, Signor Luppi says. They will live in one of the farmhouses if necessary, or lease some of the estate, only the villa must be given justice as a work of art.'

'If only they knew what they were talking about,' said Sally. He watched her pick up sketches and discard them, searching for something. She was always energetic after they had made love.

'You make me feel tired, just watching you,' he said.'Don't you ever sit still?'

'Ah – found it.' She pulled a sheaf of papers from under the bed and sat on the carpet with her back against the mattress frame.

'At least I've got my way over the style of the panelling,' Joseph told her. 'They're eager, for now, to agree to everything, in case I decide to leave after all.'

'How long will it last though?'

'Oh, until the next crisis.' He rolled over and kissed her ear. 'You smell nice. Come back to bed.'

'No. I've got work to do.' She began scribbling on her designs, altering a line here and there.

'You'll be going home to England soon,' he said after a while.

'And then you'll be all alone with the terrible Luppis. Poor Joseph.'

'I shall miss you.'

'Come on. You can't pretend there has ever been anything more than bed between us.'

'Yes there is. I like you.'

'And I like you. But that's all it ever can be. You know it is.' She pressed her hand to her breast. 'I have a broken heart. I still miss that rotter who wouldn't leave his wife. And you—' she returned to her drawing – 'your love life is complicated.'

'Not that complicated. Not any more.'

She looked at him and laid down the papers and her pencil. 'Then why don't you ever stay the night?'

'I told you. I don't sleep well.'

'Did you go to bed with the marchesa?'

'Once or twice.'

'And stay all night?'

'That was different.'

'Because you were in love with her?'

'No. Because I wasn't.'

'It doesn't make sense. You don't love the marchesa, but you spent the night with her. You don't love me, but you won't stay because you "sleep badly".'

'It wouldn't be fair to you.' He hesitated. 'I have bad dreams because of the war.'

'Is that all?'

He shook his head. 'I'm not always right in my mind. There have been times when I went berserk. They called it shell-shock.'

She put down the sheaf of papers and, kneeling by the bed, rested her chin on her arms. 'Is she married?' she said, looking into his eyes.

'The marchesa?'

'No. The woman you're in love with. The carpentry set at Christmas. Did that have something to do with her? Is she married to someone else?'

'No. She's not married.'

'Does she know about the shell-shock?'

'Yes. She knows.'

'Oh—' Sally looked at him for a moment, then she went back to her drawings. 'Forget her. She's not worth it. If she really loved you it wouldn't matter about the shell-shock. If you love someone you can get round any difficulty.'

Chapter Sixteen

It was the summer of 1923. George asked Esther to marry him one evening after they had been to the theatre. She was thirty-three. She reflected that it was almost six years since Christopher had died. How long ago their life together seemed: it was static in her memory now, like a sun-drenched, two-dimensional picture, bleached of its power to stir her emotions, except now and then, with a poignant thread of memory that she couldn't quite grasp. Would her pictures of Joseph do the same in time? she wondered. No. They would grow darker. The brightness would fade and the shadows would deepen.

George waited patiently. He sat, holding the steering wheel of the car very tightly. Esther saw that he had invested a lot in this moment. He was nervous, pretending to be casual about the proposal. 'We seem to get along so well,' he had said. 'Why don't we make it a permanent arrangement?'

He cleared his throat. 'If you don't like the house . . . if Ursula's presence is still too strong, we could move.'

'No. I like your house.'

'I know you don't love me,' he said quietly. 'I don't even know whether you've forgotten the chap you left behind . . .' He tried to joke, and, when Esther did not answer, went on in a rush, 'But I love you and I'm very fond of Cassie. I think she would accept me.'

'Oh, George.' Esther rested her hand on his. 'I do love you in a way. I'm just not sure it's the *right* way.'

'I know.' He smiled. 'Look. Don't give me your answer right now if you don't want to. Think about it. Why not take some time off from the works? You haven't had a break since you joined me. You need a holiday.'

'Thank you.' She leaned towards him and George turned to her and seized her face in his hands and kissed her. With a sudden tenderness she kissed him back, then climbed from the car. 'I'll ask my parents to look after Cassie. I'll go away for a few days,' she said. 'I'll do some thinking and walking. I promise I'll give you a proper answer when I get back.'

Esther went down to Bath and booked into a hotel. She felt a need to talk to Christopher's mother. She drove the few miles to Norbrook House and felt a quickening of anticipation as she entered the estate.

She had not seen Hugh and Marjorie for well over a year and did not know how welcome she would be. Hugh had sounded surprised, not unwelcoming, but a little distant when she had telephoned from the hotel.

There was no such reserve in Marjorie's welcome. She ran to meet her, swathed in chiffon, the cigarette in its holder, her black hair a little blacker and slicked into a curl on her forehead. 'Darling. Guess what! I saw some of your pots in Bath the other day, in a very exclusive shop. Darling, you're famous! There was a little plaque next to them. It said "Esther Norbrook Ware". I felt so proud I could have died. Where's Cassie?'

'I didn't bring her.'

Marjorie's face fell. 'Oh, but you know how little we see of her.'

'I'm sorry. I'll bring her next time. I promise. We'll come during her holidays this summer.'

'I shall hold you to that.' Marjorie linked her arm in Esther's and squeezed it. 'Hugh has gone to Bristol in the aeroplane. He's still got the bug. So we can have a lovely long talk, just you and me. Hugh said you wanted to talk to *me*, not him, which is nice, and very flattering.' She hugged her arm again. 'Oh, this is lovely! Like old times. Come inside . . .

'So, what's it all about?' Marjorie said when they were seated in the conservatory.

Esther turned to her anxiously. 'A friend has asked me to marry him.'

Marjorie laughed. 'Darling, I couldn't be more delighted, but you don't need our permission. Christopher has been dead for ages now. You were bound to marry again one day.'

'I know, but I can't decide whether I want to marry George. He's my business partner and we get on very well the way things are. I'm afraid of committing myself, I suppose.'

'Are you afraid you'll be hurt again?'

'Perhaps,' Esther said. She had loved Christopher without reserve, she had loved Joseph passionately and with disastrous results. 'Or perhaps I'm even afraid of hurting George.'

'There's always a risk with love,' Marjorie said.

'Yes, but how great a risk should one be prepared to take?' Esther remembered that she had accused Joseph of cowardice because of his caution. She hardened her heart, recalling Joseph's bizarre domination by Julia.

'Why – you must risk everything!' Marjorie said. 'You risked everything on Christopher and he was killed. That could have destroyed you.'

'But I didn't know I was taking a risk when I married him. How could I know that in a few years the world would be at war?'

'We don't know anything about the future. It's a good job we none of us know what's in store. Good Lord – Hugh's plane might fall out of the sky today, or next week. Loving someone is always a chancy business.'

260

'It's not only me. There's Cassie to think of too.'

'Cassie will adapt. She's strong. And she's growing up. We miss her you know.' Marjorie paused. 'You *should* have brought her with you.'

'I wanted to talk to you alone. I *needed* to talk to you, Marjorie. I don't know why.'

'I do. Because you can't talk to your mother. How is the old battle-axe?'

Esther smiled.

'You don't love him, do you?' Marjorie said suddenly. 'That's what it is?'

'I suppose it is.'

'Because of Christopher?'

Esther shook her head.

Marjorie became business-like. 'Well – let's see. Love might grow.'

'Yes, I think it might.'

'Or you could be making a terrible mistake. But never mind. We can always divorce bad husbands these days.'

Esther laughed. 'Oh, Marjorie. You make a very good devil's advocate.'

'Does he love you? Is he warm-hearted – or is he a cold fish?'

'Oh no. George is a dear. And, yes, he loves me. He has loved me for some time. He's older than me, but not much over forty.'

'Do you like him?'

'Yes. A lot.'

'Do you trust him?'

'More than anyone I can think of.'

'Then why not marry him and to hell with it?' Marjorie jumped up. 'I'll get some champagne. There. We've made a decision. That didn't take long.'

'Marjorie. You're absolutely priceless.' And just like Christopher, Esther thought, remembering his sweeping decisions, his lack of seriousness, as Marjorie ran to call for champagne and glasses.

Talking to Marjorie hadn't settled anything, Esther realised when she left Norbrook House that evening, but seeing her had helped to put things in perspective.

She spent the next day driving through Somerset, thinking a little, as she had promised George she would, but mostly enjoying the unprecedented freedom of being on her own, with no deadlines to meet, no responsibilities of looking after a child or directing her team of workers. George had been right – she had needed a holiday.

She felt a simple pleasure in driving, in the purr of the motor and bowling along the winding lanes with the hood down and the wind in her hair. She would buy a new car, she decided. Christopher's Morris really was ancient. It was time she started behaving like the designer of a company with her own range of production. She would swank a little, buy something sporty. She thought involuntarily of Joseph's passion for cars, his odd quirks of flamboyance that had contrasted with his austerity. There had been so many contrasts in him. Too many, she realised.

She pulled her mind back to the subject of George. Perhaps she should simply toss a coin. It was an idea worthy of Marjorie, and she told herself not to be frivolous. One really must take the subject of marriage more seriously. But it was impossible to be serious when it was such a glorious day; when the trees were in full leaf, and the hedgerows were full of flowers and insects and the scent of meadow grass was everywhere.

In the end Esther tossed the problem of marriage aside altogether. Ideas for a new range of pottery had begun to come to her, designs based on the sinuous lines of trees. She and George had been thinking of getting up a stand for the British Industries Fair the following February. What better than a totally new range of dinner sets, breakfast sets and tea sets to launch her pottery on to a wider market? She was still thinking about the exhibition when she halted for lunch at a village inn. She never travelled without her sketchbook and she opened it beside her on the table as she ate and began to draw. The inn was old-fashioned, with beams across the low ceiling and cracked, smoke-stained plaster. The sandwich she had ordered was thick and stuffed with pickles and cheese. She ate greedily, reflecting how her mother would have disapproved of the gluttony, the 'doorstep' sandwich and the impropriety of entering a public house alone. There was a photograph on the wall, a picture of men in hunting breeches surrounded by a pack of hounds under a huge beech tree. Esther's gaze wandered to the tree's tracery of branches and an image of the avenue of beeches on the way to The Dovecote came into her mind. She finished her lunch and returned to the car and, spreading out the map on the seat, saw that she was less than ten miles from the Dorset border. She had the whole afternoon in front of her. Why not spend it gathering more ideas?

Did it matter that the avenue of beeches was so close to The Dovecote? Esther asked herself as she drove through familiar towns and villages. The thought of returning should have been hateful, yet it wasn't. She felt a growing excitement as she neared the long stretch of road where the beeches spread their green canopy, and she remembered only the mysterious beauty of that stately parade of trees.

It was like driving through the endless nave of a cathedral lit by green stained-glass windows. Ideas for shapes and lines and colours flooded Esther's mind. She pulled on to the grass verge at the side of the road and, in a fever of creativity, began to sketch ... A whole series of jugs and plates, cups, saucers and dishes began to take shape in her mind – in wonderful, shimmering greens that must look as if they were lit by a magical glow. She remembered Julia's insistence on exclusivity – that people should pay for style. Julia was wrong. Why shouldn't functional pots be just as beautiful as art pieces? But she must make George see

262

them as she saw them, and she must get the colours and the glazes exactly right.

After half an hour Esther threw down her sketchbook and bent her head over the wheel. Her right hand felt cramped and her head throbbed with the concentrated effort of getting her ideas down on paper before they, or the light, or the inspiration began to fade. It was very still under the trees, there was an atmosphere of hushed, almost religious concentration, the only sound was the gentle soughing of the wind in the rippling leaves and branches above.

Esther raised her head and listened to the wind and let the tranquillity and enchanted atmosphere steal through her. She remembered how Cassie had been captivated by the road the first time they had driven along it, sitting rigid beside her, almost as if she had been in a state of religious ecstasy. And there *was* something awe-inspiring about those immensely sinuous, sweeping tree trunks that had once beckoned them on to The Dovecote.

After a while Esther started the car and drove on. She told herself that she should find somewhere to stop and turn the car, but the road ran for miles with no convenient turning places and, even when she reached open countryside with abundant farm-gates and crossroads – offering ample opportunity to double back – Esther felt a curious reluctance to depart from the familiar route leading to the sea.

It wasn't until she reached a signpost reading 'Winmouth' that Esther at last came to her senses. She pulled the car to the side of the road and sat, trembling with the realisation of what she was doing. Another mile and she would reach the cottage where she had stayed the first time she had come here. Only a little further, and she would drive past the gates of The Dovecote.

All at once, it seemed as if there had been nothing arbitrary about her expedition that afternoon, nor had it merely been a creative exercise. It was as if she had come this far on purpose, because she had needed to see The Dovecote again. Was it true? Did she have to make sure she had put the place behind her before she could make a decision about George?

Esther drove on and parked the car near the cottage where she had stayed. There were a couple of children in the garden; they stared at her then went on with their game of hitting a ball to one another. She walked quickly along the road and followed The Dovecote boundary downhill, slowing her steps only when she neared the gates. She became more cautious; the last thing she wanted was to meet anyone. She imagined Rowena or Meg – or even Julia – coming out through the courtyard and she almost turned back in fright.

The courtyard was empty, bathed in sunshine and shadow. Julia must have restocked the dovecote, Esther realised, for there were doves again, strutting and cooing on the roofs of the barns. It was as if nothing had happened, nothing had changed and no time had passed since she had last been there. The gate squeaked as Esther pushed it open and birds flew up from the roof with a clatter of wings.

Esther clung to the gate, her heart banging against her ribs. What was she doing here? Had the afternoon among the beech trees turned her head? She closed her eyes, and she could still hear the birds in the courtyard. At last her heart and the drumming in her ears grew quieter. She had done it. She had returned and nothing terrible had happened. No tears. No yearning for Joseph. She felt a sense of resignation come over her as she pulled the gate to; and at once she heard footsteps come into the courtyard.

It was too late to dart back against the outside wall. Violet, recovering first, said, 'Mrs Norbrook? Esther – is that you there? What a fright you gave me!'

Violet came to the gate and opened it. She wore a pinafore and looked the same as ever, a little heavier perhaps. 'I've got a proper job here now. I help permanent in the kitchen. Julia lets me stay overnight. Come in. She'll be thrilled to see you!'

Esther gave a disbelieving laugh. 'You really mean it, don't you?'

'Why shouldn't I mean it?' A flush of colour spread across Violet's face. 'Julia tells us we're not to bear grudges. We *love* one another. We're only human. We make mistakes sometimes, but in the end none of them matter.' She sounded as if she had learned the phrases by heart. She waited. 'Are you coming in?'

Esther shook her head. 'No. I was near. That's all. I just wanted to see the place again.'

'But, if you haven't come to visit us . . .'

'I was laying a ghost.'

Violet recognised the sarcasm but the bitterness in Esther's voice seemed to frighten her and her colour deepened. 'Oh, please, Esther, you mustn't keep making jokes.'

Esther softened. 'I'm sorry . . . I can't forgive Julia.'

'You should. Julia was ever so sad after you'd gone.'

Esther shook her head and moved away, then she turned back again to Violet, remembering the painting Julia had sent her at Christmas and the note, still clear in her mind though she thought she had dismissed it: . . . *I have lost Joseph. Do I have to lose you as well?* 'I'd be grateful if you wouldn't tell Julia I was here.'

Violet flushed again. 'I won't if you don't want me to.'

On impulse Esther said, 'It's nice to see you again. It really is. And I'm sorry I left you and the others at the pottery.'

'It doesn't matter. I'm happy working in the kitchen.'

When she reached the top of the hill Esther saw that Violet was still watching her from the gates. The girl raised a hand as Esther turned away. Something about the gesture and the still figure in its flowered overall made her feel unsettled, though she could not tell why. She knew Violet would tell Julia that she had been there, and that too was unsettling.

As Esther drove back through the avenue of beeches the sun was sinking low in the sky. She was feverish with the intense exertion of the afternoon. Thoughts crowded her mind. A memory of the uniformed figure at the seance rose again and again before her eyes, shadowy, elusive and faintly menacing. She imagined Julia arranging the seance, plotting with Joseph, telling him what he must do to convince everyone that the spirit world was against their relationship. She saw again the uniform hanging in Joseph's room and the dead dove on the floor of the wardrobe.

She thought of all the times when she had refused to face the evidence of his instability – his secret surveillance of her, his revelation that Julia and he had been lovers, his veiled warnings not to get involved with him, and his half-hearted attempts to break away from Julia ... and then the anonymous note, 'Keep away.'

These and other thoughts filled her head as she drove through the darkening countryside, until, when she reached her hotel, her past feelings for Joseph had gone and she knew that she had wiped out all regret.

She returned to Birmingham the next day and went straight to the factory. George was in the firing shop. He turned as she walked in through the door. 'Esther—' He took her arm and they went to his office. 'I thought you'd be gone for longer. Is anything wrong?'

Esther sat on the corner of his desk. How worried he looked – and tired. There were small crease lines at the bridge of his nose and at the edges of his mouth, and his eyes were shadowed. When they were married they would take a holiday together, she decided. They would go somewhere romantic and peaceful.

'Has something happened?' George said. 'Tell me. Don't try to spare my feelings, I don't think I could stand it.'

Esther smiled. How could she have doubted that she should accept him? How could George be anything other than the man before her: honest and uncomplicated. 'Yes,' she said happily. 'Something has happened. I've made a decision. Darling George, I'll marry you.'

When Esther announced she wanted to go somewhere romantic for their honeymoon, George said he would organise it. They would take Cassie with them, and she must leave it all to him. It would be a surprise.

A fortnight before the wedding, he came into the design office, looking almost boyish in his excitement. He rocked back on his heels with his hands in the pockets of his tweed suit and grinned at her. He was so pleased about the wedding that he had wanted to tell everyone, and had even put an announcement in *The Times*. He placed an envelope containing the train and boat tickets on her desk. 'I can't keep it a surprise any longer. Here – what do you think?'

Esther opened the envelope and, glancing down at the tickets, felt a chill of alarm creep through her. 'No. Not Italy.' What quirk of fate could have made him choose Florence?

George laughed, thinking she was joking with him, then his smile faded as he saw that she was not. 'But it's all arranged.'

'Then you'll have to rearrange it. I'm not going to Italy.'

'Are you worried about the political situation?'

'No ... Anyway, I'm sure the newspapers exaggerate.'

'You think Cassie is too young for Florence?'

'A little. But it wouldn't do her any harm.'

'What then?'

She looked at the tickets again, not knowing what to say, settling at last for, 'It has too many associations with the past.'

He pulled up a chair beside her, immediately apologetic, his face tense with concern. 'What an insensitive idiot I am. I didn't realise. Is it to do with Christopher?'

Should she lie and say that it was? It would be so much easier than telling the truth. 'No,' she said. 'We never went to Italy.'

'What is it then?'

'Why are you being so persistent?' she said uneasily. 'Does it matter where we go?'

'Yes, it does. It's dashed difficult now it's booked.'

She looked away. 'I just don't want to be reminded of Italy.'

'But you've only this minute said you've never been there.' He looked at her questioningly. 'You've told me so little about yourself, Esther. Especially about the time when you left Dorset.'

'And I hoped you wouldn't ask me.'

He was contrite again. 'And I shan't. So long as it doesn't interfere with our happiness.'

Esther reached out her arms to him and drew his face to her to kiss him. 'It won't. But – let's not go to Florence.' She handed back the tickets. 'And we shan't ever talk about Dorset. Please. I'd rather not.'

A fleeting uncertainty crossed George's face, then he put the tickets in his breast pocket. 'All right. I promise.'

'How about Scotland?' George said a few days later, coming into her office. 'Any bad thoughts about Scotland?'

'None.'

'Then I'll confirm the booking. Edinburgh for a week, then the Highlands for the rest of the month.'

'The whole of October?' Esther said in dismay. 'What about the pottery? I need to get the new designs organised for the London exhibition.'

'A fortnight then altogether. You're a slave driver.'

'Scotland. Grouse and heather,' Esther said with satisfaction, for autumn in Scotland might inspire new ideas for her pottery.

'Shall we shoot? Shall we behave like toffs and bag a few game?'

Esther saw a row of dead birds upon a table with their necks wrung. 'I'd rather not,' she said steadily. She smiled. 'I'm bound to be bad at it, and it might upset Cassie.'

'Golf then.' He pronounced it 'goff', tapping out his pipe in the ashtray on Esther's desk and looking pleased with himself.

'Yes. I'd like that.'

'And walking. We'll hire a help to keep Cassie entertained while you and I go for long, sentimental walks among the heather and quote Robbie Burns to one another.'

'The call of the curlew,' Esther said, laughing as she echoed his mood. 'Mountains and lochs and Scottish mist, and Scotch whisky, and men in kilts playing bagpipes.'

Esther was contented. She told herself that if this was happiness, it would do. She could live without the agony of being in love, the dreadful uncertainties, and the feeling of being torn apart.

Cassie wished her mother had worn a long, lacy wedding dress – like the one in the magazine pictures of Princess Elizabeth when she had married the Duke of York. But Esther looked lovely anyway, she conceded, with her hair cut short and permanently waved, fitting her head like a golden cap under a little veil of net and flowers; and she wore a beautiful sea-green coat-dress that showed her legs and ankles and was silky to the touch.

There were crowds of guests; almost everyone from the factory had come to see George and her mother get married, and there were various customers and business people, none of them people Cassie knew. And then there were the distant relatives – cousins and half-cousins – most of whom she had never met. Giles was there. He kissed Esther, shook George's hand very vigorously and said that he could heartily recommend marriage. He had his arm round his wife's waist and she was smiling up at him, and Cassie felt a warm glow of satisfaction to see that Giles was really happy at last.

She was glad Marjorie and Hugh had come, though one could almost feel the animosity between her two grandmothers. Cassie loved them both dearly, but she had to admit that to put them side by side at a wedding showed both of them in a poor light. Marjorie wore purple trimmed with fur, and she talked very loudly; Cassie overheard her grandmother from Larch Hill say to her grandfather, 'Whatever does that woman think she looks like?' The register office had scandalised Esther's mother, who did not consider any ceremony outside a church a proper wedding. Cassie – still earnestly religious – found herself in agreement, and she confided to Marjorie and Hugh that she didn't believe Esther could be properly married in the eyes of God.

Marjorie looked at her and gave a little peal of laughter, saying, 'Lord, Child. How old are you? Fourteen or forty?'

'Thirteen,' Cassie corrected meticulously. 'I shall be fourteen at Easter – when our Lord died for us.'

Cassie was caught up in the general confusion as everyone left the register office and began throwing rice and confetti. She stood on the pavement at the bottom of the steps, feeling briefly isolated, even a little neglected as everyone concentrated on Esther and George. The register office was in the middle of Birmingham; several motor cars were parked by the kerbside, and cars and buses and horse-wagons passed along the street. Cassie's attention was attracted by a horse, the brasses on its harness gleaming in the sunshine as it was led by a gypsy along the road. Cassie wandered along the pavement, following the man and his horse a little way from the wedding party, until they turned off into an alleyway and headed towards the canal. Cassie pictured the canal basin, where barges were tied up and dogs ran around everywhere and people hung strings of washing and shouted to one another in rough voices. Reluctantly she turned round and walked back slowly towards the crowd of people on the pavement.

Cassie halted. From where she stood her view of the opposite side of the street was free of traffic, and she had noticed a woman, dressed as if she were one of the wedding guests in a smart red costume and a pudding basin hat, standing on the corner of a side street. The woman was not looking at Cassie but at the wedding group, and she was staring with a fixed intensity at Esther and George who were laughing as they climbed from the pavement into the car. It was Julia. For an instant Cassie was sure of it. She stood, frozen with terror. Then she realised that she must be wrong, for Julia always wore long shabby skirts and cardigans and this woman was dressed very fashionably.

Esther called out from the car and George, climbing out again on to the pavement, was beckoning. 'Come on, Cassie. Do you want to be left behind?'

Cassie began to hurry towards them, glancing across the street as she ran, but, in the few seconds when she had been distracted by George, the woman had vanished.

'What were you doing back there?' Esther said, pulling Cassie against her side. George climbed into the car after her and teased her, saying she had been in a dream. Cassie sat between the two of them. She could smell George's tobacco and her mother's perfume and the scent of the flowers in Esther's bouquet. She knew she couldn't tell her mother she thought she had seen Julia, so she told her instead about the man and his horse and the beautiful brasses that had gleamed in the sun. She imagined life on a canal boat, noisy, exciting and romantic – it made her think of Italy, where Joseph had said everywhere was full of colour and people shouted at one other all day long. 'Perhaps – ' said George, laughing a little ' – like a sweep at a wedding, a gypsy and his horse will bring us good luck.'

The wedding breakfast was laid out in a huge marquee in the garden. Cassie liked George's house; it was full of spiky palms in pots and heavy, red plush chairs and sofas. It was saved from resembling her grandparents' house by its 'artistic' wallpaper and curtains – chosen by George's dead sister – and by its wallcases of books and fine pottery and the paintings in gilt frames, which anyone could tell were genuinely cultured instead of merely being in 'good taste'.

The garden had a shrubbery down one side; dark paths led to the side fence, with glimpses of the garden of the house next door. Bored with the speeches, the adult conversation and brays of laughter, Cassie wandered in and out of the bushes for a while when everyone had finished eating. She could still see the lawn, and could study the guests more closely, watching in case the woman in the red dress reappeared. Not that she believed now that the woman had been Julia, nor did she want to see her, but Cassie felt a little sorry that no one else from The Dovecote had been invited to the wedding; she had been fond of Rowena and Freddie, and she thought that Peter and even Meg would be sad not to have been there to see her mother happy at last.

It seemed strange, Cassie thought, that after the holiday in Scotland, George would be her father and George's house was going to be their home. She liked George, but there was something too stiff about him, even when he laughed, as he was doing now, chatting with guests by the entrance to the marquee. George never lounged, Cassie reflected, comparing him mentally with Joseph. And George was smart, whereas Joseph had been elegant. George was clever and intelligent and hardworking, while Joseph's brilliance had seemed effortless. Cassie felt a familiar hollow ache in her heart as she thought of Joseph's brilliance. She pictured the workshop with its exquisite pieces of furniture and she imagined Joseph coming towards her across the lawn, here at the wedding party, smiling, laughing, saying, 'Isn't this ripping? I bet you never thought you'd see me here . . .'

Would he be sad, if he knew Esther had married George? Cassie wondered. Or pleased – as she had been pleased for Giles – to know that everything had worked out well? She had told the girls at Heather Park that Joseph was a famous playboy and that it was a swiz he had gone to live in Italy, because he had been going to teach her how to design furniture; she said that when he came back, she was going to be his student, and some of them had believed her for a while. She too had almost begun to believe it; but now she rarely showed off Joseph's photograph. She kept it under her pillow at home, and she would lie in the dark and feel for its comforting dog-eared corners whenever she felt lonely.

Cassie turned her attention from the lawn and wandered among the azaleas and the rhododendrons. She saw a figure in the next-door garden; a boy with a shock of ginger hair, and a red v-necked pullover that clashed with it, was watching her through the palings from the other side of the fence.

'What are you staring at?' Cassie said angrily. 'Hasn't anybody ever told you it's rude to snoop?'

'It's not snooping if I'm in my own garden,' he answered quickly. 'And besides, you're all making such a devil of a noise a fellow can't help noticing something's going on.'

Cassie stood, disconcerted by his counter-attack. 'Who are you anyway?' she said, more to maintain the upper hand, than because she was very curious.

'I'm Christopher David Henson,' the boy said. 'But I'm always called David.'

Cassie felt a reluctant stirring of interest. 'My father's name was Christopher. Only he's dead now. He was killed in the Great War,' she added importantly.

'Mr Ansfield's your father now, I suppose. I've seen you before. You *are* coming to live here?'

'Of course.'

'Isn't it a bit odd – going to your own mother's wedding?'

'A bit boring really. Nobody notices me very much.'

The boy hesitated, then said in an offhand way, 'You can come and talk to me if you get bored ever. At least, when I'm not away at school. I'm at home now because I've had the chickenpox, but I've got to go back in a few days.'

Cassie moved closer to the fence and studied him properly. He looked quite nice close to; there were no obvious signs of the chickenpox, though his hair still clashed horribly with the awful pullover. 'OK – thanks,' she said at last.

He put his hands in the pockets of his trousers and kicked a stone against the fence. 'I like your dress.'

Cassie stared at him in surprise, but said nothing.

His face took on a pinkish hue – which made the mismatch of hair and pullover even more noticeable. 'See you then.' And he turned and dashed away.

Cassie looked down at her outfit – a straight, cream silk dress with a square neck – and the white stockings that were already wrinkling round her knees. There was no accounting for taste, she told herself, pulling at her hat with both hands to adjust it more firmly on her head, but she felt a glow of satisfaction as she walked back to join the guests.

Cassie had been ambivalent about the prospect of a holiday in Scotland, where they stayed first of all at a very smart hotel in Edinburgh. George had hired a dull, Scottish woman called Agatha as a companion for her; she was fat and not very bright and Cassie couldn't understand her accent, and when she did understand what she was saying, Cassie still pretended that she couldn't. It was no good protesting to her mother that she was too old for a glorified 'nanny'.

It wasn't too difficult, however, to give Agatha the slip in the labyrinth of corridors in the hotel. Cassie bullied her unmercifully, and threatened to tell George and Esther that Agatha had lost her if she didn't do exactly as she said. She spent afternoons stalking the other guests, making up stories in her head about Hun spies and going up and down in the lifts, while Agatha searched for her in tears. In the end Cassie would grow bored and allow herself to be found. She would bribe

270

Agatha with sticks of soft Edinburgh rock to go out with her into Princes Street, and they wandered up and down past the shop windows, devising outfits for each other from the displays of fashionable clothes.

Sometimes Cassie went sightseeing with Esther and George – to see St Giles's Cathedral, or to climb the steep hill to the castle and watch the soldiers in their kilts playing bagpipes. Sometimes Esther, bored with playing golf, would let George go on his own to the golf course, and stayed with Cassie at the hotel. She spent every spare opportunity drawing, planning ahead for her new range of pottery, eager to get back and to start production. She showed Cassie some of the designs that she was laying out in detail, marking in the shapes and colours for the paintresses to copy. She did it in secret, when George was out, because she said she thought he would take a dim view of her bringing her work away with her, even though – now they were married – they were going to run the factory almost as equal partners.

The week in the Highlands was more dreary; Agatha kept a sharper eye out and there was less opportunity for escape. Cassie was obliged to walk round lochs, or go for rides in a chilly pony-trap while Agatha pointed out the scenery and extolled the dubious glories of her native country.

Cassie had noticed a change between George and Esther during the second week of the honeymoon. It rained a lot in the Highlands, everyone became bad-tempered, and Esther was edgy about getting back to the factory and about finishing her designs.

George went fishing very early one morning, leaving Esther still in bed. She allowed Cassie to go to her room for breakfast and dismissed Agatha for the morning; they sat eating toast and marmalade, with the pottery sketches spread about on the counterpane.

Esther, in silk pyjamas and her hair not brushed, was propped up on pillows with her drawings on her knee; Cassie sat crosslegged on the bed in her dressing gown, with sheets of paper and a pencil, drawing a dining table and chairs, based roughly on designs she remembered from Joseph's workshop.

Esther, examining her sheets of designs in turn, felt a broadening sense of relief knowing that George would be gone for some hours. She paused for a moment of guilt. Only married a fortnight and already she was cherishing her time without him? How very unromantic she was. She reminded herself that marriage to George had little to do with romance – nor passion either she recalled, thinking back to their intermittent love-making. The imperfections of that side of their relationship had made them irritable with one another, for, though she had accepted him with goodwill, Esther knew she had shown him very little fire. The knowledge made her uneasy. A distasteful notion of charity suggested itself. She dismissed it quickly, and gave herself instead to the pleasure of having the whole morning to herself with Cassie's undemanding company.

The hours ticked away, and Esther forgot all sense of time or place and even that Cassie was there. She did not notice when it was almost lunchtime, nor that she was still in pyjamas, until the moment George returned.

She glanced up with a vague, preoccupied smile. George stood in the doorway, dressed in his fishing hat and looking faintly ridiculous in plus-fours. It was too late to hide her sketches.

'What's going on?' He pretended to be amused but it was clear that he was annoyed.

Esther was defensive. 'It seemed a perfect opportunity to get on with some work – I have to be ready for when we get back.'

He shut the door and, walking to the bed, picked up one of the sheets of paper. 'Is this what you've been doing every time you've cried off coming out with me?'

'I had to. The London exhibition will be on us as soon as Christmas is over. Besides, it's all going round in my head.'

'You're supposed to be on honeymoon,' he protested.

Esther laughed, not realising that this was a mistake, nor that her next remark would provoke a bitter anger from him. 'I wouldn't call fishing and golf much of a honeymoon, George. But, now that you know, could you let me finish? I'm so *near* finishing. Just another hour?'

'No, dammit, I won't. Look at you! Look at Cassie. You're like a couple of hobbledy-hoys. It's twelve o'clock and you're neither of you even dressed.'

'Oh, don't be so stuffy, darling.'

George took off his hat and cape and hung them on a hanger outside the wardrobe. He spoke very carefully and patiently. 'Who's fault is it that we came to Scotland? If it was a more romantic holiday you wanted, I offered you that in Italy and you threw it back at me.'

Cassie stared from one to the other at the mention of Italy. George no longer seemed to notice she was there, and Esther's face had drained of humour. Cassie did not understand what George was so angry about. She only knew that Joseph was connected with Italy. Did this quarrel have something to do with Joseph?

'We were talking about the pottery,' Esther said with a chill in her voice. 'Don't let's bring anything else into this.'

George backed down as quickly as he had flared up in anger. He raised his hands in protest. 'I'm sorry. I'm sorry.' He stood, looking unhappy, trying to resist whatever thoughts and feelings were in his head. 'If you'd simply said about the exhibition ... I didn't know it worried you that much.'

'It doesn't.' Esther returned to the drawings. 'So long as I can keep up with things.'

'We could have organised the time better.'

'I didn't want to spoil the honeymoon.'

'No,' George acknowledged heavily.

Cassie's sympathies were divided. She felt the old familiar pity for George, who still looked unhappy, but she understood very well her

272

mother's intense involvement in her drawings. She too never wanted to stop once she had begun, and to be called away for a meal or to go somewhere with Agatha seemed to be an intrusion of meaningless conventions. Yet, she understood George's unhappiness as well. It was a kind of jealousy, she supposed. George wasn't jealous in the way Rowena had been jealous over Freddie – there was never any meanness or spite in George. It was more a feeling of being shut out.

George looked at Cassie, and suddenly he smiled. 'And what about you, Cassie? Are you keeping up with things?' He walked to her side of the bed and stood for a long while, looking down at her furniture designs. At last he said with an air of grave surprise, 'You know, these are really very good.'

Esther glanced up from her work. She had not until then expressed any curiosity about what Cassie was doing.

'Borrowed I should guess . . .' George handed Esther one of Cassie's drawings – of a dining suite in the modernist style. 'But still – very good. She's captured the flavour of some of the more *avant garde* fashions.'

Esther stared at the sketch and threw Cassie a sharp, searching look.

'I'm going to work with wood,' Cassie told George. 'I'm going to be a furniture designer when I'm older.'

George laughed, his sour mood had dissipated. He ruffled Cassie's hair. 'And why not?'

Esther handed back the drawing to Cassie without saying anything.

George put a finger to his lips. 'I shall make myself scarce for an hour.' He bent to kiss Esther and she turned with a vague smile and offered him her cheek.

'Thank you, darling.'

'See you both at lunch.' George left the room and closed the door with the barest, softest click.

Esther continued drawing without looking at Cassie. After a while she said, in an almost absentminded way, 'You are not going to be a furniture designer.' Her mouth was set in a firm line, and Cassie knew that she meant it.

273

Chapter Seventeen

Rowena had been nursing a conscience. She knocked timidly on Julia's door. 'I've got something to confess.'

'Come on in.' Julia was painting a small landscape of the beach and cliff, unlike her usual style. 'It's for Esther,' she said. 'A belated wedding present.' She seemed happier these days, Rowena reflected, ever since she had read to them the announcement from *The Times* about Esther marrying her business partner.

'It's Esther I've come to see you about.' Rowena felt her cheeks grow hot. 'I mean, my confession is about Esther.'

Julia smiled. 'We all know our link with Esther has only temporarily been broken. She's constantly in our thoughts. Mine too.'

And Joseph? Rowena wanted to ask. Did Julia still believe that her estrangement from Joseph was temporary? She pulled her mind back to her confession, remembering her jealousy, her prayers that Esther would go away from The Dovecote and leave her and Freddie and everyone else alone. 'I'm going to write to Esther and ask her forgiveness.'

'You did nothing very terrible,' Julia said calmly, not looking up from her painting.

Rowena uttered a gasp of astonishment. 'You mean, you know?'

'That it was you who sent her a note telling her to keep away from us? Let's say that I guessed.'

'Oh, Julia you are a saint.' Rowena sank on to a stool and leaned against the wall. 'You never said anything to make me feel bad about it, even though you've known all this time.'

'You were unhappy, dear. You thought Esther would turn Freddie's head. But you were thinking of Joseph as well – you told yourself how much happier he would be if Esther didn't come back ... I understand.' Julia paused, thoughtful for a moment, then continued painting. 'You tried to keep her away because you thought it would be for everyone's good. And, it's true – if Esther had taken more notice of our negative feelings about their relationship, perhaps Joseph would still be with us.' Julia laid down her brush. She turned to face Rowena and suddenly her eyes were hard and cold. 'But you *were* wrong to try to drive her away. Esther was sent to us, and it was my duty to keep her here and help her in every way I could. You tried to interfere with that duty.'

'I'm sorry,' Rowena faltered.

Julia's expression softened again. She went to Rowena and placed a comforting arm around her. 'Oh, we were all to blame when things went wrong. We all made mistakes. Even me . . .'

'Oh, no—'

'Even me,' Julia insisted. 'I allowed my feelings for them to intervene. I gave my emotions too free a rein.' She looked out of the window, where the doves showed very white against the roofs of the barns. 'Write to Esther,' she said with a catch in her voice. 'Tell her we all wish her well and . . . Say that we all ask her forgiveness.'

Esther read Rowena's letter and let it fall on to the book in her lap.

'Anything wrong?' George asked, lighting his pipe with little whistling sounds and a smacking movement of his lips. He pushed it to the side of his mouth and smiled at her with a look of inquiry.

'Not really,' Esther forced herself to smile. 'It's a letter from The Dovecote – where I had my pottery in Dorset – it's from Rowena. She's just cleared up a mystery for me.' After all this time, she added silently. She couldn't tell him about it. She could never bring herself to tell him all of it. She looked again at Rowena's letter of apology and her heart beat quickly with anxiety. Rowena's jealousy had led her to an act of spitefulness, so that she had sent a message saying 'Keep away from The Dovecote'. According to Rowena, Julia too asked for forgiveness because of 'the mistakes she had made'.

If she had been wrong about Joseph over the note, what else might she have been wrong about? But it was too late, Esther told herself fiercely, too late to think like that. She glanced at George as he bent to pick up his used matches from the hearth and throw them into the fire. They had changed since coming back from honeymoon, she realised, seeing herself and George, seated either side of the hearth, saying little, because they fitted so comfortably together that little needed saying. They had ironed out the irritations of the early weeks, beginning to adjust to one another's limitations. She had fitted easily into the house with its pleasant furnishings, she had adapted to George and his pipe and his slippers. How like Mr Baldwin, the Prime Minister, he was, she reflected – rather handsome, rather kindly, rather dull. And she too had become rather suitable, rather matronly, rather wifely. She had almost imperceptibly grown into his life since coming back from Scotland. Until now. She looked at the letter. She nursed it in her lap for a moment then, leaning forward, placed it in the centre of the coals, where George had tossed his matches. She watched the paper burn. As she glanced up, George raised his eyebrows in a mild question. She looked down at her book, avoiding his eyes. He would not press her and she was grateful.

A parcel arrived from Julia before Christmas. There were presents – the small painting of the bay at Winmouth for Esther, a trinket box made of silver for Cassie, a 'Sherlock Holmes' pipe for George.

'I shan't use it,' Cassie declared, putting the silver box back in its wrapping paper. 'I don't like it.' And she left the room abruptly.

Esther looked at the landscape. Why? she asked herself. Why – after she had managed to part her from Joseph did Julia now want to be involved in her life again? And what had Rowena meant about the mistakes *Julia* had made? Did Julia now regret persuading Joseph to masquerade as Christopher?

George was the only one who was pleased with his present. 'How clever!' he exclaimed. 'You must have told her that I like a pipe.'

'I told her nothing. Julia is psychic,' Esther said dryly.

George looked at her, uncertain whether or not she was joking, but Esther was reading Julia's letter enclosed with the parcel. '... I so regret not seeing your designs taking shape, but I follow any snippets of news I can glean about you from all my contacts. Perhaps I might visit the factory in Birmingham one day ...'

'She got what she wanted. Why can't she let me go?' Esther folded the letter and put it back in its envelope.

'And what was that?' George asked, spreading a piece of toast with marmalade.

'Mmm?'

'You said, she got what she wanted. If she wanted you to leave The Dovecote, why does she now want to get in touch again?'

'She didn't want me to leave The Dovecote,' Esther said irritably.

'Then why ... ?'

'Oh, George – does it matter?'

'I've never asked you why you left Dorset. I've respected your wish not to talk about it. Don't you think you might confide in me? I'm not as shockable as you think.'

Esther looked at him, so tolerant and uncomplicated. He was right, she owed him an explanation. 'I left because Julia had driven me and Joseph apart.'

'You and ...'

'Joseph Kilburn. He's a furniture designer. I fell in love with him, but he was under Julia's thumb. More than I had supposed. Oh – it was a disaster. Everything went wrong.'

'You mean, it was Julia who broke up your love affair?'

'I thought you'd guessed.'

His face was tense. 'No, not really – I realised you and Julia had quarrelled. But I thought the rest ... I thought you had decided for yourself it wouldn't have worked.'

'I suppose I did. But Julia saw it first ... and so did he.'

George went back to his toast. Esther began to pack up the wrapping paper that had held Julia's gifts. She went to the door with it in her arms.

'Esther—' His expression was still tense. 'What did Italy have to do with it? And why were you reluctant to talk about him for so long – even after we were engaged?'

'Joseph left Julia and went to Italy.' She hesitated. 'But it doesn't matter now. Let's forget it shall we?'

Cassie hated Julia for sending the gifts from Dorset and trying to stir everything up again when they had settled down to living with George. She had begun to enjoy school, now that she was less of a newcomer at Heather Park. She had become 'serious', in that she wanted to shine, and yet she was aware that academic achievement was only partly satisfying. She wanted, above all, to be a designer. It was always there at the back of her mind that one day she would meet Joseph again and he would set her on the right path.

She would scan the newspapers, imagining that she might one day read a paragraph of news that Joseph Kilburn, the well-known international designer, had returned from Italy and that he was visiting Birmingham ... And then, one day, she would bump into him by chance walking along Corporation Street, and he would say, 'Good God, it's Cassie! What are you doing these days?' And she would tell him about her plans to become a designer.

Cassie took Joseph's photograph from her handkerchief drawer; she no longer slept with it under her pillow. She stared at the figure in the light-coloured suit standing by the dovecote, and she remembered the morning when she had found the doves lying in the courtyard. Her mother had assumed Joseph had killed them. How could she think that, if she had really loved him? His hands were in his pockets and he was smiling at her in that special way of his. The memory was fading a little, she realised. It was harder to recall his voice, his laugh, the way he had really been, rather than her memory of him, fixed by the image in the photograph. Had he killed the doves? For the first time Cassie allowed herself to consider the possibility, for someone must have done it. It occurred to her then that Joseph was far away, that there would be no paragraph in a newspaper or chance encounter in the middle of Birmingham, and that she would never see him again. She put the photograph back in the drawer. If she was going to become a designer, she would have to do it by herself.

'My mother says your mother was one of Mr Ansfield's paintresses before he married her.' The boy-next-door was sitting on the front wall when Cassie set off for Sunday School one day shortly before Christmas.

So, he had come home for the Christmas holidays. Cassie halted to confront him. Echoes of her early days at Heather Park and the damning accusation, 'second-rate', ran through her mind, as she considered what he had said about Esther. She regarded him coolly. He seemed taller than when she had first met him on her mother's wedding day. His voice had deepened, she noticed. She gave him a mental score of seven – presentable – on the boyfriend scale adopted at Heather Park. But she couldn't let his remark about her mother go unchallenged. 'My mother is very talented. She knows far more about designing pots than you ever would.'

'Keep your hair on. I didn't mean anything by it.' He slid from the wall as she turned to march away, and he walked beside her along the pavement. 'You've got rather a temper, haven't you?'

'At least I haven't got red hair.' Cassie tried to sustain a mood of hostility, though without quite knowing why it was necessary.

'I wish I had black hair like you,' he told her disarmingly. 'A fellow takes a lot of ribbing at school over being carroty.'

She looked at him. 'You talk funny.'

'Do I?'

'As if you've got a plum in your mouth.'

He frowned, not sure whether this was a compliment or an insult. 'Well, I'm older than you,' he said, as if this were an explanation. 'I'm fifteen. I'm going to study medicine and be a psychiatrist when I leave school. How old are you, anyway?'

'I'll be fourteen at Easter. When our Lord died for us,' Cassie added automatically. She glanced down at her gloved hands gripping her Bible tightly.

'I say, are you a bit pi?' he asked curiously.

'Yes. Aren't you?'

'I'm an agnostic. Lots of fellows are agnostics or atheists at my school.'

They had reached the church. 'Then more fool you for following the crowd,' Cassie said, blushing furiously and feeling a surge of satisfaction as she tossed her head and walked away from him.

To her surprise, he was waiting for her when she came out of Sunday School.

'Do you really believe in all that stuff?' He fell into step beside her, as if it were the most natural thing in the world that he should have sat for an hour in the church porch.

'Yes,' Cassie said, suddenly aware that she wasn't sure that it was true. 'At least, I do when I'm singing hymns, or when I'm in church and it's still and quiet, and when I see the candles on the altar and can almost hear God's voice in my head.'

'And when don't you believe?' He seemed genuinely curious. She saw that he wasn't mocking her.

'When I think of Joseph, and everyone who died in the Great War, and I wonder what it was all about and why some people suffer more than other people and why life isn't fair.' She stared at him in surprise. Whatever had made her say all that?

He didn't seem surprised by her outburst. 'You can't use that as a reason. The war was caused by men, not God. *If* he exists,' he added carefully. 'Who do you know that has suffered more than other people?' he added after a while.

'Joseph,' Cassie said quickly. 'It's not fair about Joseph. Nor for my mother.'

279

'And who's Joseph?'

'He taught me about wood.' Cassie told him about Joseph's workshop at The Dovecote and about her ambition to be a furniture designer. 'My mother is one of the best ceramic artists there is, by the way,' she told him. 'She wasn't just a paintress. She had her own pottery in Dorset before we came here.'

'Then why did she marry Mr Ansfield? Did she fall madly in love with him?'

'My mother doesn't love George like that,' Cassie said scornfully. 'They just like each other a lot.'

They were silent for a while and Cassie thought how nice it was to be able to talk so sensibly, without all the giggling that went on when anyone at Heather Park talked to boys. 'I think my mother still loves Joseph really,' she confided suddenly. 'It's all very romantic and tragic.' And she told him about having to leave The Dovecote because Joseph had nightmares after the war, and how it wouldn't have been fair to her and her mother to have to look after him when he was sick.

'Shell-shock,' David said, nodding perceptively. 'It happened to a lot of fellows in the war.'

'Does it get better?'

'I think so. If the person isn't too badly affected.'

'So, you mean Joseph was wrong? He could still have lived with us?'

'I don't see why not. Perhaps he didn't really want to.'

'Oh, but he did,' Cassie said earnestly. 'And I'm sure my mother still loves him.'

'Perhaps you ought to do something about it.'

'He's gone to Italy. And anyway, she's married to George now.'

'She could get divorced,' David said loftily. 'My parents are divorced. My father lives in South Africa.'

Cassie looked at him with a new respect. How wonderful it must be, to be like David, and to be able to make everything seem so easy.

'I wish I could stay on in London with you after the Industries Fair,' George said.

Esther had been supervising the packing of Esther Norbrook ware into tea-chests for the Fair and for a separate exhibition and demonstration stand in a London store. She flopped into a chair in his office. 'Don't be silly. You always say how you hate London. Anyway, one of us needs to get back here for the factory.'

'It's important to you. The first proper exhibition of your work. I don't like to think of you doing it on your own.'

'I shall have Cassie, and Miriam and Irene from the painting room for company.'

'That's another thing. Is it a good idea to drag Cassie along?'

Esther laughed. She smiled at him fondly, feeling a surge of affection. 'Oh, George. I do love you, but you're like a maiden aunt sometimes. Cassie is nearly fourteen. It will be fun for her. She's growing up fast. It will do her good to see London.' She stood up and glanced at her watch. 'I must fly. They should have finished packing by now. I have to make sure they keep the consignments separate.' She paused. 'Don't look so hang-dog. We shall be together for a whole day at the Industries Fair, and I shall only be staying on for a few nights. You'll have your bachelor days back again until I get home. You can fill the sitting room with a fug of smoke and revel in the peace and quiet. You'll love it. You know you will.'

The new range of ware had attracted a lot of attention at the Industries Fair. Esther said goodbye to George on a wave of euphoria as he headed back for the Midlands. She and Cassie helped Miriam and Irene to unpack her pots and set up a stand for a practical demonstration of painting, the next day in the Knightsbridge store.

Esther smiled a little at the memory of George's reluctance to leave them alone in London; she watched Cassie stow wood-shavings back into the packing cases, from which the shop staff and paintresses had removed the exhibits. It was true that Cassie was growing up; she was almost as old as some of the shop girls and was beginning to look like a young woman. Esther was glad to have proved George wrong over bringing her to London, for Cassie was loving every minute of it.

Esther stood back to survey the arrangement of pots on stands and on shelves, gesturing with her hands to the women – a little to the left, a slight turn. With the correct lighting – and the lighting was perfect, accenting the translucent greens and shimmering patterns under the glazes – it was going to be all that she had imagined.

Esther watched Cassie, on her knees, scoop more packing into her arms to the amusement of Miriam and Irene. She said to her, 'A little less hard labour perhaps, Cassie, as befits a Heather Park girl and the daughter of the designer?'

Cassie stood up. 'But I love helping.'

'We shall have to find time to get you some more clothes for the evening reception tomorrow.' Esther regarded the patches of wood-dust on the knees of Cassie's stockings.

'Do I have to dress up in frills?'

'No. Something more sophisticated, I think.'

Cassie beamed. 'Oh, yes, rather.' She flicked a long curl of wood-shaving from her dress. She picked it up and held it to her nose. 'I love the smell of the wood-shavings. It reminds me of . . .' She looked at Esther in alarm and checked herself, then she continued with a sense of defiance. '. . . It reminds me of Joseph's workshop.'

Esther moved away. 'That's a long time ago. We said we would forget.'

'*You* said we had to forget. I wish he knew about your solo exhibition. He would be so pleased for you. I know he would.'

'Cassie!' Esther turned on her angrily.

'Well, he would.'

'You don't know what you're talking about,' Esther said quietly. 'Now come on. We've done enough in here. Let's get you some clothes for tomorrow.'

Cassie began to enjoy herself as she went with Esther from shop to shop. She had thought buying clothes with her mother would be a trial, but standing in front of the long mirrors in her underslip, choosing from all the prints and fabrics, she was allowed to flounce and preen. It was like being someone very grand and famous, having a free choice from all the store had to offer. She tried on everything the sales assistants produced for her, pretending to be very particular as to style and colour, until, growing exasperated at last, Esther chose a velvet dress for her with elbow length sleeves and a short skirt, in subdued greens and greys that toned with the exhibition pottery. It was embroidered with pearl beads, like hoar frost on winter foliage.

'It looks like camouflage,' said Cassie, peering into their bags of purchases in the taxi on their way back to the hotel. 'It's almost as nice as yours. But you'll look the best – as befits the designer and the mother of a Heather Park girl.'

They smiled at one another. Cassie was secretly more pleased with the new outfit than she pretended. 'When you are watching birds you have to wear some sort of camouflage,' she said after a while. 'So as not to frighten them. Joseph taught me that,' she added, and looked swiftly out of the taxi window.

Esther was perplexed by this new defiance in her. 'Cassie, whatever has got into you this past day or two? You know I don't want you to talk about Joseph.'

Cassie turned from the window. 'Well, I still miss him. I can't help it. He was my friend as well as yours. David says that people with shell-shock can get better. And I don't see why, just because he was sick, we had to go away.'

'Is that what Joseph told you?' Esther said.

Cassie bit her lip and her eyes were bright with tears. 'Well, it's true, isn't it?'

'It's only half the truth. Joseph did strange things. He helped Julia do strange things. It was obvious that he couldn't really have loved us.'

'What sort of strange things?'

Esther hesitated. 'He dressed up and pretended to be a ghost.'

Cassie, remembering the boxes of dressing-up clothes at the bottom of the stairs beneath Julia's studio, released a burst of sceptical laughter. 'But that's silly. It was a gag . . . Surely—' Her heart began to flutter in her breast. 'Wasn't it?'

Esther shook her head. 'He pretended to be the ghost of your father. Not for a joke – though that would have been bad enough, but because Julia believed the spirits ought to show me a sign that Joseph and I were wrong for one another. He did it to frighten me, because Julia had told him we shouldn't live together, and he thought she was right.' Why was she talking about him after all this time? Esther wondered. She had forgotten him. She had put it all behind her.

'That's a terrible thing to say about him!' Cassie protested. 'I don't believe it. You know Joseph wasn't like that. He would never have sided with Julia against us.'

'But he did.' They had reached the hotel. 'And that's the last – I mean the very last time I want to hear his name.'

The room was filling quickly. Cassie watched Esther greet people. Her mother looked beautiful in a straight black and gold dress with wide embroidered sleeves, quite different from the overall she had worn when she and Irene and Miriam had given a painting demonstration for the press, but she looked just as proud and confident, as if she knew that the pots were the best she had done. Cassie jigged up and down on her heels with excitement as she was introduced to people. She was so glad she had come, so glad her mother had brought her, and yet there had been a distance between them since Esther had told her why they had left The Dovecote.

The revelations about Joseph still spun in her head. How could her mother believe such rot? How could she have believed it for all this time without questioning it? Had she really at no time stopped to tell herself that Joseph wasn't capable of such a thing – that it wasn't in him to do something so wicked? Joseph had loved them. Did her mother have such little faith in love?

'Are you enjoying yourself?' Miriam whispered.

'It's gorgeous,' Cassie said distantly. 'I'm going to have my own exhibition one day when I'm a famous furniture designer.'

Esther had overheard her and she swung round in anger, but Cassie moved away as some friends of her mother bore down on them, people Esther had known from her work at The Dovecote. Cassie watched them greet Esther as if they hadn't seen her for years. She watched from a safe distance as the woman dabbed at theatrical tears and said in a loud French voice, 'How Julia would have loved to see this! I'm so sorry you two quarrelled. But Julia, she quarrels with everybody. It never means anything. What was it about, *ma cherie*?'

'Oh – nothing worth talking about,' Cassie heard Esther say.

Nothing worth talking about. Cassie repeated the words over and over in her head. She walked towards one of the shop assistants who were acting as waiters, standing in doorways with trays filled with glasses. Ignoring the orange juice, Cassie took a glass of champagne. The boy winked at her and she tossed her head at him and walked away with a swing of her shoulders. She leaned moodily against the shop counter and sipped at the champagne. She would never, never forgive her mother, she told herself. She made a vow to herself that, what was more, she wouldn't let her get away with it. One day she would get to the bottom of what had really happened.

The reception was half-way through and some of the spectators were beginning to drift away when Cassie, finishing her third glass of champagne, turned to see a woman striding through the crowd. She was very tall and angular and the sight of her made Cassie's head reel.

She pushed her way towards Esther and, reaching her, seized her arm. Her grip tightened on her mother's wrist. 'Don't look. Don't look now. Julia is here!'

Esther gave a gasp of fright as she turned to see Julia crossing the room.

'She was at the wedding,' Cassie gabbled. 'I should have told you.'

Esther turned back to Cassie. 'What are you talking about? Of course she wasn't at the wedding. We didn't invite her.'

'I saw her. She was watching you and George from across the street.'

Esther felt a chill creep through her body as she realised that Cassie was telling the truth. 'Why didn't you say anything before?'

'I couldn't be sure. And then I thought I'd imagined it. Julia always wears old clothes. She looked different . . .' Cassie tailed off. 'Like she looks different now.'

Julia looked magnificent, Cassie was forced to acknowledge as Julia came, or gave the impression of sailing towards them. She wore a gold crêpe-de-Chine dress and a long coat embroidered with beads. A gold-feathered head-dress bound her hair tightly to her forehead; her hands were encased in gold gloves as far as the elbows, and bracelets jangled at her wrists.

'Darling! It's marvellous! Absolutely! Well done!' Cassie quickly side-stepped Julia's arms as Esther was swept into an embrace.

'How did you know about the exhibition?' Esther said accusingly.

'Who doesn't know? My darling, you are taking everyone by storm. They are so modern.' Julia swung round to survey the pots. 'I knew you could do it.' Her eyes were large with emotion. 'Didn't I always tell you?'

'Yes, you did,' Esther said quietly. She stood, rigid with anger. How dare Julia come here and behave as if nothing had happened all that time ago?

'And I was right. I was right about everything. You should have listened to me sooner.'

'You can't mean you're taking some of the credit for all this?' Esther said in astonishment.

'You are married. You are happy. You are working. What has it taken – three years? Haven't you prospered since I took you in?'

'I've also suffered a lot of unhappiness,' Esther lowered her voice. 'And Cassie too. Heaven knows what it did to her.'

Cassie opened her mouth to tell them her opinion about what it had done to her, but Julia interrupted. 'I suppose you mean because of Joseph.'

'Of course I mean Joseph!'

'You would only have squandered your talents with him,' Julia said

284

dismissively. 'You would have destroyed each other. Tell me it isn't true.'

Esther shook her head. 'It's you who destroys people. You manipulated our lives because it suited you.'

'Because I *cared*. I knew what was best for you. You and Joseph could have both been happy at The Dovecote, living separate, creative lives, if you had only listened to me.'

'Joseph did listen to you,' Esther said coldly. 'What more did you want from him than that sort of unthinking devotion? I suppose I should be glad, for his sake, that he had enough nerve – or sense of conscience – to get away from you in the end.'

Julia looked puzzled for a moment, then she narrowed her eyes. 'I've written Joseph off since he went to Italy. I failed. There, I freely admit it. But, Esther, I didn't fail with you.'

Esther laughed in disbelief. 'I was rather hoping you'd written me off too.'

'After the way I nurtured you and introduced you to the best people? I can't let go that easily.'

'I was grateful. I still am grateful . . .'

'And you've not let go either. I know, you see, that you came back to The Dovecote last summer.'

Cassie stared at her mother. Esther had been back to The Dovecote? Why hadn't she told anyone? Why go there . . . Unless she had lied about wanting to forget? Unless it was true that she still loved Joseph? Cassie remembered David's deceptively simple solution to the situation – that Esther could get divorced. His challenge that she should do something about it seemed more imperative than ever. And yet, what could she do, when Joseph was in Italy, and her mother pretended she didn't care any more? And what about poor George? It was all very well for David to talk glibly about divorce.

Julia seized Esther's hands. 'I was so glad you had come back to The Dovecote. But why didn't you come in to see us?'

'I didn't want to see you. Can't you understand? I can't believe you're taking what you did so lightly – as if it didn't even happen.' Esther eased her hands from Julia's grasp.

'You betrayed me, you know,' Julia said. 'You and Joseph – you trampled on my feelings for you both. But I've forgiven you. We all love you, Esther. And we love Cassie. How she's altering.' She turned to Cassie. 'You show promise of your mother's beauty. I hope you're still drawing. Don't leave it too late to develop her talents, Esther. You could send her to us in a year or two . . .'

Cassie looked at Esther in alarm and her mother smiled a reassurance at her and shook her head in disbelief. 'Cassie, go and fetch some canapés, will you?'

Esther watched as Cassie walked away. Suddenly she gave a laugh. 'Julia you are mad. Absolutely mad. And I must have been crazy ever to have come to you, let alone allow Cassie anywhere near you.'

285

'You were. Remember? You were crazy with grief.'

'Yes.' Esther was sober.

'I am a little mad. It's true – yes, I know it,' Julia said. 'A wise person learns to understand themselves before they try to understand others. There is a kind of sanity in recognising one's own madness, don't you think? Better than people who go around believing they are terribly reasonable and well balanced?' She lowered her voice. 'And I'm not so crazy that I'm ready to commit suicide by drowning myself in the sea. I watched you from the cliff that day, you know, after I'd first met you. I knew then that our destinies were linked, right from the start.'

'You watched me?' Esther's mind gave a lurch.

'I often watch my doves. It's part of my duty of caring – to know when they are disturbed – lonely rather than seeking to be alone, sad rather than solitary. You see, I may be mad, but I've enough wisdom to know that life always holds something back in reserve for us when we are struck low. That our sadness will pass. That there's always hope.'

'You were the one with Joseph's binoculars?' Esther's thoughts returned to the first time she had swum in the bay, she remembered the flash of binoculars from the shore, and the other times when she had sensed she was being watched. She had even suspected Freddie until . . . She remembered those last hours at The Dovecote when her fears about Joseph's dependence on Julia had been confirmed.

'Oh, Joseph didn't mind my borrowing them.' Julia waved a hand airily. 'He knew how much I liked to keep a close eye on everyone. Joseph understood me. That's what made it so hard when he went away . . .' She bit her lip. 'It was terrible for me – and when you left.'

'Julia,' Esther said coldly. 'You arranged a seance. You showed me Christopher carrying a dead dove in his hand. You faked a *ghost* to frighten me, to try to persuade me that you and the spirits knew best. Why don't you admit it? Because if you do you have to see yourself for what you are? Manipulative, egotistical, a fraud. What did you expect me to do – stay and thank you both?'

'I wanted to save you,' Julia said. 'There was no trickery about it. The spirits came to warn you. I had to do something. I *knew*, you see, Esther. I knew what was best for you.'

Esther looked at Julia in despair. What if her very first impressions had been correct – that Julia was sincere, that she really did care about each one of her 'doves', that everything she had done – the management of her protégés, the orchestration of the seances, her hold over Joseph – she had done out of love and not self-interest? 'You are dangerous,' she said. 'I'm almost beginning to believe you.'

'But why shouldn't you?' Julia's expression of hurt was unfeigned. She glanced across the room. 'Oh – I can see Gerard and Monique. I must say hello.'

'How long are you staying in London?'

'I shall go back tonight.' She kissed Esther and clasped her hand lovingly. 'But I shall be in touch now that we're friends again. I shall

come and visit you at your factory. We are friends, darling, aren't we?'
She did not wait for Esther to answer, and in fact Esther could not
answer. She felt powerless as she watched Julia walk away.

Julia visited them a few weeks later. She telephoned one day and said
that she was travelling north. 'May I stop off and see you at the factory?
I should love to see where you work now.'

'I don't think . . .'

'I know you must be busy, but I shan't stay long. A flying visit, that's
all. Besides, I haven't met George.'

'I don't want you to meet George,' Esther said in dismay.

'Darling. Don't be churlish. You can't keep him all to yourself.'

Esther wavered, and was lost; Julia took her silence for assent. 'I'll be
there about four. I can find my own way. It can't be difficult, and I'm
sure everyone's heard of Ansfield's.'

Esther stood with the telephone in her hand. 'Julia is coming to visit,'
she said heavily, as George walked into her office. 'Here. At the
factory.' She folded her arms and paced the floor. 'Why didn't I tell her
she couldn't come?'

'Why are you so agitated?'

'Because she's going to cause trouble. I know it.'

Esther watched the clock creep past four with mounting apprehension.
Why hadn't she stopped Julia from coming? She could have been rude
to her, told her straight out, 'I want nothing more to do with you.' What
was it about Julia that paralysed her self-will? Esther saw a movement of
shadows on the rippled glass of the partition between the corridor and
her office, she heard the sound of voices and the tread of heels on the
linoleum, and she grasped the edge of her desk as she waited for the
knock on the glass. One of the typists put her head round the door. 'A
visitor – it's a Miss Brassington. Is it all right?' she mouthed. 'She says
she's expected.'

Esther nodded. 'Yes. Show her in.'

Julia was dressed in a flowing red costume with kimono sleeves and a
black pill-box hat with a feather that accentuated her height and
threatened to topple as she embraced her. Her lips matched the
vermilion shade of her jacket. 'Darling – everyone's still talking about
your exhibition.' She let her gaze wander round the office. 'So, this is
where you work. I've tried so hard to picture it.' Her glance came to rest
on a glass showcase of flame design pottery. 'Your first. It was good. It
was extremely good.'

'But I've moved on,' Esther said. 'Julia, I *have* moved on.'

'I know, darling. And I'm glad. I couldn't be more pleased at the way
things have turned out.'

'Couldn't you? Wouldn't you rather I'd stayed under your wing?'

'It doesn't matter now. It was fate that you should marry who you
did. And now we're friends again I can still keep a loving eye on you.'

Esther drew her breath through her teeth impatiently. She moved away and went to the outside window. Girls from the downstairs decorating shop were carrying trays of plates across the yard. How could everything seem so normal when Julia was sitting here in her office and talking about keeping an eye on her? She thought of Julia and Joseph, imagined them planning the last seance together – how he should stand, the lighting, the finishing touch of the dead bird. Or had Julia given all the orders and Joseph, perhaps reluctantly, merely gone along with them? But not refusing to take part, Esther reminded herself, not protesting that it was all too bizarre and too cruel. She turned from the window and, leaning against the sill, steeled herself to ask her next question. 'Have you heard from Joseph?'

Julia frowned and looked down at her gloves in her lap. 'He never writes.'

'I'm surprised.'

'Why?'

'I have to admit it, I'm surprised – glad, but surprised – that he could cut himself off so completely like that.' Esther held Julia's gaze and Julia's eyes flickered with hurt. She bent her head again and fiddled with her gloves. 'You faked that last seance,' Esther said quietly. 'I found the uniform and the dead dove in Joseph's room. You talked about learning to understand ourselves the last time we met. Do you, Julia? Do you understand yourself at all?'

Julia was silent. She did not seem to hear. When she eventually looked up she smiled again, picking up her gloves from her lap. 'Well. Am I going to see your workrooms and meet the famous George who has won your heart and taken over your talents, or not?'

Esther turned away in exasperation; tears misted her eyes as she looked down into the yard. Suddenly she saw the futility of it all. What did it matter any more? This was her life – the pottery and her partnership with George. Like Julia, she should ignore what had happened, instead of letting it eat away at the back of her mind. When today was over Julia would be gone. She need never see her again. There was nothing to be gained by going over and over it all. She turned back to the room and showed Julia to the door, saying as they went into the corridor, 'George has won my heart, but I look after my own talents these days.'

George fell at once under Julia's spell. She looked exotic, she was at her most charming and he was flattered by her attention and by her enthusiasm for everything she saw. Esther went through the motions of explaining the work of the paintresses and their current production. She talked mechanically, telling herself that in another half-hour Julia would be gone and she could forget she had ever been there.

'You've been very good for Esther, George,' Julia confided as they went to George's office after a tour of the factory. 'She has suffered great sorrow and disappointments in her life; she has learned to recognise the mistakes she has made, and she has been very brave through it all.' She looked at Esther fondly and her eyes were bright with emotion. 'Darling, I really think the process I began is completed. You deserve your present happiness.'

Esther released a sigh of exasperation. There was an awkward pause. George sent for tea, and one of the apprentices brought it with a clatter of tea-cups. 'Will you come for dinner with us this evening, Julia?' George said amiably, unaware of Esther's look of outrage.

To Esther's relief Julia refused the invitation: she said that she had to be in Liverpool to meet a potential client that evening on behalf of one of her doves.

'But why don't you both come to The Dovecote soon?' Julia addressed the invitation to George. 'You and Esther could come for a holiday. I didn't tell you,' she turned excitedly to Esther. 'I have a new project. The others think it's marvellous. Guess what! We are going to open The Dovecote as a hotel next summer. Rowena will do what she does best, presenting jolly good food; guests will be able to take part in the classes . . .'

'And the seances?' said Esther with heavy sarcasm.

'Yes, that too if they want.'

'Seances?' queried George.

Esther turned to him. 'Yes. There's something I haven't told you about, darling. It's actually rather unusual. Julia is a sensitive.'

George looked from one to the other with an expression of puzzled amusement.

'She puts on side-shows. Calls up the dead. What do you think of that?'

'Well, I don't know.' George laughed lightly with embarrassment.

'Esther,' Julia said sadly. 'You know it isn't like that. How can you still be so sceptical?'

'Because – as you know – I remember everything so well,' Esther said harshly.

Julia finished her tea and stood. 'And so do I.' That cold intensity, which Esther had half forgotten, burned in her eyes. 'I remember you when you first came to me. You were a tormented, grieving little creature. Seeing you now – so alive, so full of confidence and ambition – has only convinced me further that everything that happened was for the best.' Her manner softened again. She turned to George. 'I should like to commission some pots for The Dovecote. We must talk about it. I'll telephone.'

'A bit odd that,' George said with a nervous laugh when Julia had gone. 'A bit of a character. Does she really hold seances?'

'Yes,' Esther said flatly. She remembered Julia's spirit voice telling her that Julia was her friend, that the spirits wanted to help her, and she felt cold and hard inside. She looked up from her desk. 'George, I won't have anything more to do with her. If Julia telephones or writes again I

289

want us to make every excuse we can think of not to see her.'

'Because she's a spiritualist? Well, each to his own, darling, but . . .'

'I want to drop her.'

'I say, now hang on. She's just talked about commissioning work from us. She could be a valuable customer. In fact, I have to say, I think you were silly to have cut yourself off like you did.'

'You know why I left.' Esther felt exhausted and close to tears.

'Yes. Because of a love affair. Surely that's irrelevant after all this time . . .' He held her gaze. 'Isn't it?' Esther sensed the tension in him as he waited for her answer.

'Yes. It is. But still . . .'

'I thought she was charming. Jolly nice. You said yourself it was all for the best. I really think you should keep in touch. I can't imagine her doing anything out of spite.'

'She didn't. She does everything for everybody's own good,' Esther said.

Chapter Eighteen

Another spring had come and gone and Joseph wondered what he was doing still in Italy. The Fascists had won an overwhelming victory in the elections that year. The government of Italy was fast becoming a dictatorship with all the oppression that went with it. And still people like the Luppis spoke glowingly of Mussolini's achievements.

It wasn't even as if he felt at home here, Joseph told himself. The climate was pleasant, the work was deeply satisfying, but he felt his position as a foreigner, and, after Sally went back to England that spring, he became more acutely aware of his isolation. He began to dread being alone, returning at night to his farmhouse under that close ceiling. He was afraid of his old dreams returning, though they had not haunted him for months. Instead, his waking hours were troubled by thoughts of the war.

Had he been a coward? The old question kept recurring, and he would go over every detail, minutely examining his behaviour. It was true he had been afraid, had gone into a funk, had crawled back to the lines instead of following his men. But afterwards, he remembered, hands had held him back, voices had restrained him: 'There's no use ... no point to it.' So what should he have done? Performed the ultimate sacrifice? Like the brave Australian sergeant who carried men to safety until a bullet hit him in the back. Was that what it was about – the Christian ethic of laying down one's life for others? Or was there, as in most things, a self-interest behind conspicuous bravery – the need to show one wasn't a coward? Men had been obsessed with it. Greater than beating the enemy had been the need to prove one wouldn't give way to a cringing, cowering terror. Every ordinary soldier had the vague notion that he should aim to become a hero. Every proven hero with the title to wear a medal on his breast sweated in fear of being revealed in the next crisis as an impostor.

He remembered the man beaten to the pavement in Siena and the crowd standing by. There too hands had restrained him, and there too he might have pushed his way free, might have submitted to a broken rib or tooth perhaps – nothing so terrible as a bullet in the back or drowning in mud alongside his comrades – but enough to prove he was a man and not a coward.

By the summer Joseph had completed the work on the upstairs

panelling of the Villa di Sogni. He was glad it was over. Living with the Luppis had become unbearable: Signora Luppi was forming ambitious plans for a picture gallery at the villa and they had begun to squabble about money again. The obligatory demands on his time in attendance at dinner parties with the Luppis' friends, and the Fascist-dominated conversation were also becoming tedious.

'I must tell you,' Signora Luppi said on one of these occasions, turning from the guest beside her to address Joseph. 'I have had a letter from our friend the Marchesa di Malfi. She is going to marry again.'

Joseph's thoughts flew at once to Roberto Falzon. Surely not? A permanent alliance between the young architect and the marchesa would be disastrous. Even Maria would recognise that. 'Who?' he said. 'Who is she going to marry?'

Signora Luppi turned to the others and Joseph saw that she had come the point of her revelation as she said in Italian, 'He is a man close to *Il Duce* himself. They say he has the ear of Mussolini on many occasions.'

Maria was clearly seeing her way into the best society, Joseph thought wryly, and asked, 'What of Roberto?'

'Roberto?' Signora Luppi's colour had heightened with the telling of her news, for connection with *Il Duce* bestowed a certain importance, even if it was only by proxy.

'Yes. Roberto Falzon. You once employed him as your architect.'

'Oh, him – the Bolshevik. The Marchesa di Malfi was bound to dismiss him six months ago.' Signora Luppi too dismissed Roberto with a negative wave of her hand.

Joseph waited until the guests had left before he approached her again. 'Where has Roberto gone? I didn't know he had left the marchesa.'

'Of course you didn't know. I had not told you. And Maria asks that I should not tell you. She says you think she is fickle. She says you shout, "I tell you so" . . .'

No, Joseph thought. Maria had not wanted him to know that she had dropped Roberto because of his Socialist sympathies. He remembered Roberto's letter, his insistence that a few weeks or months of joy were worth any pain that might follow. 'Poor Roberto,' he said out loud; and, silently, 'Poor fool.'

Signora Luppi tapped his arm with her fan. 'I hope you are not going to quarrel with Maria about it,' she joked. 'Or we shall have to think how long you stay at the Villa di Sogni.'

'The work is finished,' Joseph said. 'At least the men can complete it without much supervision. I think, Signora Luppi, I should end things here as soon as possible.' Surprised at how easily the decision had come, Joseph felt a sense of relief. He realised how much he had wanted to leave. The Luppis and their friends were not bad people, only stupid: they would go on ignoring stories of violence and intimidation, to suit their conviction that Mussolini embodied the greatest hope for Italy. And perhaps they were right, but he had had enough.

'Giuseppe – I was teasing when I say we must think how long you stay...' Signora Luppi's mouth formed a slack ring of dismay.

'But I share Roberto's anti-Fascist sympathies, Signora,' Joseph said. 'Very much so. It's becoming uncomfortable for me here. I can see what I should have seen months ago – that it's time I left.'

'Giuseppe – no!' She had begun to weep. 'Back to England?'

The Luppis told everyone that Joseph had not been the person they had hoped. His declared alliance with the anti-Fascists had completed this disillusionment. 'We have learned our lesson and shall never give our hearts to anyone again as we did with Joseph,' Signora Luppi told her friends. 'We were too close,' Signor Luppi said, with a meaningful sigh. 'He had become like a son to us and, as we all know, children always hurt us in the end.'

Joseph booked into a *pensione* near the marchesa's Villa Rosa for a few days. He wandered through the town, debating whether to see Maria to find out where Roberto had gone, when by one of those odd quirks of fate, as he was passing through the main piazza, he came upon the man he had once seen attacked by Blackshirts; he was sitting beside the fountain surveying the passers-by.

Joseph sat next to him. 'Good day, *signore*. Do you remember me?'

The man turned his head slowly. His expression was cautious. He stared at Joseph, recognising his Englishness; the wariness vanished, though his look was still blank.

'How is it with you? How is your little girl?' Joseph said.

The man grew pale. '*Signore*. I remember. One summer . . . a year, two years ago?'

'I'm glad to see you fit and well. Is the situation in your town worse or better since that day?'

'Oh, it is not so bad,' the man assured him; his cautiousness had returned.

An idea occurred to Joseph; he said eagerly, 'I wonder if you have heard anyone talk of a friend of mine? I am returning to England soon and I should like to say goodbye to him. His name is Roberto Falzon – an architect – he was working at the Villa Rosa. He would perhaps have friends among you Socialists.'

'Please. I am no longer involved with politics.' The man glanced about him hurriedly. Joseph saw a look of shame and sadness enter his eyes. 'I am a widower, signore. I need to work. I have my little girl to think of . . .'

'You don't have to explain. I understand.'

'You despise me.'

'No. Of course not. Who's to say . . . ?' Joseph faltered, embarrassed, not knowing how to ease the other man's sense of humiliation, and unaccountably he felt near to tears. 'Who's to say what we should or should not do when hard pressed.'

'I hate myself.'

'No. You must not,' Joseph said fervently. 'You've done a very brave thing. You've put aside your self-esteem and your peace of mind for the sake of your child.'

The man smiled weakly. 'I thank you for those few words, *signore*. I shall try to remember them.'

Joseph stood to shake the man's hand and say goodbye, and the other said quietly, 'The architect you are looking for. I knew him. He is working for a printer in Bologna. I tell you where. He has friends. Many friends.'

Joseph, driving north, headed for Bologna the next day. It was July: town and countryside alike quivered and suffocated under a fiercely blue sky. The dust raised by the car wheels joined the bluish cast veiling the hills, the olives and vineyards, and those relentless sentinels, the cypress trees. He reached Bologna and booked into a hotel, then went on foot in search of the printing works in the narrow, noisy streets.

'Roberto Falzon? Who is asking for him?'

'A friend. Tell him Joseph Kilburn is here. He knew me when he worked near Siena.'

The youth disappeared and returned. He beckoned to Joseph to follow him into the print-shop, where the crash and thump of machines in the close, semi-darkness was deafening. Men, working at the printing presses, glanced at Joseph with mistrust as he passed.

Roberto was at his desk. Sheets of drawings, posters and programme sheets lay scattered about. He came towards Joseph with open arms, his face and hands stained with printers' ink. He had aged in two years and had lost his boyish look, Joseph noted.

'My friend. My old friend.' They hugged one another; Roberto patted Joseph on the back, and Joseph, shocked to see the change in him, found it hard to speak. 'Come.' Roberto put on his coat. 'We must talk.' He led the way to a side-door, waving a hand to one of the printers who nodded but said nothing.

'Is it all right?' Joseph asked.

'To leave? Of course. I have friends here. They know it must be important.' He held the door open and they walked out into the noise and glare of the street. 'And *it* is important, Joseph. You are like a breath from the past, when times were happier. Ah, you've no idea how I have suffered this past year. Love! You were right. It's for fools.'

They went to a bar nearby, where the air was thick with the smell of garlic and cigarette smoke, and noisy with the sound of voices raised in laughter and argument. Roberto selected a table near the door. 'I have friends here – but one never knows,' he explained, indicating the ease of exit.

'It sounds very sinister.'

Roberto shrugged. 'It can be. But mostly life goes on as usual, without trouble. Except for women.'

'I'm sorry about Maria.'

Roberto shrugged his shoulders. 'Women are shallow. They have no brains and no hearts.'

'I'm even sorrier about what is happening to your country.' Joseph drank the wine Roberto had ordered. 'And to see where you are working. Can't you get work as an architect?'

'With commissions for people like the Luppis and the marchesa?'

'Come with me to England. I'm on my way home. You could get out from all this mess for a few years. Come to England with me and work at what you do best.'

Roberto shook his head and smiled. 'No, Joseph. My life is here.'

'At a print works?'

'You think we print only advertisements for health salts and concerts? There is important work to be done. I love my country, Joseph. I must help to fight against the *Fascisti*.'

'And get yourself beaten up one dark night, or dumped in the river?'

'If necessary.'

'You're an idealist.'

'Yes, I suppose one would say that.'

'I admire you. I even envy you in a way.'

Roberto laughed. 'I guess you do. You've had your war. Your time is over. Now it is my turn.'

'Let's hope it's a different sort of war,' Joseph said, and felt a foreboding for him.

Joseph arrived in London on a wet day in August. As he walked out from Victoria Station to the din of traffic and the cockney shouts of flower-sellers and news-vendors, the baking heat of Italy seemed a million miles away.

And yet, almost six years after the Great War had ended, London had changed, he was forced to acknowledge after a few days. The pace seemed faster, brasher. There were advertisements for cigarettes and motor cars. Women strode about with an air of purpose, smoked and laughed in public, walking arm-in-arm and wearing make-up. The war veterans on street corners jogged consciences with their bleak stares and trays of matches; and the huddles of men in street caps with the hunched shoulders and hopeless humiliation of the unemployed seemed to suggest that even here a political shake-up – more profound than seeing a Labour government come to power – might not be out of the question.

Joseph telephoned Exeter and checked on his equipment in store; he picked up old contacts and made appointments with former clients, initiating a few leads towards new commissions; and he began, through various estate agents, to search for a property out of London where he might re-establish his workshop. 'Come and live here, old son,' Colin had said, when he learned he was looking for somewhere. But Joseph knew that he couldn't go back to that – any more than he could go back to The Dovecote.

He hoped Julia didn't know he was in England, though it wouldn't be long before the word spread, he realised. Would Esther hear it too? He thought about her often now he was back. It seemed he need only catch a train or drive up to Birmingham and he would be able to pick up a trace of her. He had heard, casually from one of his former clients, that her reputation as an artist-potter was gaining in strength.

He had not realised how much she still haunted him until he saw her picture one day in a Knightsbridge window. He halted and stared at the press photograph beside a shop display of Esther Norbrook ware. The news-cutting was to do with an exhibition held at the store earlier that year; the photograph showed Esther, with a couple of women workers, holding paintbrushes and smiling into the camera.

Joseph stood for a long time, his gaze shifting from the photograph to the pottery, decorated in misty greens with a translucent glow under the shop lights. It was a far cry from her early flame series.

He was drawn again and again to the photograph. She smiled out from the picture with a serene confidence. She had cut her hair, he noticed, but otherwise she looked the same. He wanted to see her. The memory of her was intense, as if no time at all had passed since the morning she and Cassie had walked out of his life.

He went into the store and approached one of the shop counters close to the window display. He chose a plate and watched while the assistant did up the parcel with string.

'I believe "Esther Norbrook" is becoming very popular.'

'Why yes, sir. It's selling ever so well. Mrs Ansfield herself came down for a day with some of her girls and they put on a little demonstration right here in the store. You can see her picture in the window. It caused a lot of interest.'

Joseph took the parcel and paid for it. 'Did you say Mrs Ansfield . . . ?'

'Yes, sir – oh, I see.' The woman laughed, thinking she understood his confusion; she explained that 'Esther Norbrook' was a trade name. '. . . Mrs Ansfield was called that before she got married.'

Joseph walked from the store with the plate under his arm. It had begun to rain, and after a few minutes the brown paper was sodden. So she had married her company employer. She hadn't wasted much time, he reflected bitterly. He hailed a taxi and climbed in, giving the address of his hotel to the driver. That was that then, he told himself. The final seal. Suddenly he wanted to weep. Had he really been hoping to see her again? He realised now that he had. He felt a deep, unreasoning hostility towards the fellow she had married. George Ansfield. Mentally sound, you could be sure of it. A safe bet instead of a mental cripple. Had Ansfield served in the war? Or had he stayed safely in England making pots? Or perhaps he had found a post in some cushy bunker behind the lines.

A man, peddling cheap neckties, with an empty sleeve pinned across his chest and a DSO on his civilian coat, stood outside the entrance to the hotel. Joseph bought one of the man's ties, thrusting a guinea into his good hand. It isn't fair, he wanted to yell as he went up the steps of the hotel. Why should some have been pushed into the worst of it while others came through it unscathed?

In spite of his resolve not to pick up old habits, Joseph was tempted by the idea of living in the South-West and he found a house in Devon. It was close to the sea but within easy reach of Exeter and the rail link to London; a small Georgian manor house with a cluster of outbuildings. The main building needed structural work, but Joseph was glad to immerse himself in its conversion; he wanted to be busy, to indulge himself in rational activity for a long time.

He had been living there for less than a fortnight when a car pulled up outside one afternoon, and a woman stepped from it, gazing around. She was pretty and fair and slim and when she saw his startled look of recognition she gave a whoop of laughter. 'Hello, Joseph. You sly old thing. Why didn't you tell me you were in England instead of leaving me to find out all by myself?'

'Sally.' Joseph felt a slow stealing of pleasure as he hugged her and led her into the house. 'How did you find out?'

'I was talking to some people in London the other day and they told me you'd been spotted.' She looked round the hall and followed after him into the sitting room where she sat on the dust-sheeted sofa, swinging one leg over the other. 'You're like one of those elusive birds that only appears in certain habitats every few years.'

He laughed. It was good to see her. 'I didn't know you were a bird-spotter.'

'I'm not. But *you* are, apparently. Your friends have been telling me all about you. But it was still a devil of a job to find out where you were living.'

'And now that you've found me?' he said, looking at her fondly, thinking she was the first good thing that had happened to him in months.

'I want you to make me some furniture.' She looked around at the freshly plastered walls approvingly. 'I'm thinking of living round here actually.'

'What a coincidence.'

'Not really.' Sally gave a roguish peal of laughter. 'Oh, dear. Is that shameless?'

'Absolutely.'

'Do you mind?'

'Sally, darling. I couldn't be more delighted.'

Esther had been troubled by a restlessness since exhibiting her pottery in London. Her reputation as an artist-potter had begun to grow swiftly, and she had tried to persuade George that they could show her pots at the Paris exhibition the following spring. 'Ansfield's is a small

Midlands pottery. We have no hope of exhibiting,' he had protested, when she had pressed him on the subject, and the most she could persuade him to do was to agree to go to Paris for the opening week – without her pots.

She was ambitious, Esther realised. She had tasted success and she wanted more. She tried to be a good wife as well as George's business partner, but she really wasn't sure these days that she was cut out for it. And sometimes George was so maddening, with his conservatism, and his natural caution, his refusal to wear Oxford Bags, his delight that autumn after the election when the Tories were 'back at the helm'. Even his uncanny resemblance to the Prime Minister, with his pipe and his reputation for steady dependability, was becoming infuriating. She did not remember that married life had been so difficult when she was younger, nor that she had felt so stifled, nor needed to make so many sacrifices. She could only suppose that she had grown too used to her independence. And perhaps there were, besides, too many thoughts of what might have been.

One point of contention between them would not go away. Julia had begun to send brochures from The Dovecote, advertising its opening as a hotel and inviting Esther and George to go there for a holiday. She had repeated her request to commission some pots, and George kept nagging Esther to reply. 'You ought to write to her. I think she's being extraordinarily generous. Has it occurred to you that you treated her rather badly? Have you thought about that? You *do* treat people badly. You disregard their feelings.'

'You don't know what it was like,' Esther replied. 'Why won't you take my word for it when I say we should have nothing more to do with her? It's not like you to be so unreasonable.'

'But it's like you,' George said with none of his usual patience. 'Dashed unreasonable sometimes, Esther. It makes me feel unsettled.'

'All right. We'll take on a commission for her if you think it's so important.'

'You can't do a commission without knowing what the customer wants.'

'I know The Dovecote well enough inside and out to know what would suit it. I don't need to go there.'

'Don't be ridiculous.'

'All right then. You go.'

He hesitated. 'You know I couldn't talk to her about our designs. Besides, it's *your* designs people want. It's you Julia wants.'

'Yes! And she's not going to get me. Not again!'

'They are arguing more and more,' Cassie told David, after overhearing the tail end of a quarrel. He was home from school for Easter. It was a Sunday, but Cassie no longer went to church. In the year since she had got to know David, she had swiftly abandoned religion.

'It happened with my parents before they were divorced,' David said

298

prosaically. 'It was a struggle with them all the time as to who was going to be top dog.'

Cassie considered David's assumption seriously. Was George jealous of her mother's success? Certainly he would not have expected, when he invited Esther to join him, that her pots would become so popular. And, for all his sweet-natured charm, George needed to be in charge. As Cassie had grown older, she had begun to realise that George would always come second to her mother's work – or to anything else Esther might consider more important than their marriage. Was a simple power struggle at the root of their disagreements?

Cassie didn't know who it was had told her mother Joseph was back in England. The fact was, they all of them knew – George as well – that Joseph had returned. So, perhaps it was George's unease about Esther's past that had begun to drive a wedge between them, thought Cassie.

'Joseph is home from Italy,' she confided to David with a casualness that hid her real feelings. The news had set up a fervour of activity in her mind. Despite her friendship with David and his influence on her as far as religion was concerned, Joseph was still Cassie's idea of the ideal, romantic hero. She had not quite abandoned a secret hope that one day she would be walking along a street and there he would be, walking towards her in his light-coloured suit, smiling in his special way from dark-fringed eyes, laughing as he swung her into his arms.

'What are you going to do about it?' David asked her in his customary way of getting to the point.

'I don't know.' Cassie thrust her hands in her coat pockets as they walked through the park. Her mother was unaware that she and David met every Sunday; she imagined Cassie still attended church. Cassie saw no reason to disillusion Esther, or to let her know she had embraced atheism with the vigour she had once reserved for Sunday-school attendance. David had said that God was invented by man, because questions such as, Who are we? and, Where do we come from? were too hard for people to understand except in human terms. 'Something exists: *ergo* someone must have made it,' he had said. 'So, by the same argument, one cannot believe in a God who created the universe, because if the universe cannot exist without a creator, then neither can a God. There would have to be an even more powerful God somewhere, who created the God with which we are familiar, and so on, *ad infinitum*.' Cassie was so much impressed by this and other arguments that her passion for religion had evaporated almost overnight.

It was pleasant meeting David every Sunday and having a secret from her mother; it appealed to Cassie's passion for intrigue. They sat on a park bench and she considered his repeated challenge to 'do something' about Joseph. 'When I said we should try to get in touch with Joseph, that perhaps we should get to the bottom of what really happened, my mother told me to grow up and not be so silly.' Cassie remembered Esther's anger and knew that she *had* grown up, and that it was her mother who was being silly.

'Over-reaction,' David said, nodding wisely. 'It means she wants to get in touch with him really. Your mother would be a very good subject for psychoanalysis. What was he like – this Joseph?' he added after a while.

Cassie did not know how to answer. How could she sum up in a few words the way Joseph had dazzled her? She remembered his sadness when he had said goodbye to her, and that other, wartime sadness in him, for he had witnessed things no one should see. She remembered his vitality and his joy, so often suppressed by the shadow of the war, but which had nevertheless broken out from time to time – in his love of jazz and fast cars, his taste in clothes, his sudden laughter when she had said something to surprise him. She told David about Joseph's knowledge of sea birds and the way he had isolated himself from the rest of the people at The Dovecote, living like a monk in his cottage on the edge of the cliff.

'A hermit,' David teased.

'No. There was a severe side to him – it was in his furniture too. But his furniture was beautiful rather than grim. He was an artist. He inspired me to want to design furniture.' Cassie remembered those brief periods of happiness in Joseph's workshop and fell silent.

'Guess what,' she said after a while. 'I'm to be allowed to go to the Exhibition of Decorative Arts in Paris next month. George says it will be good for me to see something of Europe. Lucky he never said anything about me wanting to be a designer or my mother would have a fit and say I can't go.'

'You really mean it, don't you?'

'About designing furniture? Of course I do.' Cassie knew there would be battles over wanting so desperately to study design, for her mother was just as desperate that she shouldn't do it. 'After I've taken my School Certificate I shall start pestering them in earnest to let me apply for the Royal College. Meanwhile, there's Paris to look forward to. Imagine!' She clasped her gloved hands beneath her chin. 'The Eiffel Tower! Notre-Dame! The bridges, the river! And the exhibition! It spreads over both sides of the Seine. Think of it – all those fabulous exhibits – fashions by Chanel and Poiret! There's a fountain, fifty feet high, all lit up at night! And there'll be glass, pottery – and – ' she closed her eyes in rapture – *'les pièces de résistance* – the furniture!'

'Don't forget me, will you, while you're in Paris?' David said a little wistfully.

Cassie looked at him and saw that he was blushing. She stood up. 'I'll send you a postcard and embarrass you in front of your friends by signing it "Fifi". Come on. Race you to the park gates before they close.'

Cassie had been given permission to be away from school for a whole week, for Miss Collins, her art teacher, had convinced the headmistress that it was all in a good cause. 'I'm envious, Cassie,' she had said. 'It will be a unique experience for you. The very best of international design will be on show. Come back with lots of ideas, won't you?'

Cassie wished George and Esther could be happier with one another as she stalked the slippery decks of the Channel steamer. She was pretending to travel alone, that this wasn't her first trip abroad but that she was an international art connoisseur with a retinue of staff – George and Esther – attending to her travel plans below decks. She pulled her new, rather fashionable suede hat closer to her head and wished she was old enough for a cigarette holder – she was sure that everyone in Paris carried long cigarette holders. She leaned on the ship rail, wrapping the fur collar of her coat round her ears and closed her eyes in bliss as the salt spray stung her face.

She so much wanted everyone to enjoy it all, she thought as the train took them through the flat French countryside and villages. She was impatient with Esther and George's silence beside her in the railway carriage, and with the journey, restless for the train to reach the heart of Paris – until, at last, they arrived at their hotel.

Cassie, hardly able to believe such luxury existed, had a suite all to herself. She unpacked swiftly and bathed in scented water in a room full of mirrors, then switched on all the lights in the bedroom so that it blazed with colour. Wrapping herself in a white bath towel, she walked from one room to the other on the deep soft carpet. She came to a halt in front of one of the glittering mirrors and let the towel fall, surveying her reflection dispassionately. Her hair fell damply, curling to her shoulders, echoing the dark triangle of hair between her thighs, and Cassie recognised, with a sense of pleasure, that she no longer had the body of a child. She felt a tingling glow of excitement; for she was in Paris, where anything could happen.

She turned away from the bathroom and, returning to the bed, laid out the new silk pyjamas her mother had packed as a surprise present. She was no longer an art connoisseur, but a film actress – she had 'It' she told herself, remembering the fierce arguments at Heather Park over girls who had 'It' and those who were sadly lacking in the department of sexual appeal. She draped herself on the bed, imagining that Valentino might at any moment walk through the door. Then, tiring suddenly of playing a vamp to thin air, imagining that her mother – rather than the great lover – might knock on her door and summon her to dinner, she jumped up and began to dress.

Esther too felt herself respond to the atmosphere of Paris. The chill between her and George had begun to thaw as soon as they arrived.

Was it work that had come between them? Esther wondered, trying to analyse what had been happening to them. Were they simply too busy to pay enough attention to one another? Or had the knowledge that Joseph was in England made them wary of close communication? It was Julia who had dropped the news about Joseph casually into one of her letters – though, of course, there would have been nothing accidental about it. Esther had sensed that Julia was testing her, trying

301

to discover whether she had heard from him. Julia had written that Joseph was living not fifty miles away from The Dovecote, yet he had not been to see them and – when Meg had made inquiries – he had made it plain that he wanted no contact. '... When are you and George coming to The Dovecote to visit us?' she had added. 'I am getting impatient with your excuses. You must come this summer.'

The Dovecote was another point of contention between them, for George wanted to go; he couldn't understand her reluctance. Esther refused to tell him – would not tell him about Joseph. She had a strong suspicion that, like Cassie, his initial reaction would be one of disbelief, that he might even laugh at her or wonder about her sanity if she said that Joseph had pretended to be Christopher's ghost. If only she could dismiss the whole business, instead of letting it simmer at the back of her mind, like a poisonous brew concocted by Julia.

But now, in Paris, all that seemed far away. She began to relax at last, seeing George too visibly loosen up over dinner as Cassie chatted excitedly about all the landmarks she had heard and read about.

'I'm so glad you persuaded me to this trip,' George said. 'You know, I only wish now we had tried to submit some of your pots.' He looked sheepish. 'I wonder if I've been guilty of professional jealousy.'

'If you have, I don't hold it against you.'

'Next time,' he promised.

'You mean we'll come again!' Cassie gasped, her cup of joy threatening to brim over.

'Who knows? We have your mother's link with Galeries Lafayette. And what about New York? We really should be looking internationally. I've been too cautious. The whole world is at your feet, Esther darling.'

Cassie's eagerness was infectious, Esther thought as George smiled at her over the dinner table, and, reaching out simultaneously, as if with one thought, their hands met and held one another.

That night they made love with a sweet and tender sympathy, leaving them spent and Esther astonished at the feelings that had woken in her. She sat beside George the next morning as they toured the sights of Paris in an open car. Remembering their intimacy, she was aware of the birth of a deeper aspect to their relationship. She must not lose him, she thought, for they were strong together. There was something unique in their partnership, different from anything she had ever known: George was one of those rare creatures who believed instinctively in the equal position of women. He understood her ambition and her need for a sense of independence. He accepted her right to combine marriage with success in her artistic career. And she loved him, she realised, as she thought again of their love-making. This new feeling would grow and nothing and no one – not even Julia – would be able to come between them.

Cassie could not tear herself away from the furniture. Never – except in

Joseph's furniture at The Dovecote – had she seen such innovative designs. She was familiar with the old Arts and Crafts Movement themes and the curling, naturalistic lines of Art Nouveau. This new artistic expression was geometric, sweeping, jarring, colourful. It demanded that one look and look again.

Cassie wandered away from George and Esther, who were locked excitedly into ceramics and pottery. She walked from one exhibit to another and stood before a stand of bedroom furniture: the mirrors and dressing table were deceptively simple in shape, their surfaces inlaid with fan-shapes of mahogany, the mirrors clean circles, intersected with geometric lines.

The streamlined forms were so like those of Joseph's furniture in the rooms at The Dovecote and in their flat above the studio that Cassie wanted to tell someone, 'I recognise this style. I saw it first. It's like that of the greatest designer I know. And it's my style too. This is where I belong.' Suddenly she felt a shock, a little thrill of real recognition. She stepped closer and read the labels. It *was* Joseph's – a whole stand of 'Joseph Kilburn' furniture. Cassie was feverish with discovery.

There was a pile of cards on one of the tables – of the kind that business people handed to one another, printed with a name and address. She picked one up and slipped it in her pocket. Then she turned from the furniture and saw Joseph.

He was standing with a man and a woman. The woman, fair, freckled, very pretty, hung on Joseph's arm. The man looked like a Frenchman, overweight and mustachioed. Joseph leaned against a pillar with a cigarette in his hand. He wore a cream-coloured suit and two-tone laced shoes with brown toe-caps. He was beautiful, dazzling. It was exactly how Cassie remembered him from the first time she ever saw him and her heart rushed upwards and crashed in her ears. She felt as though she were floating as she walked across the floor space between them, until at last she stood before him. 'Joseph it's me! It's Cassie!'

Joseph turned with a half-smile at the sound of her voice and stared at her without speaking, as if he too were in a daze.

Sally, amused by the interruption, looked Cassie up and down, taking in the flushed face and startling dark eyes and the girl's air of barely suppressed delirium. 'Joe, darling. Shouldn't you introduce us all properly?'

Joseph recovered, but the sensation of being in a dream remained. What on earth was Cassie doing, standing there in front of him, like some rare and precious image from his past? His voice broke a little as he introduced Cassie to Sally and to his promoter.

'Why are you here, Cassie? Has it really been so long? You look almost grown up.'

'I am grown up. I'm fifteen,' Cassie said indignantly, and suddenly Joseph laughed. And that too was exactly as she remembered, Cassie thought, as she looked and looked at him, knowing she had a silly smile on her face. It was like something from a fairy-tale – except for the freckled woman standing next to him, smug, with her arm linked through his.

Cassie was aware that Joseph had stopped looking at her and that he was staring over her head. She turned and saw that Esther and George had come into the furniture section of the hall. The colour had drained from Joseph's face. 'Of course,' he said softly. 'You would hardly be here on your own.'

'I'm with my mother,' Cassie said as Esther approached. 'And my stepfather,' adding anxiously, 'Esther is married now.'

Joseph looked at her with a bleak little smile. 'Yes. I know.'

Cassie saw that her mother had turned a fiery red and was gripping George's arm tightly, but, having begun the journey across the hall, there was no turning back. Everyone smiled very politely as Joseph went through the introductions again. The Frenchman excused himself after a moment or two and wandered away.

'I'm very impressed by your designs,' George was saying to Joseph.

'Thank you.' Joseph drew on his cigarette and avoided looking at Esther.

Sally glanced from one to the other. She began to talk, praising this and that in the exhibition. Had George and Esther seen the Chanel designs yet? Wasn't Paris just amazing? Cassie began to warm to her after all, for at least she was doing her best to stop everything being horribly embarrassing. After a laborious five minutes of this, George said, 'Well – we must move on...'

Everyone smiled again and said polite goodbyes, just as if they were all the merest acquaintances who had met in town, thought Cassie as, reluctantly, she followed George and Esther and they walked away.

They had reached the next exhibits when Esther halted. She turned an agonised, pleading look on George. 'I'm sorry, but I have to talk to him. I can't leave it like that.'

George said nothing, but he let go of Esther's arm. Cassie watched as her mother ran back the way they had come, then she looked at George, who was staring after her with an ashen face. Cassie slipped her hand in the crook of his arm, her heart aching for him, but knowing she could do nothing.

He turned to her and patted her hand. 'Shall we walk on?'

Esther found Joseph standing where she had left him. He had his back to her. His hands, the cigarette discarded, were thrust in his pockets while the woman he had introduced as Sally talked to him steadily in a low voice; she turned when Esther approached and gave her a cool, hostile glance, then murmured something to Joseph and he swung round to face her.

'I—' Esther's mouth dried. She could think of nothing to say.

Joseph glanced at her hands, twisting her gloves, and at the ring on her finger. Esther wished the other woman would go away. She looked up and her head reeled with unspoken accusations.

'Cassie has altered,' Joseph said.

Esther gave a laugh of bitter disbelief. So they were going to continue to behave as if they were mere acquaintances. 'Yes,' she heard herself say, conscious of the woman beside him. Who was she? Were they lovers? 'Cassie is quite the young lady these days.'

'She has a look of you.'

'Thank you.'

He frowned, looking strained. 'Well. I'm glad you are happy. Your husband – he seems a decent chap.'

'Yes. George is *very* decent,' Esther said emphatically. 'He's been very good to us. I am *very* happy.' She wanted to weep. How could they stand there talking about George when there was so much else to say? Why had he done that for Julia? She wanted to scream. Why so elaborate? Why so cruel? Why hadn't he simply told her he didn't love her? She could bear it no longer and burst out, 'Why did you do that dreadful thing to me? How could I have believed you loved me and then have been so wrong? It doesn't make sense.'

'I don't know what you mean,' he said, frowning. 'You made a free choice. You were the one who left – who decided you'd had enough.'

Sally looked from one to the other. 'I guess it's time I made myself scarce.'

'No. Don't go—' Joseph restrained her.

Sally smiled. 'Darling. I'll find you later. You'd better get this little . . . misunderstanding sorted out.'

Joseph watched her go.

'Who is she?' Esther said.

'I met her in Italy, when we were both at a low ebb. We live together.'

'Shall you marry her?'

'No,' he said levelly. 'We are just friends.'

'And lovers,' Esther said, knowing that she was close to becoming hysterical, that at any moment she would begin to create a scene.

Joseph looked at the ring on Esther's finger. 'Yes. Sometimes. Though I don't really see why that should concern you now.'

'The fact that you've found somebody you can live with? I find it interesting at least. It does make me pose the question: Why her but not me?'

'She accepts me.'

'So did I accept you.'

'But you made the decision to go,' Joseph reminded her. 'It was you in the end who left.'

'And do you wonder – after you went to such insane efforts to convince me we shouldn't live together? Pretending to be Christopher. The uniform . . .'

He stared at her. 'I hope you realise I don't know what you're talking about.'

'My God!' She laughed. 'I couldn't believe it. I *didn't* believe it to begin with.'

Joseph said fiercely. '*What* uniform?'

'Pretending to be Christopher.' It was like a grotesque dream. She would go on having to repeat it, locked in a sort of nightmare. 'I saw you! At Julia's seance. You were dressed like Christopher in full uniform. Don't you think that's monstrous? Don't you even feel badly about it now? I thought I understood you a little, but how could you!' She was breathless and white with anger. He stared at her and the expression in his eyes caused a trickle of fear to enter Esther's mind. She thought again of Julia's refusal to admit to any trick. What if she were wrong? What if she had lived under a dreadful misapprehension all this time? 'You were there,' she insisted, suddenly calm. 'I didn't imagine it. You appeared at the seance dressed as Christopher. And it wasn't the first time – I saw you on the stairs to Julia's studio. Don't you remember I ran after you? And then I saw you in the garden, I thought you had the uniform in your knapsack.'

He took her by the arm and shook it angrily. 'Don't you understand? I've no idea what you're talking about. I guessed something had happened – spirit contacts, voices perhaps. I don't know what Julia has in her repertoire. But I thought she had convinced you – like she had convinced me – that we would be making a ghastly mistake if we stayed together. Because of the doves. I thought that was why you went – because I killed the doves.'

'I found your uniform in your room,' Esther went on, feeling hysteria threaten to rise in her again. 'You were there. On the stage. Dressed as my dead husband! I saw you.'

Joseph let her go. 'I have to take this in, Esther. I thought . . .' He passed a hand across his eyes. 'I assumed you left because you realised you couldn't live with me after all – and because of Cassie, after what happened to the doves. I thought you didn't say goodbye because you wanted to make it easier for us both.'

Esther drew in her breath slowly. 'And so I did. Oh, perhaps you've forgotten the rest – perhaps your illness made you forget everything afterwards. I don't know, and I can't pretend to understand. I only know that I wish to God we'd never met like this. Why now – after all this time?'

She turned away and he did not try to stop her. The past minutes had bludgeoned his mind like repeated blows from a very heavy instrument; he reeled from them. To see her again had been shock enough. To learn they had parted because of some peculiar mistake, or fantasy, or deception of Julia's, was too cruel; he couldn't work out the truth behind it. She thought she'd seen him dressed as her dead husband? Her imagination? The mind playing tricks – or some sort of theatrical performance of Julia's? But, if it had been a trick, why hadn't Esther seen through it? And then – to have gone away without telling him, without saying anything or giving him a chance to deny it? To let such a gross misunderstanding come between them was unforgivable.

To be the creator of such a misunderstanding was worse, he told

Chapter Nineteen

In his diplomatic way, George did not question Esther about what had passed between her and Joseph in Paris; but the incident lay like a weight between them, oppressing every conversation and putting a constraint on their new-found intimacy.

Back at the factory, Esther threw herself into her work with a determined energy to forget Joseph; but his reaction to her accusations nagged at her constantly, building a slowly increasing suspicion that she had been wrong all this time. She had been wrong about his watching her through his binoculars, wrong too about the note, sent by Rowena. She had been wrong about so many things. But if the figure at the seance hadn't been Joseph, then who? It was as if the answer was there at the back of her mind somewhere, as if she only had to remember something that had happened, something she had overlooked at the time, and a fog would lift and reveal everything clearly.

She tried to recall exactly what she had seen that day, and realised that nothing had proved Joseph's guilt except her own certainty of his domination by Julia. And yet Julia had admitted to nothing, had not once talked of Joseph's taking part in the seance – only her sadness at his leaving. Esther felt weak with misgiving when she recalled how readily she had jumped to conclusions. Had it been she who had thrown away a chance of happiness – Joseph's as well as her own?

Cassie wanted to talk about meeting Joseph. She been overjoyed to see him, then depressed after they left Paris. She wrote to David at his school and he encouraged her to get to the root of what had happened at The Dovecote. It was very important, he said. '. . . The only way to free oneself from past events is to face up to them. I should say it is essential for your mother's peace of mind, to find out what really happened.'

For a while Cassie became obsessed with it. 'I *have* to talk to you on your own,' she would say, with sufficient schoolgirl drama for Esther to avoid discussing anything to do with Joseph. 'It's important.'

'No, it isn't, Cassie,' Esther said. 'Joseph is a subject long since dead and buried.' She closed her mind to the memory of meeting him in Paris. She would forget it had happened.

Esther went to London that summer to see a customer. Walking along Bond Street she was brought to a halt by a group of paintings in a gallery window. 'Peter!' she gasped aloud, for there was no mistaking the style or the subject matter of the pictures. She stared at the flurries of wings, recognising the startling violence; then she saw the lumpish shape of Peter himself, inside the gallery with his back to her.

She looked away from the window. She ought to walk on, but she was tempted to glance again at the figure inside the gallery and discover whether Peter was alone. At the same moment, he turned and saw her; in the next, he was on the pavement beside her. 'Esther! Esther, this is wonderful! Come inside!'

Reluctantly Esther left the street and the door closed behind her, shutting out the traffic, enveloping them in a silence among the paintings of the doves. The gallery attendant nodded at them, then moved into a back room. 'It's been a long time,' Peter said. 'We have missed you. Julia has missed you most of all.'

'She wants me and George to visit,' Esther said, as she walked beside him from picture to picture.

'You should. Yes, you should. Why not let bygones be bygones?'

Esther halted. 'Would you be quite so forgiving if it had been you and Meg Julia had tried to part?'

'But she wouldn't have succeeded,' he said with simple logic.

Esther felt her face flush fire. So, Peter thought her love for Joseph hadn't been strong enough under test. Was he right – for what use was love without faith? They walked on in silence. Esther halted before a painting of a pair of birds sparring, their feathers stained red. 'Why do you make them seem so brutal?'

'Because everywhere there is violence beneath the surface – even in the dovecote. Birds peck at their rivals. Love is not gentle. Underneath there is always a hunger for domination. It is our task, as human beings, to harness the brutal side of our human natures.'

Esther smiled. 'If anyone has succeeded in that, Peter, it must be you.'

'You still think Joseph killed them, don't you?' Peter said, looking at the doves.

'I'm sure he must have done. But that in itself wasn't why I left. Oh, Peter – to be honest, I don't know what to believe any more.' And she told him about meeting Joseph in Paris.

'He wasn't lying,' Peter said. 'Joseph wasn't there at the seance. I don't think he even knew what had happened that day; he left The Dovecote soon after you did.'

'Then tell me – what did I see?'

He smiled at her and his faded eyes were gentle. 'Why, Christopher, of course.'

'Oh, Peter!'

'It was. I know.' Peter set his jaw and Esther saw that he wouldn't be swayed. Did he know the truth? she wondered, as they continued slowly round the walls of the gallery. If he did he wasn't going to say. He would remain loyal to Julia.

Esther left after a while. 'Think about it,' Peter said as they parted. 'Wasn't Julia right all along? You are happy in your marriage,

310

successful. Aren't you better off as you are than if you had gone off with Joseph? Come and see us sometime, darling Esther. Mend a few broken bridges.'

Sally had been up to London and returned one evening unexpectedly; Joseph heard the sound of her car from his workshop. He preferred the workshops when they were empty at the end of the day. He would walk in the semi-darkness among the half-finished pieces that constituted the day's work, enjoying the familiar scent of resins and French polish, and appraising the progress made by the individual apprentices. It was the time when he did most of his thinking.

He went out into the evening air and made his way through the garden to the drive at the front of the house, and felt a lift of his spirits as he saw Sally. He realised how accustomed to her company he had become.

'Tired?' He helped her from the car.

'Just a little.'

He was absorbed by a project he had thought of that day, and did not notice that Sally avoided his eyes. Nor did he puzzle about the embarrassed half-smile she offered him as he kissed her. He wanted to tell her about his plans. 'I'm thinking of taking on more apprentices,' he said as they walked towards the house. 'Students who want to become craftsmen. Not only local people. It's an idea my father always had, but he didn't live long enough to carry it through.'

'A school?'

'In a way. Perhaps half a dozen at a time. They would have to live in.' He paused. 'How would you feel about that?'

She did not answer him at first.

'After all, this is your home as well,' Joseph said. 'At least, for as long as you want it to be. I need to know that you feel OK about it – I mean about having other people live here.' He followed her into the house.

'Has it occurred to you that you'd be "doing a Julia"?' Sally said over her shoulder.

'No.' He gave an ironic laugh. 'No, it hasn't.'

She turned at the foot of the stairs. 'Joe. I have to talk to you. In a minute. I'll wash and change and then I'll be down.'

He stared after her. Her face was pale in the light from the hall, her expression very serious. Joseph felt his heart deaden a little, knowing at once that something had happened and she wasn't going to stay.

He went into the sitting room at the front of the house and stood by the window, looking out at the darkening lawn studded with topiaried yew trees. It occurred to him that to many outsiders he must seem successful; his name was known internationally; he owned a fine house; he had a team of serious craftsmen producing his designs. And all at twenty-eight. Yet what had he achieved in his personal life? He was at peace, he supposed. He rarely had nightmares these days for, like most of his contemporaries, he had at last begun to come to terms with the war. Distance tended to alter one's perspective and, while he could never forget the men who had died, the events of each passing year jostled with sympathetic insistence to crowd out the worst of the images and obscure the horror; the present was taking over from the past.

So, he was over the war, but what about love? Would it have lasted with Esther? he wondered. He heard a sound in the hall and turned. Could he and Sally have found love with one another? It was too late for that, too, he thought, as she came into the room.

He forestalled her. 'You're leaving.'

'How did you know?'

'I remembered Italy – when you said you were coming back to England. They are the only times I've seen you so serious.'

'He's leaving his wife, Joe. Remember the bastard who wouldn't give up his home comforts? He's said he can't live without me. We've been meeting again.' She was trembling. 'He means it this time. He's going to get a divorce. I've been seeing him every day. Oh, Joe – we're just crazy about one another.'

'I'm very glad for you.'

'Are you?' Her eyes sought his. 'Do you know, I really think you might be. Why are you being so nice? I was so afraid to tell you.'

'What did you think I'd do?'

'Tell me I'm an idiot, I suppose. I don't know.' She moved her hands in a helpless gesture. 'I don't want to leave you. We get on so well together, but what else can I do?'

'You have to go where your heart is.'

She came to him and he folded her in his arms. 'I love you,' she said. 'Does that sound crazy?'

'Not to me.'

'I'll come to visit you. And I *do* like your idea about taking in more apprentices – a woodcraft school. I think it's a splendid idea.'

It would take his mind off things, Joseph thought wryly.

'Will you be all right on your own?'

'For goodness' sake, woman,' he laughed. 'It's not in your nature to agonise.'

'No. It's not. Oh, Joe!' She swung away from him. 'I'm *so* happy. I can't believe it.'

Joseph's life fell into a fresh pattern after Sally had gone. He opened the Furniture Craft School that October with half a dozen students, and appointed a tutor who had trained under fellow craftsmen in the Cotswolds, as Joseph had under his father. Sometimes he thought of Esther and Cassie, and sometimes he wondered about Julia and what had happened the day Esther fled from The Dovecote, but as soon as the speculations began, he pushed them out of his mind. It was good to be busy, to concentrate on his passion for the beauty of wood and be working at what he loved most, quietly expanding and at the same time teaching others to believe as passionately as he did in trying to achieve perfection of design. It was unproductive to dwell on the past.

Cassie passed her School Certificate with Honours in several subjects the following summer. It was David's last summer before he went to University College to study Medicine in London. They spent days cycling in the lanes of Warwickshire, or walking along the canals, talking about when he would be a psychiatrist and she a furniture-maker.

'Are you getting serious about the Henson boy?' Esther asked her one day, for the days of hiding her friendship with David had long-since passed.

'No, of course not,' Cassie laughed.

Was it true? she wondered on David's last evening at home; she knew she would look forward to his next holiday, and she had promised to go on writing to him in term-time, as she had when he was away at school.

'Another two years and you'll be joining me,' David said. 'If you manage to get your own way about the Royal College.'

'Oh, I shall get my own way,' Cassie told him. 'I've got George and Miss Collins at Heather Park on my side. My mother wants me to go to university after taking Higher School Certificate, but she's only being obstinate because of the way she felt about Joseph.'

David did not say anything. He always went quiet when she talked about Joseph, Cassie noticed; he no longer pushed her to get to the root of things as he once had. But Cassie could not forget about meeting Joseph in Paris; the enforced silence about the incident had alienated her from her mother and only made her want to talk about it all the more with David. She kept Joseph's business card with his photograph in her handkerchief drawer. The memory of seeing him, the knowledge that he was in Devon, creating beautiful pieces of furniture like those she had seen in Paris, glowed like a beacon of inspiration in her mind.

'George has become quite an ally over my becoming a furniture designer,' Cassie said. 'He's argued and argued for me to go to the Royal College. They have the most awful rows about it.' Cassie had heard her mother and her stepfather quarrelling about her future until late into the night. She had gained a renewed respect for George, whose high-principled nature always made him set aside all personal considera-tions. 'He's so unselfish,' she told David. 'He's the most unselfish man I know – except for Joseph,' she added quickly.

'What about me?'

'What about you?' Cassie laughed. 'You're just David.'

'Is that all?' He looked so clearly disappointed that Cassie pulled his hair in fun and said, 'Yes. That's all. That's quite enough for anyone too, thank you very much.' But she was blushing as she said it, and for a moment she perceived that it would be as easy to hurt David as it would be to make him happy. The awareness gave her a sense of power. She felt the soft strands of red hair under her fingers; their touch sent a prickle of tension through her body, and she felt an urge to press her hand more gently against his head and to hold him quite differently.

Esther felt herself besieged on all sides. She could not understand why the school, usually so keen on getting their girls into university, were encouraging Cassie to go to the Royal College. Cassie's art teacher seemed to be at the heart of the campaign. She had obviously bombarded the headmistress with her opinions that autumn, so that the head began sending letters home and had a long and grave interview with Esther; she said she was surprised that Esther was taking such an entrenched stand, being a designer of such obvious integrity herself. 'Cassie has the brains for more academic study,' Esther protested weakly, avoiding the woman's eyes.

Cassie was tearful, sullen, and Esther knew she had begun to hate her for her opposition.

'Cassie's future is in design, and anyone with half an eye can see it,' George said angrily, after Esther's interview with Cassie's headmistress.

'But it doesn't have to be in *furniture* design. She could come into the pottery if she doesn't want to go to university,' Esther said, taking off her coat and hat and jabbing the pins in the crown. She hung them on the office hat-stand and sat at her desk, pretending to look for some papers. 'And if she goes to London I shall lose what little influence over her I still have.'

'That would happen wherever she went. Are you afraid of her going to London? Or are you frightened of losing her to something that makes you feel uncomfortable?'

'Both. This ambition to make furniture is a childhood whim – a hangover from The Dovecote. I know her better than you do, George. She still has a romanticised view about it all.'

'You mean about Joseph Kilburn?'

'All right. Yes! About Joseph Kilburn.' She looked down at the desk. Her hands were trembling. She gripped them in her lap and said levelly, 'I'm afraid, if she follows a career in design, she might meet him again – she might bring him back into our lives.'

'Don't you think I've thought of that too?'

'Have you? It was bad enough for me after Paris. I can't go through all that again.'

'And what about me?' George's voice had a measured anger in it. 'We must always consider *your* needs, mustn't we – your work, your art, your emotions? Everything comes second to that. It always has. Even Cassie.'

'It isn't true.'

'Then let her study what she wants. She has talent.'

'I can't, George,' Esther wailed. 'You don't know what it would do to me – or to us.' She looked at him, seeing his openness, his love for her, his unshakeable trust in his own feelings, and she envied him, wishing she could trust herself with such conviction. If George could risk

314

everything, then why couldn't she? She knew that George was afraid she was still in love with Joseph, that he was afraid of losing her. And it was true that she brooded still, wondered what had actually taken place the day she left The Dovecote. She had drifted in a sort of limbo since meeting Joseph again, making work or Cassie's future the excuse for her conflicts with George; she resolved things in the only way she knew how, by withdrawing, by burying herself deeper in the pottery business.

And the pottery was absorbing. They had come unscathed through the previous year's General Strike – largely because of the loyalty of George's workers. Esther was determined that her own range of tablewares would survive the current slump in trade and the fall in the market. They wouldn't go under as so many other small firms were doing. 'That's all you came back to me for, wasn't it?' George once said to her after a particularly bitter argument. 'Your pottery means more to you than anything.'

'You knew it was at the time. I didn't pretend any different,' Esther said. And so it was now too, she realised, in spite of their moments of intimacy and the times when she counted her good fortune and knew she'd secured a good man in George. Oh, she knew she cared for him, but she was too frightened, and often too physically tired to deal with the problem between them. She was so afraid of destroying what they had built together that she was powerless to tackle her feelings about Joseph. Confront Julia, a voice told her. Julia knows exactly what happened. All you have to do is go to see her, make her tell you what you saw. But Esther knew she couldn't rake it all up again. She didn't have the courage to go back. It was a matter that lay unresolved at the back of her mind – and might have remained so for years, if she had not caved in suddenly over Cassie going to the Royal College.

Cassie had approached the headmistress with a tearful impression of an artist under siege – which might have convinced her to put her in for RADA instead of the Royal College of Art. The head telephoned Esther, suggesting that she was not only being unnecessarily obstructive, but she was possibly blighting her daughter's future; and Esther, acknowledging at last that she was outnumbered, weary of the long battle, suddenly gave way.

Cassie was accepted by the college. She embraced London and student life with a sense of having been marking time until that moment. She had her hair shingled, wore Russian boots, and shocked the distant, ancient aunt of George's – with whom she was boarding in South Kensington – by becoming a flapper. She threw herself into energetic discussions about the merits of the *Bauhaus* and futurism, about prohibition, trade unions, Virginia Woolf and D. H. Lawrence, Mae West and Garbo, over cheap cups of coffee and endless cigarettes in shabby cafés. Sometimes she danced to jazz and the Charleston with David, who was in his third year at University College. On Saturdays they went to the cinema and laughed at Laurel and Hardy and then ate ice-cream sundaes in the Lyons Corner House at Marble Arch. David was not like the boys of her own age, who seemed so young and green and awkward – 'like unseasoned wood', she told him. And yet, even David seemed a little dull when she thought of Joseph with his slow smile and glamour.

One day, after Cassie had been at the college for several weeks, one of the tutors, talking about lines the students might follow after leaving the course, mentioned apprenticeships under well-known craftsmen. He dropped Joseph's name into his lecture and spoke of his workshops in Devon – as an example of one of several leading artists who were training graduate students.

To hear Joseph's name in the context of the college was oddly shocking. Cassie sat for a long time, her heart pounding, hearing nothing of the rest of the lecture. She remembered Joseph's card which she still carried around with her like some sort of talisman. It was then she made up her mind to go to see him.

'I don't know why I haven't done it before,' she told David excitedly when she met him that Saturday. 'I suddenly realised that Joseph and The Dovecote will always be an unfinished episode in my life – in all our lives. It's up to me – up to us, to do something about it.'

'You can leave me out of it,' David said a little sulkily. 'I never even knew him.'

Cassie wasn't listening. 'Just think!' she said breathlessly, 'I could have telephoned Joseph at any time, but I haven't done it. Why? Because of my mother and George. I've colluded with my mother in suppressing her feelings about Joseph. It's as if Fate decided I should wait until now.'

'I don't see that Fate has much to do with it either,' David said, pushing his spoon round his empty sundae dish. 'Simply because some fellow mentions him in a lecture.'

'Oh, David. Don't be a killjoy,' Cassie wailed. 'Why aren't you on my side?'

He stood up and paid the bill. They went outside without speaking and walked along Oxford Street, past the lighted shops.

'Don't you think it would be good for everyone if we were to find out what really happened when my mother thought Joseph pretended to be my father's ghost? Bring it all out in the open?' Cassie persisted.

'Isn't it all rather too silly and too long ago to be bothered about?'

'I thought everyone should "seek access to the hidden things in their subconscious". What happened to your ideas about facing the past, releasing the negative side of old experiences?'

'Cassie. Some things are perhaps best left buried.'

'That's not what you used to say. You told me I should *do* something.'

'I was only a kid when I thought that. I didn't know then how disturbing digging up memories can be.'

'But she *loved* him, David. My mother really loved him. And he loved her. Don't you think they should have a chance to find out what that means?'

'And I love you,' he said suddenly. He halted and swerved round to face her. 'I think I've loved you since you were a gawky kid, when I saw you peering through the fence at your mother's wedding party.'

'You were the one who was doing the peering,' she reminded him. She smiled. How handsome he had grown. She knew that girls at the college envied her having him as a boyfriend. 'You wore an awful red pullover.'

'And you weren't really gawky. You looked really pretty. You were the prettiest thing I'd ever seen. You still are. I want to kiss you,' he added softly.

'You'd better do it then.' Cassie stepped back into a shop doorway and offered her mouth tentatively, trying to behave as if it was not the first time she had been kissed.

The experience left her breathless; she stared at David with wide eyes in the shadows of the doorway, falling back against the support of his arm. Then she said, 'You beast! You've done that before!'

'Well—' She knew he was blushing in the darkness.

'Who with? I thought you said you'd loved me since I was a gawky kid of thirteen.'

'Oh – come on, Cassie . . . You can't really mind.'

Cassie laughed. She loved to tease him, she realised. It was so easy to make him do just as she wanted. She tipped back her head to look at him in the darkness and settled her shoulders more comfortably against the weight of his arm. 'You'd better do it again,' she said. 'I obviously need the practice.'

Joseph found it difficult to order his thoughts after Cassie had telephoned to say she was coming to see him. Just as his life had levelled out, here was something to complicate it again. Until that moment he had succeeded in rationalising his past and present existence. The war had been a trauma for millions besides himself; he had survived and could at last bear to examine the scars. The Dovecote, once a source of emotional support, was an episode he regretted, but it was behind him. Esther had been his one great love; he had lost her. Sally had left him but they remained friends. He could live without women. His work was his only passion; the challenge of developing new ideas and of communicating them to others had become the only important motivation.

He recalled Cassie's voice on the telephone. She must be eighteen by now, he calculated, but she had sounded excited, with that childish eagerness for an adventure that he remembered so well when she had been twelve. 'Let's go to the cliff and watch for kittiwakes . . . Take me to see the heath butterflies . . . Let's all go to the beach before the regulars come.' Her enchantment drifted from the recesses of his

317

memory and made him smile involuntarily. He remembered that it was Cassie who had brought the first chink of joy into his life again; he had watched her pleasure in simple things, seen her delight in nature, taught her how to handle wood and respect its idiosyncrasies. He had observed her lack of cynicism with a kind of wonder, recognising her trust in his own dependability – the trust of a generation untainted by the great deception of the war. Something inside him had begun to blossom when she was around – a sense of hope; for it was through Cassie as much as Esther that he had given himself permission to love again.

She was right, he thought, reflecting on their telephone conversation. The events at The Dovecote would always remain a mystery unless they rooted out what had happened – what exactly Julia had been playing at, as Cassie put it.

He found himself looking forward to her visit as the days passed. She arrived on a Sunday and he drove to the station to meet her. She looked very neat and determined as she stepped from the train, her dark hair hidden under a cloche hat. She had Esther's strong jaw and wide mouth, he noticed, but there was less of a guarded look in her dark-fringed eyes, instead, a look of expectancy, a puppyish eagerness. She glanced about her, then saw him, and she became a radiant, whirling creature, all arms and smiles as she ran to greet him. 'Joseph! Joseph. For a minute I thought you'd chickened out.'

Joseph's heart turned over as she flung herself into his arms.

'I don't know what you said to her, but my mother was very upset after the Paris exhibition,' Cassie told him when she was seated in his car.

'I know. I'm sure it would have been better if we hadn't met again.'

'Oh, don't say that.' Cassie looked at him with shining eyes. 'I thought it was so wonderful to see you there. I missed you dreadfully when we left The Dovecote. I cried and cried but I had to do it silently. She wouldn't talk about you, you know.'

'I missed you too, Cassie. I thought about you both a lot.'

'I remembered everything you taught me. I'm still going to design furniture. It's marvellous being at the Royal College. George has helped – ever so. He used to laugh about my drawings, but then he said I should be encouraged. It was my mother who didn't want me to be a designer.'

'Because of me.'

'I think so.' Cassie looked away, remembering the deep hurt she had felt because of Esther's opposition. 'It was so selfish of her, you know. My mother can be very selfish and pigheaded sometimes.'

'It seems I wronged you both very much without knowing anything about it.'

'She thought you had pretended to be a ghost, you see.'

'She told me. But that's so ridiculous.'

'She thought you had dressed up as my father. You did it because

Julia had such a strong hold on you. You did it to put her off you because of your nightmares.' She looked at him and this time there was a challenge in her eyes. 'Did you?'

'Of course I didn't.'

'She found your army uniform. I know it was there, because I saw it too once in your room. And there were the poor birds...'

Joseph stared out through the windscreen with a sudden feeling of disconnection from his surroundings. The doves. No one could explain them away. 'I must have killed them, Cassie.'

'I don't believe it,' Cassie said, her eyes filling suddenly with tears. 'You loved birds. You loved so many things. It wasn't fair.'

Joseph showed her over the workshops and Cassie breathed again the wonderful aroma of planed wood. 'Isn't it odd, how smells can take you back?' she said. 'I love your house. It's the sort of house my mother and I used to tell ourselves we would live in one day. Much nicer than The Dovecote.' They crossed the yard to a pair of french windows; the mullioned surround was crumbling, coated with grey and yellow lichen; three large, squat urns spilled a skeleton of cotoneaster branches on to the cobbles. 'Oh, it's so lovely to be here! I feel—' She spread her arms as if to embrace the house, the courtyard and Joseph. 'I feel as if I belong here. Do you know what I mean?'

'Yes, I know,' he said, for she caught at his heart, standing there, her cheeks flushed by the November wind. He tried to reconcile this fascinating young woman with the child he had once known; she was the same creature, and yet she was so much changed that he found himself confused by his reaction to her.

They went indoors and she told him about her course at the college. 'You are *famous!*' she told him. 'Everyone wants to get on to one of your workshop apprenticeships.'

Joseph smiled, guessing that she was exaggerating, but flattered nonetheless.

'We *have* to find out what happened that day,' Cassie said, when she was seated in his sitting room. 'I've thought and thought about it. My mother's convinced she saw someone dressed as my dead father. I used to tell myself she must have imagined it – when people are upset they can believe all sorts. I used to imagine I saw you sometimes. You'd be there, standing on the corner when I came out of school. Or flying past in the Bentley and I would be in a crowd of people – too late to call out to you and let you know I'd seen you. I used to pray – I prayed a lot in those days – that you would turn up and everything would be the same as it had always been and we could all live together like my mother had promised. And then she married George.'

Joseph was transported suddenly to a wet day in Knightsbridge – a shop girl wrapping a parcel for him, telling him that Esther was married. He had tried to hate her husband, he remembered, but after meeting him, even that small comfort had been denied him. 'Did you know that Esther thought she had seen me pretend to be the ghost of your father once before, at the first seance she went to?' Joseph said.

Cassie shook her head.

Joseph remembered Esther's almost hysterical accusations when he had met her in Paris. 'She said it was on the stairs to Julia's studio. Could she really have seen someone then too, do you think?'

'Yes!' Cassie said excitedly. 'There's a stair from Julia's studio leads straight to the seance room. It would have been easy for someone to get from one place to the other. I found it once when I was creeping about on my own. I was kid enough to believe I'd get into trouble for being there, so I've never told my mother about it.'

They stared at one another.

'Could Peter or Freddie have been the "ghost"?' Joseph said, drawn again to the possibilities that had turned themselves over and over in his mind since meeting Esther in Paris.

'They wouldn't – would they? Besides, they'd have been there, sitting with the others at the seances.'

'Then I don't see how we are ever going to know the answer.'

'Unless we confront Julia – make her confess and tell us about it.'

'Oh, no, Cassie.' Joseph saw what she had been planning.

'But don't you see? We have to convince my mother that *you* didn't have anything to do with it.'

'I can't believe you are still so naïve.' He went to the window, his stomach churning with the thought of seeing Julia again and reviving old emotions. Suddenly he stooped to open a cupboard under the window-seat and pull out a wooden box. He blew the dust from the lid, nursing it thoughtfully in his arms. He had forgotten about it until now – except for bringing it to England and putting it away in the cupboard. He remembered the loneliness that had made him go into the shop and buy the present for Cassie, and the resignation that had prevented him from posting it. The memory sent a wave of longing through him for the past to be undone.

Cassie came to the window and touched the lid of the box curiously. 'What is it?'

'A tool-set.' He opened it: the tools were arranged neatly on a bed of blue felt. 'I bought it for you one Christmas in Italy. I didn't send it, of course. I knew all the time that it was too late to go back.' He closed the lid. 'I bought it in a moment of sentimentality. And I won't be caught like that twice. Not even for you. We can't turn back the clock. It's too painful all round.'

'That's the sort of thing David says,' Cassie said, unperturbed. 'But he's wrong.'

'And who is David?'

'He's a medical student. He's going to be a psychoanalyst. I've known him for ages. I expect I'll marry him one day.'

'Well, David sounds very perceptive to me,' Joseph said, turning away.

'No. No!' She caught his arm and the agony of her expression, her disappointment struck at him like a knife. 'It's never too late to put things right. We've *got* to talk to Julia.'

Joseph hesitated, for a moment believing her. Why hadn't he confronted Julia before now? Was he still so much afraid of her influence on him?

'Can I keep it?' Cassie took the box from him and lifted the lid again.

'Don't be silly. You'll need more sophisticated tools now. I'll buy you some this Christmas if that's what you want.'

'No. I want to keep these.' She looked at him with shining eyes. 'You bought it for me. You were still thinking about us all that time. And you're wrong – it's not too late to go back.'

They avoided discussing their reason for driving to Winmouth until they were almost there. Was it all rather pointless and childish? Joseph asked himself, regretting the fact that he had given in to Cassie and allowed himself to be drawn into her enthusiasm for the dramatic.

Cassie clasped a hand to her heart as they neared the village. 'Oh! We're there! I feel *so* nervous.'

Unwilling to approach The Dovecote immediately, Joseph parked the car near the war memorial in the village square. A crowd of people were coming out of the church and the Unitarian chapel. He waited until it had thinned a little, then climbed from the car. Cassie followed. Wreaths of poppies still lay around the memorial a full week after Armistice Day. Cassie approached it and stood, silently reading the names of the dead. 'Do you still have bad dreams?'

'Hardly ever.' Joseph remembered that the Armistice ceremonies had always triggered an attack. Could he really dare to hope they were over?

'It must have been terrible. People nowadays want to forget it ever happened – or else pretend it was all rather magnificent.'

'There are some who are prepared to tell the truth.'

'And then everybody says they are too gloomy and morbid.'

'Perhaps they are. The best way is simply to move on.' Joseph turned away from the war memorial, remembering the purpose of their visit. Cassie had planned to march up to the house and challenge Julia about the seance, but he felt a strong reluctance, now he was here, to go anywhere near The Dovecote. The church and chapel crowd had dispersed and a lone figure was coming down the hill. A memory stirred – the day Esther had left The Dovecote; he had walked along the shore and through the village; the same figure had come towards him down the road that morning.

'Isn't that Violet?' said Cassie. 'Hello, Violet. It's us.'

She had been crying the last time, Joseph remembered. It hadn't occurred to him to wonder too deeply about it, but now the memory struck him as odd.

321

'What are you doing here?' There was a wariness in Violet's expression.

'We've come to see Julia.' Cassie turned to Joseph with a sudden burst of inspiration. 'Violet would have been at the seance that morning. Perhaps she knows something about it . . . Violet, we want to know what happened the day my mother and I left The Dovecote. You see my mother thought she saw a ghost . . .'

Violet stared at her and shook her head. She hovered for a moment like a large grey bird about to take flight, then, pressing her hand to her mouth, she fled across the road. They watched in amazement as she ran up the chapel steps and disappeared inside the building.

'Well, what do you think of that?' Cassie swung round, her eyes bright with a sense of melodrama. 'Is she frightened because I mentioned "ghost", do you suppose? I think *not*! She definitely *knows* something, don't you think?'

It was a game to Cassie, thought Joseph. An adventure, like the ones that had caught her imagination when she'd been a child. She had already half forgotten the issues at stake. But he was remembering more clearly now, seeing the girl that morning: Violet's hair had been scraped back from her face into a wispy sort of bun. She was a large girl, tall and well built, some might say masculine in her appearance. He glanced swiftly at Cassie. 'Stay here.' He crossed the road to the chapel.

The door swung silently open and he stepped inside, closing it behind him. He saw Violet at once, kneeling in a pew near the harmonium. Her hands were clasped and her head was pressed over them. Her shoulders heaved with distress.

Joseph walked slowly up the side aisle and sat in the pew across the gangway from her. After a while he said, 'Do you want to tell me about it?'

Violet shook her head violently.

'You might as well. I think I've guessed anyway.'

'It had always been all right before,' Violet sobbed. 'People were *pleased* to see their loved ones. No one ever made a fuss. Julia said I was helping them. She said I was helping that time, too, but it didn't seem like it – all the fuss there was afterwards. I got frightened. I took off the uniform and put it back in your cupboard – only there was the bird . . . I didn't know what to do with it.'

'One of the doves?'

'I was supposed to carry it – to show it was the spirits had done for them. I didn't know how to get rid of it though, so I left it in the cupboard. I meant to go back for it, I really did. And then Esther went away and you went away and Julia was so angry and miserable about it all.' She looked at Joseph, her eyes wide with fright. 'Esther found the dove and the uniform, you see. Julia was furious with me for getting everything wrong.'

'It wasn't the first time you had dressed up in my Army uniform for Esther to see—'

322

'Oh, honest. I never wanted to. The first time, I was only supposed to stand on the stage – to show how her husband was there, still looking after her. Only she left the meeting early. I thought I still had to let her see me, so I went to the attic stairs. I really thought she would want to know he was there in one piece on the other side. But then she came chasing after me and I got frightened.'

'So why didn't you stop then?'

'Julia said we had to convince her. She said you would be bad for her and she would be bad for you, and the spirits wouldn't be pleased if we didn't help.'

'Was it you smashed her pots?' Cassie said, walking down the side aisle towards them from the back of the chapel.

'No. I didn't.'

'It was Meg who broke your mother's pots,' Joseph said to Cassie. 'She told me once. Meg was jealous because of Peter. She thought he was paying her too much attention.'

Cassie sat beside him. 'Rowena was always very jealous too.'

Violet turned to Joseph in fright. 'I thought it was you. They said you did queer things.'

'Is that why you thought I would be bad for Esther?'

'Yes. Julia said we had to save her before it was too late.'

'And the doves?' Cassie said intently. 'Violet, do you know who killed the doves?'

Violet dried her eyes and stuffed her handkerchief back into her coat pocket. 'That was Julia. She saw your mother and him come back from London together that night and she went and lost her wits.'

Joseph felt a tension deep in his mind suddenly release its hold. Julia had killed the doves? Relief flooded through him. With a sense of euphoria and sadness – for, more than anything, the death of the doves had convinced him that he and Esther should part – he heard Violet continue, talking to Cassie as if he were no longer there.

'... Poor Julia. She told me it was a great blow to her when she saw him and her together like that. She tells me everything. She trusts me with all her secrets. All that work, all that love she'd given them both. She thought it had all been for nothing. So she went crazy and killed the doves – one for everybody in The Dovecote, "her life's work in ruins". Only she told me it must have been the spirits done it really – that they'd possessed her. They don't always work in the way we expect. She fetched me up to the house and showed me the birds in the kitchen. She said the spirits needed more help and I was to dress up again as Esther's dead husband. The spirits wanted Esther to know she mustn't be with Joseph any more.'

Joseph tried to imagine how Esther must have felt when she believed he had masqueraded as Christopher. Had she at last been convinced that he was unbalanced? He remembered the doves, Cassie holding them in her arms. Had that been enough to make Esther believe he would take part in the grotesque charade of Julia's seance? He felt a continuing sense of hurt. How *could* she have believed it, if she had loved him?

Violet turned to him. 'What are you going to do about it, now you know?'

'Do?' He stared at her. She was a simple-minded, superstitious girl; she probably still believed in all the mystical side of it, even after being involved in the management of the spirits. He looked round at the plain little building. 'I shan't do anything. But if you want some advice, Violet, I should say you'd be better off spending your Sundays here, instead of up the road.'

Cassie ran after him to the car. 'What now?'

'I can't talk to Julia after this. Besides, there's no point. We know all there is to know.'

'*We* know the truth, but my mother doesn't.'

He looked at her. 'Oh, Cassie. Can't you see it's much too late?'

Cassie was silent as they drove from Winmouth, then she changed the subject, talking about London, her friends at the college, David – who she said was in love with her – but Joseph sensed that her mind was elsewhere, planning, scheming. 'I think my mother ought to go back to The Dovecote,' Cassie said when they reached the railway station. They sat staring ahead through the windscreen of the car.

'What for?'

She looked at him. 'What do you mean, what for? It would set her straight – put her mind at rest about what you did – or at least what you didn't do.'

'What for?' he said again, angry with her. 'What exactly are you expecting to happen, Cassie? I was going to marry her! Shall she leave her husband, and shall we all live happily ever after – except for poor old George of course?'

'We could at least all be friends again,' Cassie pleaded. 'George too.'

He got out of the car and slammed the door in exasperation. 'Cassie, I can't believe you see it all in such simple terms.'

'You owe it to her – and to me – to put things straight. Give her the chance to face the truth and how she really feels. She's still mixed up about it all. Believe me. She hasn't forgotten. Julia keeps inviting her to stay and she won't go back – not even to plan a commission for some pots.'

Joseph's mind was spinning. He knew there was some truth in what Cassie said. Hadn't the war sent him berserk before Julia had helped him face the things he had seen? Time had done the rest – but the healing had begun then, with talking it through, revisiting the experience.

'Let me at least tell her about seeing Violet today,' Cassie coaxed. 'I could suggest she goes back to have it out with Julia. You see, I've got an idea about how to do it – you and me and my mother would be in it together, we'd be in charge. And Julia will realise that she shouldn't have done it. We'll show her she didn't really win.' Cassie was persuasive as she sensed the weakness in Joseph's hesitation. 'You owe me something,' she pleaded. 'You both do, for the way you ran away from one another like that.' Tears shone suddenly in Cassie's eyes; she turned away so that he should not see as she brushed at them with her gloved hand.

A knot of emotion seized Joseph's throat and he could not speak. He saw that the whites of her eyes were a bluish colour, like fine china, the irises greenish-grey, huge with tears. The short time he had known Cassie as a child flooded back – their walks together, her enthusiasm for everything. He realised that she could probably persuade him to do anything to make up for the hurt he and Esther had caused her.

'I don't know what you mean about showing Julia she didn't win, but I suppose I can't stop you telling Esther about what happened today,' he said at last.

'And if I can get her to come to The Dovecote – will you come too? Will you meet her?'

He nodded, for a part of him wanted to go along with Cassie's craziness, he realised. And he wanted Esther to know the truth. 'So long as you tell her exactly what you mean to do and she agrees.' He did not dare to ask himself, *What then?*

Chapter Twenty

Cassie waited until she went home for Christmas before she did anything about her plan to reunite Esther and Joseph. She told David about it as they travelled to Birmingham together on the train.

'It's all about facing fears, mending destructive attitudes,' she said. 'I think Joseph is going to co-operate if I can only get my mother to see the sense of it.' She wiped a patch in the condensation on the window with her glove.

'Why are you doing this?' David asked her after a while, looking up from the book he had been reading. 'I mean – what's in it for you?'

'Is this the psychoanalyst talking?'

'Yes. Nobody ever does anything with a purely unselfish motive.'

'I want my mother to be happy.' She beamed at him, believing it, seeing herself embarking on a final quest for Esther's peace of mind.

'You mean you have a romantic, sentimental idea that if you take your mother back in time you can wipe out everything that's happened between then and now. And for you, the glow of rosy childhood will return? Well, I'm telling you, it won't work like you think.'

'Oh – I hate you when you're like this,' Cassie said crossly.

'Like what?'

'So pompous and superior.'

'And what about Joseph?' David went on after a while. 'What if they do still love each other? It's dangerous. People could get hurt – and they'll blame you for it if they do.'

'They must have their chance to find out how they feel, resolve things. It's all so *unfinished*.'

David recognised the pleasure Cassie was getting from making things happen and being at the centre of an intrigue. It made him uncomfortable. He wondered for a moment whether he was growing a little tired of the way she swept everyone along in her wake as she rushed headlong into some scheme, however crazy. 'You're not a tiny bit in love with this Joseph yourself, are you?' he said condescendingly.

'I've always been in love with him.' Cassie turned again to the railway carriage window and stared out into the darkness. 'But not in the way you mean.'

He did not answer and she felt angry with him, and, for a moment confused. How did one distinguish between adolescent and adult love? She wasn't even sure that what she felt for David was love, so much as liking to have him around – except when he provoked her, she told herself, like he was doing now. It was exciting when he kissed her, she reflected. And sometimes she wanted to do more than kiss and it was David who said they must be careful. She respected him for that. Oh, and he was clever and easy to talk to. But he didn't make her blood sing, she realised. She thought of the tide of happiness on which she had returned to London after seeing Joseph again.

'You forget, he was my mother's lover,' she said after a while, turning to face him.

Still David did not answer, but pretended to read his book.

'And he *must* be at least thirty by now.'

He looked at her. 'I wonder who you are trying to convince?'

The festivities were over. George had gone to play golf on the afternoon of Boxing Day, and Esther and Cassie were left alone. Cassie wandered restlessly round the sitting room, examining the Christmas cards in turn, exclaiming at those she recognised – her mother's family connections, Hugh and Marjorie, Giles and Margaret. Marjorie had scribbled a note to say that Hugh was going to fly his aeroplane in Australia next year. There was a card from Julia and the rest of the commune. Cassie picked it up, using it to broach the subject uppermost in her mind.

'Don't you ever want to know what happened?' She fingered the card, a photograph of The Dovecote in a rectangular frame of holly leaves, an obvious promotional picture for the hotel. 'Peace at Christmas' was overprinted in gilt letters. 'How can she put that on her Christmas cards when she created such chaos?'

'Whatever else she may be, Julia isn't a hypocrite. She believes in what she does,' Esther said sleepily from the settee. George was trying again to persuade her to go back to Dorset and make her peace with Julia. He had some idea, picked up from Cassie no doubt, that she had left things unfinished after meeting Joseph in Paris, that she would always be restless until she could put it out of her mind for ever.

Cassie came to sit beside her. 'Aren't you ever curious? You must know by now that Joseph didn't do those things you thought he'd done. Don't you ever feel guilty about the way you misjudged him?'

Esther looked at Cassie and wondered at her tenacity all these years. She remembered how important Joseph had been in Cassie's life at that turning point between childhood and adolescence. She knew she ought to stop her before she started on her pet hobby-horse in earnest, but she was mellowed by good food and wine. 'I don't suppose we shall ever know now,' she said. 'Perhaps I didn't see anything really. Perhaps it *was* my imagination.'

'But we do know!' Cassie seized her hands. 'It was Violet. I went to see Joseph and we met her and she confessed to it.'

'You did what!' Esther pulled her hands away, appalled by what

328

Cassie had said. 'How did you know how to find him?'

'I picked up his address card in Paris. And they know about him at the college. Listen. Just listen! We talked to Violet and she admitted that *she* dressed up and pretended to be my father's ghost.'

'Cassie!' Esther leaned back weakly against the settee. 'Cassie, I don't know what you're talking about, but this isn't fair of you.'

'It wasn't fair to Joseph if you ask me. He loved you – and you went away without giving him a chance to explain. You owe him something.'

'What? What do I *owe* him?'

'An apology. To get it all straightened out and be friends again.'

Esther shook her head in exasperation, but slowly the implications of what Cassie had said had begun to sink in. The confusion of happenings, forming a gigantic puzzle, like a heavy mental knot at the back of her mind, began to unravel and slip into place. Violet had pretended to be Christopher? Violet was tall and muscular. In a poor light, with a cap covering her hair, and in khaki, she would have passed for a man. Esther tried again to recall the figure she had seen on the stage – not much more than an outline behind a curtain – and before in the shadows of the attic stairs, so indistinct that she had convinced herself she had imagined it. The only certain feature had been the Army uniform. She remembered the day she had driven to The Dovecote after George had asked her to marry him. She saw Violet standing in the road with her hand raised in an odd gesture of farewell. It had been the same gesture and the same image as the one she had seen on the stair. She searched Cassie's eyes, bright with passion and conviction. 'It's true, isn't it?' she said sadly. 'What you're telling me is true.'

'Yes! Every word.'

Esther gave a long sigh and closed her eyes, feeling tears prick the back of her eyelids as she thought of her obstinacy about what had happened. She remembered the way she and Joseph had once loved one another, the intensity of their feelings and her own assertions that their love could overcome all obstacles, even Julia. How could she have let the abnormal atmosphere of The Dovecote so completely cloud her reason?

'We should go back,' Cassie said. 'The three of us have to confront Julia about what she did. I know you ought to go back. It's important for you both. I've been reading David's psychiatry books. If you don't face your bad experiences, you never stop feeling unhappy and guilty about them. I know Joseph thinks so too really, only he's too decent to ask you himself.'

'Joseph thinks! Joseph thinks!' said Esther in a last-ditch attempt at self-defence. 'If he hadn't been so much under Julia's thumb, I'd never have jumped to the conclusions I did. Who is he to tell me what's important for me after all this time?'

'For you *both*! And he's not trying to make you do anything. He's as much mixed up and worried about it as anyone.' Cassie looked at her mother in despair. She *did* want her happiness, she realised. The glamour was fading from Esther's spirit, and she had looked ill and tired over Christmas. David was wrong to accuse her of acting out of selfishness.

'And what about George?' Esther said heavily.

'What about him?' Cassie said, feeling guilty, for she knew the question was important.

'Don't you think he deserves some consideration in all this?'

'I don't want him to be hurt. But I know that if you and Joseph truly loved one another, you should try to put things right or you'll never forgive yourselves. 'Do it,' she said earnestly. 'For me. Go back to The Dovecote and confront Julia. I've had an idea to shake Julia up. I've told Joseph about it and he says he'll go if you will.'

Esther looked at her. For a wild moment she was convinced that Cassie was right and she had lived too long with this shadow over her. She thought of seeing Joseph again. She didn't know what hare-brained scheme Cassie had thought up, but if Joseph had agreed to it – if he could face seeing her and, more significantly, Julia again, shouldn't she at least do the same? Didn't she owe him that much?

'I know who killed the doves too.' Cassie repeated what Violet had said about Julia seeing Esther and Joseph come back from London together.

'I really believed he could have done it in the end,' Esther said, half to herself. 'The strange thing is, that part of it didn't seem to matter at the time.'

'But it did to Joseph. He believed he'd killed them. Don't you see? He thought if he could do that, he might hurt us as well. It's the one reason why he let us go without a fuss.'

Yes, Esther realised. Perhaps it had been the only reason in the end. Cassie was still watching her expectantly. 'All right,' Esther said quietly. 'Tell me about your idea.'

The Dovecote had altered only a little in its new role as a hotel. Doves cooed in the yard. The gardens were perhaps a little tidier, endowed with a more conscious sense of being on show; and a band of heavily gilded letters above the entrance, proclaiming 'The Dovecote Hotel', betrayed a recent concession to commercialism.

Cassie squeezed her mother's hand as they entered the hall. 'You know what you have to do?'

Esther realised that Cassie was treating this as if it were a full-scale theatrical production. Her own mind was devoid of excitement and her heart banged anxiously under her ribs. Why had she agreed to it? Why on earth had she come? For Joseph? For Cassie? She tried to examine her real motives for coming back. She heard a footstep on the stairs and, looking up, Esther felt a jolt of apprehension. Could she really go through with it?

Meg came down the staircase to greet them. She wore a cardigan and pearls and looked hardly any different. She halted in confusion when she recognised Esther. 'Why ever didn't you tell us you were coming?'

'But we did,' said Cassie. 'My mother made the booking.'

'I don't understand.' Meg crossed the hall and scanned the hotel ledger with a worried frown. 'We have a few guests left over from Christmas, but it's rather quiet at this time of year. So, I remember . . . Yes. Here it is. I do have a booking for the weekend, but it's in the name of White.'

'That's us,' Cassie said cheerfully. 'My mother likes to travel incognito, now she's famous.'

Meg stared at her, the frown deepening to suspicion. 'Cassie, stop it. Esther, what is this – a joke?'

'We didn't want Julia to know in advance that we were coming,' Esther explained.

'Where is Julia?' Cassie asked.

'Taking a painting class. I'll fetch her,' Meg offered. 'She'll be so pleased. She has wanted you to come for ages. She really wants to be friends again, Esther. I'm so glad you've decided to forgive and forget.'

'No, don't tell her,' Esther said hurriedly. 'I mean – let's settle in first. Where have you put us?'

'Overlooking the garden. The rest of us – except for Julia and Violet – live in the outbuildings now. Freddie and Rowena have your old flat. Peter and I have a flat above Joseph's workshops.' She frowned at the mention of Joseph and looked at Esther anxiously. 'I haven't put either of you in Joseph's old room.'

Esther was saved from saying anything in reply as Freddie came into the hall from the garden. 'Esther? Well, I say! This is absolutely topping! And, Cassie, is that really you? Do the others know you're here?'

'They haven't told Julia,' Meg said. 'They've come as hotel guests.'

'We're travelling incognito,' put in Cassie.

'I say – what a jape!' Freddie beamed at them.

'He doesn't know quite how much of one,' Cassie said softly to Esther as Freddie picked up their suitcases and they followed him up the stairs.

'Cassie—' Esther said angrily. 'This really isn't a game.'

No, it wasn't a game, Cassie thought as she laid out her clothes on the bed, remembering David's anger when she had told him that she was going ahead with her plan to persuade Esther and Joseph to meet at The Dovecote. 'If you go through with this, you and I are finished,' he had said. 'It's crazy. It's childish, melodramatic, and its vindictive towards that poor, deranged woman you call Julia. You don't know what you're doing. I can't think why your mother and Joseph have agreed to it.'

'Because they loved one another and Julia made them spoil that love,' she had said, adding self-righteously, 'And if you loved *me* you'd see that I'm only trying to help them put it all behind them.'

'If you believe that, you can convince yourself of anything,' he had said.

Cassie changed out of her travelling clothes, then sat on the bed to wait. She heard the luncheon gong and the sound of people making their way to the dining room, and, looking at her watch, went to the window. She could see the corner of the lawn and the gate into the courtyard by the barns. The sight of the doves perched on the roof-tiles brought a lump of sadness to her throat. She held her breath with the tension of waiting, and released it in a sudden gasp as she heard the sound of a car. A few minutes later, Joseph emerged from the courtyard and walked across the lawn towards the house. Cassie opened the window and waved, calling in a whisper, 'It's all clear.' Then she closed it and, opening the door to her room, stepped silently into the corridor.

Julia's eyes lit with gladness as she met Esther in the dining room; she seemed unaware of the stiffness in Esther's greeting. 'Meg told me you had come.' She hugged her, then stepped back to regard her critically. 'You've put on a bit of weight. It suits you.' She paused. 'Meg hinted at an air of mystery. That's not like you.'

'No. I have to admit, it's more your style than mine, Julia,' Esther said.

'It's been a long time, but I'm glad we got there in the end. That *is* why you've come? We are going to be friends again – mend bridges, as Peter says?'

'In a way.'

'But where's Cassie? Meg said she was with you.' Julia glanced round the dining room. She swung back to face Esther as the small knot of guests began to take their seats at the long refectory table. 'Where would you like to sit? As you can see – we're still like one big family here.'

Esther regarded the table and the other pieces of furniture with Joseph's distinctive touch. She stroked the silk-smooth finish, remembering the first time she had seen it and the awe with which she had regarded his work.

'The guests all mingle in,' Julia was saying. 'It's like a house party. It works very well.' She hooked her arm in Esther's. 'I'm so glad we're together again. The Dovecote thrives on friendship – on differences settled, imagined hurts forgiven.'

'I can almost forgive the intention behind what you did, but I don't think I shall ever forgive the way you did it,' Esther said. 'Invoking Christopher's spirit, passing on messages . . .'

'Oh – you're a confirmed sceptic.'

'Well, I'm not a fool.'

'We won't argue about it. I admit – I regret some things . . . But you agree it was for the best? You are happy?'

'Oh, yes. I'm happy. There may even be something in what you say. That it all worked out for the best.'

'It's true. Joseph would never have achieved as much as he has if the spirits hadn't intervened. He's in Devon, you know. Did you know?

Have you heard from him? He never comes to see me.' An expression of sadness crossed Julia's face.

Esther turned away. 'Joseph achieved what he has because he left you, Julia. Not because he and I were forcibly parted.'

Peter had come into the dining room. He lifted a hand in a gentle wave and came across the room to kiss Esther. 'I'm glad you listened to me. We'll talk later,' he said, pressing her arm affectionately and drifting away towards Meg.

'I loved Joseph so much,' Julia said. 'I loved you all. And Cassie ... Where *is* Cassie?'

Esther moved towards a middle-aged couple with a vacant seat beside them. She smiled at the woman guest, gesturing to the chair next to her, 'May I?' then she turned again to Julia. 'Cassie has a sick headache after the journey. She's lying down. Perhaps she could have a light lunch later?'

Esther waited until everyone had eaten and the guests had gone into the drawing room for coffee before she said that she would go upstairs and see how Cassie was feeling.

She paused for a moment on the landing, her heart beating hard against her ribs, knowing that Joseph would be nearby. Was he too regretting all this, wishing he had not come, blaming her perhaps for giving in to Cassie? Why *had* they come? she asked herself. What did each of them expect from this reunion?

After a while she returned to the drawing room. Julia was by the sideboard – Joseph's sideboard – on which were laid out cups on linen runners and two large coffee pots; the guests moved towards them and chatted to Julia.

'How is Cassie feeling now?' Rowena asked Esther. 'Dear little Cassie. She never, ever used to be ill.'

'She is much better,' Esther said. She turned to Julia and drew her aside so that the others should not hear, saying in a deliberately baffled tone, 'I heard sounds from the meeting room while I was upstairs, Julia. Do you still use it?'

Julia's head jerked up sharply. 'What sort of sounds?'

'Voices. I distinctly heard voices.'

Julia looked round, mentally counting heads of the guests assembled. There was a pause as she murmured, 'How could anyone have got in there?' Then she turned swiftly on her heel and made for the door.

Meg hurried after Esther into the hall. 'What's going on?'

'Nothing,' Esther said quickly. 'Stay here, will you, and make sure nobody notices anything?' She followed Julia to the first floor.

'You imagined it.' Julia listened self-consciously outside the meeting room door and, throwing Esther a puzzled look from narrowed eyes, she indicated with an impatient movement of her hands that they should go away.

'Perhaps someone has locked themselves in there?'

'Impossible,' Julia said with a frown.

'Aren't you even going to look?' Esther regarded her coolly, though her heart pounded in her ears and she had begun to feel sick with apprehension.

Reluctantly Julia drew a key from her pocket and opened the door.

The room was in darkness. Esther shut the door behind them, blocking out the light from the corridor. A glimmer showed between the open stage curtains; there was a rustle of movement and, as the light brightened, a figure appeared from the gloom at the back of the stage.

Julia gave a gasp and sat down suddenly on one of the chairs as Cassie, dressed in a white nightdress, a veil hiding her face and shoulders, drifted slowly to the centre of the platform. She certainly looked the part, Esther conceded, as the ghostly figure stood rigid for several seconds, then raised one arm to the accompaniment of a tinkling sound of bells. Pointing out into the room and swinging round to face Julia, Cassie cried in ringing tones, 'Welcome, friends, welcome. I am your Spirit Guide.'

Esther's heart beat so violently that it seemed to rise into her mouth; she walked to the stage and, grasping its edge with both hands, turned to see Julia's look of fury as the 'Spirit Guide' called out, 'I have come here today with a message for Julia.'

Julia stood and walked to the stage to stand beside Esther. 'Who are you?' she said angrily. 'Though I think I hardly need ask—'

'I am the prophetess, Cassandra,' Cassie called in the same resonant tones, beginning to relish the role of a materialised spirit. 'Chum of Moses and Elijah – and I have come here today to show you the error of your ways.'

Julia turned a tragic, injured look on Esther and said under her breath, 'I'm deeply hurt, Esther. If this is supposed to be a practical joke—'

'The message is –' Cassie interrupted – 'don't trifle with the spirits, Julia, or one day your deeds may come back to haunt you.' She stepped aside and a second figure, standing deep in the shadows at the back of the stage, moved forward into the light.

Esther caught her breath, for though Joseph wasn't dressed in uniform, but in a pullover and slacks, she was instantly transported to the last time she had attended a seance in that room. She remembered the fear that had paralysed her will that day so that she had only been able to stare in horror at what she saw.

Even today, dressed as he was, the figure beside Cassie could as easily have been Christopher as Joseph, but it was not fear that made Esther sway a little on her feet. She hadn't seen him since meeting him by accident at the Paris exhibition. She thought she had prepared herself, but she had anticipated only that she might be afraid; she had not accounted for other emotions that might engulf her. Joseph seemed in that moment to stand as a cipher for all those young men whose lives had been squandered by war. Tears slipped down her cheeks, and, struck by the futility of the misunderstanding that had separated them, she grieved suddenly for her own past, for Joseph's burden of his lost men, and for all the abandoned lives and loves of a whole generation so wronged by the war.

'Cassie – get down at once!' Julia cried. 'And as for you . . .' Her voice tailed off as she contemplated Joseph; he stood in silence, his hands in his pockets – next to Cassie and yet distant from her, as if waiting with a patient respect for her next move.

'Do not resist us with your negative thoughts,' Cassie cried in a booming, deliberately 'ghostly' voice. 'Oh – do not mock the great spirit forces, Julia, or they will be angry. Trust your Spirit Guide. Feel the energy flow, the cosmic vibrations . . .' She tipped back her head under the heavy veil, both arms outstretched as if to feel her way to the front of the stage. At the same moment, deciding that enough was enough, Joseph stepped forward; he put an arm round Cassie's shoulders and said something close to her ear. Cassie tipped her head on one side. 'It seems I must leave you now. The spirit world calls and being in two dimensions is jolly exhausting. But I shall leave you with these thoughts . . .'

Esther walked across the room and snapped on the light. With a rattle of bells Cassie lowered her arms. 'I don't know why you made me stop,' she said irritably, throwing back her veil. 'I was beginning to enjoy myself.'

Julia sat down again on the nearest chair. Esther turned to face her. 'Well – I think you've got the idea. And we've certainly seen this sort of thing before – ghostly figures, Spirit Guides. There's really no need to go any further.'

Julia turned a tragic face to Esther. 'The spirits will be so distressed—'

'Julia – you're a fraud.'

'I can understand Cassie. She always was a naughty child. But you – and Joseph. How could you be so heartless! Why have you done this to me?'

'But it's nothing to what you did to us, Julia.' Joseph came to the front of the stage and jumped down. 'Perhaps it *was* a bit melodramatic, but you operated *us* as if we were puppets in some drama you'd conceived. You seemed to think you had rights over our lives.'

Esther looked at Julia and felt a sudden wave of pity for her. 'You *were* wrong to do what you did,' she said gently. 'You must see that now?'

'I admit, I made some mistakes – went too far, but I couldn't bear the thought of losing you both. And I couldn't bear to think that you would both suffer. You were so obstinate, Esther. When Christopher couldn't make you believe he was trying to get through to you, I knew he expected me to show you proof of his loving intention. Sometimes people need to see a spirit form. It provides a channel of communication through which the real spirit can pass. I did what I did out of love.'

Esther did not answer.

'I'm not a great artist like Peter, or you or Joseph,' Julia continued. 'But I have the gift of love. I'm able to inspire people so that they bring out the best in themselves. I could have done so much with you if only you'd let me.'

'But you destroyed us,' Esther said sadly. 'I didn't know it was Violet up there on the stage that day. How could I? I thought that it was Joseph pretending to be Christopher. I thought you and he had schemed . . .' She broke off, realising that Julia wasn't even listening. Cassie's attempt at a moral lesson, dealt with all the self-importance of youth, wouldn't make any difference. Julia would see only the cruelty behind the elaborate performance. And perhaps she was right to do so. They shouldn't have come back to The Dovecote.

Julia looked at her with a sad smile. 'You were so promising. I had such high hopes for you. And I thought things had worked out well for you in the end when you married George. But now, after today . . .' She stood up. 'I pray the spirits will forgive you all. You don't understand love, Esther. You never will.' She went to Joseph and, standing before him, touched him gently on the cheek with the palm of her hand in the old proprietary way. 'You were my best dove. You'd almost begun to understand the self-sacrificing nature of love. Esther took that achievement away from me.' Then she went to the door without a backward glance and walked from the room.

'Well!' Cassie was the first to speak. She turned to Esther and Joseph, still flushed with excitement, waiting for their judgement on what had happened.

Esther offered her a taut smile in response, unwilling to commit herself to a verdict. It had been so important to Cassie that she should bring them here, hoping that something would be resolved by it, but Esther doubted it was as simple as that, and the recent scene had left a sour taste in her mouth, as if, even now, Julia had gained a moral triumph. She glanced at Joseph, who leaned against the stage, his arms folded as if deep in thought. He did not meet her eyes. She allowed herself to speculate on his side of it. Had Joseph come here only because he had been swept along by Cassie's enthusiasm – or had he hoped for something more?

Suddenly Joseph looked up. 'Cassie – would you mind leaving us for a moment?'

Cassie went out into the corridor and walked to the head of the stairs. Below, the drawing room buzzed with conversation. She heard the click of a door and saw Meg come out from the dining room and close the door behind her; she glanced up as she crossed the hall and did not seem surprised to see Cassie in her nightdress. 'Julia's told me what happened. What on earth have you been up to?'

'It was an experiment,' Cassie said. 'It was important for Joseph and my mother.'

'You should be careful, young lady – playing around with the spirits. Poor Julia – she's very upset.' Meg turned away and went into the drawing room, closing that door too, reducing the noise of conversation to a murmur of sound.

Cassie felt a strong reluctance to move from the gallery. Had the episode been therapeutic or a disaster? Had her 'ghost' been too silly? David had called it melodramatic, and so had Joseph. Panic swept through her. From the beginning, Joseph had been grim about coming back, only agreeing to do it because she'd persuaded him that Esther wanted him to come. What if he'd only gone through with it to humour her – as he might have humoured her when she was twelve? But she wasn't a child any more, and she didn't want Joseph to look on her as a child.

What *had* she wanted? Revenge on Julia? That had been part of it, she supposed. She wondered what Julia was doing, all alone in the dining room. Weeping? It was hard to imagine. Cassie tried to resurrect the triumph she had felt on seeing her collapse, but instead she was aware of a curious sense of anti-climax. So, what had she wanted? she asked herself again; and it occurred to her that David had been right to question her motives. Had she expected that, after today, everything would be as it had been before – bathed in the rosy glow of childhood? If so, the glow seemed calculated to include only her mother and Joseph, for she felt let down – as if things had gone wrong and she was left out in the cold.

Why had her mother and Joseph gone along with her idea? she began to wonder. Had they persuaded themselves that any scheme, however melodramatic and childish, would serve if it might bring them together again? They would use her as an excuse: 'It was Cassie,' they would say, laughing about it in later years. 'Dear, silly Cassie with her fanciful ideas. If it hadn't been for her we should have gone on as we were and never have found one another again.' They would look at her fondly. 'And now, instead – we shall be together for always.'

Was that really what she had wanted? Cassie asked herself, close to tears. She became alert as she heard footsteps approaching the open front door. She leaned over the gallery rail and her heart leaped with anguish, for she could see a figure enter the porch. He looked up and Cassie's worst fears were confirmed. 'George!'

Her stepfather came slowly across the hall towards the foot of the stairs. 'Well, don't look so terribly pleased to see me. What are you doing in your nightdress? Aren't you well?'

Cassie glanced along the corridor at the closed door of the seance room, and she realised the enormity of what she had done. In all of this she had only given a token consideration to George – who had been so good to her, who had tried so hard to be a proper father in the past few years; he had supported her about studying furniture design; he had loved Esther faithfully, knowing her heart belonged to another man. And now it was she who had dealt him the most terrible blow by bringing her mother and Joseph back together. 'Oh, George.' She felt an enormous wave of remorse.

He laughed. 'Didn't you guess I'd be coming? To be honest, I'd almost decided to join you at the last minute this morning, but I couldn't get away from the pottery early enough.'

Cassie opened her mouth but no sound came out.

'Where is Esther – upstairs?'

'Oh, George!' Cassie croaked.

A look of concern crossed his face. 'Is she all right?' He started up the stair towards her.

'Yes.' Cassie found her voice at last. 'That is . . . I think she's gone for a walk.'

George halted. 'I'll go and find her.'

'No.' Cassie gripped the rail of the gallery tightly. 'You don't know the way.'

He shrugged, then continued up the stair. 'Well, then. You'd better show me to her room.'

Esther leaned with her back against the wall, glad of its support. Joseph smiled uncertainly and Esther remembered a time long ago when he had rescued her from the sea and she had watched him come towards her, looking so like Christopher. Was that why she had loved him so intensely – because he had seemed like Christopher – but without Christopher's obvious flaws? Without the flippancy, the overriding arrogance, and – as it had proved – without Christopher's deceit.

'Thank you,' she said. 'Thank you for going along with all that. It can't have been easy. Such a crazy piece of dramatics. I still don't know why you did it.'

'Cassie asked me,' he said simply.

'Yes. She has a very persuasive way with her.' Nothing had changed in the meeting room, Esther noticed, looking around her at last. Did people still gather in the courtyard for the monthly seance meetings? She looked at Joseph. He too looked the same – not much older really. 'I owe you an apology.' Was that all she could say? How inadequate after all this time.

Joseph looked at her, searching her face, his eyes expressionless. He did not move from the stage and Esther left the wall and sat on one of the chairs, remembering the seances she had been to, Julia in a trance, the intense atmosphere when the others had held hands and waited for the Spirit Guide to speak.

'There was an element of revenge about today,' Joseph said.

'On Julia.'

'On Julia – and on you. I suppose I wanted to say to you: Look. Is this what you thought you saw? Is this what you threw away our happiness for?'

'We would have parted anyway if I'd listened to you. You were the one who kept arguing against us being together,' Esther reminded him.

338

'I was wrong. And you were right, by the way. The nightmares and memories have diminished over the years.'

'Cassie had an idea that if we came back here together it would stop me feeling so negative about what happened. The notion's very theoretical.'

Joseph smiled. 'I believe she has a friend who's studying medicine.'

'David. He wants to be a psychoanalyst.'

'Perhaps we could have done with him around a few years ago.'

They were silent, and Esther felt a sense of sadness, knowing that their reunion should not be like this – so cold and sterile. She tried to think back to what they had once shared, but it was as if she had buried it under the years of bitter separation. They had become different people in the meantime.

'It's over. Isn't it?' Joseph said.

'Does that make you unhappy?'

He eased himself from the stage. 'Relieved, in a way. I was a coward about seeing you again after Paris. I didn't know what would happen. And I was scared of coming back here. The strange thing is – I felt absolutely nothing when I saw Julia. No sense of awe. None of disloyalty. And no memories of the war.'

Joseph was surprised to discover how little emotion he felt about meeting Esther too. It was good to see her again: she was just as lovely, yet less lovable, somehow; perhaps less overtly tender. The core of attraction that had been at the centre of their relationship had gone.

'You've never been a coward,' Esther said with some of her old spirit. 'You had no idea why I'd backed out of a commitment to you, but you let me go because you thought it was better for me and Cassie for it to end that way.'

He turned suddenly to the door and let out an exasperated, 'What a waste!'

'Isn't life made up of lost opportunities? We just have to make the best of what's left.'

'Do you love George?'

Esther stood up. She did not answer at first. When she did, she did not want to see his expression and looked down at her hands. 'Yes. More than I can say.'

Cassie tried to act normally as she showed George to Esther's room. 'Mother will be ever so surprised to see you,' she said faintly.

George glanced round the furnishings with critical approval. Esther's nightdress lay on the bed. Her suitcase stood open on the floor. He turned to Cassie with a wry smile. 'Well, I don't think she'll be all that surprised, seeing as it was Esther's idea that I should follow you here.' He studied Cassie's face with sympathy as several emotions flitted in disarray across it. He went to the suitcase and Cassie saw that Esther had packed his pyjamas and shirts. He began to remove things carefully and place them in drawers. 'Cassie. You didn't really think she would do something as important as this without consulting me about it first, did you?'

'I don't know. I—'

'We agreed it was for the best – especially now – that she should come down here for a holiday and get what happened all that time ago out of her system once and for all. I've wanted her to do it for ages.'

'You didn't mind about Joseph being here?'

'I had my doubts about it.' A look of uncertainty crossed his face. 'For lots of reasons. But Esther said you were determined on it – and she had a strong feeling that she should come back now, at this particular time. One has to obey these feminine intuitions.' He closed the drawer of the tallboy and opened the bedroom door for her. 'And now, if you don't mind, I should like to change out of my driving clothes. And you might think about putting on something more suitable.'

Cassie went along the corridor and changed quickly out of the nightdress into a dress and cardigan. She returned to Esther's room and waited for George in the corridor, trying not to think about Esther and Joseph together in the seance room. 'What particular time?' she said impatiently when the door reopened. 'You said Mother thought she should come back now – at this particular time.'

George went ahead of her along the corridor. He paused at the top of the stairs and Cassie saw Esther below them in the hall, standing by the entrance porch; she leaned over the stair rail and scanned her mother's face anxiously. Esther looked tired, but her weariness broke into relief as she caught sight of George, and he ran down the stairs to greet her.

Cassie followed more slowly, watching them, seeing George's arm slip round her mother protectively. Esther's body seemed to sink into his side, as if briefly letting go of something and relinquishing herself to his strength.

Cassie confronted them. 'You said, "at this particular time". What did you mean?'

George turned to her, and his solemn, patient face broadened suddenly into an exuberant smile. 'Esther is going to have a child.'

'It's true,' her mother said.

'But you're too old.'

'No I'm not. I'm only thirty-eight.' Esther's spirit momentarily asserted itself, then sank back into the protection of her husband.

Cassie gave a sudden laugh.

'What's funny?' Esther asked.

'I was just remembering Julia saying you've put on weight. She's supposed to have so much insight, but she didn't even know you're going to have a baby.'

'Julia ... I was beginning to worry about her,' Esther said with a small frown. 'Were we too hard on her? Where is she?'

'She doesn't seem to be suffering very much,' Cassie said. She could see Julia through the open door of the drawing room among a group of hotel guests; she was talking, smiling, gesticulating with her cigarette holder, as always at the centre of attention. Cassie turned to Esther, a fresh anxiety stirring in her. 'Where is Joseph?'

'He went outside. He didn't want to meet Julia again.'

Cassie went to the door and looked out into the garden. She didn't know what her mother had said to Joseph. Had she told him about the child? Would he be heartbroken because he had lost his one true love, or angry with her for arranging the meeting when so little had come of it?

'Where are you going?' George called.

Cassie turned with a swift reply. 'Out. I have to talk to him.'

'Let her go,' Esther said softly.

George turned to her, touching her hair with a tender gesture. 'I guessed you were with him.'

'Did you?' Esther looked at him and wished she could make him understand how much she loved him. 'You're always so knowing. So patient.'

'You don't know how afraid I've been all day. I thought everything might have been over between us.'

'Have I really made you so unsure of me?' Esther reached for his hand. She had arrived at a point of stability, she realised. She could look back on experiences – on her life with Christopher, her love for Joseph – and examine them without flinching. Perhaps, in George, she at last had what she wanted from marriage – for she saw now that a certain distance between men and women was inescapable: there was no such thing as a perfect love. George recognised his failings and had accepted them, and hers too – for her own character wasn't without its limitations; a certain detachment, a protective shell had been necessary for her to maintain a notion of independence.

There was a sudden commotion of sound at the door and they turned as a young woman came into the hall. The newcomer shrugged off her coat to reveal an overall splashed with clay; she was fair, with aquiline features and large eyes, their deep hollows hinting at some past tragedy or illness; she stood looking at them with interest and a hesitant, trusting smile.

Julia came out from the drawing room. She cast a brief, cold glance at Esther and then allowed a warmth to creep into her expression. 'George. I didn't realise you would be here.' Julia's attention flowed to the girl in the doorway; she went to her and put an arm round her, smiling tenderly. 'This is Alison. She came to us before Christmas. She's a sculptor, and she shows tremendous promise.'

Esther turned again to the newcomer, taking in the clay splashes, the air of vulnerability and hint of melancholy in the trusting eyes.

'Hello,' the girl said. 'Julia's been so good to me. I'd begun to lose faith in there being any kindness left in the world until I met her . . .' The girl's eyes brightened and she bit her lip, then she smiled suddenly. 'Have I missed anything? I didn't realise how late it was getting until it occurred to me that everyone would have gone for lunch. When I'm working on a sculpture I seem to get carried away.'

'Oh, I don't think you've missed much.' Julia flicked a glance again at Esther. 'Not really.'

They all shook hands and Alison excused herself, saying she must wash after being in her workshop. Julia's gaze followed her along the corridor to the kitchen, where Rowena and Freddie could be heard arguing comfortably.

Esther, watching Julia, was aware of a perverse emotion, a sudden and unexpected flow of affection towards her. 'Poor girl,' she murmured to George. 'I hope she knows what she's letting herself in for.'

Julia did not hear. Still looking after Alison she said, 'As you can see, The Dovecote has a new injured dove. She's very like you, Esther. She has suffered so much and needs our kindness and love. We must take care of her.' She turned to smile at her; and Julia's expression was no longer cold but held a fond invitation to share her conviction. Already she has almost forgotten, thought Esther in amazement. And forgiven? Yes, that too. And so had she, she realised with an even greater sense of wonder.

'You don't know how terrible it has been for me, to have to count you as a failure, Esther,' Julia said. 'But we shall be patient. Life goes on. With this one we shall succeed.'

Cassie did not know what she expected to find when she ran out from the house in search of Joseph. A shattered heart in need of consolation? She could not see him in the garden, though his car was in the courtyard, and she imagined him, alone on the cliff path, walking blindly in his distress. She pictured him as he reached the point where they had once watched cormorants together, pausing to contemplate the rocks and shore below. The wind tossed the branches high above the tree-walk and its roar joined with the crash of the sea. The image of Joseph on the cliff grew more vivid, so that Cassie, suddenly afraid for him, began to run.

The door to his cottage was wide open and Joseph was inside, leaning with one arm on the shelf above the fireplace, staring into the empty fire-grate. He turned as he heard Cassie in the doorway. 'Hello.' He smiled. 'I wanted to take another look. I was remembering how I used to live here – like the old man of the woods.'

Cassie was so glad, so relieved he wasn't grief-stricken, that she couldn't say anything at all.

'Look.' He held something in his hand. 'I've wondered whether they were still here. I went in such a hurry all that time ago that I left a few things behind. I thought Julia would have got rid of them, but she left everything exactly as it was.'

'Perhaps she thought you would come back one day ... What is it?' Cassie went to him and saw that he held a pebble and a seashell in the palm of his hand.

342

'Mementoes.' She took the pebble from him and his hand closed slowly over Esther's shell, remembering. A peace offering.

The stone was calcite, white and cold and very smooth. Cassie remembered that Joseph had chosen it one day from a bucket of pebbles she had collected on the shore.

'What did you do with the carpentry set I gave you?' he said, as if the one gift had reminded him of another.

'It has pride of place in my room in London. It's the most beautiful present I've ever had.'

'And so is this,' he said, smiling again, prising open her fingers and retrieving the pebble. 'Don't you know a present, once given, can't be taken back?' He put the pebble in his trouser pocket and moved away.

'I'm sorry,' Cassie said suddenly. 'This whole thing seems to have turned out to be a bit of a catastrophe as far as you're concerned.'

'Not really. Perhaps you shocked Julia out of her self-importance a little. And your mother and I had to meet again one day. You made that happen. I'm glad you did.' He looked round the cottage. 'Poor Julia. She brings out the best and the worst in people. I've treated her abysmally, you know.'

'*Poor* Julia? How can anyone possibly feel sorry for her?'

'Because she's lonely. She needs people more than the rest of us do.'

Cassie wondered whether, in a roundabout way, he was telling her that he didn't need anyone and that it was all right about Esther. Cassie remembered when she had first known him and he had been so alone. No one could want to go back to living like that, could they?

'I remember I thought it was very romantic here,' she said suddenly. 'I used to lie awake and think of you, all by yourself in your little cottage on top of the cliff.' She looked at him. 'But there's nothing romantic about it at all really. Everyone needs someone. People shouldn't be all alone.'

He did not answer and his face was turned away so that she couldn't see his expression. Cassie was afraid the remark had struck too deeply and that he was more upset about her mother than she had thought. She did not know what to say and, feeling disoriented, said the first thing that came into her head. 'You needn't have worried about me because of your nightmares. They never frightened me, you know. I heard you call out sometimes. I would open my window wide and listen and then I'd cry sometimes because I wanted to comfort you.'

Joseph looked at her and said, very seriously. 'Dear Cassie. What a tender little thing you were.'

'I want you to see that you didn't have to stay away because of me. I suppose I don't want you to blame me when you think about it in the future. I suppose that's why I wanted to get you both back here, so that at least I could say I'd done my best. David says everything we do has a purely selfish motive.'

'He's right. There were lots of reasons why I stayed away. I realise that now,' Joseph said.

'Perhaps you didn't love us, after all.'

'Oh, I loved your mother passionately. Don't imagine I wasn't sincere about it. We could have been happy – and would perhaps have stayed happy. But we missed our chance.'

'What about me?' Cassie said rather piteously.

He looked at her. 'I've always loved you, Cassie. You brought joy into my life at a time when I thought there was no delight left in the world. Then, when you telephoned and came to see me . . . you made me see how much we had all changed, and that one shouldn't try to hold on to the past.'

'You mean you don't care for me any more?' Cassie said, feeling her spirits fall.

'No. You idiot. I mean I saw you – and Esther – in a different light.' He changed the subject then, and would not be drawn any more on what he had meant. He looked at his watch. 'You'd better get back to the others before they send out a search party.' He moved from the fireplace and waited for her at the door. Cassie felt a strong desperation to stay with him, to go back with him to his house, so that he wouldn't be alone. Of course, he wasn't really alone, she reminded herself as she waited for him to close up the cottage. His house and workshops were well staffed, and he had the apprentices boarding with him.

'Had you thought what you will do after your final year?' he said as they made their way through the walk under the trees.

'Try for an apprenticeship, I suppose.'

'There's a place for you at my workshops, if you want it.' His voice was strangely diffident, as if he thought she might say no.

Cassie's heart was so full that she could not speak at first. Her eyes swam with sudden tears and she couldn't see where she was going; stumbling over a tree root she felt Joseph's arm round her, holding her steady. He took her hand and they picked their way together over the tree roots until they reached the lawn.

He dropped her hand then and she felt him draw away from her. When at last she said she would love to work with him, he had become distant and business-like again. 'Good. We'll talk about it when the time comes.'

'You'll write to me, won't you?' Cassie said, before she went indoors.

Joseph promised. He watched her, though she did not know he was watching as she ran into the house. He walked across the lawn to the courtyard, his heart beating erratically, realising that he had wanted to hold her when she stumbled against him, to hold her and never let her go again.

The doves fluttered about the ledges of the dovecote with their soft, vibrating call. The pale afternoon sun caught their wing and tail feathers. He remembered when he had first seen her; she had been hiding in one of the barns and had stepped into the sunlight – like a breath of spring in autumn.

When had he recognised that his feelings towards her had changed?

In Paris – seeing her appear as if from nowhere? And then again, when she came to him in Devon with her determination to turn everything on its head? He had begun to understand the precious quality she had brought with her when she first came into his life, how much he owed to her eternal optimism. He knew now that he wanted Cassie's brightness with him always.

A feather, blowing lightly in the wind, floated from the roof to land at his feet. He picked it up and stroked the soft down, remembering a white feather handed to him a long time ago – another world.

As he drove back along the coast road he could not rid himself of the memory of Cassie, her eyes swimming with tears, the whites very clear, the irises a greeny-grey. He began to plan for the year when she would come to his workshop and realised that he had learned to hope again; she had taught him that. He saw the fields on either side, grey and brown with winter, the hard ploughed ridges and mist veiling the dark, skeleton trees; and throwing back his head he wanted to shout, with an irrepressible need to celebrate that he was alive.